THE LOONEY BIN

by
Stan Kapuchinski

ISBN-979-8-218-27249-4

Library of Congress Control Number: 2023915805s

Cover design by: Nazia Hameed

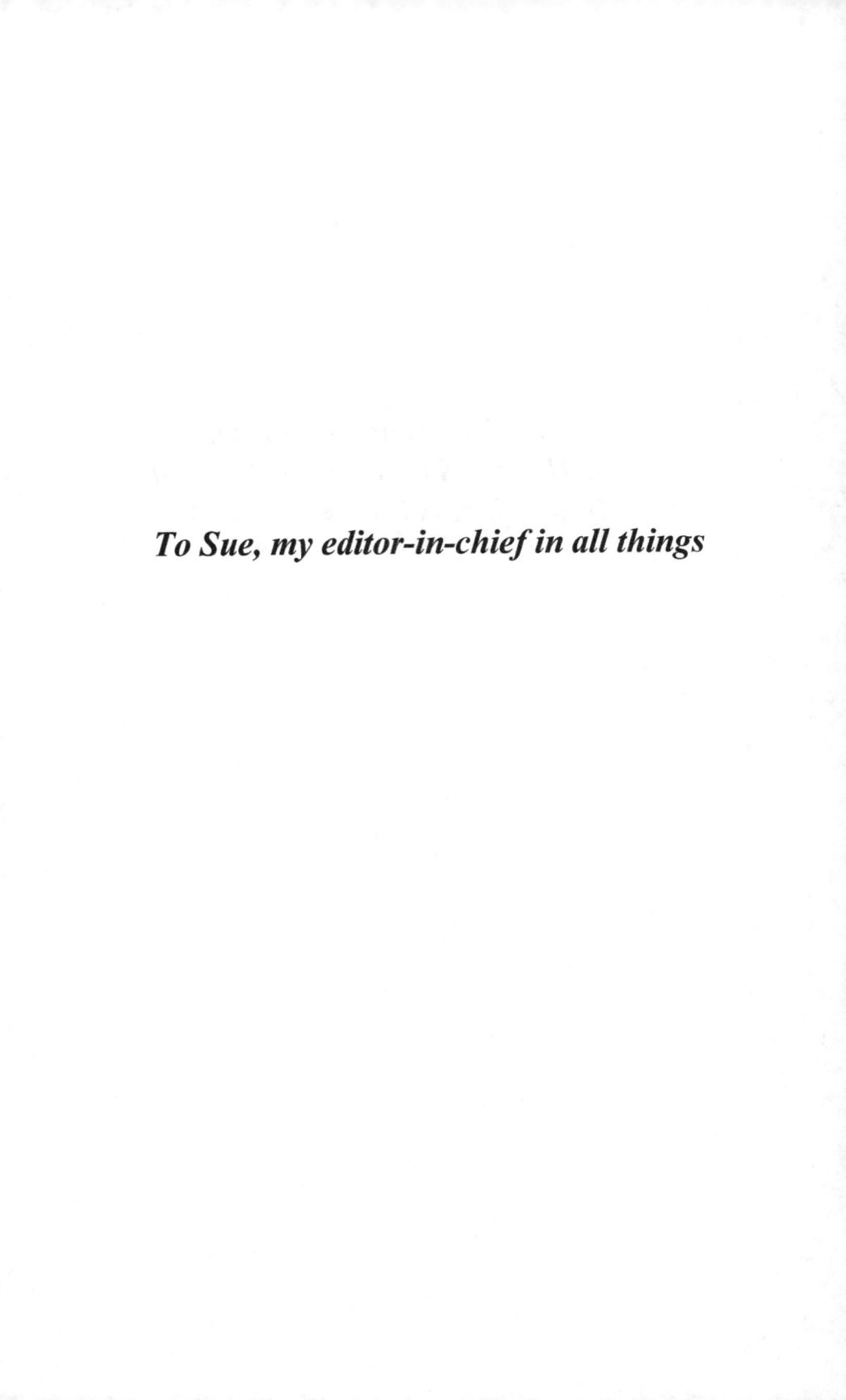

To Sue, my editor-in-chief in all things

Everybody Has Emotional Baggage.
Some Have A Small Carry-On While
Others Lug A Steamer Trunk.

Table of Contents

---

[1] Wm Shakespeare, Act1, Scene 4, *King Lear*
[2] T.S. Elliot, *The Love Song Of J. Alfred Prufrock*

---

[3] Calvin, *Calvin And Hobbs*, Bill Watterson
[4] Wm Shakespeare, As You Like It. Act3 Scene 2

---

[5] Charlie Brown

ONE

You Can Tuck It In, But Your Past May Not Want To Go To Sleep
Where Bonny Reflects and Jack Deflects
<u>Defense Mechanisms:</u> Psychological Processes
That Reduce Anxiety;
Mental Tricks That Help You Keep Your Balance

"I thought I was going to see the li'l baby Jesus today."

She quickly closed her book and met his eyes. "Excuse me, Jack, but what did you just say?"

He gave her a wry half-smile and nodding said, "Bonny, my love, today, I really thought I was a dead man."

She stared at him. "Jack, what are you talking about? What happened?"

"Only that this patient pulled a gun on me and aimed it right at my head."

"At the clinic?"

"Yeah. Right in my office during an appointment. Can you goddamn believe it? He was sitting about three feet away from me, but that freakin gun seemed a lot closer…and much bigger than it was. Much, much bigger."

Bonny pressed her hands together and raised them to her lips. She let out a deep breath. "Oh my God, Jack. Why'd he do it? Was this a new patient? An old one? Holy mother, what did *you* do?"

"His name's Brad. I've been seeing him off and on for depression. Today, he comes into the office, plops down and stares out the window without saying a word. So, I decide to wait. You know, see if he's going to say anything. That's when I notice he's wearing a raincoat."

"A raincoat? In this Florida heat?"

"Right. I wondered that too. He'd always come in wearing a polo, chinos and loafers."

"So?"

"So, finally, I say my usual, 'How're you doing'?
Silence.
'Brad, anything happen since we last met?'
Silence.

'What's with the raincoat? I didn't see any rain in the forecast.'
More goddamn silence.

Bonny, I'm hearing the AC-grate's rattling, the fluorescents buzzing and guys cutting grass outside, but all I'm getting from him is his sullen silence. I'm thinking, 'Hell. Is this appointment going to be like our others? My trying to pull things out of this stubborn pain in the butt?'

Then it happened. His right hand goes into his raincoat and slowly pulls out this shiny, black gun. He raises it up to his eye and aims it…at *me* for chrissake. And there it is, the muzzle of a pistol pointed right at my face. I look at the gun. I look at Brad. I look at the gun. I look at Brad. The bastard wasn't staring-off now. He was looking at me straight down that gun's barrel with this wise-ass grin."

"Jack, what did you do then?"

"Well, like out of reflex, I reached out and tried to push the gun aside. As I did, he said, *'Don't do that,'* in this flat, threatening voice." Jack smiled. "You can bet I put my hand down pretty fast. Now it's me staring in silence. I saw the gun was a revolver. So, brilliant me tries to see if there were any bullets in the cylinders. Then I think, 'you idiot, all he needs is one bullet in the chamber to kill you. Crap.'

And Brad? Not moving. Just sitting there with the gun at his cheek and his eye sighting down it at my head…smiling at me.

I was totally fixed on that deep, black-hole at the end of the barrel. I'm thinking if I tried to lunge at him or run, he could shoot me before I left the chair. I looked to see if he had his finger on or off the trigger. Ha, like that would've reassured me. Bonny, talk about feeling powerless. I was freakin frozen.

Then, and I've no clue how much time's passed, he pulls the gun back and looks at it, all innocent. Like…like it's an ice-cream cone and he's wondering where to take his first lick. When he started moving it again, I know I yelled, 'Brad, don't *do* it'.

And do you know what he does?"

"No, Jack, I don't."

"He lowers the gun and starts to put it back inside his raincoat. As he doing that, he starts laughing and says. 'Huh? Don't do *what*, Doc? Gee, I just thought you'd like to see it. They sure make these reproductions look real nowadays, doncha think? '

Next, he stands up and leaves, without a word. Oh, and on his way out, he makes another appointment. Maybe he's got a goddamn replica bazooka to show me next. Jesus."

As she hugged him, Bonny said, "My God, Jack, that's incredible. And this horrible, what should I call it, 'thing', 'experience', 'traumatic event' happened this afternoon?"

"Yeah. I saw the rest of my patients and came home. Figured I'd tell you the story, then go sit out on the lanai with a vodka/tonic."

She stepped away to look at him. "Wait a minute. This guy pulls a gun, aims it at your face and you think you're about to be killed?"

"Yeah?"

"Then he leaves and you just move along and finish your day? How does that happen? I'd have been pretty shaken-up."

"Bonny, I had patients scheduled and some paperwork to finish. I got on with things. What else was I supposed to do? Although I did want to run after him and smack that grin off his face.

Anyway, have you noticed? They're back. Driving home, I got behind this old fart driving five miles-per-hour and saw a granny whose head was below her steering-wheel. Honey, the 'Snow-bird invasion' is upon us. "

"Thanks, Jack, for that news-update, but I'd rather hear how you're doing."

"Bonny, I'm fine. Really, no shit, I'm *fine*. I just need to analyze what's going on with Brad. The clear transferential issues, his displacing his underlying anger to me instead of who he's really pissed at." He laughed. "You'll like this. Driving home I began thinking about taking martial-arts classes. Then it hit me how I was rationalizing. Like, if I knew Kung-Fu, I could've, with lightning-fast moves, grabbed that gun away and had him cowering on his knees. Crazy how the mind works, huh?"

"Mm-hmm. That ole, crazy mind of yours rationalizing away. It's adorable."

"I think so."

"Well, Jack, I don't. I'm thinking how really scared and helpless you felt and how you're going to downplay it with your 'I'm fine' garbage just like you've done before. You're good at that."

"Bonny, why do you have to start busting my chops? I just

wanted to share a story with you."

"Why? Because when I ask you how you are, I get, 'Oh, I need to analyze…' as an answer. Jack, a guy aimed a gun at your head and you thought you were going to die. *I'm* upset. *How are you?*"

"It wasn't fun."

"That's pretty articulate."

"Look, I'm supposed to control the session. Today, the patient was in charge. Not good."

"A patient with a gun," she said.

"Okay. Okay. I'll admit that for those few minutes I was a little scared. Happy?"

"Hmm. So your being frozen *wasn't* because you were afraid? It was because, let's see, the AC was too low?"

"Jesus Christ. Stop. I'm fine. I'm okay. I'm handling things. Got it?"

"You've never mentioned this guy before. Have you been seeing him long?"

"A few months. I picked him up at the Clinic after the University's psych-unit discharged him. He'd tried to hang himself from a garage pipe that broke when he put his weight on it. He fell, hit his head, went unconscious. His father found him, called the EMT's. After Medicine cleared him, they transferred him to Psych. I saw him a few times, but then he left for the US Naval Academy. After they asked him to take a leave of absence because of his depression, he came home and I started seeing him again."

"Gee, Jack, I feel so much calmer now knowing my husband's treating a suicidal guy with a gun."

Jack shrugged. "Actually, I don't know if he's still suicidal because he won't discuss it. In fact, the stubborn shit won't talk much about anything. And if he does, it's smart-ass comments like, 'Aren't psychiatrists supposed to help people? Let me know when you start, Doc?' Or, 'Your diploma says, Jack Rackham, MD. Where'd you get that MD, online?' Outside of his being a pain in the ass, he wasn't worth mentioning," he smiled, "until our little tête-à-tête today."

He looked outside. "Ah, I hear the lanai calling to me, 'Come, Jack, relax, have that drink.' I just hope those little rascal no-see-ums aren't around. Man, when they start biting. Hey, Bonny, come look at this sailboat going by on the canal."

Bonny drummed her fingers hard on the tabletop. "Jack, I don't care about some sailboat. I care about how *you're* doing. And, so far, all I've heard is that you're... *fine*. Well, I'm not buying into that." She paused. "And you know why."

After a long, dramatic sigh, he turned and found her eyes fixed on his. "Bonny, you just had to bring up that crap from the past, didn't you? I'm telling you right now that that's *not* an issue. The issue is my interpreting the psychodynamics behind Brad's behavior today. Why would he use a gun to show me he was in control? He was already running sessions with his not talking. Was I getting close to something? Did he need to distance me? And then there's all his pent-up rage. At what? At whom? Now do you get it? What's important here? Or do I have to speak more slowly in monosyllables?"

She glared at him. "No, I get it. Your anger at me says it all."

"Goddammit, Bonny, I'm fine. Just let me do my job, will you?"

She stared at him, unmoved. "Okayyyy, so that pent-up anger, needing to feel in control? We're talking about Brad, right?"

"Yeah?"

"And ...your feeling powerless? Frozen in your chair?"

"Mostly my surprise. And confusion about what I was gonna do next." He laughed. "I added some drama to the story for you."

She raised her hands in surrender. "What can I say? I'm not the expert on the human mind, am I?"

"No, Bonny. *I* am."

"Okay, Jack. Although *you* may have everything under control, may *I* share two concerns?"

"Like I have a choice?"

"The first is how much this... this 'incident' might upset you. Your experiencing something like that and not be affected? I don't think so. But, okay, you say you're fine and I'll have to accept that, at least for the present.

Now, since this guy's already made one serious suicide attempt, it's likely he's going to try it again, right?"

"Yeah, but...."

"My second, deeper concern is that if this fellow succeeds this time...."

He shook his head. " Won't happen."

"Jack, humor me. If he *does* succeed this time, how's the 'Expert' going to react?"

"Can't let that bullshit go, can you."

"Jack, face it, you don't deal well with suicide. Your twin-brother killing himself? Your needing therapy for depression afterwards?"

"Bonny, when I told you about his suicide, I said I was upset, but 'normal 'upset. It was my parents who thought I was depressed so I did the therapy for them."

"Of course. Because you were fine, huh? That's why you hid the suicide and your depression from me for years into our marriage. And only told me when? After…."

"But I *did* tell you. Anyway, I worked through his suicide long ago."

"*Really*? You worked it through so well that when your two patients killed themselves three weeks apart, your getting depressed, cancelling appointments, isolating at home, gambling…."

"That was day-trading."

"Had no connection with your twin?"

"No."

"No? Geez, Jack. That's when you finally told me about your brother's suicide. How the patients' killing themselves stirred-up memories of your brother's suicide. How that was causing a depression just like you had after your brother died. That's why I'm saying you don't deal well with suicide."

"Bonny, how about some credit for seeing Dr. Lankersham that last time. We did some good work together."

"Oh? The psychiatrist I dragged you to? I thought he was restarting your engine getting you back to work. But then you come home one day and, without our discussing it, tell me you're selling your practice, *our* home and, surprise, we're moving to Florida where you'll work in a psych clinic."

"Bonny, where are you going with this?"

"That our moving here had something to do with your therapy."

"Jesus. C'mon, babe, we'd always talked about moving to Florida to get away from those freezing winters."

"Jack, the whole move, especially your not talking to me about it, was so out of the blue, I did wonder if Dr. Lankersham was getting too close to something and you reacted, *really* reacted." Bonny paused. "Crazy how the mind works, huh? I remember our sitting in his office. Him describing your tendency to run from emotions and feelings you're uncomfortable with. What words did he use? Denial? Avoidance? Rationalization? You just rationalized something about Kung-Fu? Overpowering Brad?"

Jack looked outside. "Yeah, yeah."

"Please, Jack, I really need you to hear me, to know where *I'm* coming from."

He half turned to her. "Okay, what?"

"Jack, if something does happen with this guy, I am *very* worried that you, *we* will go through the same problems we had up north."

"Bonny, Lankersham helped me see some things. But his provoking me to move because he was getting too close to some dark, deep problem inside me? Nuh-uh. *No.*

And my not talking with you about the moving? I wanted to surprise you. I thought you'd be delighted with the change."

"Uh-huh. 'Delighted' isn't quite the word I'd use."

"And Brad? Nothing's gonna happen. He'll come around once I get through his resistance."

"Jack, you should terminate him. I'm very serious about that. He's made a significant suicide attempt and he'll likely do it again. He's threatened you with a gun. He's antagonistic. And he's not engaged in therapy. Where do you draw the line?"

"Dammit, Bonny, it's what I do, help confused people. And this guy's definitely confused. Look how he comes to our appointments, then pushes me away."

"Mm-hmm. And what if the next time, he doesn't push, he blows you away? Jack, where's your head? You don't *have* to keep seeing this guy."

"Yeah I do. He needs my help."

"Right. And you need to help him? No matter what."

"All right. All right. I hear you. I'll think about what you said. Okay?"

"Thank you. That's all I'm asking, Jack. That you seriously think about my concerns."

"For chrissake, Bonny. I told you I will. But right now I'm taking my vodka/tonic and going out onto the lanai…where nobody'll bother me."

TWO

Tell Yourself Enough And You'll Come To Believe By And By
Where Fancy Tames Her Bangles While Jim And Jack Tangle
Rationalization: Justifying Actions Or Feelings With Logical Or
Even Admirable Reasons; One More Cookie Couldn't Hurt

After tap-dancing around the cigarette butts, coffee cups and gum on the sidewalk, Jack pushed open the spit-encrusted glass door of the *Palm University Mental Health Clinic*.

Once inside, he warmed to the Clinic's coming to life. Receptionists were checking-in people. Patients were already sitting and waiting. There was one guy, probably a druggie, wearing a tee-shirt shouting, 'Say <u>YES</u> to Drugs Or Go Fuck Yourself' on its front. A woman sat alone in a corner, head down, tears on her cheeks. Kids were romping while a support-animal growled. Spying a female drug-rep gearing-up to tell him about her company's newest miracle drug, he nodded and disappeared into Fancy's office.

Fancy Muwamba, the Clinic's office manager, stared intently at her computer screen. Wooden bangles with green, yellow and orange designs hung from her wrists and matched her necklace. An orange, yellow and black dress with a broad, abstract print wrapped around her ample figure. Her dreadlocks with polished wooden combs took a sinuous path around her head.

A clamor of files, family pictures, fresh flowers, coffee cups, pens and paper-clips, a wooden elephant, a half-eaten apple and her 'thought-for-the-day' calendar hid Fancy's desk. Jack had first thought the calendar was a sappy collection of soothing, religious bullshit. But when he read, 'Everyone appreciates your honesty until you're honest with them. Then you're an idiot!', he knew they shared a similar appreciation of humanity.

"Morning, Fancy, how does the world find you today?"

"Well, Dr. Jack, if I knew this was hide-and-seek, the world wouldn't be finding me at all. But, since I need that paycheck, I'm here and you've found me."

"Love your dress. The vibrant colors. And your hair. I bet that's a real project for you in the morning."

"Why, thank you, Doc. The dress is an African dashiki. This one's a little different because the print's more abstract. My 'dreads' aren't a big deal. I wrap them around and the combs hold them. I'm doing a modified 'rasta' style today."

"How do you type with all those bangles?"

She smiled. "Simple. I just push them up on my arms, say, 'Stay' and they listen. They're not like you lazy psychiatrists who don't finish notes, don't get prescriptions done and don't stay on schedule with our consumers."

"'Consumers'. I hate that sugar-coated word. I'm a Doctor. I treat patients, not shoppers at Walmart."

"Doc, that's way beyond my pay grade to worry about. Anyway, your charts and patient list are in their usual place."

Fancy kept a table near her desk where she'd stack the charts and a list of names of scheduled patients for each Clinic psychiatrist and therapist. He checked his appointment list. "Hmm, how many poor wretches am I saving today?"

"Dr. Jack, we've scheduled twenty-five consumers to receive your services. It don't make no never mind to me which ones you save. That's up to you."

"Fancy, I assume you'll be taking your usual nap at ten while I'm slaving away?"

"Only if the manicurist shows up on time before."

Jack grinned as he read her thought-for-the-day, 'I'd agree with you, but then we'd both be wrong'.

"Fancy, if you need me before I start seeing patients, I'll be in the staff-kitchen treating myself to some coffee-syrup likely reheated from yesterday. See ya later."

Her bangles clacking, she smiled. "You'd better, Dr. Jack, with your charts all complete."

***

Holding his mug with, 'Never Fear, The Doctor Is Here' on it, Jack entered the staff kitchen. The room was small with a miniature, rust-stained sink overflowing with unwashed cups and dishes, a microwave that had borne an internal food-explosion and a counter infested with scattered crumbs, spilled coffee, sugar and ants. Four beat-up, orange plastic chairs clung to a wobbly table that was always sticky.

"Why Dr. Bizby, my learned colleague, any coffee left?"

"Good morning, Jack," Jim Bizby said looking into the coffee urn. "Well, if your reality testing includes brown syrup as coffee, then yes, here be coffee."

"That'll work. It's only when my spoon stands up in it that I won't drink it."

"You're a true gourmet , Dr. Rackham. How're you doing, Jack? Aren't you early this morning? Miss your gym work-out because of a broken shoelace?"

"Nah. Bonny and I talked longer at breakfast so I skipped the gym and came here. You know, I sorta missed my daily dose of eau de Ben-Gay that the old farts working-out exude. It's either that fragrance or overkill with Old Spice to cover the Ben-Gay."

"Well, Jack, at least the guys are out there."

"Thank you, Doctor, for that unsolicited lesson in tolerance."

"Hey no charge. Professional courtesy."

"Jim, since we're discussing things that assault the senses, I've gotta ask. In the two months since you moved here from Cleveland, how many of those outrageously gaudy Hawaiian shirts have you bought? I don't believe you've worn the same one twice."

Jim Bizby was wearing wrinkled, khaki cargo-pants that fell over red, high-top sneakers and socks with parrots on them. His six-foot three height accentuated his shirt. "Ah, dear colleague, such an observant question demands an answer. Since my wife, Anne, and I arrived here in paradise, I've purchased not a few of these snazzy-yet-tasteful shirts. This one with white orchids on the deep-violet background is one of my favorites.

You know, if I'd worn this to work at The Cleveland Analytic Institute, my stuffy colleagues would've turned their pictures of Freud to the wall. The daily uniform there was a plain grey suit, white shirt or, if an analyst was in a zany mood, a light-blue shirt and a solid tie. Doing analytic therapy, one had to be plain to, you know, 'facilitate the transference'."

"Uh-huh. The blank page, the non-person to whom patients transfer their issues which you discuss. Then, they see where their thinking went awry and everyone's happy. Neat trick when it happens."

"Well, I think my casual look makes my patients feel more comfortable."

"You're going for the 'real person' look?"

"Yep. And I've found doing psychotherapy here, my patients still involve me in their emotional conflicts despite my vibrant, elegant shirts."

"Or maybe it's your shirts that get them going. I'm thinking you must feel pretty liberated away from there?"

"I do." Jim hesitated. "Jack, can I tell you something?"

"Sure."

"Um, I am not the most assertive guy. I can dither over a decision forever. When something disagreeable happens, I generally take the 'flight' versus 'fight' option until the problem passes. Cleveland fed right into my passivity. Just follow their rules and there'd be no conflict to run from. It got too comfortable. That's why I had to get out of there. I needed to face life more, not run from it."

"Good for you, Jim. And, ah, thanks for sharing that so early in the morning." Jack smiled. "So, I'm presently talking with a once desperate man, hitherto trapped in the, 'tyranny of the shoulds', who's made his heroic escape?"

"Working on it."

So the shirts…?"

"Yep. Like my Uncle Joe'd say, "When you keep your eyes closed, you miss a lot."

"Uncle Joe?"

"My favorite uncle. A farmer who worked everyday of his life. Raised five kids, loved his wife, drank beer and watched sports. He had a gift for seeing through the bull."

"Sounds like a good guy."

"You bet he was."

***

"Hey Jim, ever have a patient pull a gun on you?"

"A few psychotic in-patients have thrown things at me, but I've never faced a gun. Why?"

"Yesterday, one of my patients pulled-out a revolver, pointed it at me. It was a replica, but I didn't know that."

"Holy-moly, Jack, what'd you do?"

"Ha. Just sat there, wondered if I was going to die."

"Was he a violent guy? Paranoid? No, no, first, how are you doing? That would've scared the pants off of me."

"I'm fine. But I need a little advice on what to do next. He's a guy in his late teens who made a serious suicide attempt by hanging some months ago. I saw him a few times after his hospitalization. Then, he left for the Naval Academy, couldn't handle that and returned home. I've seen him a few times since. He resists treatment. He won't take meds and won't engage with me. He's either staring out the window or insulting me. Pulling the gun was a deviation from his usual presentation."

"Although threatening you with the gun is consistent with what appears to be deep-seated anger. Wow. Any idea what's eating at him?"

"Jim, read my lips. The shit won't talk with me. I can speculate, but I really don't have a clue."

"But he keeps coming back. You must be having some kind of effect on him."

"Right. I'm so effective, he aims a gun at my head. That's not quite the progress I was," Jack grinned, "shooting for."

"Glad *you* can smile. Hmm, that gun. Pretty extreme. A real power play on his part. I wonder...."

"Jim. Before you start getting into some analytical 'wonderings'. I'm looking for some concrete suggestions on what to do next."

"Well, there are clear transferential issues. But you know that."

"Yeah. And?"

"He's trying to distance you. But you also know that."

"Uh-huh."

"And he wants you to get angry with him, which you are."

"The bastard pulls a gun on me? Enraged might be a better word. C'mon Jim, give me something I don't already know."

"Okay, Jack. Let's talk about your countertransference."

"Why? That's obvious. Jim. What'd be more helpful are some ideas what might I do in the next appointment? Duh?."

"You're talking about your anger?"

"What else could there be?"

Jim waited a few seconds. "Jack, I need to see if we're on the same page about counter-transference."

"What-the-fuck? I don't need a lecture, Jim."

"No, no. I just want to be sure we share common ground here, okay?"

"Yeah. Sure."

"In psychotherapy, our patients can elicit feelings in us as we interact, our countertransference. The seductive woman who could be arousing? The passive-aggressive guy who ticks us off? If we're not careful, their behavior triggers in us the same responses they get from everyone else and then the therapy goes nowhere. We're supposed to use our own feelings, our countertransference, in the therapeutic process. Why does she *need* to be coy and suggestive? Why does he *need* to provoke to get an angry reaction? And then, well, you know the rest."

"Thanks for your pithy tour of countertransference, but I'm there. His bullshit provoked, really provoked me. My problem is to get him to talk about what happened."

"But what about your other feelings?"

"What other feelings?"

"The ones I know you'd rather not talk about. Feeling scared, confused, powerless staring at a gun. You couldn't let yourself get angry then. That came after."

"Goddamn soon."

"But what about your sense of failure at not controlling things? Your guilt over not connecting with this guy? Feeling helpless and frustrated as his psychiatrist? And…what about your possibly feeling grateful to him for not killing you?"

"*What?*"

"You'll need to reconcile being enraged at him while simultaneously being grateful to him for not killing you. And, of course, you'll be ticked at yourself for feeling grateful. All while trying to help him. Yikes."

"You bastard. You think this is funny?"

"No, Jack, I don't. And beyond these more obvious feelings, I'm more concerned about the darker side of countertransference."

"The *dark* side? C'mon?"

"What we've talked about are your conscious feelings. It's the subconscious ones that can be the real stinkers."

"Jesus. You're really on a roll now? Okay, what're those?"

"Patients can also evoke baggage from our past that can hinder our helping them. Jack, my father was an angry, abusive, SOB drunk. That's where a lot of my passivity comes from, not wanting to get hit in the mouth again for doing something. When I later had patients like him, I discovered I didn't deal well with them. My subconscious anger from the past was the reason. It stripped me of my objectivity."

"But I know I'm pissed at him. That's conscious and I'll deal with it."

"That's because he wasn't being a good patient and listening to the doctor. And, okay, he aimed a gun at you and scared you. But the degree of the anger you're manifesting is going way beyond that. It's overdetermined. I'm thinking his making you feel so helpless touched something in your subconscious that's making you so irate now."

Jack stood and shook his head. "Goddamn psychoanalysts."

***

Jack waited until his breathing slowed. "Screw it. Can we sit down? I need to fill you in on some stuff."

"Sure. There's still time before patients."

After brushing aside the crumbs on the table, Jack laid his hands flat and looked at his friend. "Jim, you shared something earlier. Let me do the same?"

"Certainly."

"When I practiced up north, I had two patients who killed themselves a few weeks apart. One was a very depressed young mother. She always told me she'd never kill herself because she'd never leave her three-year-old daughter motherless. Well, she did. The other was a young guy like my patient now, depressed and thinking suicide for months. I'd wanted to hospitalize him, but didn't because he swore to me he wasn't suicidal. He hung himself."

Jim shook his head. "Jack, you know that you can't stop someone if they decide to kill themselves. And they'll tell you anything so you won't interfere."

"Yeah, yeah. But knowing that doesn't make you feel better."

"Agreed."

Jack hesitated. "Okay, here's the rest. I had a fraternal twin-brother, JD. He hung himself when we were fourteen. We were very close until our teens when it became clear to me that he was the smarter twin who people liked more than me. And I resented him for it. After he died, I did the guilt thing for not being a better brother, had some therapy and moved on. Well, when those two patients killed themselves, the guilt over my brother resurrected itself.

So, Jim, I know about subconscious feelings. And if one's driving me, it's wanting to avoid feeling responsible for someone else's dying. Brad might kill himself. And the reason I'm so pissed, what you call my 'overdetermined' anger is from my frustration in not getting through to him." Jack smiled. "Plus, you bastard, you haven't given me any advice."

\ Excellent, Jack. No deep issues. Your only flaw is wanting to prevent another suicide. How noble."

"Okay, Jim, I know you've some asshole comment to make. Get it out."

"Just don't let your heroic need to rescue blur your objectivity. Brad may not want to change. Brad might kill himself. Trying to help him, great. But, trying to rescue him? That's about your guilt. And it's irrelevant. Jack, this isn't about you."

"My trying to help the guy is about *me*? Jim, you are so freakin far off the mark."

"Jack, I've gotta' go. When you see this guy? Tell him why you think he did what he did and what you believe is going on in general. He'll likely deny it and laugh in your face. But you need to get these things out on the open. Then, reaffirm to him you're there to help. There. That's my advice."

"You stinker. Something short, direct and not over-analyzed. I guess you can be decisive."

***

Walking to his office, he stared down at the faded, tile floor. The shit just keeps coming, first Bonny and now Jim with that smug, 'It's not about you, Jack' crap. They don't get it. They just don't get it.

He looked up. Dr. Felicity Steele, the new psychiatrist at the Clinic, was coming down the hallway. This was, what, the third time he'd glimpsed her few weeks here? There was that one time. He'd passed her office and saw her reading a Bible. The Bible? She was wearing a white, long-sleeved blouse, buttoned-to-her-neck, black plain-front pants, a black belt and flat, black shoes. What stood out was the two-inch, gold cross lying on her chest. He saw no make-up on skin so white it had a bluish hue. She'd pulled her black hair into a short, pony tail. She could be attractive. But she'd have to drop that grim look. Black and white must be her thing.

As they approached each other, he saw her rigid walk, almost rubbing against the other wall. She stared straight ahead.

"Good morning, Dr. Steele."

"Oh. Good morning." She pressed herself closer to the wall. No eye contact.

"Isn't this weather great? It's another day in paradise, isn't it?"

"Dr. Rackham, God has given us a sunny day. But remember. We are not in paradise. That which surrounds us may appear beautiful, but it is still imperfect, as are we. Paradise awaits us with the Rapture." Her right hand was intently twisting the gold cross.

As he stood, fumbling for a come-back, Dr. Felicity Steele was gone.

Now there goes one weird woman. Jack smiled. And I'd bet she's also a vegan.

THREE

Listening Often Gives Better Support Than A Mattress
Where Jack's Limitations Vex Him
OCD: Obsessions Are Thoughts You Can't Rid From Your Mind.
Compulsions Are Actions You're Driven To Do;
Did I Leave The Stove On? Did I Leave The Stove On? I'd better
Check.

Jack took a sip of his cold coffee, spit it back into his mug, put it on the desk. His eyes went to Bonny smiling at him from the framed picture she'd given him when he'd started work. She'd been so pleased finding that frame covered in small sea-shells. "Now you'll have me and a little bit of Florida right in front of you." Jack grunted, turned to look at his appointment list. Ken Rogers, his OCD man, was his first patient. Jack shook his head.

In the waiting room, Ken's face told Jack that his sadness hadn't changed. "Ken, would you mind if I gave you a hug rather than a hand-shake?"

"As long as you don't get sick. Doc, it's okay with me."

"I'll try not to, Ken."

In his office, Jack waited until Ken sat down, then slid into his desk-chair that squeaked each time he moved.

"Have you thought about getting that fixed, Doc? It's not a big deal. A little oil. I could do it for you."

Jack smiled. "Thanks, Ken. But if I fix it, I'll have nothing to complain about to maintenance, except maybe the dead flies on the windowsills. How are you?"

"The OCD's a little better. The other, no. If I'm driving and pass somebody walking along side of the road, I still have to circle the block and go back to reassure myself I didn't hit them. Or, if there's a bump in the road, I still stop and check I didn't hit anyone."

"I thought those had improved?"

"Well, I'm less compelled to check, although a new one's sorta crept in. You'll really like this."

"Oh?"

"You know I pick up part-time jobs here and there. My most recent one is in a cemetery. I'm the guy who comes with the back-hoe to cover up the grave when the service is over. What's happening is that after I finish and I'm driving away, I start obsessing over whether the person was *really* dead. Then the compulsion creeps in to go back, dig up the grave and check. Then, what would I do? Knock on the casket and say, 'Hey, anybody home?'"

They both laughed. "Ken, it's good to see you laughing a little more. You know, I'm still amazed at how differently your OCD presented. Instead of your being obsessed with germs getting on you, you were afraid you'd contaminate others and get them sick."

"Yeah, Doc. Mary was the only person I'd touch without that fear. The roughest time was when I was a mail-carrier up north and worried about spreading disease because I'd touched people's mail. But you can see that's much better. Otherwise, I wouldn't have been able to return your hug."

"I noticed and thought it a good sign, especially with your stress over Mary's death. Significant stress like that can cause relapses. You are taking your med?"

"Yeah. Same dose. No side-effects."

"With your wife's death and your grieving, I'd like to think it's helping there as well as with your OCD."

"You're the Doctor,"

Jack leaned forward, the chair squeaked. "Ken, how are you *really* doing without her? I know how profound losing her has been for you. Did you call that number I gave you? That support group for people who recently lost a spouse? My guess is no."

"Doc, you know how shy I am. I lucked out being a mailman all those years because I didn't have to deal with people too much. I'd been pretty much a loner my entire life until I met Mary. I still think it was a miracle how we ever got together. She was just as shy as me."

Ken lowered his head. "Give me a second."

Jack waited.

"That's why I miss her so much. We weren't, you know, social with lots of friends, church and stuff. It was just the two of us, always with each other. She was part of my soul, way beyond that, 'soul-mate' stuff. Our 'beings' were one. I think it was because we both were so shy and, despite that, found each other that made our relationship so extra especial. She'd call my OCD things my "kindness for people' because I didn't want them getting sick or hurt.

Every day, I go to the cemetery and we talk. I tell her about my day. Oh, I've asked her if you can still be shy in Heaven, but haven't heard back yet. I've told her about my new part-time job with the nursing home. I'm their driver and take residents out to, like, doctor's appointments. It's a good job for me because I can't turn the car around and check if I ran someone over. She told me to stay with this job for a while."

"Do you see anyone outside of the job?"

"See anyone? Doc, whaddya mean?"

"Not like that, Ken. I meant, besides saying,' Please 'and 'Thank you 'at the grocery store, do you have any social interaction with anyone outside of work?"

"No, but I gotta tell you. Those widows in my condo complex are crafty. A couple have asked me to fix a leak or help hang a picture. Then they drop hints about making dinner to show their gratitude. I just smile, thank them and shake my head."

"Ken, you know we all need people, some sort of interaction."

"Doc, I talk with the elderly people I drive around. I like that. And it really helps as a distraction. Otherwise, I'd be thinking of Mary all of the time. You're right. People need people. And Mary was my 'people'. The one and only I needed. I think of our happy times even though it makes her not being with me all the worse and me sadder. Go figure."

"Ken, I know you won't believe this right now, but, things will get better. It'll never be like when Mary was alive, but, somehow, you will be better. With time."

"You're right, Doc." Ken gave him a little smile. "I don't believe you, but thanks anyway."

When their time was up, Jack was writing Ken's prescription when he looked up at his patient. "Ken, as I write this, I'm telling myself I'm doing something for you. But I feel so frustrated not being able to lessen your sadness and feeling of loss."

"Doc, if I didn't love her so much, I wouldn't feel so sad now, would I?"

"No, but…"

"Doc, listen, I wouldn't have traded that happiness for anything,

anything. So, it's okay I'm sad. It tells me how wonderful it was."

"You're a good man, Ken. Do you still want to meet this often? Outside of the prescription, I'm not sure what else I do for you."

"Doc, don't sell yourself short. First, you give me some of that," Ken smiled, " 'social interaction'. But, more than that, you give me hope."

FOUR

Life In Black And White Is Easy. It's Color That Makes It Messy
Where Dr. Steele Gives Compassion A Try
Empathy: The Ability To Understand and Share the Feelings of
Another; Being Sympathetic And Caring

You have failed again. Failed to manifest to others His spirit within you. You made a feeble try, but then you faltered and fled. Facing that wanton woman, you also ran. Your sins still make you weak.

Felicity sat at her desk, hand on her Bible. She raised up her eyes, whispered, "Lord, in Your infinite wisdom, You have placed before me today iniquitous people. Guide me, a weak and flawed sinner, to suffer them in their imperfections that I might lift them from the darkness where they dwell. Dr. Rackham sees but the temporal world, not beyond. His false friendliness conceals not his licentious leer. Ms. Muwamba, a Jezebel in her dress and hair, feigns kindness and caring with deceptive smiles. My Savior, give me strength to overcome my revulsion to their hypocrisy and not flee from my task to bring them to Your glory. Help me, Lord."

She recalled Reverend Billy-Ray Turner's daily Bible quote on her Ford Fiesta's radio, *With everlasting love I will have compassion on you, says the Lord, your Redeemer, Isaiah 54:8,* Today, she would show compassion for those dead in the Spirit. With compassion, she would raise them out of the abyss of their ignorance and from Satan's grasp.

***

Her first two jobs were but His preparation for the Clinic, a fertile place for His word. She had learned tolerance at the drug rehabilitation clinic with its addicts scorning and reviling her, rejecting how coming to Jesus would cleanse both their bodies and souls and give them a 'spiritual high'.

That group psychiatric practice that expected her to prescribe medication to everyone had given her determination. They scoffed when she explained how the sin of Adam destined all mankind to suffering. How, through Him, we must all learn to accept and cope with our plight until the Rapture. How drugs like antidepressants gave but a false happiness, not His happiness. It was His will when they asked her to leave.

In the solitude of her office she slowly twisted her cross.

Finding Pastor Franklin of The Evangelical Covenant Church had been a blessing. He seems a godly man sincere in welcoming her to his fold.

"Dr. Steele, I understand your father is also a minister?" Pastor Franklin had said.

"He is an Evangelical minister with a very large congregation. He is also a Bishop in the Church."

"You must be quite proud of him and hold him in high esteem?"

She gave a slight nod. Growing up, she had assisted Zane Steele with his congregation. She was his, 'earthly angel' aiding him in spreading the good news of the Bible and leading fallen-away sinners to be reborn and turn away from the Evil-One. *His* earthly angel.

Her hand tightened around her cross as she recalled the Bishop's words as he baptized those wishing to be reborn, "*Above all, love each other deeply, because love covers over a multitude of sins.*" 1 Peter 4:8

She shook her head, thought briefly of her mother but then Verity came into her mind. Verity, now in her teens was beginning to receive more attention from the Bishop. Felicity had been avoiding that.

She would call her, ask about things at home and at church. They had not talked in a while.

A noise jarred her. She looked at her clock, pushed on the arms of her chair and rose up, ready to do His work.

***

They sat in silence. Cindy Kraft, a new patient to the Clinic, peered at this Doctor with the super-organized desk intently page through her chart. Just minutes before, Cindy had watched this woman in black and white stand on the edge of the waiting room and call her name. Cindy had stood up and nodded. Realizing that her new Doctor was not coming to greet her, she walked to her.

Cindy extended her hand. "Hello, I'm Cindy. I…"

"I am Dr. Steele," the Doctor had said, turned and walked away.

Cindy guessed she was to follow and found the Doctor in the hallway pointing to an open door. Looking in, she saw a chair and guessed again that's where she should sit. Now, she watched and waited, hands tight together on her lap. The office was so sterile. Only that cross on the wall, the Bible on the desk. Give her a chance she told herself. You need the help and you've waited two weeks for the appointment. Give her a chance.

The Doctor was looking down at Cindy's chart. "From what you have written here, I see you do not take any psychiatric medications, have no physical problems and have not been treated for any past psychiatric problems. Is this true?"

"Yes. Why would you think otherwise?"

"Ms. Kraft, I asked a simple, direct question. Thank you for confirming what I asked. In my world, people may hide things."

The Doctor pointed at something in the chart with her Bic. " I note that you answered in the, 'What brought you to the clinic' question, 'Will speak with the doctor'. Why are you here?"

"I bought a condo and moved here from Rhode Island five years ago. I took early retirement and wanted to get away from the cold winters. You might know what those can be like?"

"Ms. Kraft, I am not here to discuss the weather. Why are you here?"

"Sorry. You see, my Mother and step-father lived near me up there although I didn't see them too much. He, my step-father, was the true reason I moved away after I retired much more than the weather." The Doctor said nothing.

"He sexually abused me when I was growing up. It started when I was eleven and it really didn't end until I left for college."

The Doctor, turning the cross at her neck, looked up without comment.

"About six months ago, while talking with my Mother on the phone, she told me how she was getting weaker because of her heart. How her doctor had recommended that she move to a warmer climate. Then, I hear her saying that she's moving in with me so I could take care of her. Just like that. Doctor, I'm an only child in a family, including her two sisters, that'll have nothing to do with her. So, I guess I was it."

Head down, the Doctor was writing in the chart. "Why are you here."

"I resisted, but she eventually guilted me into letting her move in with me. How she was suffering up north. How I was the only one she could rely on me to help her. How I had room with my two bedroom condo."

Stopping her writing, the Doctor looked up and glared.

"Doctor. The reason I came to the Clinic is that my step-father also came with her. He's why I fought her moving here for as long as I did."

"But you did finally submit and agree?"

"Yes. It was the 'If I die up here, it'll be on your conscience' nagging that got to me. That was four months ago and it's been hell since."

"Hell is for sinners, Ms. Kraft. Perhaps we shall pursue that later. But why has it been so difficult for you that you came to the Clinic?"

"From day one here, he…"

"Your step-father?"

"Yes. Who else? Sorry. He started making comments about my looks, things like 'You've sure matured into a beautiful woman, Cindy,' or, 'I don't remember your tits being that big. Didja get one of those boob-jobs to get more action?' He'll deliberately rub against me or brush his hand against my breast or back-side. Then he'll say, 'Cindy, why do you always stand so close to me?' so my Mother can hear. My place isn't that big so I try to avoid him by doing things like seeing my friends. But I think, 'Damn, it's *my* place, my home Why do I have to be the one who stays away?'"

"What does your step-father's behavior have to do with your coming to this Clinic?" The Doctor said, shaking her head.

"I'm sorry for not being specific. His behavior has me very stressed. Before the serious abuse started when I was a kid, he started with what my immature mind thought were compliments like how I was getting pretty and 'filling out so nicely'. His attention, at first, made me feel a little special. But then, he started touching my arm or hand which led to his skim his hand across my chest or leg. Then, he'd come into my bedroom at night to 'tuck me in'. That led to his fondling me, his fingers probing and his having me give him oral sex to 'help him cope'. That went on for several years. He's now beginning the same behaviors. And I know where they're leading."

The Doctor looked up. "So, you allowed him touch you before?"

"I did. I didn't think I had a choice."

"That's what you told yourself. Did he have sexual intercourse with you?"

Cindy twisted her hands together harder. "It was awful. He'd start by telling me how beautiful I was, more than just a step-daughter to him. How he was preparing me for being with men so I'll know what to expect and not be scared. He said that if I ever told my Mother about what he was doing, he'd say it was me who'd seduced him. He had me convinced she'd believe him over me."

"But why are you at the Clinic?"

"Your questions bring up horrible memories. Sorry." Cindy sat more upright and looked directly at her. "Doctor, there's a man who raped me, violated me, made me live in fear everyday growing up, living in my house. I'm here because my anxiety is getting way out of control. I thought I could handle the situation as an adult, but I can't. I know what he's doing. In *my* place. In *my* home. Where I had found peace." Cindy began shaking her head. "Doctor, I'm on my guard whenever he's around. I'm having flashbacks. I'm having nightmares where I see his face, feel the weight of his body on me and hear his heavy breathing as he pushes himself into me. In another nightmare, I'm in this enclosed space like a box and it's pitch-black. I can't see anything and I can't breathe. I struggle, pushing with all my might, to escape. But the walls won't give. That's when I panic and wake up sweating, gasping for air.

I've lost fifteen pounds. I'm jumpy all the time. He follows me around. I know he wants to get me alone."

The Doctor put down her pen.

"You are certain that he is being sexually inappropriate?"

"What? Doctor, are you kidding? I've been through this before. Do you think I'm imagining this? Hallucinating? I can assure you I'm not."

"Is your mother aware of what you say is transpiring?"

"She closes her eyes. I've told her, but she responds exactly like she did years ago. That I never liked him so I lie and make up bad things about him. That he's just trying to be nice. Now, she brings up my divorce. My 'ex', by the way, was a cheating drunk who'd slap me around when he felt like it. She says that maybe I'm giving off sexual 'vibrations 'to him, since I haven't been with a man for a while, Anyway, whatever I think is happening is my fault.

Oh. And I've learned there's nothing wrong with her heart. I got her a cardiologist when she moved down and went in with her to the appointment. After all the tests, he told us she has no big problems. He thought she'd be elated. Instead, she got upset, called him a 'quack' and started yelling at me. That's when it hit me what a jerk I've been. How she's been using me."

The Doctor crossed her arms. "Your Mother raised you and knows you. Could it be that she is right?"

"Right? In what way, please?"

"Might it be that you *are* being sexual towards your step-father? That subconscious motives are driving you to return to what you had with him years ago? I assume you now have no male companionship. You are divorced. You did say that you felt, 'special' in that relationship. Are you are attempting to recover that now? Perhaps that's the reason you allowed your Mother to move down here? You knew he would be coming, did you not? The man you fled from?"

"I told myself he was older. That that ugly history was in the past."

"That's what you *told* yourself. Yet, you still let her and him come. I believe your unconscious and conscious minds are in conflict and that is what is causing your anxiety."

Cindy slid her chair closer to the Doctor's desk and rested her palms on its surface making the Doctor wince. She fixed her eyes directly on the woman in black and white before her.

"Doctor Steele, I am conscious of feeling quite dumb in letting my mother move down here in the first place, especially since learning she doesn't have a heart problem. My constant worrying if he's going to come into my bedroom or when I'm in the shower make me feel even dumber and, yes, angry, mostly at myself. Yes, I did feel special with the extra attention he gave me, a kid, years ago. But, Doctor, that was very short-lived once I realized something was wrong. Having been in group therapy for abused women, I've learned that those feelings are normal. That guilt over those feeling is also normal and to let that go, which I did."

"I believe you stated you had no previous therapy. That was a falsehood."

Cindy's palms pushed harder into the desktop. She enunciated each word. "I have a sexual predator living in my condo. I am afraid. I am extremely anxious. I'm not sleeping. I'm not eating. He will be coming into my bedroom one of these nights."

"Your door has a lock."

"Yes, one of those that you can open with a paper-clip."

"Install a bigger lock."

"Doctor, it's my house. Why should I have to do that? Right now, I keep a bottle of pepper-spray next to my bed. But this is no way to live."

"You resist a bigger lock? Do you want him in there."

"Doctor, am I not being clear? I'm a prisoner in my own home."

"You can call the police."

"They're useless. They arrive, my mother describes how I get hysterical but now I'm fine. They look at me like a nut case and go."

"You can ask them to leave."

"I've seriously thought about it. But, I do feel an obligation to her. After all, she is my mother.Even though there's no love there, I know I'd feel guilty if I threw her, them out."

"Ms. Kraft, you have many excuses which allow you to keep them in your house. I see your anxiety as a consequence of your guilt. Man is born in evil and must constantly guard against it entering our souls. You were sexually active as a teen."

"You can't possibly..." The Doctor raised her hand.

"When you left home, did your lewd behavior continue? There is your failed marriage, your anger towards your Mother and, I believe, your ambivalence towards your step-father. You have admitted to the anger at yourself. These are the many seeds from which guilt grows."

"Doctor, I'm here for my anxiety. I'm not myself anymore."

"Is there a minister? A priest with whom you and your step-father might counsel? Jesus may have placed your step-father, who you say dwells in evil, before you so that you might be a light for him for change?"

29

Cindy sat back and placed her shaking hands back into her lap. "If I could, I'd solve my issues myself. But my anxiety is so bad I can't keep my attention on anything long enough.

Why am I here? For help to function better so I can resolve the outrageous situation I'm in. Not to talk about Jesus. Doctor, can you help me?"

"I recommend church with perhaps your step-father joining you. Commit to Jesus and He will forgive your sins, absolve your guilt."

"Will you please prescribe a medication for my anxiety? I'm falling apart."

"No, it is your soul that is in spiritual turmoil. Anti-anxiety medications are not for that."

"Then what are they for?"

"To dull the mind and open it to Satan."

"I shall pray for you," the Doctor said to Cindy's back.

FIVE

A Meeting Of Minds Rarely Happens
Where Sentient Beings Demonstrate Interpersonal Skills
<u>*Personality:*</u> *That Unique Combination Of Traits That Form An*
Individual's Distinctive Character; What You See Is What You Get

"Thank God you're here, Martha." Dr. Kingston-Smith was staring at his reflection in his full-length mirror. "I really need your expert eye. Be honest now. How do I look? I chose for my *mode du jour* this tan, poplin suit with the light-lavender shirt, matching print tie and pocket handkerchief. I think the colors work quite well together, don't you? But, these gold cufflinks? Perhaps they're a bit *de trop?*"

He pulled up his pants leg. "Look here.The lavender socks with the palm-tree *motif?* They really complete *l'ensemble, n'est-ce pas?* Martha, I can see it in your eyes. I do look good, don't I?"

Martha, Dr. Kingston-Smith's personal secretary, sighed. Tip-toeing in, she'd planned on leaving the meeting agenda on her boss's desk, then tip-toeing out. But he'd caught her. She straightened and appraised her boss from top to bottom.

"Dr. Kingston-Smith, I do believe y'all have outdone yourself. I only wish I knew some fancy French word to describe you."

"I knew you'd agree. You *always* surprise me having such good taste for someone who grew up around here."

"Why, bless your heart. But Doctor? Did you want your pen showing in front of the handkerchief?"

He looked down and adjusted the pen to stand out more. "I keep my *Mont Blanc* accessible to highlight items I'm reviewing with someone. When I speak, like at today's meeting, I often use it as a pointer."

"Mm-hmm." Martha dropped the agenda on his desk, turned to leave.

"Oh, Martha, two things?"

"*Yes,* Doctor?"

"I noticed one of the diplomas on my trophy wall hasn't been upgraded to my new hyphenated name. Take care of that, won't you?"

"My pleasure, Doctor."

"And order me that stronger-hold mustache wax. This Florida heat. I hate it when one end starts to droop."

"Consider it done, Doctor." She said over her shoulder hurrying from his office.

Smith stepped onto a small stool to review his look once more in his mirror. Lifting his chin, he assessed his thick unibrow that loomed over large, dark eyes, a wide nose and thin lips. *I may be short and not ultra-handsome, mais, je suis unique.* He curled each side of his handlebar mustache. *But I have the look. And, that, in fact, makes me très unique.* Smith pleasured himself curling both sides up again. He loved doing it in front of others staring-off with a pensive look.

Hopping to sit on a desk corner, his squatty legs dangling off the floor, Dr. Kingston-Smith reviewed his points for the staff-meeting. To lead and motivate his staff were his goals. The Vice-Provost's words, 'Reginald, I know you'll be going places here' still inspired him. He'd never be like his gutless parents, wasting their lives teaching and catering to those rich, condescending brats at that elite New England prep school. He'd moved on, acquired status as an MD and found his niche in administration rather than clinical practice where he'd be forced to listen to the endless whining of ungrateful patients. Here he had prestige, respect and power.

Slipping off the desk corner, he checked his Rolex, took one last-look in his mirror and twisted both ends of his mustache, giving each an extra turn. *C'est moi. Très elegant, très unique.*

Leaving, he bared his left wrist to Martha. "Instead of the gold cufflinks, I added this gold bracelet. Be honest. What do you think?"

* * *

Having a no-show, Jack went to the meeting room early to have some quiet. As he sat in one of the metal, folding chairs that surrounded the meeting table, he sniffed. It was still there, that low-grade smell of mold. Jesus, it was obnoxious. He stood up, inspected the room. Looking up, he saw the bastard, a black AC vent in the ceiling. The mothership for mold smell. And nobody gave a shit about it. Sitting down again, one of the fluorescent lights started to flicker and emit a loud, buzzing. Goddamn it.

He turned as Hester Snopes came in. "How's it goin, Hester?"

Jack took in her blousy blouse, her long, frilly dress, the dangling 'dream-catcher' earrings, her clanging bangles and sandals wrapping around pudgy feet that attached to a pudgy body. Her pink-lensed granny glasses on the tip of her nose was a nice touch. Gathering her dress in, Hester Snopes, psychiatric-counselor, took the chair that'd be right next to Smith's. Her bangles clunked against the table as she put her water bottle down and settled in.

"Hey there, Jack. Great morning, isn't it?" Hester said, fluffing-up her hair.

"That water, Hester, I don't recognize the brand."

"It's Icelandic Glacial Water, the *purest* water in the world."

"All the way from a glacier in Iceland?"

"Jack, please? It's overflowing with natural minerals and antioxidants to boost the immune system and cleanse the liver." She coughed slightly. "I feel a cold coming on so it's perfect for me."

"It'll certainly cleanse your kidneys when you pee more." He smirked. "Does it also cure cancer, slow aging and bring world peace?"

"Always the cynic, aren't you, Jack? It can't hurt to be good to ourselves, can it?"

"Right, Hester. Outside of your cold, how're things?"

Hester clapped her plump hands. "Fantastic! I've had two couples in this morning who're doing better talking without yelling. And it was me who gave them the tools they needed to do it.

I had one woman, though, who's still sad. She hasn't responded to my PAT."

"Huh? Never heard of that, Hester. You give a client a pat on the back and make soothing sounds? "

"No, Jack. It's my 'Positive Attitude Therapy'. But I've been reading about a new approach I might take with her."

"Uh-huh."

"The woman's husband died six-months ago and she's still not over it. She claims she's seen him at times since, mostly like when she's drifting off to sleep. She'll feel a presence, open her eyes and see him. I believe his spirit is there beside her."

"Do they talk to each other?"

"She talks, but so far, he hasn't said anything back to her."

"Hester, seeing loved ones after they die is pretty common,

especially in the dark when someone's falling asleep."

"But I think this is different."

"Because your PAT didn't work?"

"Yeah. See, with PAT, I first find out the client's problem.

Then, I give similar stressful experiences in my life and how I solved them. Like I told this woman how sad I was when my cat died. How I saw friends and did a little bar-hopping for socialization, went shopping and pulled myself out of it."

"How strange that she didn't buy into that."

"No. I told her how selfish she was, just thinking about herself and losing him, being alone, all the usual garbage. The stubborn woman wouldn't listen to me."

"Uh-huh. This poor woman continues to be distraught over the loss of her husband and you're calling her selfish. So, what're you gonna do?"

"Well, when she began talking about feeling his presence, I started reading about spiritualism, you know, spirits getting in touch with us from the beyond? I'm thinking that maybe I can guide her to talk with him and get him to talk back."

"Hester, isn't contacting the dead a little out of our area of expertise?"

"I don't know. Heck, since none of my usual stuff's working, maybe it's worth a try?"

"In helping people process grief, we aim to get them past their loss and back into life. But, beyond the sadness, grieving might contain anger, guilt. And these have to be dealt with. Grieving takes time. And, Hester, it has to go at their pace, not yours, I'm guessing you don't get much into psychodynamics?"

"Are you kidding?. That stuff takes time. And, I'm actually supposed to listen. Like with this client. She goes go on and on about missing him, how her life's changed, how alone she feels. It's all about her. Jack, I'll stick with my Experiential Therapy. It's more direct. Here's how I coped, it worked, do it."

"Okay. Instead of helping her bring closure to her loss and move on, you're looking to keep him around? So, if she gets lonely, she can pick-up the phone and dial 1-800-afterlife and ask for, Roy?"

"Always the smartass, huh, Jack?"

Closing his eyes, Jack waved his arms and made a high-pitched, 'oooOOOoooo' sound. "The spirits are around us....oooOOOooo...." He grinned, "Okay, Hester, let me know if you make contact. There's a dead guy I knew who owes me twenty-bucks."

Jim Bizby came into the room. "Good morning, all. What's this about the hereafter?" "Oh, Hester and I were discussing a therapeutic approach," Jack said. Jim sat down opposite him.

"Mm-hmm. All going well, Jack?"

"Life's a piece o'cake."

"Great. Any more curious weapons pop-up in your office?""Nope, not a one. Although I did suffer a paper cut injury."

"Hey." Hester said. "What are you two talking about?"

"Oh, I told Jim that sometimes I wished I'd a squirt gun to use on some of my annoying patients and he's just kidding me about it."

A noise made them turn to the doorway. Dr. Felicity Steele had been watching, listening. She walked to farthest end of the table and sat, ruler-straight, crossing her hands in front of her like an obedient third-grader. She stared at the empty chair at the table's opposite end.

"Good morning, Dr. Steele," Jim said.

"Good morning."

"In your three weeks here, I must apologize for not offering you any help settling into the Clinic. If you've any questions, we could sit, have a cup of coffee?"

"I have been here three and one-half weeks. And I do not allow stimulants into my body. I have no questions regarding the Clinic. But, thank you for your offer."

"Well, if you need any information about the area like places to shop, restaurants, let me know, okay? I like to take photos so I've driven around here a lot."

"Thank you. I have established support in the Christian community here. They have been of great help to me."

"Super. Well, if...."

"Why don't you just leave her be," Dr. Gus Cobb said to Jim as he walked to a chair. "She's already told you she has friends helping her out. You know, Bizby, sometimes that overly folksy, mid-west behavior of yours makes me want to puke."

In his early sixties, Dr. Cobb had been at the Clinic since it opened. His grey eyes, alert and penetrating, stared out from a deeply lined face that resembled a scowling, dried-up apple. Sitting, he unbuttoned the jacket of his wrinkled gray suit showing a frayed white shirt. He always wore a bow tie.

"You're absolutely right, Dr. Cobb," Jim said. "I was being a little pushy with Dr. Steele."

Cobb growled, "Pushy? Bizby, you were being damned intrusive."

"I was, wasn't I." Jim turned. "Dr. Steel, I'm sorry if..."

Fancy Muwamba burst into the room. "Good morning everyone." She stood, arms overflowing with the memos, University updates and psychiatric journal articles that Dr. Smith would soon inflict on his staff.

Maximo Hernandez, MD appeared behind her. *"Permesso, Señorita?* May I help with your burden?"

"Thank you, Dr. Hernandez. You can put them next to Dr. Smith's chair."

"De nada," He said putting the pile down, his thick, braided gold chain and cross falling from inside his unbuttoned shirt. Putting on his smiling face, Max Hernandez mouthed a, *buenas dias* to no one in particular, his eyes prowling around the room. Moving a chair closer to her, he sat next to Felicity Steele, placing one hand near hers. *"Ola, señorita.* Is all going well for you today?" Max's teeth gleamed.

"I am well, Dr. Hernandez," Felicity said.

"To hear that gives me great happiness. Please, call me Max like all *mis amigas?* You should know, *señorita,* I am very familiar with the area. Since you've just arrived, I'd be very pleased to show you around."

"Dr. Bizby has already offered me help." Felicity said. "But I have my own resources. Therefore, I shall not need to impose on you."

He brushed his hand lightly against hers. "It would be no imposition, *señorita.* Believe me. There's a local restaurant that serves excellent Spanish food and music to dance to, I...."

With his touch, Felicity withdrew her hand as though stung and wrapped it around her cross. She turned to face him. "I have no need. Thank you. Also, please do not call me, *señorita.* I am , as you, a Doctor. I wish to be addressed as such." Distancing their chairs, she turned away as Dr. Kingston-Smith entered, walked to the table's head and opened his arms. *"Bon jour, mes enfants.* Thank you for your presence."

Once seated, he stretched his arms placing his note-cards to his left and his *Mont Blanc* to his right while allowing a gold bracelet on one wrist and his Rolex on the other to emerge. He looked up at those around the table and, stroking his mustache, gave a broad grin.

"I want to thank you all for the great job you're doing in my, our Clinic. As I am constantly telling the Vice-Provost at lunch, your splendid team effort reflects your dedication to the core underpinnings fundamental to our mission. Keep up the good work.

I'll first distribute various journal articles I believe you'll find instructive as did I."

"Will there be a test?"

"Dr. Rackham?"

"On the psych articles? Will there be a test?"

Smith condescended a smile. *"Quel drôle,* Doctor. No. No test. Only intellectual stimulation Please read them in your leisure time."

"Or when I need something to help me sleep," Jack mumbled across to Jim.

"Fancy, my dear, please distribute the articles and other information."

"Certainly, sir," she said, thinking she'd soon be shredding them.

"I've also drawn-up recommendations, mostly for the doctors, describing what you should be including in your clinical notes. The State will be auditing our charts soon and, notwithstanding how excellent your clinical notes are, I want to be sure you're following Florida's best-practice guidelines. Fancy, make sure you get those out to everyone. Additionally, Doctors, to improve your efficiency, I am lessening your time with a new patient from forty-five to thirty minutes and from fifteen to ten with follow-ups."

Jack raised his hand, but didn't wait for Smith. "So, you want us writing more in the chart for State bureaucrats while simultaneously seeing more patients with whom we'll spend less time. Move the assembly line faster and increase production? Make those numbers look better, huh?"

Dr. Kingston-Smith pointed his pen at Jack. *"Au contraire.*

Doctor. You and I are both aware of the virulent expansion of community mental health problems. With this tragic increase in emotional suffering and consequent demand for services, I've taken upon myself a Herculean effort to meet this urgent need for help and fulfill our sacred mission to administer to and improve the quality of life of these tormented people. My plan will lessen the wait for mental health services and, thus, hasten symptom stabilization. With this enhanced nexus between services and needs in the social structure, I know we'll all experience an increased sense of fulfillment, a genuine 'wow' moment in witnessing our consumers smile once again."

Jack was gazing at the black ceiling vent. With all the hot air, he thought the mold colony was actually expanding.

"Am I clear, Dr. Rackham?"

Jack nodded. "Yes. I am illuminated, Dr. Smith."

Hester raised her hand. The pen moved to her. "Will the counseling staff have lessened appointment times? I'm engaged in intense therapy sessions with several clients who could profit from even more of my expertise. Since the doctors mostly do med-management, I can see dropping their client time. But we counselors have more intimate relationships with our clients that require quality time."

Dr. Kingston-Smith furled his thick unibrow and twisted his mustache. "Hester, your contribution to the Clinic team is invaluable. Within the present milieu of our deliverable modular units, I, presently, foresee no changes in your time allotments. Dr. Bizby?"

"Are there rules about firearms in the Clinic? I mean, we do treat some distraught people. And this *is* Florida."

"The University forbids firearms in any building on campus. We should have a sign about guns on our entrance. Fancy, confirm that for me. Have one put up if we don't. Why do you ask, Dr. Bizby?"

"Just wondering."

"Fancy can locate the University's dicta about that for you if you wish."

The pen pointed at Gus Cobb. "Dr.Cobb, you seem a bit disquieted. You've a question or comment?"

"Damn right I do. Two things: First, must you keep swinging that dumbass pen of yours around like you're some kind of orchestra conductor? I feel like some kid in a chorus. Second, can you stop those damn female drug reps from hanging around my office? They get in the way and they take up my time. I've no problem giving them my signature so they can leave samples. But getting cornered to hear them spout skewed data that makes their product look amazing is a waste of my time. It was better when we had male reps. If I said, 'look, no bullshit. Just give me the basics on the drug,' they would. Now, with sex helping to sell meds, we get these cutesy babes with their sweet smiles and short skirts pushing the product. Can you just keep them out of my way? Especially since we're going to have less time with patients."

Smith knew he'd never jeopardize the Clinic's relationship with any pharmaceutical company. He loved the free drug-dinners at expensive restaurants too much. "Dr. Cobb, I appreciate your concerns about the drug representatives. They do, however, supply us information on new meds and I suspect an experienced psychiatrist like yourself knows the right questions to ask to circumvent the, the…."

"Bullshit," Cobb said.

"Yes,. The reps shouldn't be venturing on their own into the doctors' office area. I'll look into that. But, please don't close your mind to new products which we might add to our psycho-pharmacologic armamentarium."

Smith took a quick breath. "I am distressed that you find my 'swinging' my pen distasteful. However, I find your analogy to my being a conductor quite apt. I direct you, my staff, to work in rhythm and harmony. I conduct, you follow. C'est évident."

Cobb grunted.

"Myself, I find speaking with the drug reps a welcome break in my schedule. They are personable people I enjoy interacting with. It increases my knowledge and experience," Dr. Hernandez said.

"Dr. Max," Fancy said, "I have noticed how you close your office door for long spells to increase your experience with those female reps. I notice because your patients start piling up in the waiting room."

"I only want the reps to think well of us. I'm spreading good will. Is that wrong?"

Fancy nodded and smiled.

Smith raised his pen. "Dr. Hernandez, keep up the good work. Everyone, if that's all there is, I shall adjourn the meeting. *À la prochaine,*"

Walking out with Jim, Jack said, "These meetings have a certain Dickensian quality to them, eh, old chap?"

"I do believe, old bean, that in future meetings, I shan't have any… great expectations." Jim smiled. "You know what my Uncle Joe'd say about Smith? 'Every donkey thinks himself worthy to stand with the king's horses.'"

***

Her face alternating between smiles and grimaces, Hester was thumb-tapping-on her iPhone. Sensing something, she looked up. Dr. Steele was staring at her from the distant end of the conference table.

"Oh, I was so busy catching up with clients, I didn't see you. I give them my number in case they're in crisis and need me."

"Ms. Snopes, it must be very supportive for them to know they can depend on you. To have someone to trust is rare. I did not mean to interrupt you. I was waiting until the staff exited the room. I dislike being among the crush as people jam together."

Hester nodded."Uh-huh." Her thumbs active again.

"You are so busy administering to your clients, I am sorry to bother you. But may I say something?"

Hester sighed. "Sure, Dr. Steele, what?"

"It impressed me when you voiced your concerns in the meeting about having enough time for your therapy clients, your fighting for them was a very assertive thing to do. At my Church…."

Hester sneered at her phone. "I just got this text from this mf-ing male client. He's sending me suggestive texts again. I'm his freakin' therapist, not some babe to hustle. You know he tried it before? And I warned him. What balls. I'll have Fancy send him a registered letter to terminate him. That'll make it official and cover my ass. I've gotta stop giving clients my number. I'm just too caring.

Oh, and just before this pervert, a woman client texts me. Over and over, she gets into relationships with abusers who push her around, bad-mouth her in front of her friends and try to control her life. And then, guess what? She gets upset and texts me. I've told her what to do a million times, but does she do it? Ha.

Wait, listen to this. One time, she did go out with a guy who seemed nice and really liked her. Know what happened? She dropped him. Why? Because, he was being *too* nice to her and she didn't deserve him. I can't believe her bullshit. Well, she's hooked-up, again, with some asshole who's treating her just like all the other assholes. She wants to know what to do. Un-freakin'-believable. Dr. Rackham told me once that her behavior was classic 'repetition compulsion', that she was 'seeking mastery over traumatic events from her childhood'. I told him, to save his snooty psychoanalytical terms for someone who cares.

All I know is that she keeps walking down the same road and falling into the same hole I tell her she can walk around the hole and even chose to walk down another road, What a dumbass.

Dr. Steele, weren't you saying something?"

"I am impressed by how Christian your caring for your patients is."

"Yeah, well thanks. I don't know how 'Christian' it is, but it's what me, Hester Snopes, does."

"Ms. Snopes, this client you were discussing, the one being abused?"

"Yeah, the one looking for love in all the wrong places?"

"I know you are trying your very best with her."

"Yeah? And?"

"Ms. Snopes, might I suggest that your client, in her quest for love, embrace Jesus? He is the Source from which all love flows. And, He does not abuse."

What the hell? This little pissant who sits like she has a rod up her ass giving me advice? Damn Christian of her. Maybe I could get her to speak in tongues? Now, that'd be a hoot.

Hester forced her biggest smile. "Dr. Steele, *thank* you. Now I've another treatment option for her. Right now, I'll keep telling her what a dumbass she is. Maybe one of these days, she'll choose to walk around the hole. Or maybe, down a different freakin street."

Dr. Steele nodded. "Ms. Snopes, you are a shepherdess tending her flock. When you see one go astray and become lost, you wish to show her the way back."

Hester nodded. What a load of bullshit. "Dr. Steele, what sparked you to talk to me?"

"Your concerns about your clients and helping them change impressed me as consistent with our Evangelical task of conversion. You appear confident, assertive and manifest strength in doing the right thing. I shall admit to you that those are attributes I strive for, but often fall short of."

"Uh-huh. I'm glad you like my style, but I've a feeling you didn't start this conversation just to compliment me."

"I wish to emulate your qualities. Perhaps you would attend a Church meeting?"

"Doctor, that ain't never gonna' happen."

Dr. Steele stood and pushed her chair in to align perfectly with the table. "Ms. Snopes, I am very interested in how you will help this ill-used woman avoid further abuse by males. How you will help her to feel less helpless. I sense you have a special interest in these kinds of women."

"I do. And it's just not therapeutic, it's also personal. I want women to stop feeling weak and helpless and to believe in themselves. To see they have choices in their lives." Hester paused, shrugged. "Okay. Maybe we can meet and have some tea sometime? But you'd have to call me Hester."

"Yes, thank you. You may call me Felicity." She turned and left the room.

After untangling her long dress caught in a chair-rung, Hester stood, looked at the empty doorway and grinned. This still could be a hoot.

SIX

Not Only Stripes And Checks Can Clash
Where We Glimpse Darkness In The Sunshine State
<u>Undoing:</u> Counteracting A Disturbing Thought By Thinking The
Opposite; Let Me Fluff Up Your Pillow Instead Of Smothering You
With It

"Jack. Glad I caught you. I've been thinking more about the guy who pulled the gun on you."

"Why? I haven't."

"The more I think about, you know, his resistance to treatment, his deep-seated anger, his using the gun to act out. Plus your frustration and how he's affecting you on a multidimensional level...."

"Jesus, Jim, spit it out."

"He's really got me worried. Can we talk more about what you're going to do? Over a beer after work at *The Lusty Pelican* down by the harbor?"

"Nah. I'm tired and I'm going home. Like I said, we've already analyzed it to death. You even made some pithy suggestions on what to do. Remember?"

"I know. But I've thought about it even more and....When are you seeing this guy again?"

"Jim, 'this guy' has a name. It's Brad. I'm seeing him next week."

"How about before patients tomorrow morning? I'll pick up some coffee on my way in. We can talk in your office or mine."

"No. I work-out in the morning. By the time I get here, my first patient is already waiting."

"Skip your work-out?"

"Hell, no. What the fuck's going on with you?"

"Jack, Brad's dangerous. He's been overtly violent already. He verbally abuses you, aims a gun...."

"A replica gun."

Jim paused. "Oh? Now it's a 'replica' gun? What are you doing, Jack? Minimizing what really happened to defend against how terrified you were? 'Oh, Jim, it was just a toy.' Very clever. Feeble, but clever."

"Just giving you the facts."

"Geez, what's coming next? That right from when he pulled the *gun* out and pointed it at your head, you knew it was a fake. How you'd everything under control all along and were merely observing how things'd play out because he was finally *interacting* with you?""Goddamn it, Jim. Why're you being so pissy?"

"Look. We both know he's not miraculously going to open up to you and discuss what happened."

"Do we now?"

"C'mon, Jack. No matter how good a psychiatrist you are, that's not going to happen. But, okay, have your appointment. See how it goes. But I've gotta tell you that if it's the same old stuff, you have to terminate him. Those red flags are waving, pal. Don't let your hang-ups blind you to them."

"Terminate him? Are you nuts? I've yet to make any real progress helping him and you're telling me to dump him?"

"Don't you mean you haven't made any real progress in *saving* him?"

"Screw you, Jim. And screw your trying to make me feel like an inept, naïve idiot. My hang-ups blinding me? I've fucking told you. I'm very aware of my issues and how to deal with them. I'm fine. It's Brad I'm concerned about."

"Mm-hmm. You sure do keep telling me how well you know yourself. And I keep wondering who you're really trying to reassure."

Jack took several deep breaths. "Okay, Jim, why did you really stop me in the hall? You were so concerned about, shit, what were you so intense about? Oh, yeah. Brad being dangerous. How did we get from that to your insulting me and telling me what I have to do with *my* patient?"

Jack, I...."

"No, no. Wait a minute. Let me tell you what I think. Here's Jim, a fine mid-western lad, who blurts out of the blue that he needs to be more assertive and decisive and no longer run from, what word did Jim use, *conflict*.

Here's Jack who, coincidentally, is facing conflict with a difficult patient. Jack needs to wrest his control back in therapy and has to make some decisions how he'll do it.

Jim, being a perceptive fellow, sees an opportunity.

Professing sincere, psychotherapeutic-based concerns, Jim pushes, goads and provokes Jack to make a decision. If Jack does, Jim can puff out his chest and tell himself that it was he who really made the decision. Jack being his tool."

"Jack, you've a rich imagination."

"Thank you. I kinda like the story. Jim living vicariously though Jack, telling himself he's the man in charge while still safely avoiding the fray. I think it's brilliant."

"Uh-huh. Readers of fantasy should love it."

Jack looked hard at his friend.

"Jim, something's not right. And it's not this Brad-gun bullshit. Your being a provocative son-of-a-bitch is not you. What's going on?"

"Right, Jack, I'm the one with the issues. Nice move."

Jack grinned. "Takes one to know one, Doc."

***

Okay, Jim, you're home. Focus now, ruminate on Jack's issues later. He turned into his house's dirt driveway. Anne wasn't waiting for him at the door with a smile, eager to tell him about what a good day she'd had. He shook his head. Why do you keep doing that, you idiot? Gotta keep that hope alive, don't you? And your guilt down.

Driving into the garage, he looked at the thick weeds and strangling vines thriving in the dirt he'd tilled and fertilized for her garden. Took me the whole day. He smiled. Well, at least I know some living thing is appreciating my labor.

Out of his car, he walked towards his one-story, stucco house. The two palm trees he'd bought three-weeks ago sat in their pots near the door, brown and dead. All she had to do was water them. No, it was me. I should've watered them instead of letting them die.

The air inside was icy. She must have the AC turned to the 'see-your-breath' temperature. Jim stood for a minute, listening, looking. The piles of unpacked boxes still squatted where the movers had put them two months ago. Small pieces of furniture crowded into a corner, enduring their uselessness. The two Florida photos he'd taken and framed still leaned against the wall. She's never going to like them. I should just take them into the office where I can enjoy them.

"Anne, I'm home. Anne, honey, where are you?"

He chuckled. She's in the great room. She always in the great room.

And she was. Sitting, eyes fixed on pictures in one of her many family albums she'd made sure to unpack. A light blanket over her shoulders, she was rocking slowly back and forth, a half-empty glass of wine next to her.

The off-white painted room was large with sparse furnishings. Two sofas opposed each other. Their end-tables each held lamps, their shades still cellophane-wrapped. One sofa had unhung curtains lying across it. Anne sat in the other. With the shades closed, no sunlight entered the room. One lamp threw-off meager light forcing the space to appear even more cheerless.

"There you are, honey. How are you?" He leaned down to kiss her cheek, but she turned away.

"Well, well, the Doctor, finally home after dealing with the loonies."

He moved the dusty curtains to the side and sat down across from her. "I saw patients with mental-health problems. That's what I do."

"And I bet everyone loves you. Thinks you're so concerned. That nice, even-tempered guy who really cares."

"I sure hope so. Anne, do you realize how cold it is in here?"

"I like cold. And I hate humidity and heat. I tell you that every time you complain. And don't touch the thermostat."

"I won't. How was your day?"

She sipped some wine and looked up. "For Chrissake, Jim, do you have to wear those flashy, stupid shirts every day? In Cleveland, you always looked so professional in your suit and tie. Here, you dress like some homeless guy who got his shirt out of a dumpster. Is growing a pony-tail your next project here in Flori-*duh?*"

Jim waited. "Anne, I kinda like these shirts. I'm sorry you don't." He sighed. "And I'm sorry that you find them offensive."

"God. There you go again with that, 'I'm sorry' crap. If you're so damn sorry, why do you keep buying them? It's to irritate me, isn't it?"

"How about I buy one that's more subdued? Or, a solid with no design? Would that be okay? Now, tell me about your day, please?"

She drained her wine glass and settled into the sofa. Looking at her husband, she grinned . "Well, when I went into the kitchen for my morning coffee, I noticed you'd left another pile of information about things to do in the area and I started reading them. There was that lovely Art Center brochure, how they offer lessons. And that booklet on adult-ed classes at the University. Wow. I got so excited, I jumped into the shower, got dressed and drove around to check things out. I even signed up for a few classes. And tomorrow, I'm going to do some unpacking and hang those curtains next to you. They've been lying on that sofa much too long. And golly gee, the people here are so friendly, like family."

Jim bent forward. "So, you did nothing, again?"

Her smile changed to concern. "Why Jim, dear, are you saying you're doubting what I said?"

"When I drove in tonight, I saw that thick dust layer still covered your car. And there weren't any tire tracks. I remember thinking the battery's probably dead and that I should check it after dinner."

"Gosh, I guess you caught me."

"Did you do anything today?"

"I did. Jeanine called. We talked until a tornado-watch passed and she calmed down. She told me how nice it was to have a big-sister to comfort her. How she wishes I were closer. Most of the afternoon I looked at a bunch of family get-together pictures from back in Ohio. Those were good times."

"Mm-hmm."

"I did go into the kitchen for lunch. And a few other times for more wine, does that count?"

"Did you look at anything I left?"

"No. I threw everything into the trash like I've done with all the other crap. Why do you keep leaving that stuff?"

"I saw that pamphlet on The Art Center and thought maybe you'd be interested in art lessons. You said once how disappointed you were when your Mother told you art school was out because you had an obligation to work in the family business and have a real job. Now you can do it. There was that University catalog listing adult-ed courses. I thought you might find something interesting in that. Meet some people? Make some friends?"

"No. I've never had any formal training and I don't want to feel dumb sitting next to someone who knows what she's doing. And friends? I have friends."

"In Ohio."

"In Cleveland. And I miss them."

"Honey, I know you do. You've wonderful memories, but we've moved. We need to establish ourselves here. Build a new life. Keep old friends, but make new ones too. I bring things home because I keep hoping you'll find something that'll interest you. We've been here two months and you've barely moved from the house except going a few times on errands with me."

"Yeah. Our togetherness time. What fun that was."

"That's another issue, us. I'm gone in the morning before you get up. We don't eat dinner together and you refuse to shut off the TV at night so we can talk a little. The last time we were intimate was in that first week after we arrived. And now you're lying to me?"

"Jim, how could it have been a lie when I I knew you'd see right through it. I was funny you about your constantly bringing home that junk about the area, the downtown, the University, restaurants, lectures, the Art Center and then finding it in the trash. I was hoping you'd catch on."

"Catch on to what? Why you won't do anything?"

"Why should I?"

He lowered his head, shook it and gave out a long breath. He looked at her. "Why? Because we live *here* now. Because I can't imagine your continuing to live isolated in this cold, dark house. And us? Our lives? I can't envision things going on like this."

"Dammit, my wine glass is empty." She turned back to him. "Well, maybe you're catching on. Our not being together, my total lack of desire to build a life here, my staying in the house, doesn't that tell you something?"

"I don't know. Your not having found anything interesting…"

"Jim, I don't care about doing anything here."

"Okay. Your behaving in a manner that suggests symbolic acts rejecting this place? Me? I don't know."

"I can't believe how you don't see things?"

"What don't I see?"

"Okay, let's finally get this straight. I *never* wanted to move here, to leave everyone and everything I had. I don't *like* it here and I *never* will no matter how many stupid pamphlets you bring home. I'm not starting anything here because we're moving back to Cleveland. Why do you think I haven't unpacked much?"

He stared, open-mouthed. "You're serious?"

"Oh yeah I am. I never wanted to come. And I want to go back."

He got up and began to pace around the room. After a few minutes, he sat, hands in pockets, and resumed his staring. "Then, why did you? I thought it was what we wanted? You felt smothered by too much family and wanted to move away as much as I did. But it wasn't that, was it? You've been lying to me all this time. Why, Anne, why?"

"I knew you had your heart set on leaving Cleveland and I didn't want to lose you."

"So?"

"So, I did what my mother advised. I told you what you wanted to hear."

"Your mother?"

"She said, 'If you want to get your way about this, don't fight him about moving. Do it. Humor him. Let him get this 'Florida fantasy' out of his system. Men need to believe they're in charge. Before you know it, you'll be moving back and he'll think it was his idea'." Anne laughed. "Nobody in my family thought you were going to stay in Florida this long. I didn't."

"Everybody knew, huh? Except me, the guy you were playing and not taking seriously. And here I thought…"

"Jim, don't you see? I did it because I love you."

"Love me? I thought you were humoring me?"

"Well, yeah. But isn't that part of love? Letting you have your way for a little bit? Stop making it such a big deal."

"Your going with me to a movie you don't like, that's humoring me. This is about trust."

"C'mon, Jim, we both know you'll be much happier back in Cleveland at the Institute, looking like a professional, not some beach-bum. And if you love me, you'll know I'll be much happier there too. So?"

"So? What? What are you saying?"

49

"Look, I've been more than patient with the heat, the cockroaches, how you dress, your pretending you like it here. How you kept on about my doing something and so tuned-out to how much I was suffering.

I'm done with the humoring. Read my lips, Jim. I don't want to be here, never have, never will. If you love me and want me happy, like you *say* you do, we move back. It's that simple, even for your overly analytical mind. Got it?"

Jim looked down, his hands clasped hard together between his legs, every muscle in his body tensed. He wanted to get up, pace, yell. He looked at his wife. My wife? My love? My help-mate?

"I do. I've got it."

"Well?"

He spoke quietly, slowly, deliberately.

"Anne, I'm quite angry at what you've told me, and at you. I'm even more saddened by it. I'm sor... No, I guess I was perceiving things differently. Right now, I just need to calm down, not let my feelings speak for me. Until then, I don't think I can respond thoughtfully to your, ah, ultimatum."

Anne got up and headed for the kitchen with her wine glass. "Yeah, yeah, I know. Showing you're upset is not your style."

"Just let me process this...." He said to her back.

"Process your ass off, Jim. And when you decide...."

"Decide?"

"Yeah, *decide*. When we're leaving this place. What've I been talking about?"

He followed her into the kitchen, "We'll need to talk more,"

"Sure, sure. About moving. Ah, there's the wine." She filled her glass so it overflowed onto the counter.

"Maybe the weekend?"

"Yeah, Jim. Whatever."

"Good. Is there any Chinese left from what I bought two-nights ago?"

"Your legs broken? Go look for yourself."

She picked-up her glass, looked at the spilled wine, shrugged and left.

As he rinsed her spilled wine from the sponge, he savored how the water warmed his cold hands and let it run a little longer. How did I miss this? I kept thinking it was a bad case of homesickness and she just needed some time to adjust. Something to get involved with. It has to be her family manipulating her to come back to Cleveland. It can't be Anne. I'll, no, we'll make this work. Just a little more time. We'll talk. But no anger, Jim. You know what she'd do with that.

He looked outside. Maybe put in a pool? Get rid of that overgrown jungle. What a stupid idea that was. Her family can visit as much as they want. Make it so they won't want to leave. He let the water continue to flow over his hands and warm him. He thought of Uncle Joe. "Jim, if you're going somewhere, you have to start walking."

SEVEN

A Fish Always Rots From The Head Down
Where Jack Sets Things Straight
<u>Denial</u>: *Refusing To Accept A Truth Because It's Too Emotionally*
Threatening; Not Infrequently, Associated With Stubbornness

"Hey, Jack. I thought you didn't have time to talk this morning?" Jim said.

"I *still* don't. But there's something I've gotta know. Got a minute?"

"Sure. Sit down. This about Brad?"

"Yeah, it is. You told Smith about the gun episode between Brad and me, didn't you?

"Jack…"

"Damn, I thought so. Things just keep getting better. First, I tell you what happened looking for some practical advice about handling him in our next appointment. Instead, I get a sermon on dumping him. Next, I go home and my darling starts her tirade about how upset I've made her along with some of her righteous garbage about my past thrown in. We haven't talked since.

Then, I come in this morning desperate for a simple, attack-free day and guess who corners me in the hall? Yes, our overdressed, undersized boss, his mustache glistening in my face. Well, maybe glistening into my chest."

"Jack…."

Jack put up his hand. "Smith was almost frothing because 'someone' had told him about the gun incident. How bout that."

Jim looked away. "I'm sorry Jack. The day after the staff-meeting, he stopped me wondering why I'd asked about guns in the Clinic. Believe me, I tried talking around it, but he kept pushing. And Jack, I'm not a good liar."

"Yeah. I shoulda remembered choirboys don't lie. And of all people to tell. Jesus. You know he doesn't give a damn about us, the Clinic or the patients? Only his precious reputation. I bet he's already planning how he'd cover his ass if a shooting happened." Jack's eyes burned into Jim's. "which, by the way, will *never* happen."

"I know you need to believe that, Jack, but if something *does* happen, it could involve staff, other patients, kids. C'mon?"

"Jim, I was really ticked-off thinking how you ratted me out to Smith. But what's really got me PO'd is that Smith's joined your crusade. Now I've three pains in the ass not suggesting, not advising, but freakin *telling* me what to do with *my* patient."

"Jack, he is our boss."

"Right. Our 'boss' didn't even ask if I had a treatment plan to help this guy. He just 'strongly' suggested I terminate hem and walked away. Like I said, he doesn't give a shit about us or the patients."

"Jack, listen. Even if you talk through the gun incident with Brad, he is *still* a risk. Why do you refuse to see that?"

Jack gave a half-smile. "Look, Jim, I hear your concerns, really. Brad is a risk. That's why I want to help him. Not terminate him and let him down. I resent being told what feelings I *should* be having through this and what I *should* be doing. He's *my* fucking patient, okay?

"Okay, Jack. Do it your way."

"Thanks for your permission because that's what I'm going to do."

"Is everything going to be good between you and Bonny?"

"Christ. You wanna stick your nose in that too? Gimme some advice? Or just tell me what to do?"

Jim let out a long sigh. "No, Jack. I'm concerned that a patient issue is intruding so much in your marriage that you're not talking."

"*She* started it. Usually, we sit and talk before dinner and I had this story I wanted to tell her about a male transvestite patient. When he told his wife about his cross-dressing, she took it pretty well. But now she's angry. Why? Because when he gets made-up, he's prettier than she is. I thought she'd enjoy the irony in it.

But as soon as she sat down, she started ranting again about all the past worries I've resurrected after I told her about Brad, his attempting suicide, the gun. It was like listening to your bullshit telling me what to do, but with some hysteria thrown in."

"Jack, that doesn't sound quite like the Bonny I've met. My image of her is of a bright, warm and thoughtful person. I never got an impression of her being a drama queen."

"Well, you weren't there, were you? It's her bringing up that past shit that really gets to me."

"Your brother? Those patients who suicided? How they affected you?"

"Yeah, yeah, yeah. How I tended to brood and isolate, my so-called gambling problem.

"Gambling?"

"I mentioned it to you. I was just day-trading during the time I was home. It was nothing. Anyway, now she's got this bug up her nose that if Brad suicides, I'm going to relapse. Like I'm a complete goddamn idiot."

"But don't you think she might have a few concerns?"

"Jim, you don't get it. She shouldn't have *any* concerns.I admit I may have been a little edgy lately trying to figure out how to handle Brad. I really want our next session to go well so we can move on in therapy. But Bonny doesn't understand that. In fact, I'm beginning to wonder if she understands me at all."

Well, she won't if you two aren't talking."

"Oh. Wanna know why we're not talking? What she did?"

Jim shrugged.

"Okay. Bonny's got this bullshit notion that I've some 'unresolved issues'. Things I've never dealt with in spite of my therapy and still eat away at me. Things *deeper* than the suicides. Jim, I can handle her raving about the past and her dumb fears about another relapse like before, but when she brought this crap up, I lose it.

I'm thinking that I'm focusing on staying positive, being understanding and supportive to her while at the same time trying to do the right things with a difficult patient. Does she give me any credit for that? No. She confronts me with this *feeling* she's had. Some crazy-ass fantasy that I'm running from some subconscious fears? That it's the reason we moved here. So I could avoid these *deep-seated* issues that were getting to me up north. Give me a fucking break.

Oh, and then, after battering me with her amateur analysis, she starts to come over to give me a hug. Like, 'You poor, poor, neurotic guy, you can get through his.' But I knew it wasn't support. It was a victory hug for her. 'Thank you, Jack, for seeing things *my* way. I know you're going to do the *right* thing.' That's when I told her.

"Told her what, Jack?"

"That I was done. Done listening to the endless bullshit recitation of her worries. I learned a lot in therapy and have dealt with it. It's in the past. *I'm* living in the present. That her *delusion* that I've some subconscious demon lurking inside me is pure garbage. I told her she had to end her bullshit and walked out of the room."

"And you haven't spoken since?"

"No."

Jim thought a moment. "Jack, this your wife, the one person who knows and loves you. Look, she moved down here with you despite her concerns, right? She only wants you to be happy. Maybe, you should consider what she's saying, even a little bit?"

"You had to defend her, didn't you?"

"Jack…."

"Jim, I know you're trying to be helpful, but just shut the hell up."

"You're right, Jack. My Uncle Joe would say, 'You never get into trouble by being quiet'.

I know you'll do the right thing."

"Count on it. I'm fine."

EIGHT

The Crow May Be Caged But His Thoughts Are In The Cornfield
Where Jim Keeps His Legs Crossed
Intellectualization: Dwelling In Lofty Places To Restrain Vexing
Emotions; Noble Thinking To Shoo Away The Naughty Stuff

After scanning her chart, Jim looked up and observed his new patient. Woman in her late twenties, history of intermittent depression, treatment by various counselors and psychiatrists over the years. Here for recurrent depression. She'd put a question mark after, 'any physical problems'.

Hearing Jim call her name in the waiting room, she'd approached him with very deliberate, almost calculated movements. 'Doctor, please, my name is *Ahndrea*, not Andrea.'

She was very attractive. Hair combed back into a knot, she'd left some stray wisps free-fall to the sides of her face Her eyes were a penetrating deep-blue. She wore a hint of make-up and a soft color lipstick which matched her fuchsia, long-sleeved blouse. No jewelry. A black skirt fell just above her knees. Jim observed her long, slender legs and quickly returned to her face.

"Doctor? Doctor?"

"Yes, Ahndrea?"

"You seemed so quiet." She smiled. "I wanted to tell you that I like your Hawaiian shirt. When one of the woman out front told me I'd recognize you by it, I instantly started feeling more relaxed. Your seeming less formal has already begun to help me."

"Thank you Ahndrea. What brings you to the Clinic?"

She slowly recrossed her legs and straightened her skirt. Jim turned his eyes to count the flies on the windowsill. She looked around the room, assessed it and looked back to him. She smiled.

"I like the pictures you've hung on the walls. Did you buy them, no, wait, y*ou* took them, didn't you?"

"Ahndrea, why are you here?"

"Not going to answer? Okay. I understand. I know you psychiatrists have to keep that, 'therapeutic distance'. I'm here for my depression. I've had it off-and-on since my teens with some episodes in college. Another bout started a few months ago. I made the appointment because it's getting worse and getting in my way."

"What symptoms are you experiencing?"

"Increasing sadness. Sitting at a light, I'll start bawling for no reason. I'm more irritable. Not at work, but with my boyfriend or, like with a salesperson, for some petty reason. Then I feel guilty and apologize. Most people I deal with don't know how I'm feeling. I can put on a good front and fake it pretty well if I have to."

"Uh-huh. The depression started in high school?"

"Yes. Prior, I'd be teenage-girl moody. Have one of those, 'I hate my hair' days once in a while, but this was worse. It'd go on for weeks. I'd stay in my room when I could. I wasn't myself. I'd be grumpy and get people at school mad at me."

"Was there anything at school or at home that might have caused it?"

"Home was a little…strict, but there was nothing I could ever identify as a cause.'"

"Did you get treatment then?"

"Ha. If you could call it that. I saw the school counselor. She was one of those, 'I'm here for you, but not really, counselors who never listened to what I was saying. It was a Catholic school, so, no surprise, her therapy always related to the state of my soul. Had I committed some sin of 'thought, word or deed' and feeling guilty? She made the same recommendation every week. Pray, Ahndrea. Seek forgiveness. She was absolutely useless and didn't have a clue."

"Then?"

"I just learned to live with it, get through each day."

"Was there any cutting?"

"No, never. Some of the girls did, mostly for the attention. Or to horrify their parents. I'd watch them in the girls bathroom showing off their scratches to each other. I knew one serious cutter. But she went to extremes to hide the slices into her body, not show them off."

"I take it they weren't your friends."

"No. What they did was dumb. There are much better ways to get attention."

"Uh-huh. So, no cutting?"

"No, that wasn't my thing. But…"

She looked away, then turned back to him as she bit on lip and widened her eyes.

"Uh, I should tell you. I did develop a little bit of bulimia."

"Oh? Please elaborate. What is, 'a little bit'?"

"Like most teenage girls, I was afraid of getting fat. I did a lot of physical exercise and watched what I ate. But, eventually, I discovered vomiting was my best insurance against gaining. I'd retch every morning at school in the girls bathroom."

"While the other girls were comparing cuts?"

"Pretty weird, huh?"

"Do you purge now?"

"Ah, sorta. It was under control, but restarted with my depression. It's not daily. It's mostly when I get really stressed about something or, of course, if I feel like I'm gaining."

"When was the last time?"

She raised her hands. "I surrender, this morning. I was freaked about coming here. You know, starting with an unknown Doctor. The questions. But before today, I hadn't barfed for several weeks. "

"That's why you put a question mark by, 'physical problems'?"

"Yes."

"Do you binge-eat before purging?"

"No. I never got into the four or five-thousand calorie gorging. She smiled. I guess I'm 'semi-bulimic'. Sometimes I'll eat more than usual, for me. I'll start to feel bloated. Then I'll hurl."

"Exercise a lot?"

"Of course. Have to run my little butt off every day, about twelve to fifteen miles. Lately, I've had to force myself. Just don't feel like it."

"Any diuretics, laxatives or enemas to keep the weight down?"

"Guilty to all the above in the past, but not now."

"Why?"

"I feel I've my weight under control with how I eat and the exercise. And the depression's decreased my appetite."

"So, presently, you're not purging for 'insurance'. You're okay with how you look?"

"Today, I think I look good. Uh, Doctor, what do you think? Do I look good to you? Do you find me attractive?" She smiled. "Or am I living in la-la land kidding myself?"

Jim hesitated. Checked his clock.

"Doctor? I'm patiently *waiting,* no 'weight' pun intended, for your appraisal. Please don't disappoint me."

"Ahndrea, what I think about how you look or, in fact, what I think about you in general isn't the important thing here. It's what you think about yourself and what you do with that."

Her smile disappeared. "That's the stock answer, isn't it? *'It's what you think about yourself, my dear. That's what's important'.* Is this what therapy's going to be like with you? Hearing overused phrases from your little handbook of psychiatric platitudes? What is it with you guys? Can't you ever speak like a regular human-being with your patients? *All* I asked was, do you think I look good. Am I attractive? Was that *so* inappropriate? Maybe I need a little reassurance from the Doctor I've just met. Did that occur to you? Or has bowing to that, 'therapeutic-distancing' commandment sucked all compassion out of you?"

Jim nodded. "Ahndrea, I try to avoid trite answers and platitudes when possible. But, you're right, I did just give you a stock answer. Because it's true. I believe reassurance and encouragement are great, for kids. And for adults too. But, when you asked me those questions, I sensed you were prodding for more than reassurance."

"This comes from someone who's just met me? Dare I ask what I *really* was looking for?"

"Approval."

She was silent for a bit. "Another cliché, Doctor?"

"To depend on others to validate you're a good person, that you measure up or, that you're attractive is tough stuff. And, it doesn't work. Even when you get that approval, it's fleeting, isn't it? Because your self-doubt won't let you believe it. So it's on to the next person. And the next. I like to work on changing self-criticism to self-approval. Curiously, I've found that not confronting what scares you, what makes you doubt yourself, leaves some people frustrated, some angry." He raised his eyebrows. "some even get *depressed.*"

"Hmm.; Imagine that," she said.

"You've already told me you're good at playing a role. Do you use those deep-blue eyes and your pleasing smile to charm others? You smile. They smile back. You laugh, they laugh. Is that how it works? How you tell yourself you've still got it? Whatever that means. That you're desirable? Attractive?"

"Well, maybe you are a little human, Doctor. Thank you for noticing my eyes and my smile. I think they're some of my key assets. But beyond that you need to know that I didn't come in here to play some *role*, Doctor."

"But how people see you is a serious concern for you. I wonder if that's somehow related to your depression?"

She slowly uncrossed her legs, leaned forward. "I think we all depend on others for feedback. 'Do I look good in this dress?', 'How did I do in that meeting?' And, of course, 'Am I too fat?'. People agreeing with us, smiling at something we say, makes us feel good. It says we're clever, we're appreciated. Isn't that what's it's all about, Doctor Bizby? People needing people? Someone paying attention gives us a nice feeling. We all need attention, don't we? I'd bet even you do, Doctor. You *seem* solid and confident. But, do *you* get enough attention? I'd bet you hang-out with people who make you feel good, no? Does that mean you're dependent on them? Doesn't that Hawaiian shirt get you noticed? Is that why you wear it?"

Jim threw up his hands. "Wow. You've so many questions about me, Ahndrea. Yet this appointment is supposed to be about you. Look, I agree. People need people in their lives. It is nice to talk, be listened to. Have someone enjoy our company."

Ahndrea put her chin on her hand and tilted her head, smiled. "But?"

"But, in psychotherapy, it's not about one liking to be noticed. That's a given. It's about to what extremes you feel you need to go to get it. You say you don't, yet I suspect that you're always 'on' playing one role or another. Like today, you tell me you're depressed. But you don't look depressed. I know, that's a big generalization, but I wonder if it's because you feel you have to put on a smile. That showing how you're really feeling would make you less...attractive? The face you present always has to look good. But, who's behind it? Who's the real Ahndrea?"

Jim let the silence go on for a minute. "Tell me about your job at the University."

"I've worked at the Budget and Finance Department as a financial analyst for the last three years. And, no, I didn't smile my way into the job."

"Do you like the job?"

"It's okay. I've been always good with numbers. They give no surprises. They're neat and orderly without drama."

"They do what you want?"

"Yes. They're logical, predictable. I like things to go as I plan."

"Getting everything to balance gives you satisfaction without people involved."

"If you say so."

"Like having your weight in balance, controlled?"

"Exactly. We all like things to be in control."

"How are things with your co-workers?"

"Oh, there's one testosterone-guy threatened by me because I'm smart."

"And?"

"I handle him."

"You mean control him?"

"No. I said, *handle*. Isn't that what we do in our relationships? If I need something done, I behave in a certain way to make it happen. I handle it. I thought that was a good thing, especially at work."

"Okay. But how do you differentiate between, 'being nice', 'handling' and 'manipulating' people?

"Doctor, what's this fixation you have about me and people? I'm talking about getting a busy secretary to type-up a report for me. Calling that manipulating would be a bit strong, don't you think?"

"I'm trying to get a feel for how you relate to people. I don't think I've ever heard 'handling' used like that. How about the women in the office?"

"I'm attractive and bright so they're jealous of me."

"So, no friends there. Any outside of work."

"No. And for the same reason."

"Men? Ever been married, engaged? Do you even want a relationship? Wait, you mentioned a boyfriend?"

She looked him in the eye. "Men disappoint me. They never quite meet one's expectations, do they? I meet a guy and think he might be decent. We've a few dates, I start to let my guard down and he does something. He doesn't show up, gets pushy, lies to me about something, gives some weak excuses then wonders why I won't let him get into my pants."

"'Let my guard down' means you begin to trust?"

"More like, not so wary. Who trusts anybody in the beginning? I need to see what he's like, get to know him first. Do you have instant trust when you meet someone, Doctor?"

"Would you say you have trust issues?"

She let out a long sigh. "Well, I certainly can't trust you to answer like a regular person, can I? Couldn't you just agree with me that people don't automatically trust someone right off? No. You get right into, *Ahndrea*, do I have trust issues. Okay, if it'll make you happy, I don't trust easily, if at all."

"Except with numbers."

She smiled. "Ah, yes. No agenda with numbers. They are what they are. You know, one of my previous psychiatrists propositioned me. He said it'd be therapeutic to have a deeper relationship with a professional whom I could trust. If we had sex, I'd see what a 'truly caring relationship' could be like. The creep."

She paused, slowly twisting a wisp of hair. "I hope, Doctor, I'll be able to trust you."

Jim gave her a thumbs-up. "Of course."

"I haven't been married or engaged although I've no end of men hitting on me. I've a boyfriend. He's nice, predictable and not too demanding. He thinks he wants to marry me."

"So, he's decent?"

"Ha, so far."

"I assume he must love you if he wants to marry you. Do you want to marry him?"

"We'll see."

"Do you love him?"

"We'll see."

"How do you handle him?"

"Why I give him what he wants of course. I'm an excellent cook. And I'm a good lay."

"So, you dangle the marriage possibility, good food and, ah, good sex to keep him on the hook? People needing people?"

"Doctor, why do you keep attacking me? Is this some form of psychotherapy you think helps because it's not helping me. What you just said was harsh, like you're judging me. I thought psychiatrists weren't supposed to do that."

"We're not. It was a bit harsh, wasn't it? I usually try to slowly develop some trust, not distance. I'm sorry."

"Thank you." She leaned towards him and whispered. "Then, I'll be honest with you."

Jim leaned a little towards her. "That'd be nice."

"I'm purging more than once in a while like I said. I'm so embarrassed about how I've lost control. That's why I told you that little fib earlier. I'm doing it every morning. It's upsetting because I don't have to. My weight's okay. I'm just *doing* it. Why am I hurting myself? I don't know." She looked down into her lap. "I just don't know."

"Ahndrea, thank you for being honest with me. Like I said earlier, I'd think your increased purging is related to your depression. Any ideas what brought the depression and the purging on?"

She slowly uncrossed her legs and clenched her hands on her lap. "I don't. What *really* bothers me is that I used to be able to handle these things. But that's not happening. Doctor. That's why I had to come here. I can't lose control."

"You said before you didn't think there was anything when it started. No loss? Your parents? Abuse? Anything?"

"No."

"Did past psychotherapy give you any insights?"

"Are you kidding? My past therapists were mostly women. They labelled me a drama queen and let it go at that. Some of the psychiatrists tried some therapy, but most just gave me an antidepressant and ogled my legs."

"Did any medication help?"

"Not much. Maybe a little. I don't know. I don't remember. I would if something did, wouldn't I? I know I refused the ones that could cause weight gain."

"Did you talk about the bulimia?"

"Uh, no. Never." She crossed her legs not pulling her skirt down as far as she could. She gave him a little smile. "You're my first," she said.

"I see." Jim said looking at his windowsill to check if any more bugs had died there..

"That's a compliment, Doctor. Remember, I don't trust."

"So, Ahndrea, neither medication nor therapy, although you hid your bulimia, helped?"

" No, actually, something did help. One time, I borrowed some Adderalls from someone. I wanted to see if the medicine's appetite reduction side-effect would work for me. And, Doctor, it did. It took away my food cravings so I stopped worrying about overeating. I stopped hurling. I felt better and my depression disappeared. But the main thing was I felt good. Not, 'speeded up' good, but normal, at least what normal is for me." She put her hands together in a prayerful way. "I was wondering, really hoping you'd consider prescribing the Adderall?"

Jim shook his head. "No, I can't. Using psychostimulants as diet pills was a fad years ago. But so many people getting addicted to them stopped that. I don't think so. Anyway, they're not indicated for depression."

"But I *felt* better. I wasn't purging and my depression *vanished*. Isn't that what you want as a Doctor? Making me better?"

"Ahndrea, of course I want to help you feel better. But I've concerns that the Adderall might've given you a high and a false sense that your depression had lifted. A depression you've never really dealt with. I give you some pills. Depression goes. Problems gone. But not really. Do you see?"

"No. Why do you prescribe antidepressants? Isn't it to help people get back to their normal selves. Then they're better able to talk about their depression? Aren't we talking about the same thing here, except it's Adderall not an antidepressant?"

"An antidepressant does help some people better participate in psychotherapy."

She shrugged. "Okay then. Why can't you do that with me? With the Adderall? The medicine made me feel better and stop retching I did *not* have a high from it."

Jim compressed his lips and shook his head again. "No. I do not see that as an option at this time."

Slowly, she leaned back into her chair, bent her head down and began to cry softly. She whispered. "I'm feeling really down. I purge every morning even though the only thing that comes up is an acidy fluid. I've a pain in my chest, I think, from the acid. I'm not how I want to be. There's something I know can help me." She raised her head to look at Jim. "And you, Doctor, refuse to prescribe it. I've never had any addiction problems. I've had opportunities to try both crystal meth and coke which I know decrease appetite. But I would *never* do them."

"Andrea...."

She lifted her hand to stop him. "Doctor Bizby, It wasn't easy for me to come for help." She sneered. "Now that I'm here, I find I'm dealing with a Doctor who says he wants to help me, yet seems stuck in some medical rule book, paralyzed to do anything. I guess your fear of thinking outside of the box outweighs your desire to free me, your patient, from my suffering. Or are you too scared about what others might think if they found out. I've researched this, Doctor, and I know that stimulants have been used to treat depression off-label, haven't they?"

"*Yes,* Ahndrea, for depression, *not* bulimia."

"But, isn't that what we're talking about, my depression? You even said the depression was causing the vomiting. Help me, please? Don't you have an obligation? Took some oath? I was so hoping I'd find someone who'd be different, be the one who'd finally help me. But he's afraid to bend a rule. Or that he's going to turn me into an addict." She paused. " It looks like I'm not the only person in this room with self-doubt, am I, Doctor?"

Jim let her cry for a few minutes. He pointed to the box of tissues near her. She took three, dabbed at her eyes.

Leaning forward with his elbows on his thighs, his hands steepled, he looked straight at her. "You *are* good."

Still pressing the tissue to her cheek, she raised her head, tipped it a little and narrowed her eyebrows.

"What do you mean, I'm *good?*"

"Ahndrea, you're absolutely right. I *am* supposed to be empathetic, caring and trying to help you feel better. And I'm also apprehensive about using Adderall for your depression and certainly for the bulimia. As you spoke, I sensed my concern for you increasing. At one point, I was feeling so drawn-in by your distress, part of me wanted to hurry and do whatever I could to lessen your suffering."

"But you didn't."

"No, I remembered what you said about how you get things done. You handle people."

"But that has nothing to do with this. I only want your help."

"I know you do. But yet I'm leery about how you're going about getting it."

The tears had stopped. "I'm sorry? You're leery about *how* I'm asking for help?"

"I apologize if I'm being unclear. When I commented on to what extreme people need to go to get what they want? Your moving descriptions of your anguish, your trouble trusting people, your bad experiences with therapy, how things being out of control are so immensely harrowing for you, made me wonder if I'm being handled."

"What? Aren't I supposed to tell you my problems? *You* kept asking me why I was here. I'm baring my soul and you're making it sound so very vulgar. Like, like I've some evil plan to entrap you. You have a rich fantasy life, Doctor."

" Ahndrea, I want to help. You can trust me to do what I think is best, but don't trust me to do what you want. That's why I'm commenting on your behavior. I think you were your role-playing today. And it was to get Adderall. I want you to know, you don't have to play any roles to get my help. I'll do it without all that."

She'd been tearing the tissues into little pieces and letting them fall to the floor. There was no smile.

"Doctor Bizby, you keep attacking me? Why? Are you always such a bastard with your patients?"

"I calls them as I sees them."

"Now glib comments. How creative."

"We have a few minutes left."

"Right. Beat me up and throw me out. Never mind how *I* feel? How *I'm* going to feel the rest of the day? *Please*, prescribe me the Adderall?"

"Good move."

"What?"

"Throwing in more guilt at the last minute. No, I'm not giving you the speed. I'll give you an antidepressant if you'd like."

"No thank you, I'll pass. I've told you they really didn't help. But I know *you* need to prescribe something for me, don't you? So you can tell yourself you did something."

Jim sat back and crossed his legs. "I want to be clear. I believe that when you drop all the smoke and mirrors behaviors, we'll be able to talk about you. The independent Ahndrea who likes being in charge. The needy, dependent Ahndrea looking for approval. How the assertive Ahndrea gets angry when she's thwarted from getting her way. And the seductive Ahndrea. I'm curious if being,' a good cook and good lay 'just isn't working for her anymore."

She stifled a smile. "You talk a good line, Doctor. Ha, *you're* good. Now I'm the one feeling... handled." She raised her eyebrows. "I still wish you'd consider that medication. You know, you are my *last* hope?"

"We can talk about it. Next week?"

"I wonder. Can we meet sooner? I'd like to get working on this. Plus, I want to see if you'll be as much of a bastard as you were today. And, oh, I want to see if you use the word 'thwart' again."

Jim had to smile. "You are a charmer. From wretchedness to anger to smiling in an instant."

"Thank you, Doctor. I'll take that as, *reassurance*."

"You can tell them out-front to make the appointment sooner."

After they got up from their chairs, she put out her hand. Jim hesitated, then took it.

She looked into his eyes. "See you soon,"

"Yes."

As she left, she lightly touched his arm. "I'm sorry if I seemed demanding. I'm moody you know." She smiled. "Doctor, I'm confident you'll do what's best for me. Thank you."

As he watched her walk down the hallway, her heels clicking on the tile, Jim sighed. She does have nice legs.

Jim pictured Uncle Joe shaking his finger. "Jim, only an idiot believes he's beyond temptation."

NINE

Everyone's Reality Is Different
Where Hester And Felicity Exchange Verbals
<u>Isolation:</u> *Building An Emotional Chasm Between What's Forbidden*
And What's Acceptable; Hiding Mephitic Emotions From Yourself

As her pudgy fingers continued hitting more than one letter, Hester Snopes kept texting and wondering where she could get a phone with bigger keys for large-boned girls.

Dr. Felicity Steele tapped lightly on the open door. "I do not wish to interrupt. Do you have a few minutes to speak? I can return later if necessary."

Hester looked up, waved. "Come on in." Her phone vibrated. "Just let me get rid of this dumb-ass client."

Felicity sat, put her knees close together, smoothed all wrinkles from her black pants leaving one hand on her knee with the other fleeing to her cross. She surveyed the room. Pamphlets on astrology and spiritualism covered Hester's desk. One title read, *Talking With The Dead.* To Felicity's right, a small bowl emitted a vapor smelling like eucalyptus. The walls held framed affirmations. *I Don't Need Anyone to Feel Complete, I Am More Than Enough'* and, *The Past Does Not Control Me. It Is What I Choose Today That Matters.*

Hester nodded at her phone. "I'm telling this wuss to reschedule. Listen to this. She wanted a 'texting appointment' because her cat didn't show for breakfast and she has to wait around. Then she started asking me cat-questions. What am I, a freakin vet? You know, she's the type that'll never listen to me anyway because her *suffering* gets her more attention. So why change? "Damn this small keypad." She typed a few more words. "There, enough of her whining.."

Hester took a sip of passionfruit tea, wiped sweat away from her forehead into her hair and swiveled around to face Felicity more head on. She looked at the Doctor. Okay, what's this about? A day ago we talked a little and now she shows up still twisting that damn cross. Hester waited for Felicity to talk, let a minute go by, then started.

"How're doin, Felicity? Finally settled in? You've been in town, how long?"

Felicity sat erect. "I have been at the Clinic five weeks and three days. I arrived in the area a week earlier. Yes, I am settled-in. Thank you."

Hester waited. Nothing. "Me, I've been here about four years. I was born and bred in Northeastern Florida up near Jacksonville. It's got good beaches, but don't go there in the winter. It's cold. St. Augustine, oldest city in the US, is up there too. Tourists love it. You might visit it sometime. There's also a town called Cassadaga. I mention it because I think it's kinda' funny. Here I am, now interested in spiritualism and about ten miles from where I grew up was Cassadaga. Turns out it's the 'psychic capital of the world'. And I never knew about it. I'm going up there for a weekend conference, *Karma and Reincarnation.* Anyway, after high school, I went to Florida State, majored in psychology. After graduation, I interned at a clinic, got the rest of my credits and became a licensed mental-health therapist. After a friend told me about this area, I checked it out, saw I liked it and here I am, four years later."

"Your family continues to live near Jacksonville?"

"Yeah, those losers are still up there, I guess."

"You did not consider staying in proximity to where they reside?"

Hester laughed. "No-siree. I don't ever want to see those pieces of shit again. Look, a pious woman like yourself probably came from an upright, God-fearing family with Church on Sunday, Bible readings and Mom cooking Sunday dinners. Me, I came from trailer trash. I'm not criticizing. That's just the way it was. I lived in a run-down *trailer*, not a PC mobile home. This 'thing' had black mold on the outside and God only knows what lived underneath. We coulda been poster people for the 'gen-u-wine' dysfunctional family. My father, Teddy, was a nasty, complaining son-of-a-bitch. He never worked much because his rotten personality'd get him fired. He'd sit around all day drinking and feeling sorry for himself, whining how unfair life treated him. He had a pal, Jesse, who lived two trailers down. They'd sit, smoke and start drinking right in the A.M. I remember Teddy pouring beer on his corn-flakes and calling it, 'The complete breakfast' as his cigarette ashes fell into it. The bastard used to beat-up on me, my younger brother and my Mom.

Mom? Another piece of work. She'd come home from her waitressing, yell at Jesse to go mooch beer somewhere else and then start her boozing. They'd sit out front in these old beach chairs with the orange mesh rotting away, their asses sticking through the bottoms. Then, they start in arguing and he'd start slapping her around. When she got to hitting him back, he'd come inside and beating on my brother and me. After about fifty times, the cops stopped coming. I think they hoped we'd all kill each other and they'd have one less problem.

My younger brother, Zeke, got into drugs in junior-high, got arrested for possession, went to juvie, came out and started dealing and using. He's been in and out of jail, a lot. As far as I know, he's still doing opiates. You know, the little shit called about two months ago, wanted to stay with me a few days while he, 'lined up a job'? You know what I did?"

"You aided him in his job search?"

"Felicity, you've never worked with addicts, have you?"

"Yes, I have had that experience."

"Well, then you should know that all he wanted was a place to crash and see what he could steal. When I told him, 'Hell no', he told me to go screw myself and hung up. Haven't seen him since. And, ta-da, there's me.

Felicity, isn't my runnin' on like this boring you? Don't *you* have something?"

"Yes, but please continue."

"Okay. In my senior-year high school, I thought I'd found my soul-mate, Bobby Lee Turner. Lookin back, I think any guy who didn't stink of BO or beer could've been my soul-mate. But Billy Lee had a car and good weed. He never used a rubber because, 'Us Turner men got pride', so I eventually got knocked-up. Know what the bastard did when I told him?"

" That you both had sinned and should seek spiritual help and forgiveness?" Felicity said. "What? Hell, no. He started yelling. That I'd trapped him and wanted to ruin his life. Like he was Harvard-bound instead of working at the Seven-Eleven. When he turned to leave, dumb me tried to stop him so I could have my say. That's when he punched me so hard in the stomach it knocked me to the floor. He left me there lying in a pool of blood, sobbing. About an hour later, I aborted, then cleaned everything up. My parents? Dead-drunk outside.

Didn't hear anything."

"Did you seek their guidance afterwards?"

Hester stared at her. "Huh? That may happen in your freakin world, but not in mine. After some brooding, I told myself to stop feeling so helpless. If I wanted out of that life with bellyaching, pathetic drunks, I needed to get smart. So, I made myself some rules.

I'd never again allow myself to feel so helpless. Because I'm not. I have choices about my life.

I'd make a plan to escape that shithole and all those skanky losers. And I'd keep telling myself I had choices over and over. I had to believe that. Otherwise, I'd be back being trailer trash."

"I see. You vowed to transcend negative forces around you?"

"Oh, is that what I did? Okay, sounds good. I finished high school, got myself into Florida State and freedom from them all. You know the rest. I did it all on my own. And I'm proud of it.

I became a therapist to show clients they've choices in their lives to make it better. If I did it, so can they. That's why I tell them stories about myself. I show them how *I* solved all sorts of problems. It worked for me. It can work for them."

Hester took a breath and looked at Felicity still twisting that cross around and around. Could she strangle herself doing that? Hmm, 'Religious weirdo chokes self with her own cross. Film at eleven'.

"Whew, I'm done. Felicity, your turn now."

"Hester. I usually rely on people at Church for social interaction. However, I found our verbal exchange after the staff-meeting an interesting digression."

"Oh? A verbal exchange? Is that what it was? Isn't that nice. Felicity, you do know there're always people in and out of the staff kitchen to exchange verbals with."

"I have found the room small and noisy. And some of the people can become intrusive with their questions." She shook her head. "It is not a Christian atmosphere."

"And my office is?"

"As an Evangelical psychiatrist, I wish to incorporate His word into my therapy. At times, I have failed to convince the patient that a new life without mental pain, free of worry and guilt awaits them, through Jesus. I am here because I am curious about your direct approach with clients and whether your method of reshaping their ideas and beliefs might aid me in reaching my goal."

"Uh-huh." But first you'll have to keep them awake, sweetie.

"I also see you as confident and assertive, attributes I strive for."

"So, your clients haven't eagerly taken to your spreading the word? How could that be?"

"It perplexes me as well."

"Uh-huh. Can't your minister help?"

"No, this goes beyond his expertise."

"What's your Church again?"

"The Evangelical Covenant Church with Pastor Franklin on Taylor Road. That was the first place I went when I arrived"

"Uh-huh. A bar would've been my first place. You're really into your religion, aren't you? Being an Evangelical?"

"Yes. The Bible is my sole guide to salvation and my goal is active sharing of the gospel in any way I can and help others be reborn. After some untoward events in my teens, I was reborn and reaffirmed my faith in Jesus, repented my sins and turned away from evil."

Hallelujah, sister. "Felicity, why aren't you a minister in some church instead of a psychiatrist?"

"That is not allowed. Males lead, especially in Scripture interpretation. Women still must answer to them."

"Only men running things. Fancy that."

"My father, a minister and Bishop in the Church, is the sole authority when it comes to interpreting God's Word. He often preaches about the devil, sin and the fires of hell. How we are weak and prey to Satan's constant quest to corrupt us and be eternally denied His love."

"Scares the hell out of people, huh? I can see how that'd make them free of worry and guilt."

"Originally, my goal was to tend to the physical needs of people back home. But during a psychiatry-rotation in medical school, I witnessed more misery in peoples' souls than in their bodies. It was a sign. Jesus wished me to choose psychiatry."

"Growing up, you were one zealous girl, weren't you?"

"Yes."

"*And?*"

"I am from Danville, Boyle County, Kentucky. That is where my Father, the Bishop, leads The New Salvation Covenant Church. When I reached my teens, I became active aiding him in bringing people to Jesus. Presently, my fourteen year-old sister, Verity, is becoming more involved in helping father."

" Hell, when I was a teenager, religion wasn't anywhere on my list. My parents attended the Church of the Flip-Top Beer. You know, I'd hear people talking about that happiness and redemption stuff, just believe and repent your sins. But, excuse me, I still think it's a lotta crap based on fear and guilt, like your father preaches. I never saw all that believing and repenting bring them happiness."

"Faith and repentance can bring happiness now. It has for me."

Hester jerked. "*You're* happy?"

"By repenting my sins, guarding against Satan's scheming temptations to sin and spreading His Word, yes, I am happy. That is what I want to convey to my patients."

The way you light-up a room, honey. How could a client resist? Hester gave her best smile. "Thanks for that little bit of information on Evangelicals." More than I freakin' ever wanted to know. "I respect your beliefs, really. But, for me, religion is all empty promises. 'Just submit and good things'll happen. Have faith and we'll take care of the rest'. Faith? That's the bullshit religion pushes because it's got nothing real to sell."

"I have heard that from others. I understand."

Hester shook her head. "I don't think so."

"Hester, I shall tell you that I have met Satan. Only by being born again was I cleansed. And I shall tell you that I did not blindly surrender. I chose to follow Him."

Met Satan? She probably drove over the speed limit once. "Of course you *chose*, having such a righteous father and all."

Felicity looked away.

"Hey, Felicity. I've some wiener, pain-in-the-butt clients. How bout they join your Church? Hah, you tell them what to do, they do it, get praised and feel happy. If they whine, they go to hell. Give them that, 'If you're *real* good, you go to heaven crap and they might listen. Felicity, I gotta say, your cramming religion into therapy is brilliant."

"Hester, the Bible ...."

"Look, I've some things to do right now. Remember? We talked about having a cup of tea sometime after work? Let's do that. We can talk about my approach with clients. And you can enlighten me how your clients surrender their souls to Jesus, yet learn to become independent."

Felicity got up from her chair and aligned it perfectly with the desk. "That would be acceptable."

Hester came around extending her hand. "We'll have tea soon."

"It was another good digression. Thank you. Please excuse me if I do not shake hands. I am uncomfortable being touched." She turned and left.

Hester stood watching her leave. Darlin, you don't know it, but you're already touched. She smiled. I think next time I'm going to tell her the Bible says Jesus was a hugger. See how that plays. Her being so virtuous, I'd bet she believes her shit doesn't stink. Then again, she's so tightly bound up, it might just stay inside her. Good thing she has that Jesus stuff holding her together. Or is it? Anyway, I'm definitely making that date for tea. Hester grinned. Hell, 'Digressing' with that girl is freakin weirder than talking with ghosts.

TEN

Sure I'd Like Tp Have More Friends, But People Are Such Jerks
Where Jack Forewarns Of Lurking Danger
Suppression: Deliberately Avoiding Unpleasant Thoughts Or
Feelings; I Just Won't Think About That

Jim sat down, turned to the waitress and ordered a beer. "Hey, Jack. Thanks for coming. Been here long?"

"I came a little earlier before *The Lusty Pelican's* drunks start muscling in. I wanted to get a table to look out on the harbor and marina. Watch the idiots do their stuff."

"And, were you duly entertained?"

"Jim, they did not disappoint. There were some loud assholes at the next table, but, thank you Jesus, they left.

After a cruise boat docked, all the tourists got off wearing only tee-shirts and shorts. Their skin ranged in colors from dark-pink to red. If *I* saw the crew in broad-brimmed hats and long-sleeved shirts, that would've told me something. Not these jerks."

Jim placed his fingers to his forehead. "I see the future, pain and misery for many tourists tonight."

"Then, this dipstick driving a forty-foot motor yacht could not line up his stern to back into his slip, even with his wife on the stern guiding him. He'd scream, 'Dammit, Ellie, you keep making me bang into the pilings. What the hell you doing back there?'

She'd yell, "I tell you which way to go. Then you do the opposite. You're the one who doesn't know port from starboard.'

That must've pissed him off because he started to back in way too fast. She shouted to slow down, but the jerk kept going. The dock-master must've seen this moron was about to ram the pier. He ran down with some helpers and secured the boat after the wife threw them the lines. That done, the dock master very cooly said, 'Everything okay, Captain? Since we've your boat secured, you might consider turning-off your engines.' Then he turned to the wife and saluted her. "Thank you, ma'am. You did good."

Jim took a sip of his beer and wiped some foam off his upper-lip. "Well, at least that was that one positive thing to balance your suffering those all-around you."

"Okay, smartass. Before you brought your warmth, I was enjoying the setting sun's drenching everything with a luxuriant golden glow."

"Jack, did you just say something positive? Now, I'm feeling very special being allowed to drink beer with you."

"And look at you, Jim, still wearing your Hawaiian shirts and offending good-taste wherever you go."

"I am. I've made a solemn vow to fight the rampant prejudice against these shirts as art, despite anyone's criticisms."

"Oh? You've had a negative review?"

"Only one. I'm not letting it bother me."

"Fabulous. Ladies and gentlemen, will Jim Bizby, once a mild-mannered, placid, conflict-avoidant wiener, now a hard-boiled, decisive Hawaiian-shirt-wearer finally become, drum roll, *Master of His Destiny?*"

Jim smiled. "Stick around, folks, Maybe you *and* Jim will find out."

Both turned to look at the sunset.

"Jack, what's up with Gus Cobb?"

"What about him?"

"If I see him, like in a hallway, I nod, say, 'good morning'. All he does is scowl. Why's he so angry all the time?"

"I remember hearing something happened between him and his wife. But, I really don't know why he's that way."

"Doesn't matter. How goes it with Bonny? You two talking yet?"

"Barely. I've tried to keep things light, but until I tell her Brad's improving, or better yet, that I've terminated him, going near her might give me frostbite. You know, I thought by now I would've been able to talk her around and everything'd be fine. Don't count on our getting together as couples real soon."

"No worries, Anne's still sticking pretty close to home, so we're not...."

"Jim, this thing with Anne, it's more than homesickness, isn't it? Is she depressed? Is there something else going on you've never mentioned?

Jim turned to him and sighed. "Anne's not depressed. I almost wish she were. And she's not homesick like we'd think of it, missing people as you get settled into a new area."

"What is it then?"

"She wants to go back to Cleveland."

"Isn't that part of being homesick?"

"No, no. Anne *is* going back to Cleveland. That's why she's done absolutely nothing to adapt down here. It's also her way of pressuring me, no, punishing me because I haven't quit my job and called the moving company."

"Have you known all along what you should be doing? And what you weren't?"

"No. It only happened recently after I asked her what more I could to help her start doing things, get involved She told me to stop trying. That she'd moved here to humor me about this whim I'd had about living in Florida. That she was tired of doing it and we should be moving back to where we always belonged. Just let her know the moving date."

"So, your wife was lovingly indulging a whim you had, by the way, I don't see you as particularly 'whimsical', then said, that's over, time to go home? Son of a bitch."

"She's close to her family, Jack. I still think she needs some more time. I want to make this work. I know I can...."

Jack was shaking his head. "Pal, you've got some serious marital shit here. Anne's not only been bitchy to you, she's been playing you. I'm really pissed at her just hearing about it."

"I don't want to go there."

"Uh-huh. You're telling me you're not upset with her? Okay. I'll buy that if you believe it's snowing outside."

"Getting angry with her won't solve anything."

"Agreed. But lying to yourself, and me, that you're not pissed also serves no purpose. Makes you think you're going to make things all nice again."

"You're right. But look, if Anne and I have a confrontation, I'm going to have to make some decisions. And I'm not ready for that yet. Please understand where I'm coming from."

"Okay. We'll pretend that avoiding elephants in the room for as long as possible is always best. It's just hard walking around their shit." Jack grinned. "As long as you're not giving up your quest to be... *Master of Your Destiny.*"

Jim grinned back. "I promise. The quest will continue."

They raised their beers, toasted and looked off into the distance.

"How'd your day go at the Clinic, Jim? Discover any secrets in those deep labyrinths of the human minds you explored?"

"Countless, and they were all very dusty. You?"

"Usual stuff. A husband dragged in his wife who was getting more manic. He knew she'd stopped her meds when he couldn't shut her up and she'd stopped sleeping. She also gets hyper-sexual and tries to seduce every guy she meets, like the teenage bagger at the grocery. Together we were able to get her back on her meds before the real chaos starts."

"Excellent work, Doctor."

"After her, I saw an OCD guy who needs everything to be orderly. So, to see how well he's doing, I opened my drawers, scattered some papers and put my pen crosswise on my desk corner before he came in. He sat for about a minute and then closed the drawers and moved my pen to line up with the edge of the desk, but he left the papers."

"Jack, isn't that a little mean?"

"No. We've a good relationship and he knows it's my way of seeing how he's doing."

"If you say so. Have you seen the gun guy yet?"

Jack stopped smiling. "It's Brad. No, we've yet to meet."

"Just wondering what you'd do if he's wearing a raincoat next time you go out to get him in the waiting room."

"Well, dumbass, I guess I'd have to frisk him, wouldn't I? Or, maybe I'll you to do it?"

"No thanks. He's your patient. You decide."

Jack turned from the view and looked at Jim. "Hey, didn't you see some sexy new patient with nice legs the other day? Fancy told me she was yours."

"We all see new patients, Jack."

"Uh-huh. And this new patient? How'd that go?"

"She had depression and bulimia."

"And?"

Jim backed his chair away from the table. "And what, Jack? Yes, she's an attractive young woman who, and this might surprise you, has psych problems. She's had bouts of depression from her teens when she also started bingeing and purging. She's vomiting more now and seems desperate as to what she can do to control it. Okay?"

"She's had prior treatment?"

"Yes. She said meds helped minimally and therapy didn't get anywhere. Apparently, one of her past docs started coming on to her."

"Curious she would mention previous psychiatrists hitting on her right in the first appointment with you."

"Why?"

"I've found my more dramatic female patients tend to mention certain things."

Jim leaned in. "Like what?"

"Like, 'I don't know why guys are always hustling me' or, like yours, 'Can you believe it? My psychiatrist tried to seduce me'. Then there's the, 'You can't trust men because they just use you' routine as she smiles and says, 'But, I *know* I can trust you'. She'll say how *desperate* she is, how no one's *ever* been able to help her. Some get flirty, ask about you, then pouty if you don't respond."

"Jack, this is a bright woman who is significantly depressed and purging. If anyone was inappropriate, it was me."

"You? C'mon?"

"I think I got a bit brusque with her. She'd say something, I'd ask more questions. Before I knew it, I was challenging her a bit too strongly, especially it being our initial appointment. I was making psychodynamic interpretations much too early."

"So, she did challenge you? Question what you said?"

"Yes." Jim thought for a few minutes. "I know why I was abrupt with her. She was being manipulative. Like you said, she was coy. She wanted to know things about me. She accused me of not being 'human' by my keeping the therapeutic distance. She challenged, she pouted. Yeah, drama.

She kept crossing and uncrossing her legs. But that was out of her anxiety. She wanted to know if I found her attractive. She used guilt on me...."

"Wait a minute, bud. Did *you* find her attractive?"

"Well, she was nicely dressed, hair combed..."

Jack shook his head and rolled his eyes. "Jim, cut the shit. Were you attracted to her? I remember those legs of hers. And I just glimpsed them."

" I'll admit, she is attractive. And I found myself focusing on *not* looking at her legs. At the time, I think I recognized that and was being gruff with her as my defense mechanism against the attraction. I was trying to keep the session objective and clinical. I know I have, let's call it a 'therapeutic weakness', for depressed women who are hurting. That gets to me and I really want to help them. "

"Uh-huh. And, of course, her being pleasing to the eye only adds to your wanting to help this poor, struggling girl out of her wretched state? Okay, I'm glad to hear you're aware of your soft spot of hurting, depressed females. Just keep in mind the sexual component so you can deal with that when and if she pulls it on you. You mentioned she was manipulative. Was she looking to get something specific out of you?"

"I'd say meds."

"I thought you said meds didn't work?"

"I did. But she said a friend had given her some Adderalls and they helped with her mood and appetite suppression. She said she stopped stressing about overeating, stopped purging and felt better. She asked for a prescription."

"You give her any?"

"No."

"Why Jim, you didn't surrender to her feminine wiles, eh?"

"Stop with that, will you? She's attractive and engaging. Your pointing out there may be issues there'll help me remain professional and objective.Thank you."

"What're you going to do about the Adderall? You know she's going to ask for it again."

"I've treated a few depressed patients with stimulants, but never someone with an eating disorder. It is an interesting idea using the med to decrease appetite which reduces desire to eat which decreases the anxiety and depression."

"It is. Although I've never heard of them used that way. What happened when you refused? Did she use the 'You're my last hope' or 'I thought I could trust you'?"

"Both actually and that I was an uncaring bastard. Looking back,

I *was* too glib with her. That's not like me."

"Jim, you were trying to keep your distance. She's coming back?"

"She wanted to return sooner than the usual week."

"Oops."

"What's that supposed to mean?"

"More expectations of you. Or, the sooner she gets working on you, the sooner she'll get that med. You're sure she's not an addict?"

"No, I don't get that impression."

Jack smiled. "Well, Doc, given she's already elicited a number of feelings in you, I hope you're right. Just be careful."

"Of?"

"You're already seeing her sooner than usual. Be careful if you start seeing her as the last patient of the day so you'll have extra time to help her. Or, if you start fitting her in when she calls because she needs my help. Those are danger signs that you're unconsciously, or even consciously, making it more than a professional relationship."

"That would never happen. Talking with you, I've a much better perspective of the dynamics. If only she'd open up to me. Ha, I'm sounding like you talking about Brad."

Jack glared. "I'll let that pass, Jim. Unlike you, I'm aware of what's going on there."

"Well, now thanks to you, so do I." Jim smiled. Although my Uncle Joe'd say, "Two fools are no better than one."

Each sat in silence watching the sun disappear. Neither believed the other.

ELEVEN

Only The Humble And Vampires Avoid Mirrors
Where Max Only Lies When His Lips Are Moving
Narcissistic Personality: A Person With An Overinflated Sense Of
Self Needing Constant Attention And Approval While Demeaning
others; Let Me Tell You About Myself

Dr. Maximo Hernandez sat nodding his head at Celia Fuentes, his least favorite, and ugliest patient. As she babbled on, he fantasized about the female drug-rep who'd just left his office, her long, brown hair, the pouty lips and those long, long legs.

She'd teased, "Dr. Hernandez, you're always so *kind* and *generous* finding time to see me. I find it such a pleasure when we meet." She knew how to talk to him. He *was* kind. He *was* generous. He'd wanted to tell her, "*Señorita*, I'm grooming you for an even more pleasurable oral interaction in the future." But no, she was new. He'd be patient in his seduction. Max had put on his 'intent' face listening to what she had to say as he gazed at her lips and thought of what else she could do with them. He'd done his stroking his chin and nodding pose as his eyes drifted to her breasts. She'd been showing him just enough cleavage to tempt him, to tell him, 'yes'.

"Let me point out, Doctor, that, according to our data, patients have found the once-a-day dosing very tolerable with less side effects."

Would she be good in bed? Her legs wrapped around his back? What position would she like best? He was there only to give her pleasure. He *was* kind and generous.

The meeting ended, she stood. "Thank you, Doctor Hernandez. If you'll sign this, I'll leave samples for you out front." Standing next to her, he'd lightly touched her arm. Her skin was warm and very soft. He'd commented on how beautifully she dressed taking in her body one last time, undressing it.

"Let me assure you, *mi preciosa*, your new drug will be the only one I'll prescribe, if appropriate of course."

"That's all I can ask. Thank you *so* much, Doctor." Her smile told him. She knew he wanted her. Maybe they'd do it here in his office. Some of the reps loved fucking in the Doctor's office behind the locked door. As long as she wasn't a screamer, at least not here.

Talking more loudly, Celia Fuentes rudely intruded into Max's head. Her whining about her sister, Julia, hadn't stopped since she came in fifteen minutes earlier. "Doctor, she's always borrowing my things. And she never returns them, *never*. She finds fault with everything. How I look, my apartment, my coffee's too weak, the special cookies I buy for her aren't fresh enough. She never stops, Doctor. She gives me chest pain. I know she wants me dead so she can take all my things. What can I do?"

Every appointment was the same. Celia whining about her suffering, asking for his advice and then giving reasons why she couldn't follow it. Then he'd write her a prescription. That's what Celia really came for. Max looked at his watch and put on his 'sad' face. "Celia, *lo siento mucho*, our time is up. And I've an appointment I must attend."

"Doctor, you will write me the prescription for my Ativan, yes?"

"*Ciertamente*, Celia. I'm only here to help you, *si*? Remember, take a pill if you know your sister is stopping-by, to calm yourself."

"But sometimes she just shows up?"

"Then take one when she shows up, *mi querida*," Maybe put two in your bitch-sister's coffee.

"*Gracias*, Doctor. I shall pray for you,"

"And I shall light a candle for you," he said, nudging her out the door.

Now alone, Max wondered why Smith wanted to see him. Probably one of his brainless projects promoting the Clinic among Latinos. Whatever it was, he'd handle it. He always did.

***

Before the meeting, Max stopped in the men's room. Looking into the mirror, he took out his comb and ran it through his long dark hair getting the wave just right. A black, silk, short-sleeved shirt hung from his wide shoulders over tight black pants. He saw his forearm heart tattoo showed. Women always noticed it and said, "Why is there no name in the heart?" He'd smile and look into their eyes, "First, someone must win my heart. Maybe, I'll put *your* name in there, eh, *chica*?." If Smith comments, he'll make something up. He rebuttoned his shirt to the neck, but left his gold cross out for effect.

"*Señorita* Martha, it's such a pleasure to see you," Max said entering Smith's office.

"Dr. Hernandez, thank you for being on time . You know how busy Dr. Kingston-Smith is. Go right in, please."

"*Muchas gracias, señorita.*"

"Bless your heart, Doctor."

Martha, Dr. Kingston-Smith's secretary, had hobbled in to his office earlier with Max's employee file held in her gnarled hands. Born locally, Martha graduated high school, worked a few months as a roller-skating car-hop, got fed up with the red-neck humor and low tips and found herself a University job. Even after she discovered that educated University folk could be just as rude and manure-dumb as the car-hop yahoos, she stayed on. Having never married, Martha let the University fill her life during the day and her children, the chickens she raised at home, take up her evenings. Thank God for her chickens, a variety that laid blue eggs. Their only demand was to be fed and they were competent at what they did.

In her early sixties, Martha's arthritis was aggravated by her pompous-ass boss' daily complaining and looking for a pat on the head. She had stood in front of him, her body leaning to the right. "Dr. Smith, here's the file from HR."

"Thank you, Martha. Are you standing funny? Everything in good order?"

"It's my arthritis. I might've mentioned it to you a few thousand times. I'm trying to keep the weight off my left knee."

"*Dommage.* Well, take something for it, will you? You can certainly stand like when it's just us, but I'd appreciate it if you stand and walk normally when others are about. I don't want people to get the notion I mistreat you. *Quelle drôle*, eh?"

"Bless your heart, Doctor. I'll put my pain somewhere deep inside me and appear to be fine, just for you."

"That's a good girl. "

As she turned to leave, he stood, "Wait. I want your opinion on my jacket, tie and handkerchief. I thought I'd go with the black small-check sport coat, powder-blue shirt and plain black tie this morning."

"I think you look fine, Doctor."

"Yes? The crimson red pocket handkerchief? Not too, *outré?* "

"Doctor, I do apologize. This country girl doesn't know what *'oooh-tray'* means, but I do believe y'all look great. Can I go now?"

"What about the crimson red socks?" he asked raising his pants for her to see.

She concentrated on the red sock, not his elevator shoes."My oh my, Doctor, y'all sure look wonderful, like out of one of those men's magazines."

"Thank you, Martha. I like how we always agree on things. You take care of the arthritis pain."

"*Bless your heart,* Doctor."

Sitting down, Smith opened the Hernandez file. He reached for his Mont Blanc to hold and point to random pages. He liked when he did that.

Smith was on the phone when Max entered. "Yes, yes, he's here now. I'll certainly take that up with him. We're still on for lunch tomorrow? Excellent. See you then."

Pen in hand, Smith started pointing at something in the file. After about a minute, he raised his eyes and looked at Max. "Dr. Hernandez, *merci bien* for stopping by today. It's been on my radar to confab with you on how things are going, make sure we're running the same race. Please sit down."

"Thank you, Dr. Kingston-Smith. I trust your day is going very well."

"*Merveilleux.*" Smith looked back to the file.

After a few minutes of being ignored, Max said, "Is there anything specific we need to discuss?"

Dr. Smith looked up, leaned back into his chair and put his hands behind his head. As he smiled, his mustache broadened. "Max, Max, I simply want to learnt how the people on my team are doing. You've been here, what, three years?"

"About that, yes."

"You know, in that time I can't recall our ever being able to pow-wow to make sure we're united in our thinking."

"Yes, Doctor. Outside of staff meetings, we've really never met like this. I've *truly* felt the loss of interacting with you, hearing your wisdom."

"You know my door is always open to you."

Smith leaned forward and crossed his hands on the desktop. "As you likely know, my admin style is to manage my select team of clinicians by a heuristic approach. I'm not a micromanager with my expectations being that you learn experientially and grow intellectually from that. I think that's a win-win, don't you?"

"I could not agree more, Dr. Smith. I dislike someone looking over my shoulder all the time."

"Exactement. The practice of medicine is an art and how physicians display it can vary. I want my people to bloom on their own. That said, how are you doing?"

"All is good. I enjoy the patients and feel blessed that I can help them. The support staff is wonderful and the other doctors collegial."

"Your file says you're from the East coast. Do you drive there on the weekends?"

"Yes."

"A long drive, what? Each weekend back and forth?"

"Unless there's an accident, driving Alligator Alley from here to Miami isn't so bad. Listening to audio tapes on psychiatry helps pass the time. And I find the intellectual ambience here at the University Clinic very stimulating. That compensates for the long drive."

"Your family is in Miami. It must be hard on them not seeing you?"

Max put on his 'reassuring' face. "Quite simply, my wife is happy that I'm happy. She is a saint. And I believe my children appreciate me more."

"You said you find things *stimulating* here, Dr. Hernandez?"

"Yes. The many exciting people and events on campus are what arouse me along with interacting with my dedicated colleagues here at the Clinic."

"It pleases me that you find the University 's *milieu* so rewarding. However, I need to speak to you about, how shall I put it, some of the *people* you find so stimulating here."

Max sat up from his slouch. He chose to wear his 'puzzled' face. "Please, Doctor Smith, I'm not following you."

Smith steepled his hands together and rested his chin on them, careful of his mustache.

"*Hélas*, how shall I put it? *Concerned* people have reported to me that you've been seen frequently with various University staff members, female staff members, in what they termed *affectionate* behaviors on campus and off at restaurants, bars and motel parking lots. I was just on the phone with the Vice-Provost when you came in. He, and others, are concerned that you may be, their words, 'taking advantage' of these young women by your status as a doctor. His disquiet arises from one of *his* female staff who has been complaining about your treatment towards her. I don't know what that means exactly, but I shall find out. All I know presently is that I'm getting calls from a higher-up. And, Dr. Hernandez, that does not please me. If they're disturbed about staff complaints, so am I.

'Dr. Smith, I…."

Smith held up his hand. "Let me be perfectly clear, Doctor. I've no concern what you do in your private life. However, I could become quite troubled if there's blow-back to my Clinic. For example, someone filing a sexual harassment complaint against you with HR." As Smith's face reddened, one side of his mustache began to droop, the heat melting the wax.

Smith went on, "As you know, that odious 'sexual harassment' phrase is more in the news People have a way of misinterpreting gestures of kindness and approval. A supportive pat on the back can be seen as a prurient gesture. The reputation of this Clinic is in my sacred charge and I must protect that. You understand where I'm going with this?"

Max changed from his 'puzzled' to his 'sympathetic' face. "I totally understand, Dr. Smith. I, too, share your concerns about the Clinic's integrity. I will be perfectly honest with you. I do keep company with various women who work at the University. Their friendship during the week when I am so distant from my loving family fills a void in my loneliness. After reading the latest Psychiatric journals in the medical library, I may attend lectures, musical events or a movie. However, since I love to share things with others, I still feel an emptiness inside, that loneliness."

"I see. These relationships, have they ever become sexual liaisons?"

Max sighed deeply. "Dr. Smith, my respect for you obliges me to say, yes, I may have sex with these women. Being a handsome man yourself, I know *you* share the same burden. Women are attracted to you no matter what you do to dissuade them. God has gifted us. Myself, I no longer fight it. I do share physical pleasures with others. They are willing and I am willing."

"The sex? It's consensual?"

"Permit me, Doctor, but what I do goes beyond 'just sex'."

"Oh? Please elaborate."

"In our healthy social interaction, I try to bring more happiness into a woman's life. It may be a weakness, I know, that I'm such a giving person. But it's who I am. Should we have sex, I am very attentive to her needs. I see myself as *spreading the love* I have inside me to bring her joy and, I hope, fulfillment. Is that wrong? Spreading the love? Bringing happiness to someone?"

"Doctor. I don't care how much love you're spreading. Is it consensual? Or do these females feel pressured into a 'relationship'? If that's the case, it wouldn't look good for you...or me."

Max showed his 'hurt' face. "Doctor, I *exist* to gratify a woman, to pleasure her. *Of course* the woman agrees. And, if there are ever any questions, I am covered."

Smith leaned forward as far as he could. "You've insured your 'spreading the love' doesn't cause you problems? How so, Doctor?"

"I ask all the women that I keep company with to write me a letter describing how they feel about me. I suggest that they might express their love, how they cannot wait to see me again and how much they enjoyed our sexual playing, maybe even what they liked most about it. I tell them of my loneliness and how such a letter helps me through it. So, you see if anyone ever complains of being misused, I've the letter she wrote. I don't wish to be punished for my giving nature."

Smith's eyes were so wide his mustache curled up. "And they do this?"

Max nodded. "With all modesty, I tell you, yes, they do...for me."

"I am impressed, Doctor."

Max raised his hands with his palms out and gave his most innocent smile. "I can be very convincing. My right-bottom desk drawer is filled with these letters. If you wish, I can show them to you."

Smith was tempted. "That won't be necessary for now, Dr. Hernandez. I'm pleased that we have same-pageness here and reassured that you are being prudent in your activities. I'd only ask that you be more discrete in your encounters, less public. I'll allay the fears of those who've expressed concerns, especially the Vice-Provost. I'll tell them you are conducting yourself with prudence. Presently, your 'spreading the love' philosophy and the many *billet-doux* in your desk drawer will remain between us." Smith narrowed his eyes and pointed his Mont Blanc at Max. "But, Doctor, take care. Others in the University lack my imagination and tolerance. I do not want this exploding in my face despite how many love-notes you have. Should something occur, I'll not be so understanding. Am I clear?"

"Perfectly, Dr. Kingston-Smith. I don't want to add to the great responsibilities you already bear. Be assured that I'm here to do the best job I can in caring for our Clinic patients. My respect for you is boundless. I'd do nothing to jeopardize our relationship."

Hopping from his chair, Smith came around to shake hands."I am pleased that we're like-minded on this sensitive issue."

As Max turned to go, Smith said, "Ahhh, there's one thing more. Confirm for me that you have not had contact, by that I mean sexual contact, with any of our patients outside of your professional role as their psychiatrist."

Max's 'horrified' face appeared. He took in a deep breath, held it and then switched to his 'hurt' face, one of his favorites. "Sir, my integrity as a physician and my responsibility to the people I treat are sacrosanct to me. That would *never* happen. That is the truth."

"It'd better be the *truth*, Doctor. Violating a patient's trust, and by that I mean having sex with a patient, would be a heinous, and ruinous for the Clinic.Thank you for putting my mind to rest on that point."

The taller Max looked down at Smith. "I am blessed to be working under your leadership."

"*Bien sûr,*" Smith said turning to sit back at his desk.

"How did the meeting go?" Martha said as Max passed her desk.

"*Todo bien. Gracias, señorita.*"

Martha nodded. "Bless your heart, Doctor."

Recombing his hair and undoing some shirt buttons, Max looked at his reflection. You are good, very good. Smith hasn't a clue. And getting those love letters? Brilliant. Everyone loves me. I am, 'spreading the love'.

TWELVE

How Sharper Than A Serpent's Tooth It Is To Have A Thankless Child

Where Personalities Uncoil

<u>*Individuation*</u>*: Gaining A Sense Of Feeling Independent, Yet Remaining Part Of Society; Learning To Say Yes Or No Nicely*

"Sorry I had to call you, James, but that support-beast just wouldn't stop snarling and barking and was scaring the other clients. Thanks for escorting them out."

The security man smiled. "No problem, Fancy. Call any time."

"Actually, you may hear from me later, but I won't know until the client shows."

Fancy sat back taking in the scene. The janitor slowly rolling his cart back to its closet, the consumers waiting to be seen and traces of sunshine winning its fight with the grimy windows. She smiled and took a long breath.

"Good morning, Fancy. You seem pretty peaceful."

"Dr. Jim. Just taking a minute to appreciate what's happening in this moment. How I enjoy what I do. How my life is now versus another time. My kids. It all brings me joy, and gratitude."

Jim nodded. "That's a place we'd all like to be. Oh, before I forget, has Dr. Rackham arrived yet?"

"Haven't seen him. Should I tell him you're looking for him?"

"Please." Jim shifted from one foot to the other.

"Dr. Jim? Anything else?"

"Fancy, I just wanted to compliment on your style in handling things."

She tilted her head.

"You're kind. You're helpful. You're honest. Yet, you can be firm and assertive even if it means there's some unsmiling faces. You're your own person. That's a rare thing."

"Thanks for that, Dr. Jim. But don't let my fantastic smile fool you. I've had some trying times and I've had to work hard to be where I am now." She grinned. "And I still have more work to do."

"Well, I just wanted to know. I don't want to be intrusive, but maybe you could share your secret sometime?"

"No problem, Doc." She paused. "Can I ask you something?"

Jim leaned-in. "Ask away."

"When I started here, I figured the doctors and therapists were pretty well put-together. You know, because of what they do. But, you know, what I see are angry people, cold people, complainers, people only into themselves."

"Okay?"

"So how can they help our clients when they seem worse-off than them?"

Jim laughed. "You think maybe the patients should be treating the staff?"

"Just wondering, Doc."

"Fancy, learning to understand the human mind so we can treat and help people doesn't necessarily free us from our own fears and insecurities. In training, we're *supposed* to get more insight into ourselves so we don't let self-doubts, insecurities or fears get in the way when we treat patients."

"Doc, isn't that kinda what life's about, knowing yourself?"

"Yep, exactly. "

"Okay, so if the staff are supposed to know themselves better, why are they the way they are?"

"Great question, Fancy. But, alas, the answer's a long one that we'll have to leave for another time. I will tell you, though, that fear's usually at the bottom of it all."

"Fear, huh?"

"I'm sorry, but I'd better take my charts and get going. We'll talk again?"

"You bet, Doc."

"See ya."

"See ya, Doc."

She looked down and turned to a new calendar page, 'Sarcasm: curing the world one insult at a time'.

"Checking your caustic quote for the day?"

"Dr. Jack, you just missed Dr. Jim. I'm to tell you he's looking for you. How you doin?"

" Me? Like always, zip-a-dee-doo-dah. Why shouldn't I be? What did Dr. Jim want?"

She shook her head. "Sorry."

"I'll just take my patient charts and schedule."

"Dr. Jack?"

"*What*, Fancy? I've got things to do."

"Ah, I know you're seeing the client with the gun today."

"Yeah, so?"

"Do you think maybe security should be in the waiting room? You know, just in case?"

"In case he starts shooting up the place? Nothing like a little hysteria to liven things up. *No*, I don't think so, but *you* do whatever you feel is best, okay? I wouldn't want anyone feeling out of sorts."

As he left, she dialed security.

His charts scattering as he threw them on his desk, Jack turned and headed for the kitchen. After downing his shot of caffeine, he grimaced. He hadn't seen them, but there they were sitting at the table with their bull-shit herbal teas, weird Hester and creepy Felicity. Jesus, I don't need these two right now.

Hester looked up as Felicity stared down placing her cup exactly centered on its saucer."Morning, Jack."

"Hester."

"Hey, didja know I'm using tarot cards now in my counseling?"

"New hook, huh? Was that your idea or one of your spirit pals? Listen, when you're talking with one of them, couldja get me Freud on the spirit chat-line? I always wondered about that coke addiction he had."

"Sorry, communicating with the beyond wasn't too relevant with a lot of my clients, so I dropped it. The tarot cards work better drawing them into my 'positive attitude therapy'. Manipulating some cards, I get them to listen to me tell them how to trade their dumb behaviors for more positive ones. Me, of course, being a living example of that for them."

"BFD, Hester. We all do that, help people become more insightful into their unhealthy behaviors, delve into where they originated and help them make a transition from their negative actions to more self-empowering ones. Some of us focus on helping the patient make better decisions. Then, of course, there are those of us that *tell* the patient what to do."

"I simply try to help, Jack, without the big words."

Jack bowed. "Hester, your humility overwhelms me. Look, I was going back to my office, but tell me more about, 'tarot cards and therapy'." He grinned. "Maybe I can use it with my resistant patients."

"Okay, so I pull out the cards. Something they don't expect."

"I bet. They're in a therapist's office and you pull out tarot cards, *surprise*."

"I have them turn a card over. Then, I ask them what they see in the card."

"Okay."

"As I get to know the client, I stack the deck and pull specific cards I want the client to talk about. Like if she's depressed I may pull the hermit or death card. Someone with an overbearing husband, the emperor or the card with hearts with swords in them. When I want them start changing, I pull the Empress or High Priestess and push the power angle. See?. They open up. I do my thing."

"Damn, Hester. You know you're actually doing projective testing to elicit client feelings. I am impressed." Jack turned to Felicity. "You know, I'm told it can help a lot of emotionally constricted patients."

"So, Hester, the tarot cards are working out for you?"

She shook her head. "It helps some. But like I've said a million times, some say they want help, but are too lazy to do anything to change. 'Oh, Hester, wave a magic wand and make things go away. For crissake, sometimes what I want to do is wave a baseball bat."

"The unconscious mind with its irrational fears and repressed feelings can be powerful force. I've found that although people may be unhappy, they can be very apprehensive about burrowing into their minds. Often, people see themselves negatively and are afraid that therapy will confirm that. For many, it's more 'comfortable' not to face those fears and to keep the *status quo,* no matter how bad it is."

Hester made a face. "Jack, why can't you just keep things simple like I do?"

"You're right, Hester. I'm clearly not blessed with your simple-mindedness."

He turned to Felicity who'd had her head down. "And you, Dr. Steele, another day *not* in paradise? I wanna tell you how impressed I am with your perfect alignment of spoon, saucer, cup and your napkin folded so precisely. I've heard somewhere that some people believe that if everything is arranged *just* right, all is under control and nothing bad can happen. Orderliness equals mastery. But wait, isn't that called 'magical thinking'? A symptom of OCD?" Jack stroked his chin, "Hmm."

"I am well." Felicity stood. "Hester, despite Dr. Rackham's sarcasm, I still respect your tenacity in exploring ways for your clients to change their lives and overcome their pasts."

Hester nodded. "Leave your cup and saucer. I'll take care of them."

Out of the kitchen, Jack met Jim in the hallway.

"What's up, Doc?" Jim said.

"Just spent a few minutes with freaky and creepy"

"Huh?"

"Hester and Felicity. Who else?"

"Right. You're seeing the gun guy today? "

"Sure are no secrets in this place, are there? Yes, I'd be seeing *Brad* right now if it weren't for you."

"You're okay? You know how you're going to address the gun incident?"

Jack crossed his arms and glared. "You really have a bug up your ass about that, don't you, Jim?"

"Jack, it was a very significant event in his therapy."

"I'll tell you this, not that it's your any of your goddamn business. I'll do what I have to. I'll be professional. I'll listen, takes cues from Brad and comment."

"But you *are* going to mention the gun?"

"Read-my-fucking-lips, Jim. I'll see how things go."

"Okay, but…."

"But what? Please don't tell me about your concern, *again*? Please don't tell me what I should do, *again*? Jesus Christ, Jim, I'll do what I think is best." Jack smirked. "Oh, here's a thought. How about you take all your bull-shit concerns and focus them on doing something about your marital problems and stop using this issue to avoid them? Huh? Why doncha?"

"Jack, I…."

"Jim, goddammit, enough."

"You're right. You're his doctor. You do what you think's best. But if you don't mind, can we grab a beer and talk later? I'd like to hear how the appointment went. Maybe I'll learn something."

"You know, I want to say fuck off, but I'm thinking it'll give me the chance to bust your balls about Ms. Nice Legs and how she's handling you. You know how much *concern* I have about that and what you should be doing. Okay, later."

"Sure, Jack, later."

***

Slowing as he neared the waiting room, Jack started thinking of sitting on his lanai sipping a vodka/tonic. He made himself look. Brad was there, sitting away from everyone. Jack caught his breath. Thank you, Jesus, no goddamn raincoat. And nothing appeared to bulge in his pockets.

Okay, Jack, be serious. No smile, no extending your hand.

Friendliness never worked with Brad, did it? He needs his anger and suffering too much. "Brad, come back to my office."

Just as a week ago, they sat opposite, although Jack had pushed his chair a little farther back. Brad sat erect, gripping the chair's arms. Scowl-faced, he looked out the window.

"How's your week been?"

Brad looked at the ceiling. "It's been."

"Anything worth mentioning?"

"What did I say? *It's been.* That means, nothing much. *Okay?*"

"Okay. So does that mean you've been existing solely in your room? Brooding in your cave and avoiding?"

"Whatever."

"I wonder. Do you think someone cold earn a living as a hermit? Hmm. Be a night-watchman? Deliver newspapers before dawn? Be a forest ranger in one of those fire-towers out in the wilderness?"

"You're one fucking funny comedian, Doc? Maybe you should take your act on the road because you're pretty useless here."

"Brad, I'm concerned about your isolating. My provoking you seems the only way I can some response."

"Is that your best approach, Doc, showing how you care through

100

sarcasm?"

"Your depression hasn't changed?"

"Depression? I'm irritable, but depression? Nuh-uh."

"And all along I thought your being moody, pissed-off, impatient, resentful and withdrawn were symptoms of your depression, especially if we throw in your trying to hang yourself. Sure looked like depression, doncha think?"

"Sorry, Doc. Once again you've missed the boat because you don't fucking *listen*. You just *tell* me like everyone else. You know, all this *concern* crap? It's just a way to tell me what to do. Things like, 'How about a job? That'll get you outta the house' to 'Man up and get your shit together' It's all bullshit. That's why I keep to myself."

"Okay, Brad, let's talk about bullshit. When you come in here, I do listen. Since you don't volunteer anything, I ask questions. And you? You've got your three stale responses. You either rant about somebody telling you what to do, like you just did. Or, you insult me and try to get me pissed. Or, your most creative one, you stare out the window in what looks to me like some stupid-ass defiance.

I'm going to take a wild guess and say you're angry. And behind that wall of anger, I see you as very unhappy."

"Trying to make me feel bad, Doc?"

"Nope. I'm only describing your behavior." Jack paused. "You choose if you want to feel bad."

"Fuck you."

"Okay, I'm listening. What do *you* wanna do?"

"To be left alone and be *myself.* Away from everyone and everything, parents, girlfriend, friends, magazines, TV-commercials, billboards. All that shit telling me how I should behave, dress, talk, eat. Or how I should act towards them. 'Brad, you should wear more blue. You know I like you hair shorter. Brad, eat a little more. I made it special for you. Brad, you should call me more. Brad, don't be a wuss, have another beer.'"

"Damn, with these weighty forces you're up against, and you so powerless, I can understand why you'd flee to your fortress of solitude. How's that going for you? I'm thinking that bullshit's getting old."

Brad's lips tightened as he stared outside.

"You know, Brad, I don't have a goddamn clue what, 'being yourself' means. What's worse is that I don't think you do either. You go on and on about some heroic stand you're making against the world oppressing you, but I see it as you're being afraid and hiding."

Brad turned to Jack. "Yeah. From what?"

"Life. Making a thousand choices each day and realizing that you're not always right. And seeing that that's okay. Learning that you don't have to depend on others approval to define your self-worth. That you can do that. Realizing that not being perfect is okay. Little things like that.

Goddamn *doing* things instead of stagnating like you are now.

Brad, it starts with little choices that you make. Do I want to let your hair grow longer? Grow a beard? Do I dare wear something other than the polo and chinos? Have another beer or no. Then, it's college? Trade school? Job? Being in a relationship? Marriage? Kids?

`All I know is that you can't find yourself by yourself. It's that give and take with others that helps you define things about yourself, helps you to choose."

Brad leaned back and smiled. "Cute story, Doc. It was a story, wasn't it? One of those rah-rah psych-fables you tell to motivate your patients and also make yourself look so wise? Sorry, I don't quite see it as an inspiring story. I see it more as a fairytale minus the, 'And he lived happily ever-after'.

"Oh?"

"Because he didn't."

"Why not?"

"Because in my fairy tale, the hero goes out into life wanting the freedom to be himself and make his own choices, but instead finds it's a constant struggle dealing with people who want things their way and judge him unacceptable if he doesn't fucking follow along. The hero's life is filled with disappointment and pain that doesn't end until he dies. Pretty despairing instead of inspiring, huh?"

"Brad, it doesn't have to be that way. Your depression…"

"I'm not fucking depressed."

"Brad, life brings joy and life brings pain. That's the way it is. But you're talking about unending struggle and pain? Jesus."

"Doc, I learned my lesson about life with all that Naval Academy crap. You gotta do whatever *they* want. Even if you try to kill yourself, no one listens. And that's the way it is, you give in to get by. But thank you again for that great fairytale."

"Dammit, Brad, you just don't want to hear me, do you?"

"Oh, did I screw-up again? Didn't give-in to your profound explanation on the meaning of life? Should I have said, 'Wow, what a fantastic concept, Doc. Now I can live happily ever-after? Fuck that."

"Brad, why did you pull the gun on me last week?"

"Huh? What are you talking about?"

"Since we're talking about your resistance in doing things, it struck me that, despite all your bitching, you keep coming here. Then, I thought of your showing up last week and pointing a gun in my face. I'm just kinda wondering what that was all about?""Doc, I told you. It was a replica I'd found in our attic. I wanted to share with you how real it looked."

"And it did look real. And we both know that's pure crap. Remember when I reached out to push it away from face, you said, 'Don't do that.' That sure doesn't sound like a show and tell to me."

"So, now it's all about you? Do want to talk about it? How did it make you *feel*?"

"Yes, I *would* like to talk about it. I felt it was a very inappropriate action."

"What? But I was just sharing."

"Brad, doing what you did was a number of things, but it sure wasn't sharing."

"Like what? Waddya think was oozing out of my subconscious? C'mon, tell me."

"First, I believe you wanted control of me and the session. That'd make the powerlessness, the futility you feel less. For a little while, you were a master of the universe."

"Uh-huh."

"Second, I think there's a part of you that actually wants to talk, but that still scares you. The gun was meant to provoke me into terminating you. Then, you'd be off the hook and could brood about your victimization."

"Is that it? Because it sounds like we're getting into fairytales again."

"One more. With your pointing the gun at me, scaring me, controlling me, you were in a symbolic way taking-out on me all the rage and sadness that's been building in you for a long time. Oh, thanks for not bringing a real gun."

"I just wanted to scare you, Doc. And like you said, piss you off like you do to me. Let you know you can't get to me."

Jack nodded. "I have noticed that over the months."

Brad smirked. "Yep. Why talk about something that's never going to change? Hey, Doc, I hope that doesn't make *you* feel like a failure. You know, not having brought me from the darkness into your light? That you're not going to win the, 'Psychiatrist of the Month' award with the special parking space?"

"Brad, it's not about my *getting* to you. I'm here to help and guide you. To make suggestions about what I think is pulling you down. You gotta know, Brad, it's not to control you. It's actually to free you up from whatever *is* controlling you. I know you've a strong fear of being seen as inadequate. And that it feeds the depression you claim you don't have. I wish, one of these days, we could talk about that."

Brad shook his head. "Back into those fairytales again, Doc? You know, I am who I am. That's not going to change. Look how long you've been beating your head against the wall."

"Brad, people change. That's implicit in coming for psychotherapy, hope. You must some somewhere, you keep on coming."

"Okay, Doc. What the fuck. I'm be Mr. Cooperative. Whatever you want to talk about, great. Anything not let you down. How about that?"

Before Jack could answer, Brad had left.

"Ungrateful bastard," Jack said to the silence.

THIRTEEN

Life Is Like Underwear. A Change is Good Once In A While
Where Jim And Jack's Ideas Are Like Parallel Lines
<u>*Displacement*</u>: *Shifting Disturbing Feelings About Someone To A*
Less Threatening Object; Yell At Your Wife, NotYour Boss

Jim hesitated as the Lusty Pelican's waitress tapped her foot. "I'll have, no, wait, bring me the Harbor Lights Lager craft beer, a pint, please. It's time for a change, Thanks."

He'd just phoned Anne that he'd be late. "Jim, you want to choose to stay out, I don't care. I'm just waiting to hear you've made one particular choice. And you know what that is, doncha Darlin?" She'd said and hung up.

Jim saluted as Jack sat down across from him. "Hey, Jack, glad you came. Get you a beer?"

"No worries. I caught the waitress before I sat down. How was your day stamping out mental illness in our lifetime?"

"Pretty smooth. No big challenges."

Each took a sip of beer, then sat a bit in silence. Jack smiled. "Hey, buddy, have you seen that sweet young thing with the nice legs again?"

"Not yet. And her name is Ahndrea."

"*Ahndrea*? Well, isn't that special? Damn. And here I thought I was going to be able to harass you with my concerns."

"Sorry to disappoint you."

Jack grinned. "I can wait. So, how are things with you and Anne? She out of the house at all? You know, acting *normal*?"

Jim took a swallow of his beer, hesitating. "Anne's still adjusting to the move. It seems it's taking her longer than most."

"That's curious. Last I heard, she'd given you an ultimatum, 'I don't like it here. We're moving back. Tell me when you give them notice at work so I can call the mover.' Something like that? Right? That, my friend, sounds to me like she's more than adjusted to what she wants to do. What are you gonna do?"

Jim slowly shook his head. "I don't know, Jack. Part of me wants to just keep plugging along hoping something'll change."

"Change? Are you fucking nuts? You've been down here how

long?"

"Two months."

"And in that time, Jim, *nothing's* changed, has it? Although Anne did tell you she was humoring you coming here and her, of course, her ultimatum. Jim, c'mon. What's your other part wanting you to do?"

"Well, I start thinking about my alternatives. That's when I get confused, you know, what's the right thing to do here."

"Uh-huh. You know, Jim, confusion can be one handy-dandy excuse for not making a decision? 'Oh, wretched me, if only I weren't in such a muddle, I could decide. I guess I'll just wait and see."

"And what's your solution, Jack? Getting angry? Demanding? Should I threaten her? Provoke her? You could give me some lessons on that. I know you think I'm a wuss, but I *am* doing something with Anne. I'm trying to be understanding, tolerant. I'm giving her time to get used to not having her big family around."

"Yeah? Two goddamn months? How's it been working for you? Being patient is nice. Being passive isn't. Even though I know you're angry deep down and denying it, I don't mean you should start yelling and threatening. That's not you. But I do think you need to have a plan just in case Anne doesn't magically start loving Florida because I don't believe either of us believe that's ever going to happen. Look, it can't hurt to see a lawyer, find out what options you have instead of waiting and hoping. This is no way to live."

"Jack, you do remember I told her I'm not moving back?"

"And we both can see what a dramatic effect that's had. Jim, you're too nice a guy. Anne's working on guilting you into moving back. Do the, 'If you *really* love me' bullshit. Face it, pal. Fish or cut bait time is approaching. You'll come home, she'll say, 'I'm fed-up waiting for you to decide, so *I've* scheduled the movers. You can tell them you're quitting your job tomorrow."

"Moving's not an option."

Jack shook his head and smiled. "Whatever you say, Doc. Just keep plugging along wearing your gaudy shirts, taking your pictures and hoping for a miracle. That sounds like the right thing to do."

"You can be a real dickhead, Jack."

"What can I say? I calls 'em as I sees 'em."

"I thought your steadfast belief was never to give up on a person, even if they don't do what you want? Like with Brad."

"Ah, finally. I've been waiting for you to bring him up and ask about our session. Damn, Jim, very slick how you finally worked him into our conversation."

"I knew you'd get pissed if asked you as soon as you sat down."

"I don't know, probably. Even though I knew he was the reason you wanted to meet."

"So, you did meet?"

"Yeah."

"And, no gun?"

"No." Jack smiled. "I'll admit it. The first thing I looked for was whether he was wearing a raincoat. But, he wasn't."

"So?"

"The session was SOS, his same old shit. He came in sullen and testy, stared out the window and made me drag things out of him, the usual."

"You did talk about the gun?"

"Yeah, we eventually got around to that after my having to confront him on some things."

"Like what?"

"He loves to rant about people, especially me, not listening to him and telling him how he feels."

"And?"

"I just told him what he was saying was bullshit. That I do listen and it's he who doesn't talk, unless it's to bitch about something. That the only way I can get a response from him is saying something that might irritate him which includes how I think he's feeling. I also told him his staying in his room was not some heroic stand against people telling him what to do, you know, typical adolescent, 'You can't tell me what to do' crap. It was him hiding from life and afraid to grow-up. How I wished we could talk about that."

"How'd he take that?"

"SOS. That my wanting to talk about his issues was a fairytale except he wasn't going to live happily ever after."

"Because?"

"Because he couldn't see any possibility of life changing for him."

"Jack, let me ask you. Do you think sometimes when you try to get a response from this clearly resistant guy, that you did come on too strongly, you know, like you were judging him? That you'd get too close to some of his fears and inspire more anger in him?"

"Judgmental? Fuck, Jim, I told you jabbing him was the only way I could get some interaction. I am *not* judgmental with patients. I can't be. We can't be. Sure, he pisses me off with his insults like how I had to get him better so I can win, 'The Good Doctor Prize', insinuating I *needed* him to get better. Watta jerk."

"Do you, Jack? Need him to get better? Could that have been why you were so confrontative with him? Trying to push him into health and getting angry with him when he resists? Countertransference issues. I believe you know about those."

Jack made a sneering sound.

"Suicide and depression issues apparently still cling to you, Jack. Your brother primarily, your patients who suicided. I'm sure you don't want another one."

Jack's eyes bore into Jim's. "Look, you bastard, it's crystal clear to me, his psychiatrist, that Brad is presently denying he's depressed and projecting his anger onto me. That's easier for him to do instead of facing his self-condemnation for not meeting some imagined perfect person he thinks he's supposed to be. I'll deal with it. Okay? There's no question that it'd please me immensely if he felt better. But, I don't *need* him to feel better. Clear?"

"Whatever you say, Doc. So you did talk about the gun?"

"Yep."

"And?"

"Like you'd assume. He was all innocence. The gun was a replica and he was doing a show and tell. He never admitted any deep-down motives. And I didn't expect him to. But he did fess up to wanting to scare me to keep me at a distance and also piss me off. That's when I wished I had a replica to point at him, the little pissant.

"Did you suggest any reasons for his actions?"

"Yeah. That he wanted to let me know he was in charge of his therapy."

"To reassure himself that you could't him talk, even though he wanted to."

"Exactly. That he wanted to sabotage therapy by getting me so pissed I'd terminate him. And that he was displacing his anger, sadness, feelings of inadequacy and whatever else has built-up in him over the years at me."

"And?"

"Nothing."

"I told him I wished we could talk about these things, but he just made more smartass comments. Some directed at me and some, like, 'Why talk about things that'll never change'."

"You don't think he's suicidal, do you?"

"Nah. He'll sometimes throw out comments like that just to get a rise out of me. He's depressed, but I don't think suicidal. Although, Jim, I've wondered if the stubborn kid would ever fake a suicide just to spite me?"

"Jack, c'mon. That's a bit much, isn't it? We've had patients who'd do that for attention or secondary gain, but not to spite their doc."

Jack smirked and shook his head. "Of course you're right. What was I thinking? Anyway, I won't have to think about that resistant little shit until next week."

Jim walked slowly to his car. He breathed-in the sea air. He heard laughter. He thought about Jack. He thought about Anne and heard Uncle Joe. "Jim, always remember to have change in your pocket. It comes in handy once in a while."

FOURTEEN

*In A Minute There Is Time For Decisions And Revisions Which A
Minute Will Reverse*
Where Jim Anguishes Over Disturbing The Universe
<u>Wellbeing</u>: *Health, Happiness, Confidence And A Purpose; Feeling
Zip-A-Dee-Doo-Dah*

"Hey, did you see her yet?" Jack said grinning into Jim's office doorway.

Jim turned away from his computer screen. "Who?"

"Who? Ms. Nice Legs. The woman to whom Dr. Do-Right denies he has any attraction."

"Yes, I saw her earlier."

"Ah. And? Did her neediness entice you? Did she beguile you? Charm you? Delicately hint she's available for a discrete tryst?"

"Jack. Please. If you must know, her depression's worse and interfering with work. What's worse is that she's starting to have some hematemesis."

"Blood in her vomit, not a good sign. Hmm. I'm thinking the plot, not clot, thickens. Pressure's on, eh, Doc? Give her the Adderall yet?"

"No. I'm searching the literature right now for any data on using it in bulimics."

"And?"

"One anecdotal letter-to-the-editor in the APA Journal describing it helping one patient. It decreased her appetite. Then, her fear of overeating diminished and her vomiting subsequently stopped. Mood improved."

"So it might help?"

"Jack. It's only one patient."

"It's something though."

"Yeah, but…"

"So, what're you gonna do, especially with the hematemesis? If she keeps barfing, her gastric acid will continue to erode her esophageal tissue. How long before it eats into a large vessel and she has a major bleed? And here I thought you weren't a risk-taker."

"I still think she's holding back something crucial that initially precipitated and perpetuates her depression. I've been afraid that if I give her the med and her depression lessens, we'd never get to some core issues."

"But with this bleeding, it appears you can't stand around waiting for a choice to show-up eh, partner?"

"Yeah. Darn it"

"Jim, we prescribe antidepressants all the time for patients. Some return feeling much better and say, 'See ya in three months for my script' without our discussing a single 'issue'. Some want to begin to talk about things. We can suggest, but it's really not our call."

"I just don't want to miss something with her."

"Oh, such irony. Our hero, forever hiding his balls in questing to do what's right and pure, *must* decide. Will he withhold the med to pursue his fierce desire to dig into the dark labyrinth of her mind, risking her bleeding out? Or, give the med, which might stop the vomiting and bleeding, but could destroy *his* noble goal of discovering the reason for her intense, emotional struggle? Might his being too emotionally over-invested in his pretty patient getting in his way? Stay tuned, folks."

"Not funny, Jack."

"Gee, *I* thought so."

"What should I do?"

"Do? Is this a, 'Jim daring to move out of his comfort zone and make a decision' moment? I'll tell you one thing. Looking for data to give you permission to do something isn't it. Look at your options and goddamn decide. That's what we do Jim." Jack turned to leave.

"Everything good with Brad?"

"I guess. He'd never call here anyway. He's likely in his room, brooding."

Turning back to his computer, Jim heard another knock. "Dr. Jim, can I have a minute?" Fancy stood in his doorway.

"For you, Fancy, anytime."

She placed a file on his desk. "I'm sorry to bother you, but personnel sent some forms that need filling-out. Could you do them sometime today? Otherwise, they'll just keep calling."

"No worries." As she turned, he said, "Fancy, do *you* have a minute or two?"

She grinned. "For you, Doc, anytime."

Sitting down, Fancy smoothed her dashiki dress with its deep blue, white and yellow symbols and looked up. "Doc Jim, is there anything you need? Anything I can help you with?"

Jim came around to sit opposite her. "No, I'm good, thanks."

Leaning a little forward, he dropped his hands between his legs and smiled at her.

"This is going to sound dumb, but would you tell me your secret?"

"Secret?"

"Your confidence. Where's that come from? And it's okay if you want to leave and not answer."

Fancy sat more upright in thought. "Dr. Jim, since you've arrived, I've gotten a good feeling about you. You care about your clients. You listen to them, unlike some of the people around here who think the clients are here to be their audience. So, even though I don't know where you're coming from with your question, I think if I share with you a bit of my past, you might get a sense of who I am today."

She leaned back. "Okay, Doc, sit back. Let me tell you a story."

Jim did as he was told. "Please."

"I was born in a small village in The Republic of the Congo which people often confuse with The Democratic Republic of the Congo. In that part of Africa, there's always been fighting and killing, even after my country became a democracy in 1960. In 1999, murderers calling themselves, 'The Army For Democratic Justice' attacked my village. Holding our heads so we couldn't turn away and yelling they'd use their machetes on us if we closed our eyes, they forced my brother and me to watch as they stripped-off my mother's clothes, cut her Achilles tendons so she couldn't run and, after gang-raping her, cut her throat. Making my father kneel, they hacked off his head. They kidnapped me and my brother. I was fourteen and my bother was eleven. When we got back to their base, I expected to be passed around, raped, then murdered. But the leader, Joseph, took a liking to me and claimed me as his new wife. That meant I wouldn't be passed around, but it also meant that I'd become his sex-slave and servant. They took my brother off to one of their training camps to become a child-soldier. Doc, I never saw him again.

Growing up, I was feisty like my mother and it often got me into trouble. But in that place, I learned fast that speaking out could get me killed. So, to survive, I forced myself to become docile and compliant. I *had* to be passive, which definitely wasn't me, or I'd be dead. It may sound weird, but what kept me going was my being submissive, *deliberately* submissive. I played a game in my mind that I was in control of how I acted, not my captors. *I* allowed them into my hut. *I* allowed them to boss me around. Of course, I wasn't in control, but that, that illusion of control saved me. I played the game. I kept my head down, made no eye contact, did nothing that looked defiant. Those that didn't, well, they disappeared."

"How long were you there?"

"Four years. As Joseph collected more, younger 'wives', I went down the ladder as a favorite which was just fine with me. He kept us older girls around as sort of a prestige thing, like how many cattle he owned. Another girl and I had been planning our escape for a long time. So when a rival group attacked the camp, we took advantage of the chaos, grabbed our 'escape bags' and ran. One of the attackers saw us and shot my friend dead. I luckily reached the jungle cover and escaped. I survived three days in the jungle and then came up on a missionary hospital. They cared for me and eventually arranged for me to leave the country. As much as I loved my home, I had nothing to go back to. My parents were dead, my village wiped-out and I didn't know if my brother was even alive. So, I left my beloved Africa and immigrated to England as a political refugee. I lived there with a sponsor family for two years, went to University and had a part-time job. Then, as part of a church program for asylum-seekers, I moved here. I was twenty-two. I was taking some Adult-Ed courses in business management here at the University when I saw a posting for a job at this Clinic. I applied and Dr. Smith hired me. I'm still grateful to him for that. I started out checking-in patients and worked my way up to Clinic Manager. I still take some night classes."

"I didn't...."

"Doc? Two more minutes? And I promise I'll leave."

"Take all the time you need, Fancy."

"Too soon after immigrating here, I married someone I thought was a good guy. I told myself it was love, but I know now I was looking for security. I had two children by him before it struck me that

I was in the same situation as before. I was with an abusive, controlling man and back in Africa. During one of his drunken times when he was punching me into the walls with the kids crying, he grabbed a knife and started coming at me. At that moment, what screamed in my mind was a picture of those murderers in Africa, their machetes gleaming, blood-soaked and what they had done to my family and my village. Then, I was afraid. But this time I wouldn't let myself be. All the rage I had been storing up inside of me for a very long time erupted and I fought him. In the struggle, the knife dropped. I picked it up and stabbed him dead. The police arrested me, but the district attorney found I had acted in self-defense and filed no charges.

It was a violent act, a terrible, awful thing. But for me, I was saying, 'No more being afraid. No more feeling helpless. I'm taking back control of my life'."

Fancy rolled up the sleeve on her left arm. "Let me show you this."

Jim saw a tattoo on the inside of her upper arm, the full face of a lion.

"You may have noticed I usually wear long-sleeved dresses. It's to hide this. It's only for me to see and now I'm sharing it with you. In Africa, I lived in daily dread and then found myself in the same situation here." She pointed at her tattoo, then fixed her eyes on Jim's. "This tattoo is to remind me of the lion's strength, courage and bravery. And that I'm not taking any abuse like that from anyone, ever again."

Jim sat and watched as Fancy rolled her sleeve back down. "Does any of it still haunt you? I'm amazed you're not bitter from all that's happened to you."

"Thoughts, especially of my family, used to, but they're less and less now. Sometimes, I have nightmares about my brother, my trying to hug him and him pushing me away. But those are happening less. I think it's because I've chosen not to dwell on my past even though I know it'll always be inside me, somewhere. Now, I work at focusing on taking each day as it comes and dealing with the things I can and leaving the rest behind. I trying to choose what's best for me and those I love. Doc, do you think that's selfish? Like it's an 'All about me' kinda thing?"

Jim liked the warmth of the smile he gave her. "Fancy, in a way, it is. 'All about you'. But in a good way. It's about your accepting yourself as you are so, the way I see it, you get on with your life free of the 'what if's' and able to give more to others."

"Good. That sets my mind at ease. Thanks. You know, for a while, I really kept to myself. Then it hit me. I'd been telling myself I was free to do what I wanted, but I really wasn't doing anything. Where was that feisty Fancy I used to know? Well, I took the cork out of the bottle and Fancy peeked out, started speaking her mind and, Dr. Jim, I don't think she's ever going back."

"And how do get away with that around here?"

Fancy gave him a grin that extended into her eyes.

"Dr. Jim, if I could deal with people who'd kill me on a whim, do you really think this place is a challenge? As long as I'm tactful, of course."

"Ms. Muwamba, you're a remarkable woman. It's still you and your two children?""Yes, there is no man. There will *never* be a man. I have a female partner whom I'm slowly learning to trust and love. She's very patient with me. I've my two kids whom I love very much."

"Well, thank's for sharing."

"You're welcome, Doc. I don't know if I've answered your question, but now, like you docs say, 'Our time is up.'"

"See you around, Fancy."

"See you around, Dr. Jim."

Turning from the doorway, Jim looked around his office and shook his head. I need to move my desk against another wall and get a different perspective. Then I'll move the file cabinets. Maybe paint them and get rid of that awful gray. I need to straighten my wall photos and take some pictures for the other wall. Then buy a bright Persian rug for the floor. I'd better make a list. Then Uncle Joe said, "Jim, sometimes people make a plan to kid themselves they're doing something."

FIFTEEN

Two-Year-Olds And Fools Believe Life Should Go Their Way
Where Jack Has A Cancellation
<u>*Reality Testing*</u>*: The Ability To See A Situation For What It Really Is,*
Rather Than What One Hopes Or fears It Might Be; Seeing Life
Without Photo-Shopping

Jack strode into the Clinic. Neither the cloud of gray-hazed cigarette smoke nor the rotting food on the ground outside had bothered him. The dried spit on the entrance doors? No problem. Whoever said he was a complainer really didn't know him.

Fancy looked up from the piles of patient charts that the doctors and therapists would be needing, "Good morning, Dr. Jack. You seem pretty energetic this morning." "Fancy, I am not just *zip-a-dee,* I'm the full *zip-a-dee-doo-dah* this morning. And that's even before my second cup of coffee. I've already done some high-intensity training at the gym where, by the way, the Ben-Gay fumes were low. I ignored the jerks on the road and, best of all," Jack pointed at his back, "my shirt isn't drenched with sweat from a hot car seat. All's good. And you?"

"I'm doing well. Thanks for asking." She looked over at Jack's stack of charts. "From the size of your pile, it's a good thing you have all that enthusiasm."

"Bring 'em on. I'll be back to get them once I've had my cup of java." He bent to read Fancy's daily calendar, 'If I talk like an idiot, it's so you'll understand me'. "Later," he smiled at her.

"I'll be right here, Doc."

As he walked to the staff kitchen, Jack savored his good feeling. It must be because I'm handling things better. Except for Bonny. No, I'm managing her pretty well too. I talk, keep things light at dinner. I avoid mentioning the Clinic. And she doesn't ask. That's because she's just waiting for something to happen so she can say, 'I told you so'. Damn her. But I'll handle that. She's civil, but I wish she'd lighten-up on her cool distancing crap. No matter. I can wait. Two can play that game.

Jack heard Fancy's voice. "Doc, I'm glad I caught you. One of your patients is on the phone. Says he wants to catch you before you began your day. You know I usually take a message, but when he told me his name was Brad. Well, even though you've an appointment with him later, I thought you might want to talk with him. He's on line-two."

"Good call, Fancy."

Jack stared at the blinking light on his desk phone. What in the hell is this about? Some bullshit warm-up insults before our appointment? Jack picked up the receiver, pressed the blinking light.

"This is Doctor Rackham."

"Hey, Doc, how's your day goin so far?"

"Morning, Brad. It's going well."

"Just well? I'd expect everything to be wonderful. You've got that great job telling people what to do. Ops, sorry, 'suggesting' to people what to do. You probably drive a nice car, have a lovely home and a beautiful, adoring wife. At times, I bet you must feel like a, 'master of the universe,' huh? Oh, thanks for being so caring and taking my call, me being such a resistant pain in the ass and, how did you once phrase it, 'Someone who only finds comfort in hopelessness and solitude.' "

"Brad, what can I do for you? Don't we have an appointment later?"

"Hmm. What can you *do* for me? Funny, that's what I've been wondering about too. But more like what *have* you done for me. Waddya think, Doc? If you say, 'not much,' I'd agree.

But I understand, Doc. You can only do so much with a wretch like me. And I'm certainly not the best patient, am I?"

Jack looked at his watch. "Brad, why did you call? Can't we talk about this later?"

"Yeah, that's another thing I've been wondering about. Exactly why do you keep seeing me? Over the months, the futility in all this it must've hit you."

Jack paused. "Brad I keep seeing you because I have hope that one of these days you'll let me in and we can talk about you. What you're so afraid to talk about."

"Ah, hope. I think that's one of your fairytale words you use a lot."

Jack took a deep breath. "Brad, I know it's been frustrating. ..."

Brad yelled. "Frustrating? Doc, you haven't a fuckin clue.

Anyhow, the reason I wanted to get you was about that appointment later, I thought I'd call to let you know directly, because of your hope in me, that I'm cancelling it. And I won't be coming back."

"Oh?"

"Oh? That's all you fucking got, Doc?"

"Brad, my, 'Oh' is because I'm confused. Why are you cancelling? Stopping therapy? Why now? What's going on? Has anything happened? What's changed? I know it's been hard for you, but please, reconsider. At least, come in so we could talk about your stopping treatment, just today?"

Jack started to swivel in his chair. He transferred the phone to his other hand. He looked at his grimy windows. Lazy, goddamn maintenance never cleaning things. I'll get some Windex and do it myself. It looked so peaceful outside. The sunlight, people strolling to other buildings, talking. Some were laughing as they sat in the shade. Life unfolding.

"Has anything happened, Doc? *No*. Has anything changed? *No*. That's my fucking point. Since I'm not feeling any better, why shouldn't I cancel? You always talk about the same shit. What's on my mind? What have I been doing? When did the depression start? And yes, I am depressed, pissed *and* depressed. What could've caused it?

Remember? I told you last time what caused it. How it finally struck me how I've been a fucking clone like everyone else. Do what's expected. Do the *right* thing, not what *I* might want. And that that was my future. Me being one more dumbass human plodding along every day, doing what I'm supposed to so I can tell myself what a swell guy I am. How well I fit in. How everybody likes me. Maybe I'll be a success at something so I can say, 'Hey, everyone, look what I've done. I'm pretty hot stuff, huh?'"

"Brad, look, it's human nature to want to be liked and that involves people. Admit it, if your girlfriend says she likes your hair shorter, you feel better. But you do, and I know you don't want to hear this, have choices. Choices that cannot depend on others' opinions."

"Why do you keep preaching that dumbass, 'You have choices'

bullshit? Wait, I know. It's part of that fairytale happiness bullshit you sell to your patients, isn't it? Have hope and make those choices. That'll pull you out of the darkness. We both know that's not the way it works."Jack was etching 'x's' onto a pad. "Brad, come in, please, for a last appointment?"

"Okay, Doc. If I have choices, how's about this? I'm choosing to cancel today's and all future appointments. Maybe there is hope for me after all?"

"I think you know what I meant. Please, come to the appointment."

"Nah. I've made my decision and, you're right, I feel better already. Thank's for your help. Well, maybe not help, but at least for trying."

"Brad, are you thinking about killing yourself?"

"Don't you believe I'd tell you if I were?"

"No. That's why I'm asking. Do you think about suicide at times?"

"Shit. We both know I'm depressed."

"Brad, answer my question. *Are you suicidal*?"

"Like I said, wouldn't I tell you?"

"I really wish you'd come in."

"Thanks again, Doc.You take care of yourself and keep living that sweet life."

"Brad, wait." But the line was dead.

Jack stared at nothing. This didn't happen. After all I put into helping him. Shit.

Well, if he thinks I'm going to call him back right now to hear more of his, 'You can't make me 'tantrums, that ain't gonna happen. He'll show for his appointment.

Jack stood up, sat down. He brushed a piece of dirt from a shoe. They needed a shine. He torn-up the paper with the 'x's'. I really don't need this shit.

Jim poked his head into the doorway. "Jack? I missed you earlier in the kitchen. I was…hey, what happened?"

"You got a minute?"

"Sure, what's up?"

"It's Brad, you know."

"Yeah, the gun guy."

"He just called to tell me he's cancelling today's appointment and all future ones. He's pissed at me because we haven't made any progress. That it seemed pointless to continue. Can you believe it? *He* terminated treatment with me. I told you he was a spiteful shit. I should've listened to you and beat him to it."

"Okay. He's been a tough patient for you. You know, this might be for the better."

"Yeah, I figured you, Smith, and Bonny would think that."

"C'mon, Jack? You wouldn't? Even a little?"

"Yeah, okay, a little, but…."

"How did he sound?"

"Mostly his taunting self. But there were a few times when I wondered if he were suicidal and the call was his dumbass way of saying a final goodbye."

"Did you ask him if he were suicidal?"

"Jim? Of course I did."

"And?"

"He denied it. Well, he didn't really deny it. He talked around it no matter how much I pushed him on a yes or no. Kept saying he'd tell me if he ever were."

"I thought you felt his projecting his anger at you was a positive sign? That you'd go from his anger at you to what's actually upsetting him?"

"Yeah, that's what I've been telling myself. But, in truth, he continued to avoid facing his depression no matter what I tried. Son of a bitch."

"Jack, look at me. I know you feel bad not bringing Brad around. Add to that your frustration with his obstinance, his insulting you, your feelings about the gun episode and there you are. Face it, you're not going to have a good feeling about this guy. He never showed a glimmer of response to treatment, did he?"

"No. Meds didn't work and he never came close to engaging in psychotherapy."

"Was ECT or EMS an option?"

"I mentioned it, but you can guess how that went over."

"So, if you're uneasy about him, are you going to call the police?"

"Should I?"

"Do you think he's going to hurt himself?"

"Don't know. What I do know is that, if the cops show up, he'll deny it, probably be dramatic and tell them *I* was over-reacting."

"I know I've called them in the past even when the patient denied they were suicidal."

"Me, too. But my experience's been, they wanted me to make the decision to go into the hospital and went with the cops. Brad's not like that."

"How about calling the parents?"

"I'm sure he'd deny it to them. So why upset them?"

Jim shook his head. "Well, we've probably both called the police more than once to reassure ourselves and to cover our butts. But I can see where you're coming from in this situation."

"Bottom line, Jim, is that I've no firm evidence to justify committing him. I think I'll wait until our appointment time and see if he shows. If he doesn't, I call him and try again to get him to come in, maybe even reengage, such as it was."

Jim shrugged. "Not giving up yet, huh?"

"I can't. I want him better, goddamit."

"Jack, remember what Dirty Harry said, 'A man's gotta know his limitations.'"

"Yeah, sure. Thanks. See ya later."

"Maybe a beer after work?"

"Excellent idea. That should at least brighten up my day."

Jack headed for the staff kitchen. Dammit, I still haven't had my second cup of coffee. How in the hell do I respond to Brad's whining that my life's better than his? For chrissake , it is. If he does come in, I'll be supportive. But not take his bullshit behavior either. *I* need to call the shots.

As he drank from his water-bottle, Dr. Gus Cobb watched Jack slam into the kitchen.

"Goddamn it. Isn't one of the hired-help supposed to make coffee?" Jack said.

"Pot empty, huh?"

"Empty. And dirty. My day just keeps looking up."

"Arms broken, Jack?"

Jack turned, "*What*?"

"Why don't you make your own damn coffee? Unless, of course, your arms are broken."

Jack stiffened. "Gus?"

"Mm-hmm?"

"I've been wondering."

"That's nice, Jack."

"Why are you such a cranky, nasty pain in the ass?"

Slowly screwing the cap on his water bottle, Cobb smiled. "What a keen observation, Doctor. But, really, it's none of your damn business, is it? Besides, wouldn't you concur that this is a case of, 'It takes one to know one'?"

***

"Ken, how are you?" Jack focused on the patient before him, a *good* patient.

"I'm getting along, Doctor. Thank you."

"And your OCD?"

"Just fine."

"Still working part-time for the nursing home?"

"Yep. I get a kick out of those old people and some of the stories they tell. Driving them to appointments helps me fill the time. And, you know, seeing them gets me thinking how short life is."

"Did you follow up with that list of town social activities and events I gave you?"

"I go to the cemetery...."

"I know, Ken. But..."

"Doc, thanks for trying, but you know that's not me. I've never been social. I help a few people out with things at my condo complex. Some, mostly widows, invite me to dinner which I graciously decline. My wife and I were always happy just to be with each other. Now that she's gone, I'm content to be alone."

"You're not brooding?"

Ken smiled. "No. Brooding sounds like I'm sitting around angry about something. And I'm not. Mary's in my thoughts everyday. I sit out on the balcony and think about our life together, all the pleasant things we shared. That's my meditation time."

"I know the sadness is still there, your losing her."

Ken lowered his head. "Yes, it's there. But isn't that part of losing someone you love?"

"Yes, I know it'll never go away. But I'm hoping one of these days it'll lessen a little. At least your OCD hasn't worsened."

"Doc, whaddya think about my stopping my meds? Let my OCD come back? With the obsessions rituals filling my time, maybe I won't get so sad?"

Jack smiled. "How about not today, Ken? You know, I'm thinking my attention should be on your OCD and to let you grieve in your own way."

"I'm still...still missing her. Nothing will ever fill that hollowness inside me." Ken looked at Jack, "But Doc, I am better. Can we leave it at that?"

"Sure. Any problems with your medication?"

"No, but..."

There was a heavy knock on the door. "Excuse me a minute, Ken."

"Sure, Doc, I've time."

Jack opened the door and saw Fancy. "*What?*"

"Sorry. I didn't want to buzz you on the phone. There's a call from Brad's father. He said it's urgent so I thought you'd want to take it. There's an empty office across the hall if you want some privacy. He's on line-three."

"The office with the door open?"

"Yes."

Jack turned to Ken, "Give me a minute, okay? "

"No problem. I've nothing pressing at the moment."

Jack saw the phone's demanding red-light blinking. This better be good. Jesus, Brad, did you take off somewhere? Have some big blow up at home? You wouldn't have pulled that gun shit on them. Whatever it is, I know you gotta be spending your gloom. "This is Doctor Rackham."

"Doctor, this is Mr. Phillips, Brad's father."

There didn't seem to be any emotional give-away in the man's voice. "Yes, Mr. Phillips. What can I do for you?"

"Mrs. Phillips and I were out doing errands this morning."

"Yes?"

"We had lunch out at that new pizza place in town."

"Yes, Mr. Phillips."

"And then we came home."

"Mm-hmm."

"Brad knew we'd be away for several hours. We had to go to Costco. You know how long that can take. And then some other stops."

"Mr. Phillips, the office manager said there was something urgent?"

There was a long pause. Jack looked around the room. The windows in here were grimy too. The bookcase was okay. Maybe he'd pilfer it?

"I'm sorry. When we came home, I opened the garage door like I always do." Another hesitation. "And he was hanging there, just, just hanging there. Our son is dead."

Jack stopped breathing. So Brad had finally done it. Son of a bitch.

"Are you sure? I mean, are you certain he's passed?"

"Yes. He was hanging from the same cross-beam he used when he tried it before. Only that time we got home earlier then he expected and I was able cut him down *that* time… and save him. This…*this* time, I wasn't able to do that. As I was getting him down, Marge, Mrs. Phillips, called 911. The EMT's came pretty quickly. They did what they could, but said it looked like he'd been dead for a while. We're thinking he did it right after we left the house."

Jack heard a wretched wailing in the background. It stopped as a woman shrieked, "Ask the Doctor. *Why* did he do it? I thought he had gotten that out of his system. Ask him. *Why*? Ask him. Why?' Why?" The sobbing returned.

Jack's mind was racing. If Brad had been dead a while, did he hang himself right after we talked? No way. Brad had been planning this, waiting for the parents to be away. It couldn't have been anything I said. I was trying to get him in here. Pushing hope, choices. Dammit.

"Mr. Phillips, I am sorry for your loss," Jack hated that phrase. He was sorry for the pain they were suffering, the pain Brad, that selfish brat had caused them.

Mr. Phillip said, "Thank you. I called because I thought you'd want to know after your working so hard with Brad over these past months."

Jack nodded. Here it comes, first a little sarcasm, then the blaming.

"I know my son, our son, was a difficult patient. I don't know how much he talked with you. He certainly didn't share much with me or his mother. God knows we tried to find out what was bothering him. He was so bright, so handsome. Had everything going for him. You probably won't believe this, but he was a very personable guy before he got depressed. You would've really liked him. We... loved him."

Jack listened. He wanted to say, you know, Mr. Phillips, Brad could actually be quite a talker if you wanted sarcasm and insults. And you're goddamn right. He *was* a difficult patient, a real pain in the ass. He pulled a very realistic-looking replica gun on me and pointed it at my head. He probably didn't tell you. He probably didn't share with you his call to me earlier stopping treatment. All that shit part of his plan to make me feel guilty. Mr. Phillips, aren't you gonna ask if I thought Brad was suicidal? Why I didn't do anything?

But Jack said, "Mr. Phillips, you're right, Brad was a challenge and I wish we'd made more progress. But, as *you* said, he wasn't much of a talker."

His voice straining, Mr Phillips said, "Doctor, I've some things to attend to. I just wanted you to know." In the background, the crying had turned into a haunting, gasping wailing.

"Mr. Phillips, I cannot imagine the pain you and your wife must be feeling right now. Thank you for letting me know. I am very saddened by your loss."

Jack heard a quick intake of breath. Then, silence for a few seconds.

"Goodbye, Doctor. Thank you for trying to help our son."

"Goodbye sir. If there's anything I can do..." The line was dead.

Okay, Jack. Ken's waiting. Get back to work. Don't think about it. Not now.

***

"Ken, sorry for you wait."

"Not a problem, Doc."

"Okay. Let's see. Your medication?"

"Yes. Remember I cut the dose in half because that greedy drug company jacked-up the price so much."

"I do. And your OCD? Still stable?"

"No worse for wear. Hey, Doc, you okay? You went out of here one way, but now, I don't know, you seem a little somber."

"I'm good. Just something that I had to deal with. You know, part of the job."

"I'm sure whatever it is, you'll take care of it."

"Ken, why don't we stop here? I'll see you next time. And, please don't change your medicine unless we talk about it? I need you to throw me a crumb so I feel I've some say in what's going on."

"You got it, Doc. See you next time."

He handed Ken's chart to Fancy. "Dr. Jack, everything all right? Brad's father, well, he sounded strange."

"Yeah. Brad committed suicide. He hanged himself."

"Oh my. I'm so sorry to hear that. I know you talked with him earlier."

"Yeah. He called to tell me he was stopping treatment and some other things. Fancy, I couldn't talk him out of terminating with me. Or even come in for a last appointment."

"Did you think he was going to….Never mind, dumb question. You have a few patients left this afternoon. Do you want me to cancel and reschedule them?"

"No! I'll see them."

"Dr. Jack, please understand that running the clinic is my business so I'm going to suggest you take the rest of the afternoon off from seeing patients."

"Fancy, I need to…no, you're right. Please cancel and reschedule my people. Do you know if Dr. Bizby's free?"

"He just started a full appointment, so he'll be a while."

"Okay. We'd planned on meeting for a beer after work. Will you ask him to text me if it's still on and what time to meet?"

"Sure. I'll catch him when he comes out. Should I tell him what happened?"

"He'll probably wonder why I'm not here. Yes, tell him Brad

suicided. He knows who he is…was."

"Okay. Anything else?"

"Thanks, but no."

Jack rocked back and forth in his squeaky chair. Okay, now what? Hassle maintenance to clean my dirty windows, fix the blinds and oil this goddamn chair? Nah, they're hopeless. I definitely won't call Bonny. Better to tell her tonight face-to-face. Then look serious when she starts her about my not letting this get to me like before. How she'll be watching. Like she knows everything. I'll just nod, say, 'Yes, Dear, I understand.'

He tried to pull-out his lap-drawer, but it was stuck. He stood up, man against metal,

and grabbed the handles with both hands, positioned his body and yanked. It came free with such a jolt that everything inside it went onto the floor. Stupid-ass drawer.

He looked at the mess, turned and left his office, slamming the door behind him.

SIXTEEN

Animals Below Man Never Need To Blame
Where Jack Regains Righteousness And Jim Remains Constant
<u>*Cognitive-Dissonance*</u>*: Uneasiness Experienced When You Feel Or*
Do Something Contrary To Your Self-Image; The Health-Nut Who
Orders Extra-Large Fries

"Hey, Jim, thanks for coming. I've just ordered another vodka/tonic and a bottle of that craft-beer you had last time, hope that's okay?"

Jim pulled his chair in. "Excellent." Jim paused. "Look, Jack, I know you've had a rough day. If you want, we can just sit, sip our drinks and enjoy the view. If you want to talk, I'll leave it up to you."

"You know, I'd been in great mood when the day started, everything going my way. First, there was no coffee, no big deal. Then, Gus Cobb shoots me a smart-ass comment about how I behave, like he's Mr. Wonderful. After that, I had to wrench my freakin lap-drawer out with it disgorging everything all over the floor. So, I said, screw that, and drove around bored for an hour. When I got here and out of the car, the back of my shirt was dripping from that damn hot car seat. Shit. Oh, Jim, your meeting with me isn't causing any Anne problems? Don't want you feeling like crap."

Jim shook his head. "No, nothing's really changed."

"Sorry to hear that. Are you…doing anything?"

"No, nothing's changed." Jim forced a smile. "Jack, you knew when I asked about your rough day, I wasn't referring to there being no coffee, a barbed comment from Cobb or your wet shirt?"

"I know. But those things did happen to piss me off. I've been thinking Brad's suicide pretty much since his father called. I guess I needed something else to bitch about. Jim, why do I keep rehashing things in my mind? Things you and I have discussed to death. I tell myself, it's happened. It's over. There's nothing you can do now, so leave it. He caused you enough grief when he was alive."

"I don't think that's quite the way feelings work, but anyway. I presume you documented everything?"

"Yeah. After the call, I finished with a patient and then recorded everything that happened this morning in his chart. I put in his calling to cancel his appointment and stop therapy. My several attempts to get him to come in and his refusing. That he didn't admit to me to being suicidal and that I had no firm reason to commit him. I noted that I deferred calling the cops because, based on his history, I believed he'd deny any suicidality. I wrote that, because of his rejecting my many requests to come in, I decided to wait to see if he'd show for his appointment. And if he didn't, I'd call him. I also mentioned we consulted right after his call on alternatives and your concurrence with my plan. I hope that was okay?"

Jim nodded.

"Thank you. I'm just covering my ass any way I can. Now, it's one vodka/tonic down, one to go."

"I had two suicides in Cleveland. It was tough. I kept asking yourself if there was anything I should've done, could've done differently."

"Well, I went through all that soul-searching stuff after my brother hanged himself. And I did the same hand-wringing after the two patients died. But not this time. Not with this guy."

"Probably hasn't hit you yet."

"Wrong, Jim. I did everything I could to help him and he just wouldn't cooperate. Plus, with his already making one suicide attempt, the odds were he'd try it again no matter what the hell I did."

"So you're really not wondering if you would've done *anything* differently?"

"Yeah, there was something."

"What?"

"I should've terminated him a long time ago. You and Bonny were right all along. I keep replaying in my mind his long, ignoring silences as he stared out the window alternating with his insulting wisecracks about me, what a dickhead psychiatrist I was. He was always trying to get a rise out of me."

"Maybe he was testing you? Seeing if you'd be critical, judgmental. Probably what he was doing to himself."

"I thought that when we started. But you'd think at some point, I would've passed. No, he even did that shit on the phone today. Plus, his, 'Poor me,' victim-routine bitching how everyone controlled him, told him what to do. Another thing he used to justify his anger."

"And, yet, he was the one controlling things."

"Brilliant deduction, Watson."

"It's clear his behavior evoked a transferential anger in you. But right now, I think your anger is coming from your own hurting over losing him."

Jack took a gulp of his drink, spit-out the ice, drank some more. "Jim, thanks for your sincere observation, but I am not hurting. I'm *pissed*."

"At yourself?"

" Some. For thinking I could help him, but mostly at him. How the bastard duped me into believing his anger was part of his depression."

"You don't think it was?"

"No. it was his behavioral style. He was into fault-finding with everyone to put people on the defensive. When he blamed others for his problems, it wasn't a depression symptom, it was him, his *persona*. It struck me this afternoon. Brad had a personality disorder, one of those people who get off controlling others. And psychotherapy sure as hell wasn't going to get him to give that up."

"So why did he keep coming to see you?"

"To see how much he could manipulate me, make me feel guilty, get me angry.

Man, did he suck me in. All that concern about that asshole, for what? Nothing. Can you believe it?"

Jim was shaking his head. "Darn it, Jack. This isn't about you. This is about your patient who killed himself this morning." He took deep breath, "I can't accept that you really believe what you're saying right now. This has to be your past talking. Suppressed feelings Brad's death has resurrected in your head."

Jack downed his second drink and ordered another, no ice. He sprawled back in his chair and smirked. "Jim, don't make excuses for me. It all makes sense. Here's a guy who never wanted to change. Who used his behavior to manipulate and control others so he could tell himself how cool he was. And, like all personality disorders, when I challenged his behaviors, he got angry. When he realized that his method of using people, especially his not succeeding in manipulating me, was breaking down, he took out his rage on himself and at me by hanging himself."

"Uh-huh. So let me get this straight. As you confronted his behaviors, his low self-esteem, frustration and anger began to emerge. Being unable to face that, he projected his anger onto you for upsetting him. In his attempts to get you to back off, he tried ineffectively to scare you with the gun which further frustrated him. So, being unable to kill *you* for some reason, he killed himself essentially punishing his unworthy self and, by the way, spiting you. Do I have it right?"

"A little convoluted, but, yeah, you got it. He needed to punish me and himself."

Jack looked at Jim solemnly, "Jim, I truly believe he didn't want the help. He was much too invested in his behavior to change. That's it."

"But weren't you angry at your brother for not wanting your help? Thought he was an idiot for what he did?"

Jack raised his eyes and looked at he ceiling. "By the way, Jim, how are you and Anne doing?"

Jim wiped away some water that had dripped onto his pants from the glass. He took a breath. "Fair. Anne still isolates at home. But I'm not asking about it anymore." He smiled. "What's funny is that now that I'm not asking, she makes sure to tell me she didn't go out."

"Cute. She just keeps pushing the knife in deeper about her not changing, huh?"

"Uh-huh Like the other night, she cooked. When I came into the kitchen, she immediately pointed to the one place-setting saying her mother suggested she try cooking something, for when her *real* life begins again."

"And nothing for you of course?"

"No."

"Nice passive-aggressive move, Anne. What'd you say?"

"That whatever she pulls to get me to give in, it isn't going to work."

"But she is making you miserable?"

Jim shook his head. "It's not that I'm miserable, Jack. I feel more… disappointed, frustrated, unhappy about where my life is."

"Did you say anything more? Not that it'd do any good."

"I had to get something off my chest. I told her that I'm done blaming myself for moving here and feeling responsible for her 'discontent'. She made that decision with me, no matter what she says now. That it finally hit me that she's been feeding into my believing that I was an uncaring, unloving, insensitive jerk. A failure in my marriage because I was selfish and unwilling to do what she wanted to make her happy. That now I see that that's not true. That, actually, I'm a caring, loving, sensitive, giving person, even if I don't do what she wants."

"Good for you. I hope this means less wimpy behavior and more confidence from you?"

Jim smiled.

"And Anne, she said?"

"Oh, she just shrugged and rolled her eyes."

"But she'll keep pushing your buttons?"

"I expect so?"

"But why? Why does she keep yanking your chain? You've told her you're not moving back. Why not just divorce you and leave?"

"Right now it's getting her a lot of family sympathy."

"That's a reason to live like she is? "

"Jack, rather than Anne take any responsibility in all of this, in her mind it's better to play the loyal-yet-suffering martyr until her family insist she divorce me. She'll resist a little for effect. That'll get the family reminding how much she endured living with that insensitive jerk. Who could ever blame *her* for divorcing me. I see her milking that angle all the way back to Cleveland."

Jack grinned. "Why, land sakes alive, Jim, you have changed in your thinking." He let a few seconds pass. "So, how long... before you decide?"

"Divorce?" Jim said. "No."

"Holy self-flagellation, I thought you weren't blaming yourself anymore? That you admitted to yourself how unhappy you are with your life? That you're going to be more decisive? Jim, what the hell's stopping you?" Jack paused and slowly grinned. "You've finally faced what's going on, *but* you haven't worked-through your guilt feelings, have you? You still need to punish yourself? Or let Anne do it? "

Jim nodded. "Excellent point from a guy who lives in a glass house. Maybe I am suppressing feelings that are affecting my present behavior. But, at least I'm willing to consider that. Thanks though."

"Yeah? And maybe it's simply you can't make the decision to divorce this witch because it's not *nice*. And what would people say? Jim, *think*. I don't want Anne to screw you over like Brad screwed me. Remember how you kept insisting I terminate Brad?"

"Yeah?"

"Because you thought it was a futile situation?"

"Yeah?"

"Well? Never mind. Indecision always gets so boring." Jack finished-off his drink.

"So, have you seen that sexy woman with the nice legs? Let's see, our last episode ended in a cliffhanger with our hero flustering whether to give our woman of mystery a prescription for speed to help her bulimia. Not to mention she was vomiting blood. As we look in on him now, we find…Jim, that's your cue. Have you seen her? What's happening?"

"I saw her today, my last patient."

"Last patient? Full session?"

"Yeah, so?"

"Didn't I tell you not to see sexy patients at the end of the day?"

"It was after she finished work."

"Uh-huh. How'd it go?"

"She still hasn't opened up to me. That's primarily why I hold off the Adderall."

"Even with her hematemesis?"

"She's not vomiting blood everyday."

"Jesus, Jim."

"She and I seem to banter about things more than getting into her issues."

"Bantering like in teasing, funnin with each other?"

No, Jack. Like in her role-playing to always be likable or with me, the 'good' patient. How she takes cues from people, then plays a role to get them to like her or to get what she wants. That's when I think I overdid it in confronting her."

"Oh yeah? What did you do?"

"When we were talking about her role-playin I asked her if today's scene was her portraying the needy yet scheming female type in a film noir playing me to get the med. And does she write her own dialog for a scene? That put her off, yet she did admit that she's very deliberate in dealing with people."

"Not a trusting girl, huh?"

"No. And that's the kind of dynamic we should be discussing."

"So, no prescription?"

"No."

"She coming back?"

"As far as I know, yes."

"Right. Because you're a challenge to her, Jim. Hey, you're still being objective, aren't you? Ignoring those lovely legs, the long hair, that flawless skin? You know, I wouldn't want to think that confronting her as you did, which, *curiously,* isn't like you, is actually your defending against your unconscious, sexual lust for her by labelling her as a schemer so you can distance her."

"I hit a nerve mentioning your brother and you just had to get even, didn't you?"

" Nope, not me. Hey, I liked your allusion to film noir and the classic needy yet devious woman."

"Okay?"

"Oh, it made me remember you have a weakness for needy women, to help them."

"Jack, this is different.'

"Okay, just remember what happens to the helpful guy in those movies?"

"Yeah?"

"He gets *screwed.* And not in the nice way. Oh, you two shaking hands yet?"

"When she leaves, yeah. What's that supposed to mean? I'm trying to show some caring, empathy, warmth. Not be the aloof psychiatrist stereotype."

"Oh Jim, all that analytical training and you're still so naïve. All I'm going to say is just keep it in your pants."

"Thanks for your wisdom, Doctor."

"Anytime, Doctor."

"Jack, seriously, if you want to talk anytime, about Brad, your brother, how you're doing, let me know."

"Sure, but I'm excellent. Other than your misguided references to my brother, you did help me get Brad into a truer perspective. And, likewise, if you want to talk about your stubborn, bitchy wife, let *me* know."

"You provoke so subtly, don't you?"

"Just trying to get your sorry ass moving, Jim. Because otherwise, well, you're not gonna have much of a life, are you? Jack got up, a little unsteady.

"Jack, you okay?"

"Never better, Dr. Fancy Shirt. I'm singularly the most stable one in this place. Mind clear, in control."

Walking to his car, Jack started singing,

I've got the world on a string, sittin' on a rainbow
Got the string around my finger....

SEVENTEEN

The Mouse's Reality Differs From The Cat's
Where Bonny Worries About A Snake In Her Garden
Passive Aggressive: Subtle, Provocative Behavior To Put You On
The Defensive; The Mashed Potatoes Are Lumpy Again. Can't You
Do Anything Right?

Jack poured himself a full glass of wine and thought about Jim. What a freakin wuss. I I sure as hell wouldn't put up crap from a wife like he has. Jack opened the slider to the lanai. "Hey. Bonny. Thanks for waiting so I could meet with Jim. Need any more wine while I'm up?"

"No thanks. Everything okay with Jim?"

"Well, he knows his marriage is a mess, but keeps avoiding doing anything about it. But that wasn't why we met."

"Oh?"

Sliding the door closed, he moved to kiss her cheek. He had to lean down low and reach, but gave her a quick, dry peck anyway.

"If you're out here, I'd guess the no-see-ums aren't biting?"

"Not yet, but we know they're coming. Oh, I bought some bug-repellent if you ever want some."

Jack sat down across from his wife. "Good. So, how're you? Your day go well?"

"It was long and I'm tired. I just got home fifteen minutes ago. Court ran on and then I had to go back to the office. I'm defending a homeless woman being harassed by the cops who are likely being harassed by politicians who want to look good to the voters. They want her to be their pawn to show how they're cleaning up the city."

"I think that's great. Your getting justice for someone who undoubtedly appreciates what you're doing for her. "

"I'm not looking for that. What I like is that I get to go after those self-serving rat-politicians. It's like sprinkles on my ice-cream. Anyway, why'd you meet with Jim?"

"You remember my patient, Brad?"

Bonny scoffed. " You mean the Mr. Antagonism? The gun-guy? The guy I asked you to terminate because he might try to kill himself again? And maybe you too? *That* guy?"

"Well." Jack paused. "You were right."

"And how, *please*, was I right?"

Jack paused. "He committed suicide today," he said letting his words hang in the air.

Bonny's eyes widened. She reached across the table to take his hands in hers. "Jack, I'm so sorry to hear that. You worked so hard with him, it must be a real loss for you."

Jack looked down. "He was a tough case."

Her face grew puzzled."But you seem to be in a decent mood."

"Yeah, so?"

"Nothing, but you just lost a patient, a guy you've struggled with."

"Darlin, please don't tell me you're getting suspicious already?"

Letting go of his hands, she sighed. "I guess I am."

Jack crossed his arms. "Well, relax. I'm fine. Brad called me this morning, told me he was terminating and I couldn't talk him out it. Then his father called to tell me he hanged himself. I met with Jim later and we had a long talk about what happened."

"I'm glad you talked with Jim. I know he can be supportive."

Jack sat back, nodded and took a sip of wine."Of course, I was initially upset. But, in thinking about it and talking with Jim, I was able to process things and work it through. Even got some new insights about things." He gave Bonny a cocky grin. "I'm feeling pretty good about that which is why I'm in a decent, no, a good mood. And also why you don't have to be suspicious."

"Honey, I'm truly sorry you lost a patient, but…." She shook her head. "So, you're telling me I should believe your talk with Jim gave you some near-miraculous insights into yourself and suicide? And that you've already worked through losing a patient you worked so hard and long with to where you're now in a good mood? How amazing."

"You just can't just accept things as they are, can you? I know. You're wondering if I'm bullshitting you, aren't you?"

"No, Jack, what I'm wondering is how much you BS'ing yourself."

"Goddamn it. Here I thought how happy you'd be, well, perhaps not happy, but maybe 'comforted' that Brad wasn't my patient anymore. And that I'm handling his suicide.'"Look, Jack, I'm not going to belabor what my concerns are. You've heard them enough."

"Christ, yes." He mocked her voice. 'Oh Jack, you don't deal well with suicides. *We* know what happens. You feel like you've failed. You get irritable. Your guilt creeps in and you get depressed and isolate.' Right?"

"Close. But you left out your *betrayal* when you lied to me, the drama I had to put up with. And then there's that brooding. Off in your own little world. I really hate that."

"Bonny, I've got a better perspective this time."

"Jack, I want to believe you. I really do. But what keeps popping into my mind is my mother. How she wasted her life silently enduring my alcoholic, womanizing, bastard father. Winding up like her is definitely *not* going to happen to me."

"C'mon, Bonny. Who's getting histrionic now?"

"It's not drama, Jack. I'm just adding to this 'better perspective' you think you have. And also reminding myself who I don't want to become."

"What are you saying?"

"I'm saying that I've made a personal decision that I'm never again going to tolerate your past behaviors. This may sound insensitive, but your using depression as an excuse just isn't going to cut it with me anymore. You know, sometimes it seemed like you got some weird comfort moping around. I don't know. I don't know." She met his eyes.

"Jack, the point I want to make is that I *cannot* and *will* not live like we did after the last suicides. It's unacceptable."

"Excuse me, but are you giving me sone kind of ultimatum. How Jack's supposed to follow, 'Bonny's rues for a good marriage'."

She thought a moment. "I guess it is in a way. But don't we all have in our minds what we won't tolerate in a relationship? If you'd ever struck me and I said I won't accept that happening again, would you see it as an ultimatum?"

"Yeah. And I'd see that as justifiable. But what I went through was totally different. My issues were things I couldn't control."

"So you say, Jack, so you say."

"Well, so much for sharing an extraordinarily difficult day with my wife. I get a crumb of sympathy that immediately loses itself in *her* avalanche of worries and concerns. Goddamn it, Bonny, walking in the door, I was in a good mood. Thanks for spoiling it for me."

"Oh no, Jack, don't get all passive-aggressive with me. You're free to feel and behave anyway *you* choose. Just know that *I* don't have to tolerate it."

She leaned forward and grasped his hands. "Jack, I want things to be good, to be excellent between us, like it was once. That's *all* I want. Please, if you want to talk, I'm here for you, anytime, day or night. Okay?"

"Shit. You still think I'm going to crumble or something." He hesitated, then raised his eyebrows and gave her a half-smile. "Bonny, I shall be a *very* good boy. Anything you want, I'll do it."

She yanked her hands away. "See, Jack, you're already acting like an ass. I'm *very* serious about this. I will *not* put up with how you acted before. Believe it."

He extended his arms out. "Like I said, anything you want."

Bonny let out a long sigh. "Jack, this isn't a game." She pushed back her chair and went inside.

"Your servant, I, Mrs. Rackham."

EIGHTEEN

*Even If Your Heart Is Rotten, You Can Still Smell Nice On The
Outside*
Where Fancy Makes Some Noise
<u>*Righteous Indignation*</u>*: Anger Over A Perceived Injustice; A Trait
Demonstrated Mostly By Perfect People*

As Fancy Muwamba neared his office, a young drug rep, running
her fingers through her hair and smoothing down her skirt, passed her.
Uh-huh, there goes another one. She stood by his open office door and
watched Dr. Hernandez intently writing out prescriptions and adding
them to an already large pile. She saw no medical charts to which a
doctor would usually attach a prescription, just that stack.

At first, the Doctor didn't hear her knock. Her second was much
louder. Turning his head, the Doctor slowly raised his eyes. "Ah,
Señorita Fancy, it is so nice to see you. I'm sorry for not noticing you
standing there. As you can see, I have so much to do."

"Doctor, I know how busy you are. But, may I please have a few
minutes?" Fancy gave him her most pleasant smile.

Dr. Hernandez put on his 'troubled 'face, lips tightening,
eyebrows merging. He spread-out his hands. "*Señorita,* I'm so
overwhelmed in my work and sadly don't have much time to talk."

She sat down. "This won't take long, Dr. Hernandez. It's
something I feel I need to tell you. And, I'd like to do it as soon as I
can."

He gave a dramatic sigh. "If you must. I can spare you few
minutes."

"Thank you."

"Well?"

"I noticed one of the drug reps leaving your office. Since you're
so so very busy, I hope she didn't take up too much of your valuable
time. I know how intrusive they can be. They're supposed to check in
with me, but some of them, mostly the ones you see, somehow slip
by. Would you like me to be stricter with them, so you won't become
more overwhelmed?"

"*Gracias, señorita,* but they aren't a problem." He turned to resume writing more scripts.

"Dr. Hernandez, I know you're having sex with the reps during the lunch-hour. It's hard not to notice a woman leaving your office straightening her blouse and checking her lipstick."

He raised upturned palms and smirked. *"Es verdad.* I will admit that women find me attractive. It is a gift."

"Well, I'm concerned these 'activities 'are occurring during clinic hours and could be an issue."

"Señorita Fancy, these activities, if they happen as you imagine, occur during the lunch hour. That is my time, is it not? What I want to do with it is my choice. Now, may I have your permission to go back to my work?"

"Dr. Hernandez, if those sales reps want to use sex to get you to use their drug, that's their business. If patients are stacking up in the waiting room to see you while you play, then it becomes mine."

"I see my patients. There is no problem. I think we are done."

"Please, Doctor, just a few more of your precious minutes?"

"What else?" He didn't look up and continued writing.

"While you were recently engaged with the rep, an acquaintance came by hoping to catch you during lunch. Since you'd closed your door, I told her you were in a meeting and couldn't be disturbed."

"Yes? So? Do you want me to thank you for doing your job?"

"As we got to talking, she shared with me how grateful she was to you for continuing to write her narcotics prescriptions after her own doctor cut her off and the pain clinic dismissed her. She also mentioned that you write pain med prescriptions for several other people she knows on campus and they think you're wonderful too."

Dr. Hernandez put on his 'confused 'face. "Eh? I don't know anything about that. Who was this woman? Certainly as a Doctor I try to help-out needy people anyway I can. Perhaps she has chronic pain and the medical people she's seen have poorly understood how she suffers. However, I cannot remember giving her, or anyone else, narcotics."

"Doctor, let me remind you that your prescribing narcotics and other controlled substances to University people, and others is neither medically appropriate nor consistent with the Clinic's mission. We are not a pain clinic."

"And your assumption is based on what? Some drivel an acquaintance told you? Some gossip who should be working and not wandering around? She said I gave her drugs? Señorita Fancy, these are lies. She is likely a jealous woman I have spurned. Now she seeks to spread vicious stories about me."

"Doctor, I think not. She got me wondering about some of the people who wander in here that I don't recognize. They don't check in so they're not patients. I've watched them walk down the hallway to your office without talking to anyone. A short time later, they're heading out the door. They're the ones coming in for their narcotic scripts. In and out in a few minutes. What else could it be? You can't have that many friends just stopping by to say, 'Hello'.

Doctor, as Clinic manager, I must tell you that what you're doing is inappropriate, no, it's wrong."

His 'sincere 'face appeared. "*Señorita* Fancy, I am a Doctor. But I am also a simple man who, in his heart, wants to help others. If there is pain, I wish to help. Perhaps, I say, perhaps, if someone is in need, I do help, but it is very, very rare."

"So, that large pile of prescriptions in front of you?"

"For my patients, of course."

"Uh-huh. May I ask, why does your deep concern for your fellow man require cash?"

"*Qué*? Cash? What do you mean?"

"My friend told me she pays you, cash only, for your 'concern ' and, of course, the prescription. How kind you are to charge her less than she'd have to pay for pills on the street. Doctor, it appears you're using the Clinic to make money off the books by prescribing controlled substances to non-patients." She looked at the pile before him. "And I know it's more than rare."

His sincere face gone, troubled face erased, Dr. Hernandez got up and came around his desk. He stared directly down at her. For a few seconds, Fancy flash-backed to angry, brutal men who'd towered over her, glaring down deciding whether to kick her, kill her or rape her. Then, she'd cringe, shake and stare down hard at the dry, dusty ground. Today, she didn't move, didn't cower, didn't even blink. Eyes wide, they bore into his, not the floor.

His voice was loud. "You are a simple clinic manager, a glorified secretary. You do my schedules, get my charts and make sure I have enough paper-clips. You are here to serve the Doctors and... I am a Doctor, a licensed physician in Florida. I wouldn't expect you to know, but that means I can prescribe medications in this State, whatever I chose. The DEA has also approved me to order controlled substances like stimulants for ADD patients. That also means I can prescribe narcotics. If I write a few pain prescriptions, as you, lacking any evidence, allege I do, I'm doing nothing illegal. I am the Doctor and I will decide what is appropriate. Not some clinic manager who pretends to know more than her superiors. This is none of your business.

Fancy, I believe you do not want to start trouble with a Doctor. You will not win."

As he raised his hand to point to the doorway, Fancy winced, thinking he was going to slap her. Ha, old habits die hard she told herself.

" You will leave my office now."

Fancy stood up and, for a minute, let her eyes bore into his. Then, she turned and strode out. It seemed to her that in this meeting, Dr. Smooth had left the building.

Dr. Hernandez glared after her for a few seconds. He looked at his shirt, checked that it was open enough to show his gold cross. Saw some dust on a sleeve and swept it away. He smoothed-back his hair and sat down, looking at the pile of prescriptions. He had Smith under control, but he'd need to watch this puta. Maybe, start some rumors about her? Should he be more discreet about the narcotic prescriptions? Not the diet pills. Sometime, the addicts would show up sweating and shaking. People can notice them. No, he won't cut back. But he would tell his people to either shut-up or be shut-off. Max nodded, *todo bien.*

NINETEEN

It's Not Denial. I'm Just Very Selective About The Reality I accept
Where Jack Finds Himself Very Entertaining
Ritual: A Repetitive, Precise Behavior People Use To Reassure
Themselves; Human Belief In The Magic Of Their Ways

Leaving Dr. Hernandez office, Fancy quickly stepped to the side. "Dr. Jack, you sure seem intent on something? I hope it wasn't because of your appointment with Dr. Smith."

He looked up. "Fancy? I almost ran you over, didn't I?"

Jack moved to the side, closer to talk. "The meeting? It went as I'd expected. Our great leader pontificated on how my not terminating Brad , as *he* advised, and Brad's subsequent suicide have threatened the integrity of the Clinic and endangered the grandiose plans he has for it. He also fumed about potential lawsuits and how they'd reflect on him. He didn't ask if I knew how the family was doing or how I was getting along. When he finished, it was clear that I'm number one on his fecal-roster for for screwing things up. Like anyone can really prevent a suicide. Fancy, I'm sorry. I shouldn't be laying this on you"

"I'm sure you did everything you could, Dr. Jack."

"Of course I did. Will you please pull Brad's chart for me? Smith wants me to review it again to make sure everything's documented. Oh, what's this release for the medical examiner I need to sign?"

"When a client over eighteen dies, you have to give authorization to release his records. It's pretty standard."

"Good. Smith was so critical, I thought he might be pulling something so he could dump the whole thing on me if he had to."

"Dr. Jack? You doing all right?"

"Me? Absolutely. With a suicide, things get stirred up a little, but I'm fine. Why?"

"You didn't seem quite yourself when you came in this morning."

Jack raised his eyebrows. "Oh? What does that mean, not 'quite myself'?"

"Well, maybe a little short, not your usual joking self." She smiled, "No big deal."

"Fancy, I'm excellent. I'm certainly not going to let Smith bother me. And if I need to talk, I've my wife, Bonny, and Dr. Bizby as great supports. Everything's copacetic Thank you."

She nodded, "Okay" and walked away.

Jack poured himself some coffee. There were less ants on the counter today, but the sugar still crunched of sugar under his shoes. He sat down at the wobbly staff-table next to Gus Cobb who was reading a psychiatric journal. Curious, Gus was no longer in his hobo-chic, dumpy clothes. Rather, he sported a crisp, white shirt, a navy, polka-dotted bow-tie and what looked like a new seersucker suit, without wrinkles or stains. Felicity Steele, a cup of tea aligned perfectly in front of her, sat opposite Jack.

"I trust I'm not disturbing you guys?" Jack said.

Cobb shook his head and kept reading. Felicity's eyes darted up and then back to her tea. "You are not."

Jack continued to look at her. Even in her plain white blouse buttoned tightly at her neck, her dark-hair pulled back in a pony-tail and no make-up, Steele wasn't bad looking. Yet, she dressed in such an austere way? He nodded. It's gotta be some religious thing. He sipped some coffee, smiled. "Dr. Steele, are you reading the leaves in your cup?"

She looked-up. "Excuse me, Dr. Rackham?"

"You were staring so intently, I was wondering if you were unraveling your future in the those tea-leaves at the bottom of your cup."

"No. I am in thought and using my tea-cup as a focal point."

"I assume you don't believe in fortune-telling, astrology, those sorts of things?"

"I do not."

"But you were interested in Hester's talking about astrology, spiritualism, those tarot cards?"

Felicity took a restrained breath. "That was purely my interest in her using novel techniques to engage a patient, nothing more."

Jack let a few more minutes pass. "Dr. Steele, do you believe in magic?"

She looked up again, one hand grabbing her cross. "I do not know what you mean?"

"You know, unexplainable events happening in the physical world? Supernatural occurrences? Magic. Simple tricks like finding a quarter behind a child's ear or grand illusions like making an elephant disappear. There are superstitions like not walking under a ladder or crossing your fingers 'for luck'. What about horoscopes and Hester's tarot cards? I know people believe they magically tell the future. Others have a saint's statue on their car's dashboard to ensure divine protection while driving?" Jack grinned. "I've even heard some people open their Bibles randomly, point to a line and *actually* believe God was transmitting a message to them for that day. I'd say those folks believe in unearthly, even what might be called supernatural ones."

Felicity's body stiffened. "I do not believe in magic. It is entertainment performed by people who use distractions, slights-of-hand and other ruses to mislead people who find being tricked amusing. I do not. And, your last example mentioning the Bible involves faith in God, Who is real, not a deception. You were in error using it."

Jack scratched his head. "Okay. Then please explain to me Jesus' miracles? I strongly suspect you believe they happened? His curing lepers? Making the blind see? Cripples walk? And, His never-to-be-forgotten rising from the dead? The Bible describes these events as supernatural. If He were around today, I think He'd be seen as some superhero with special powers. So, if you believe in miracles, Dr. Steele, then...no, never mind. I guess I just don't understand how you view magic and the supernatural. I'm sorry."

As Jack spoke, Felicity had been slowly pushing her chair back, teacup in one hand, the other slowly twisting her cross. "Dr. Rackham, magic is an illusion, a deception. The supernatural is entirely different. It involves a fervent belief in a Divine Being who works outside the boundaries of the physical world.

I wish to say that, in the past when we have conversed, I have noted your derision and disdain. I must tell you that presently I find it most offensive that you imply that Jesus was a magician. To me, that is blasphemy. Jesus *is* a Superhero, my Spiritual Superhero and Savior, my God and my Lord. And the Bible is His Word."

She stood to leave.

"Please, Dr. Steele. I'm like you. Well, not *like* you. But I don't believe in magic either. It *is* all tricks and gimmicks. I sincerely apologize if I appeared to blaspheme. That wasn't my intention. I know you're very involved in your religion and I guess it was my clumsy way of learning more about your beliefs. You're an Evangelical?"

"Yes, we believe in spreading the gospel's Word to enlighten our fellow man about his becoming corrupted by Adam's sin. That he must take the Christian direction. Be born again, repent his sins and abandon the evil that abides in him. This will insure him a place in Heaven when the Rapture comes. I, myself, was born again. It is my mission to convert others do the same. I trust that helps you to understand?"

"You were 'born again'?"

"Yes, in my teens."

"Weren't you already part of the fold? What did you have to repent and turn away from? Speeding a little over the limit? Telling a chubby girlfriend she didn't look fat? Letting your mind wander during Bible study?"

Dr. Steele pushed her chair back into the table careful to align it evenly. After scrubbing her cup and saucer and placing them in a cabinet, she turned to Jack.

"Doctor, I believe that all your mocking and judging have left you egregiously insensitive to what lies within a person's conscience, guilt they may bear from their wickedness. I was reborn and repented *my* sins to cleanse my soul. That reaffirmed my turning away from evil and those who were evil."

"I see," Jack smirked. "So, I guess inviting you to a magic show is out of the question?"

"You are correct. I believe those deceptive illusions stealthily breed false ideas of what life is into vulnerable people. That one can make happiness, success, finding trust occur, magically, with little effort. Life is not that way.

People need to know the truth. That life on earth is one of pain, struggle and the need for repentance. People need to know that their denial of their evil natures makes them stray from the Truth and into the arms of Satan."

Jack reflected a minute. "Holy-psychotherapy. Dr. Steele, I think you've found something we can definitely agree on. Two things our patients need to face in therapy, truth and denial. But, alas, that's where we part because I think our conceptions of what trust and denial run far apart.

I agree with you, life can bring pain. And because of their emotional pain, our patients come to us for help. However, I don't believe that pain and suffering are an inherent part of life because some guy ate an apple that pissed-off God Who subsequently took his anger out on humanity forevermore. Unless, of course, they repent.

Dr. Steele, I find many of my patients are distressed because they feel something is wrong with them. Maybe it was how they were treated as a child? Were they abused? Ignored? Whatever. The *truth* I want to convey to them is that there are reasons for their feeling unworthy, unloveable, imperfect, deficient or inadequate. Reasons grounded in the *temporal* world. Reasons that we can uncover in therapy. The *denial*? It's that they refuse to accept themselves as they are, a little flawed, having a few blemishes and not being the best dancer. Denying they're imperfect just like everyone else and don't have to live up to some perfect self they evolved. My job is to help them accept who they are and lose the fear of just being themselves, warts and all. And that they've a right to be happy. Life can be a bitch, that's just the way it is. But, Doctor, it's definitely not because someone's innately evil."

Jack looked at Felicity. She stood, hand tightly grasping her cross.

"Truth or denial? You know, Dr. Steele, I like that phrase so much, I might use it with patients. 'What'll it be folks? Acceptance of the truth that you don't know everything and may have a few shortcomings, like the rest of the goddamn world, and find some peace? Or, deny it and keep kidding yourself into exhaustion that all is well.' Yep, I like it."

She still hadn't looked at him. "Dr. Steele?" "Dr. Steele?"

"I am sorry. My mind was elsewhere." She left the room.

In the silence that followed, Gus Cobb looked up from his journal, "Your know, Jack, she's right about one thing."

"What's that?"

"Your derision. Your disdain. You can be one caustic bastard in general, but why do you have such a bug up your nose about her? And

Hester too. You just can't stop yourself from making some cutting remark about them, can you?"

"You saw what just happened? We're having a nice conversation and Dr. Praise-Jesus walks out without a word."

"If you'd talked to me like that, I would've walked out too."

"Like what? I was being sociable."

"Jack, that's bullshit. You were taunting her. But, you *were* slick. Starting out talking about tea-leaves, then segueing into magic, illusions, the supernatural. But you really wanted to get her going about religion and her beliefs so you could jeer and sneer. Why, Jack?"

"Gus, please? I wasn't harsh. Teasing maybe."

"You gonna answer my question? Or keep bullshiting me?"

"Okay. Be they vegans, exercise freaks or religious nuts like Felicity, I've a thing about self-righteous zealots. They're rigid, insensitive and dogmatic. Their way is the *only* way. And if you don't agree, there's something wrong with you. You heard her? We're all corrupt, for chrissakes, bad, shameful, wicked right from birth needing to seek forgiveness for something we never did. We need to be reborn. Why? To buy into a religious system that tells you you're still flawed?

Nobody wants to feel that they don't measure up. Don't we all run through our minds how we could've done this or should've said that better? I think religion feeds into those self-doubts.

Gus, it's all a scam. 'Hey, pal, life gotcha down? You know it's because you're bad. You're immoral, deceitful and tainted by sin. Wanna make it all go away? Just come on down to Jesus and make Him smile.' But that doesn't happen, does it? According to Steele, the suffering just continues. Do you ever see any exuberance, enjoyment of life in her? A speck of a smile? She's been reborn, but to me it's like she went back to hide in her mama's womb. Dammit, Gus,

we're supposed to eliminate that, 'I'm bad' thinking in our patients, not perpetuate it."

Gus had been watching Jack closely. "I'd agree. Dr. Steele does have a hard veneer."

"Veneer? How about a fortress wall? She...."

Gus put up his hand. "Jack, my turn. You 'teased' her about her being reborn in her faith."

"Yeah? So?"

"Did it ever occur to you that she may have done something that *she* felt particularly guilty about? And that she's still not free of it? That her self-control, her cool aloofness, even her plainness all have to do with that? That they're her ways of coping, protecting her from something?"

"Yeah. But what about her and patients? She has no empathy, no understanding, no warmth. They're all sinners. We can handle her. But can they?"

"I'll grant you that about the patients. But, your handling her? That seems to consist mostly of ridicule, criticism and scornful judgments. Jack, why does *she* bother you so much?"

"Gus, I told you. It's her...."

"Nah, I don't think so. Certainly, on the surface I get it. But there's something about her that really pulls at you."

"Gus, I don't have a clue where you're going with this. I thought I was just a witty guy expressing himself."

Gus sighed. "I don't know. You're probably right."

Jack sprang up. "Want more coffee? I'm going back to the office"

"No thanks."

"Good call. I expect it'll be pretty shitty anyway."

Gus stood and moved to face Jack. "Before you leave, I'd like to tell you something."

Jack tasted his coffee and made a sour face. "I knew it. It's crap. Sure, Gus, what's up?"

"I want to thank you."

"For making your day a little brighter?"

Gus smiled and leaned in closer. "I know I've been an exceptional pain in the ass over the past months. I've been abrupt, cantankerous and ill-tempered not only with staff, but, also, sadly with my patients."

"Yeah. When I asked you why you were such a pain, you said, 'It takes one to know one'? What was that about?"

Gus laughed. "Didn't get it, huh? Well, since you arrived, I've watched you bitch about so many things. I figured you had your own baggage and I didn't want any part of it. Then, that day you asked me why *I* was so nasty, it hit me. I didn't like your bitching and moaning because I'd been seeing myself in you. Of course, at the time, you didn't see it that way. Like you, I was angry at others for not measuring up to my expectations. But when I really took stock of myself, I saw I was upset with myself for falling short.

You see, eighteen months ago my wife divorced me. She told me I no longer 'brought her joy' and left. The short story is that she was right. I'd failed her in not letting her know she was special. Her leaving shot my ego to hell. But, instead of dealing with my loss...and my failure, I got bitter and irritable. It was a lot easier to blame everyone else for something than to face my inadequacy. It's incredible. Forty years I'm doing psychiatry and I didn't see it in me. What an idiot. Once I saw that, my attitude and life's changed."

Jack walked towards the door. "Yeah, I did notice your new clothes, without stains or wrinkles. Great. But Gus, I gotta go."

"Just so you know, Jack, your being a pain in the ass saved me from being an unhappy, bitter, old fart. So, since it takes one to know one, I'd like to do you the same favor. There *is* something eating at you. I know it because I've been there. Don't let it get you like it did me. Truth or denial, Jack?"

Jack made a show of checking his watch. "Gus, thanks for all that great sharing. But really, my joking, my wit, my teasing have been with me a long time. It's my way coping. And the attention I get's not bad either."

"Understood." Gus smiled. "Just wanted to share my wisdom. You doing okay since your patient suicided?"

"Jesus, does everyone know about that?"

"It is a small place where that's front-page news. How are you?"

Jack turned and splattered coffee onto his shirt. "Shit". Wiping it, he said, "I'm fine. I'm fine. Thanks for asking. You know, Gus, I think I'm gonna put a sign up on my office door. It'll say, 'I'm fine. Thank You For Your Concern. Don't Come Back'."

"Good to know you're doing so well," Gus said. "I've lost a few patients and each one stuck with me for a while...." But he was talking to an empty room. He shook his head, Remember, Gus, it took you a while to catch on.

TWENTY

Suffering Is The Soil From Which Purity Grows
Where Ahndrea Soothes Her Doctor
<u>Abuse:</u> Regular & Repeated Mental Or Physical Cruelty On
Another; How Weak People Reassure Themselves

Jim was staring at a bee battering itself over and over against his office window.

Ahndrea cleared her throat and pushed out her lower lip. "Dr. Bizby? Have I lost your attention?"

He turned. "Sorry. I guess I got a little distracted."

She smiled as she sat across from him. "Well, you looked so serious, I guess I'll forgive you *this* time."

Before the appointment, Jim had called Anne to coax her out to a monthly town event, 'Harbor Walk'. After he'd described shops and galleries staying open, music on the streets, free samples of food and wine, his wife gave a sneering laugh. "But, Jim, *dear*, it'd be nothing like Cleveland puts on" and hung up. He started thinking of Uncle Joe, 'Jim, I get to where I'm goin' by walking away from where I've been'. He knew where he wanted to get to, but that walking away part was still paralyzing him.

And here was Ahndrea. Her playing coy and avoiding any talk about her past was getting old. And then there was that darn bee.

"How've you been, Ahndrea?"

She waited. As she crossed her legs, Jim noticed her high heels and remembered the sound of their clicking on the tiles as they walked to his office. He waited. "Ahndrea?"

She raised her head and eyebrows in an appraising manner. "Oh, I have your attention now? Let's see. My depression's worse with my decreased concentration interfering at work to where my boss has noticed. And I'm not vomiting every morning. Other than that, I'm just *fantastic*. Thank you for asking."

"I can hear frustration in your voice. Is there anything specific you'd like to talk about?"

"Doctor, you're hearing sarcasm, not frustration. And what I'd like to talk about? How about my depression, the hurling and what you're going to do about it?"

"Is blood still in your vomitus?"

"Yes, but not every day."

"Is there more blood? As I told you, the bleeding could become a life-threatening event."

"The barf has tinges of blood. But, like I said, it's not every day."

"It doesn't scare you?"

"If it doesn't scare you enough to prescribe the medication, why should it scare me?" Jim waited.

Ahndrea folded her hands on her lap and stared at them, hesitated. She slowly lifted her head to meet his eyes and . She gave Jim a hesitant smile. "I guess my depression and bulimia didn't just happen out of the blue, did it?"

Jim shook his head.

"I know deep down I need to talk about my past. To hear out-loud, finally, all the wretched thoughts, feelings and images I've imprisoned in my head over the years."

"That would be nice." Jim smiled. "As long as you're 'Ahndrea' and not playing a role in some scene that shows only what you choose to reveal."

She feigned a hurt look. "Doctor, how could you say that? I've found my playing overly needy or being coy doesn't work with you. You know, you're one very hard person to manipulate." She smirked. "I'm being honest there. Does that get me any points?"

He nodded. "Let's say it's a start, okay?" He leaned forward. "Now, you were saying something about talking about your past?"

She ran her hands down the front of her skirt several times to smooth out any wrinkles. Her silence drowned-out the sound of the bee still ramming into the window. "I'm scared."

"Ahndrea, I know this can be hard. You've been playing roles so long, let's find out who you really are, okay?"

She sat back, crossed her arms and let out a deep breath. "Growing up, I was constantly abused. But it wasn't the usual suspect like my father, an uncle or some other male. It was a woman, my mother, a truly vile person who exuded cruelty. It wasn't until I was older that I fully realized what a sadistic person she was. Her abuse was physical and emotional, although, on occasion I'd call it sexual too."

"Would you tell me more, please?"

"I grew up in a very, *very* Catholic household, a bleak place devoted to piety, prayer and penance. Being pure through penance was what Mother lived for. She found a sick solace in her suffering. I think it made her feel more sanctimonious. My house held no love, no kindness, no compassion, no warmth. I can't remember ever being hugged." Her voice hardened. "My only physical contact with Mother was when she beat me. Every day, I could expect a hard slap or punch. When I was older, she used a leather strap."

"What reasons did she give for hurting you?"

Ahndrea turned abruptly to Jim."There were no *reasons*. It was just one thing, that I was bad. From a little child, that's all I heard. That I was a sinful, wicked, disobedient, spiteful girl. I was three, four-years-old? I didn't even know what those words meant. But I knew that I didn't feel good about myself. Today, I'd say that I felt somehow defective and not worth caring about. Do you understand?"

"Yes."

"The beatings were for your 'sinning'?"

"Yes, a beating and then a penance. Mother always dressed in black. I still carry an image of this huge, black mass with these hideous lips spitting-out what an impure, disgraceful little-girl I was as she hit me." Ahndrea took a breath. "I can still feel her wet saliva on my face. Yuck."

"And your being beaten was your penance?"

"Doctor, we're talking about a religious sadist who called her violent and brutal behaviors purifications. The beatings were only a warm-up for her.

Mother would make me kneel for hours, hands held perfectly together praying to this immense statue-of The Virgin whose hideous face scared the hell out of me. She prayed next to me and would slap me if I slouched or let my eyes wander. There were days she wouldn't feed me. Once, she burnt me with an iron to let me know what Hell is like for sinners."

"Ahndrea, you were how old?"

She shook her head. I don't know. It all ran together." Ahndrea stiffened, but I know when I got older, the worst penance started. Mother loved bleach, you see, because, 'it purified'. On occasion, her depraved mind 'knew' I was having 'impure thoughts'. That's when she'd drag me into the bathroom, undress me and force me into a tub filled with water and bleach. Then, she'd start washing me all over with a brush. It left my body raw."

Jim winced. "Ahndrea, what she did...."

She held up her hand. " It gets better. When I said Mother washed me all over, that included my genital area. When she reached that area, she'd scrub harder chanting , 'dirty little-girl, smutty little-girl' over and over as she stroked. If there was sexual abuse, that was it."

"Ahndrea, this woman tortured you."

"If you'd call brutalizing your daughter day and night, I'd agree."

They both sat silent for a few minutes. Ahndrea took a sip from the ice-tea she'd brought, blotting-up any water that had dropped from the glass. Jim continued staring into her face, transfixed by her story.

"Where was your father in all of this? He had to know what was going on?"

"Think about it, Doctor. If you were married to a woman like Mother, where would you be? Not home. Father owned a small manufacturing company. He was either traveling to schmooze his buyers or he was 'working late'. As he left for work every day, he'd pat me on my head and say the same, exact words, 'What a perfect, beautiful daughter I have'. Then, he'd leave. No kiss on the cheek, just that dumb pat on my head. I *know* he saw the welts, bruises and my bleach-bath reddened skin, but, you know, he chose *not* to see. He had a business to run, didn't he." Ahndrea shook her head. "He was a very weak man totally dominated by that odious woman. You know, I can't recall their ever touching each other? Makes me wonder how I ever came along. I know she resented me because, well, I was a cute kid. She probably begrudged me for that stupid pat on the head too."

"That, 'pat'? Was it really stupid?"

She brought a finger to her lips in thought. "You're right. In the beginning, it did mean something. Getting his attention made me feel special. I remember imagining things like, after he patted me on the head, he 'd say to Mother, 'You're not going to hurt my beautiful little girl anymore' and I'd be rescued. But when I eventually saw he wasn't going to do anything, it lost its meaning. No, actually it made me resent him. He was supposed to be my superhero. But, he was never,

never there for me."

"Perhaps that explains your low expectations of men now? Why you have to 'handle' their behavior? Can't trust"

Ahndrea tightened her lips.

"What about school? Did that give you some escape from your hell at home."

"I attended an all-girls, Catholic grammar-thru-high-school, run, of course, by fascist nuns. In class, they thought themselves strict making us be silent, sit up straight and keep our eyes to the front. A ruler across the knuckles if you misbehaved. For me, it was a piece of cake."

"Ahndrea, didn't anyone there notice signs of abuse on you body?"

"No. Mother always dressed me in clothes that hid what she'd done. And before you ask, I never told the nuns anything. They believed Mother was a devout, saintly woman. I knew if I told one, she'd hear about it and the strap would come out."

"I understand."

"Anyway, I was bright. I was respectful. I did well. I graduated, went off to college and freedom. Or so I thought until I got depressed. I probably was depressed all along, but it wasn't until after high-school that it got in my way."

"It's likely you couldn't allow yourself to feel anything while you were still at home. Your fear, your feeling powerless, your guilt about being this bad person and maybe some anger were too threatening to you. Imagine those feelings erupting with your avenging Mother around?"

"I *had* to hold it all in, didn't I? Or else. You know, Mother used that strap on me until I left for college." She stopped and shook her head. "Wow. You know, I *never* tried to stop her. Why didn't I, Doctor? Why didn't I grab that strap from her hand and start whipping her? Watch her cower. See her feel pain as I did. I was definitely big enough. Why didn't I?"

"Ahndrea, she'd instilled in you an immense fear of her. That was one thing that stopped you. Plus, I believe that a massive amount of suppressed rage was ballooning inside you as you were maturing and seeing things differently. Perhaps a part of you was afraid that if you started hitting her, you wouldn't have been able to stop. That you might even kill here if you let it out. Since that was unthinkable, you *had* to keep everything locked inside."

She stared out the window while Jim waited until she turned back to him.

"Is that why my bulimia started in late high-school?"

"I'd say so. Unlike other teenage-girls, you couldn't yell at your mother, stamp your foot say, 'I hate you' and then go off to watch TV. I think your beginning to binge and purge was the way you found to cope"

"Couldn't I've just smoked some weed? Something less weird?"

"Remember you told me your mother'd starved you as punishment? Think of bingeing as your way to rebel, to assert yourself, to show yourself *you* were in control of something, not her." Jim paused. But...."

"But?"

"But you also felt guilty doing it."

"She really had me, didn't she? And the purging?"

"It also served to help you feel in control of something. But it also symbolically reassured you that you had control when you let go, when you purged. Does that make sense?"

"So, since I *had* to hold it together, my purging allowed me to let things inside of me out in another way?"

"Yes, a less threatening way."

"But not without some guilt?"

"No. Her constant beating into you that you were a bad person left its scars, inside and out. She was your conscience." Jim paused. "And I suspect she still is."

"What are you saying, Doctor? I've been away from her for a long time. I'm a grown-up. I live my life. I make my own decisions, I do what I choose. And there's no guilt or punishment involved."

"Oh? Then what do call your depression? Your purging?"

"You bastard. I do not want to believe Mother's still influencing my life. I can't."

They sat in a long silence.

Her voice mocked him. "Okay, Doctor. Just how is Mother still controlling me?"

"Every day. How you interact with people."

"I interact with people very well, thank you."

"Yes you do. As long as your role-playing gets them to like you, find you engaging, attractive and gets you attention. If the world loves you, then you can't be bad, can you? But all you're really doing is living your life fighting off your mother's curse. That's how I see her as still controlling you."

Ahndrea made a low cackle. "And here I thought I was the one controlling things. And my depression now? The purging?"

"What do you think?"

She took a long pause. "I think…I think that when things might not be going my way or I'm not charming everyone and getting those smiling faces, I begin to doubt myself."

"And?"

"I can almost hear her voice screaming that I'm bad. That's why nobody likes me. And then I get depressed. But why the purging?"

"An old coping habit you fall back to when stressed. Remember, it gave you a sense of control, of letting go and a dash of mother's guilt. But it doesn't work anymore because your real feelings are coming nearer to the surface."

"So, Doctor, what do I do?"

"First, you need to exorcise the,'I'm bad' spirit that still haunts you."

"Oh, is that all?"

"No. You also really have to be what you said earlier, 'I'm a grown-up. I make my own decisions. I do what I choose. Without guilt.' And I'd add, without maneuvering for others 'smiles' to confirm you're worth something."

"Is that all?"

"Yes."

"You know that's all very scary for me?"

"Yes. Revealing your real self can seem risky at first. The upside is that you'll realize you're not as bad as you think."

"And the downside?"

"That you're not as perfect as you'd like everyone to believe."

Ahndrea smirked, twirled a wisp of her hair. "But, Dr. Bizby, can't I stay perfect for some people?"

"Andrea."

"Can I call you Dr. B?"

Jim thought. "That wouldn't be inappropriate."

"How about Dr. Jim?"

He shifted in his chair. "I think not."

"Okay, Dr. B. it is. Oh, there I go, already relapsing into being flirty and not a grown-up. Sorry."

Jim looked at his clock. "We do have to stop. We've gone way over."

She sat and looked at him.

"I'll write you a prescription for Adderall at the dose you'd tried in the past. If there's a problem, please let me know."

A wide smile filled her face. "Thank you. And thank you for not making me beg again. I know I called you a bastard, but you're a kind man, Dr. B. So, I can't call you Dr. Jim, ever?"

Jim continued writing her prescription. "No. Your parents? Still alive?"

"My father died seven years ago from a heart attack. Mother? She's still alive and, no, I have no contact with her. I hate her and that's that. She lives in a Carmelite convent. If you haven't heard about the Carmelites, I'll tell you that they're not party animals. A few years ago, she sent me a picture. She was in profile on a prie-dieu in her black habit, with her beads wrapped around her fingers, eyes looking up to heaven. In capitals on the picture's back, she'd written, 'Always stay pure in your soul and your body'. My first impulse was to tear it up. But then I found a match, lit the picture and watched it burn. I put Mother's ashes into the garbage disposal. It felt good."

"Well, Ahndrea, now all we have to do is kill the wicked-witch inside you."

TWENTY-ONE

A Great Cause Of The Night Is Lack Of The Sun
Where Felicity Stumbles Onto Feelings
<u>*Repression:*</u> *The Mind's Pushing Unwanted Thoughts And Feelings*
From Awareness Into The Unconscious; Keeping That Dark Stuff
Deep Inside

"Dr. Steele, thanks so much for all the help you've given our little congregation since your arrival in Florida. When I think how draining it is for me to shepherd my small flock, I'm amazed how you find time for us after caring for those poor, sad people at your clinic. You are a paragon of dedication to Him."

Felicity was placing hymnals in perfect rows in the pews of The Evangelical Covenant Church. "You are welcome, Pastor Franklin. I exist to do His will and spread His Word."

He gave her a warm smile. "I'm thinking, Dr. Steele, ah, may I call you by your Christian name, Felicity?"

"If you wish, yes."

Well, Felicity, I'm thinking that you must've been a great help to your father, Bishop Steele."

"I did whatever Father directed me to do."

After Pastor Franklin put another number on the hymn-sign for next Sunday, he stopped and turned to her. "Oh, my gosh, I forgot to tell you. The other day when I was going over my Sunday sermon the phone rang. It was Bishop Steele calling me out of the blue. After he introduced himself, and, I must say, he has one powerful voice. I bet his sermons are rousing. Well, he asked about my modest Assembly. Imagine, such a high-up clergyman showing an interest our church. Anyway, he asked about you. How you're fitting into the congregation, your activities here, what we talk about. I was so impressed by his concern about you and your well-being. But...." Pastor Franklin raised his hand to his chin in thought, "I thought something a little strange . More than once, he asked whether you'd shared anything, 'deeply personal' with me. I told him no, you hadn't. That, after exchanging daily pleasantries, we talk about what things you need to do and you get right to your duties without much further conversation. With that, he sort of grunted, said, 'Good, good' and rang off. He left no message for you. I assumed that's because you speak with him often. It was a little curious though. But then I put it down to me be nervous talking with a *Bishop*."

Felicity stood very still, hands tightening on the hymnals she'd been holding. "That is curious, Pastor. Thank you for telling me. Did Father speak about anything else?"

"Golly, now that you mention it, he did. After I told him how much you were helping me here, he said he was so exhilarated, yes, that was the word he used, *exhilarated* that your younger sister, Verity, right, was becoming mature enough to help him and fill your place. That they'd already been spending some extra time together so he can educate her in the things she'll need to do for him. He lauded you again in how you eased his burden. How he relied on you, trusted you. He was hoping to shape your sister to be, 'just like you'. He used those very words. From the way he spoke, I'm certain he misses you."

Felicity dropped the hymnals and let them scatter on the pew. She moved to face Pastor Franklin head-on. "I am sorry to ask again. But, was that all Father said?"

"That's all I can recall, Felicity. Praise for his two beautiful daughters."

He looked at her more closely. "Felicity, is everything okay? I've seen that troubled look on others. Do you need to sit down or something? Some water?"

"What? Thank you, no. I am well. I apologize for my behavior. Pastor, may I finish-up later?"

"Certainly, Felicity, although it looks like you...." But all the he heard was the door closing.

In the Church's parking lot, Felicity sat in her car and stared ahead, not seeing or hearing anything around her. Trying to keep her mind blank, she clenched the steering wheel ever harder, her hands becoming white.

It was that patient, Cindy, whose step-father continued to abuse her sexually. She had triggered something. Something she'd long ago entombed inside herself. Then, Dr. Rackham confronting her about her religion. About truth. About denial. That had turned a trickle of feelings into what she was fighting off now, emotions she could not allow herself to have. Except, now Father and Verity were complicating things.

Sweat running down her forehead and back from the sun's heat focused her. She started her car and blasted the AC. She must do something. She must make the call. She had to, no matter what. She knew it would set things in motion. Things she, as a Christian woman had lied about. She had lived in denial too long. She needed to be calm, in control.

Felicity speed-dialed Verity's number. The phone rang several times. The car's heat seemed to be sucking her breath out of her.

"Hi, Felicity. What a great surprise, a call from my big sister in Florida. Sorry I took so long to answer. I was finishing up dusting and polishing Father's pulpit. There are all these spots on it where his hands rest. I want it glistening when he gives his Sunday sermon. How *are* you? How's Florida?"

"I am fine, thank you. I am at the Church that I attend here. The Pastor told me that Father called here and mentioned you had begun to help him."

"Yes. Father said that now that I'm growing into, 'the bloom of young womanhood', I can be of great help and support to him. He doesn't see me as a little girl anymore. Isn't that great?"

"Yes." Felicity hesitated, searching for the right words. "Verity? Of late, various occurrences here have made me think more about you."

"Well, isn't that nice. I think of you everyday. How much fun you must be having, sitting around a pool, working on your tan. You know, I've never seen you in a bathing suit. Since you moved to Florida, we haven't talked as much as we used to and I miss that."

"I have been very occupied here. I shall call more."

" Great. It'd be nice to know my big-sister still remembers who I am." Hearing only silence, Verity said, "I'm sorry. I know you don't like kidding."

" Verity, you mentioned Father's observing your maturing. And it is a blessed thing as God guides you into womanhood. Is everything going well at home, at Church? Father has been…normal? There is nothing occurring that you have found different? Uncomfortable for you?"

"Heavens no., Felicity. I come home after school, help Mother, then we eat. Father mostly talks about an upcoming sermon or something to do with Church. After dinner, just like when you were here, Mother, Father and I sit and do a Bible reading. Then, I do my homework and go to bed. The usual stuff. Why do you ask?"

"And when you go to sleep, get into bed? Nothing…different?"

"Felicity, what are these silly questions about? Normally, I read in bed for a little until I get sleepy. Then, I turn out my light." Verity paused. "But, you know, lately, after I've shut off my light, Father has stopped by my door and asked me if I'm okay, whether I had any questions about the Bible text we discussed."

"Does he enter your room?"

"Ha, funny you ask. He's sorta coming into my room a little bit more each night. I tell him I'm fine and that I'm sleepy. Then he says, 'goodnight' and leaves. Why are you asking these freaky questions because this is not seeming like a plain old social call."

"That is all Father does?"

"Yes. Felicity, that's all. Why? Are you okay? You're scaring me."

Felicity rubbed her ear that hurt from her pressing her phone so hard against it. "Yes."

"*Really*? You sound different. Not like, well, *you*."

"I am fine. Is Father in the Church with you now?"

"He is. You know I drive now. When I get home from school, I use Mother's car to drive here. Father's already here when I arrive."

"Is there anyone else there helping?"

"Nope, just the two of us. He comes out from his office every once in a while, says what a wonderful job I'm doing and gives me his ' hug of encouragement'. That's what he calls it. The Church is so beautiful right now. It's so quiet and the sun is streaming in through the stained-glass window behind the altar."

Felicity needed air. Escaping her car, she began pacing back and forth on the hot pavement gripping her cell with one hand and her cross with the other.

"Verity, I am going to ask you to do something special for me."

"Sure, no problem."

"Since you have Mother's car, I wish you to leave Church and go home, right now. Please."

"Felicity? Why would I do that? There are still things for me to do. Father wants me to…."

"Verity, I shall explain why I am asking you to do this at some future time. But, please, right now, do as I ask."

"I think you're just jealous that Father asked *me* to help him while you're way down there in Florida."

"No, *no*, Verity, it is not that. Please believe me."

"Felicity, I'm teasing again. Why are you alway *so* serious? Okay, I'll do what you're asking even though I don't have a clue why. You know, you definitely sound weird."

"I shall explain, but not today."

"I'm positively going to hold you to that. I'll just tell Father I'm leaving…."

"Verity, no. Do not do that. When Father asks you later why you left, tell him that I called because I needed something immediately, like… like my very first Bible that I left by my bed. I wanted you to send to me."

"Felicity, that would be a lie. You know I can't do that. And I'm totally surprised *you* would suggest that."

Her pacing stopped. "You are right. Tell Father the truth. That I called and asked you to leave and go home. When he asks why, tell him I did not explain, but I just asked you to go."

"Okay, but only because you're my big-sister and I love you. I'll go now, after telling Father."

"I know you must tell him, Verity. But…."

"Felicity? But? But what? What's wrong?"

"But, promise me you will leave, whatever Father says to you. Please, promise me you will leave?"

"Okay, okay. I will. Boy, you sure sound serious, even for you."

"Thank you, Verity. I shall speak with you again very soon."

Felicity found herself facing the Church. She stood unmoving, her eyes transfixed on the cross looming high over her. She felt a wetness in her hand. Opening it, she saw the blood. She was bleeding from where her gold cross had dug deeply into her palm.

TWENTY-TWO
A Real Secret Is The Truth You Hide From Yourself, Not Others
Where Rain Cannot Quell Disquieting Forces
Anxiety: A Physical And Emotional State Caused By Real Or
Imagined Fear; You Can't Keep A Good Worry Down

Hester Snopes looked up from the *Maddy's Tea Room* menu as Felicity hurried into the room. "Well, isn't this a hoot, your being late instead of me. You didn't have to rush, though."Hester grinned. "Unless Satan was chasing you. Ops, sorry Felicity, but that was just too good to pass up. How you doin?"

Even though it didn't stock her favorite Manuka Honey for her tea, Hester had endured and met with Felicity here a few times. Hester did most of the talking, some gossip about the Clinic staff, but mostly about her 'positive attitude therapy' and how much her clients loved her. She couldn't say that she 'liked' meeting with Felicity, but the woman's weirdness still kept her entertained. Hester called Felicity, 'Robot Woman' and liked to see if she could get any rise out of the her other than that Jesus crap. She still wondered why Felicity met with her. She'd talked about becoming more assertive, more confident, but had yet to mention it in their conversations. Go figure.

"I am sorry that I am late and kept you waiting."

"I hope no burning problems for you? Hey, you okay? You don't look your usual self." It certainly was a little change from Felicity's usual flat puss.

Felicity caught her breath. "No. Some Church duties detained me."

"Good. I was beginning to worry." Knowing she didn't sound that sincere, Hester reached to pat a hand that Felicity immediately pulled away.

"Sorry. I forgot about that touching thing you have. Say, your hand is cold. Didn't know that could happen in Florida. And that's a pretty mean cut on your hand?"

"Yes, I scratched it on some metal. It is better now."

"Okay. Let's order. You can wrap your hands around the cup to warm them and maybe help soothe that cut."

Stirring her tea, Hester watched Felicity arrange her spoon, napkin and place mat into perfect symmetry. She wanted to reach over and move something out of order, but held back. Felicity seemed too intense.

Hester put her cup down. "Felicity, you do seem different. I was wondering, did Dr. Rackham upset you earlier? I was walking by the staff-kitchen and saw you in there with him and he was sounding like his usual jackass self."

"He was asking me about my beliefs and practices as an Evangelical Christian, but what started as a discussion progressed to his being critical."

"That's Dr. Rackham, isn't it? Even though he jokes around, that judgmental bastard always has some sarcastic remark. Is that what's bothering you? Look, if you'd rather not share?"

"It is not the first time someone has challenged my beliefs. I have learned to cope with it."

"Good. You know, I think Rackham's got his own problems and deals with them by dumping on others. I tell my clients who do that to go look in the mirror instead of at everybody else."

"There was something Dr. Rackham said that does keep going through my mind."

"So Dr. Bug-Up-His-Butt did bother you? You know, he was probably just looking to provoke. Forget it, Felicity."

"He said something about truth or denial, that people avoid things they fear in life, the truth, and use denial or one of the other minds defense mechanisms"

"Yeah. I see that everyday with clients. Me? If I'm bothered about something, I just use rationalization and bullshit myself out of it. Felicity, Rackham's one of those guys that should be looking into the mirror. Let it go."

"I had succeeded in doing that."

"Great."

"But then other events today made his words return. They have made me reflect on my life and my family, especially my sister."

"Help me out, here Felicity. Are you just talking about things in general? Or is there something up with your sister or family that's bothering you?"

Felicity put down her teacup. "I am disquieted, Hester, not

bothered."

There was a long silence. "Felicity, I sure don't know what the damn difference is between being bothered and disquieted, but I've gotta say, you're weirding me out right now."

"I apologize for making you uncomfortable. My mind is in conflict about whether I shall discuss something with you or not."

"Okay. Let me know when you decide. But, please don't take too much freakin time."

"Hester, I am a very private and serious person. I strive for strict, self-control in my life and to follow His Word. I allow myself little time for social interaction."

"Uh-huh. I kinda noticed that. That's why I was so surprised when you wanted to meet for tea. But then you said you wanted to talk about your becoming more independent, more confident and how I might help. Then it made sense."

"That is true, Hester. My hope has been, through our talking, that you would be a resource to help me develop more assertiveness to make choices."

"Yet, Felicity, we haven't talked about any of that, have we? And, given your need for control, I wasn't going to bring it up."

"Yes, I have been lax in that regard."

"You know, Felicity, you rushed in here. You're 'disquieted'. Now you're bringing up becoming more confident. Has something happened? Something in your life and now you've gotta be assertive? Make some choices? And because those actions are a tad out of your comfort zone, you're looking for some guidance now. Right? But you're not confident enough to decide whether you want to tell me anything? Man, there's gotta be something funny in this."

"Yes, going outside of my established ways makes me most uncomfortable."

Hester laughed. "Well, honey, the thought of sitting here until my ass starts throbbing from this hard chair and watching you make things on the table even tidier will make *me* most uncomfortable. So, you can tell me what's going on or not. If you do, I'll let you know what I think. Otherwise, I'm outta here."

Felicity nodded solemnly. "I understand. May we leave here and walk outside? It would be more private."

"Okey-dokey. I'll pay the check and meet you outside."

**

As they walked, the huge oaks lining the street shaded them. Hester noticed the moss on their branches began to stir as the wind picked up. "Felicity, we've been walking ten minutes and you haven't said a word. I thought we were supposed to be talking. That is, you were supposed to be talking about what's bothering you so much? Rackham's crap? Something about your sister? Is she in some sort of trouble?"

"Hester, I am thankful for your patience. I am trying to make logical sentences in my mind as not to confuse you."

"Yeah. Yeah. Could you just spit-out what's going on and drop the drama?" Hester snorted. "I'll do my best to keep up. Plus, it looks like rain and I don't fancy getting caught in that. Damn, I should've brought an umbrella."

Felicity looked straight ahead. "I need to talk about my sister. But first, I must tell you about myself and my upbringing."

"Don't I already know that part? Strict, religious home. Father hotshit minister in an Evangelical church, lotsa Bible and lotsa Jesus? You've a younger sister, Charity?"

"Her name is Verity."

"Verity, huh? Cute. Felicity and Verity. Does she live up to her name as much as you do? Anyway, you left home, went, I bet, to some Bible College. Then, medical school, psychiatry school and here you are."

"That is basically true. But I must impart to you some other things."

"Okay, start imparting."

After they walked a little further, Felicity stopped. Hester turned and saw her still staring ahead, her chest rapidly rising and falling.

"Hester, my father raped me when I was fourteen years old." She started walking again, but faster and more deliberate. Staring ahead.

"Hey. Wait up. He *what*? *Raped* you? Your *Father*? Bishop Fire-and-Brimstone? Felicity, how long did it go on?"

"Father began inappropriate behavior towards me much earlier, after I started helping him at Church When I began to mature

170

physically."

"How much earlier?"

"I was thirteen. In the beginning, he would give me what he termed, 'hugs of encouragement' for helping him. Any physical contact was rare in my family so, initially, I felt uneasy. But, and it shames me to say this, I came to welcome the hugs."

"That's not surprising seeing it was the only affection you ever got in your family. And the bastard took advantage of that. Just an innocent hug from Daddy."

"As I lay in bed, he began to stop at my door. He'd ask if I were okay. Did I have anything I wanted to discuss about the Bible reading. Then, he would come to my bedside, stand over me and we would talk. That led to his sitting on the side of my bed next to me."

"So freakin smooth. I'd bet he'd already seduced other girls."

"He began quoting Bible verses about how the father was to love and lead his daughter to adulthood. How a daughter needed her father for direction, preparing her for life. His proximity was, at times, comforting. It was a closeness I had not experienced with Father. I believed we were establishing a new bond."

"It was a bond all right. The shit was grooming you for sex."

"He began running his hand lightly against my arm. He said he sensed my tension from the day and wished to calm me. I began to pull my blanket up higher so it covered my arm. But he would reach up and pull it down, to touch me."

"You felt something wasn't right?"

"Yes. I still liked the closeness, but now it was stirring discomfort in me. I was confused. I felt guilty because Father was trying to be supportive, yet I was no longer comfortable with it. I felt guilty because I knew, deep down, it was not…right. And more guilt for thinking Father was…. "

"Doing bad things to you."

"Yes. But I could not let myself think that."

"Because they're true," Hester's voice now louder, more intense. "I know. I've been there."

"I began closing my door and shutting off my light pretending to be asleep."

"Let me guess, he came in anyway."

"Yes,. He said he knew I wanted to talk."

"That's when you felt powerless, isn't it? When the real fear began."

She nodded. "I was afraid to do anything that might anger him. Of what he might do to me. I would lie in my bed rigid, staring at the ceiling, praying that I would not hear the sound of the door opening and his footsteps. But he came. He would enter my room. I would feel his weight on my bed. There was an odor about him."

"Felicity, that was just plain ole lust oozing off that pervert."

"He began to talk about my becoming a woman. How it was a glorious part of God's plan. He spoke of seeking spiritual guidance through prayer and the Bible as to how he might perform his task as a loving father in educating me spiritually and physically."

"And?" Hester puffed as Felicity walked faster.

"He quoted the Bible, *Train Your Child in the Way She Should Go, Proverbs 22:6* as he touched me. He started with my hair, down my arm, across the top of my chest. I could feel a dampness and realized it was from his sweaty hands on my skin. He touched my breast on the outside of my pajama. Then his wet hand went inside."

"And you?"

"I was paralyzed with fear. I was trying very hard to keep my breathing steady. But I could not move. I was thinking how could Jesus let this happen? What had I done?"

"Did you shout out? Yell for help? Do something to get him to stop?"

"I desired to, but I was frozen. How could Father be doing this? He reached between my legs. I was so rigid, they were locked.

He said, 'Daughter, this is His will, for me to show you the way. My hand is His hand. How can I prepare you for the sensations of the flesh if you resist what He has ordained? I must ready you now that you are becoming a woman, to show what is right in a man and woman's flesh becoming one. It is His hand. Resist not the will of the Lord'."

She let out a long breath. "It was then I submitted."

"It didn't stop there, though, did it?"

"It did not. The next time he had me touch him. He stood over me, unzipped his pants and presented his penis as he spoke of man being made in God's image. He took my hand to touch him. I remember his wet breath on me as he told me to stroke it. I did it twice. When I began to sob, he left the room. The following night, he returned. Without a word, he mounted and penetrated me. That happened many times, in my room and then at Church."

"Felicity, I am truly sorry for what that self-righteous hypocrite did to you. How did you cope through it all? Was there anyone there for you?"

"I went to school. I did my chores. And I had my Bible."

"And to survive, you also shut off all feelings."

"I had my Bible and Him."

"And I'm sure that brought you much consolation. You know what he did was wrong, don't you? That you're blameless?"

"What I know is that evil occurred in my life."

Hester waited. "Felicity, your father was a disgusting hypocrite who took advantage of his position to sexually and emotionally abused you many, many times saying it was God's will. If there was evil, it was him." Hester knew there'd be no response.

Both silent, they walked a few more minutes side-by-side. Felicity turned. "Hester, I must tell you all to clear my soul."

Hester stepped back. "What? There's more?"

"You have told me you have endured similar things."

"Yeah, I've been sexually abused. But not by my dickhead father. It was a married guy who lived three trailers up from ours. I was thirteen and pretty developed for my age. He sweet-talked me. Said I was sexy, looked more like a woman than a girl. Man, was I dumb falling for that BS. When he started getting rough with me and I began to avoid him, he got mean. Said if I didn't keep screwing him, he'd cut-up my face so bad that no man would want me. That's when I got real scared. Then I got pregnant and the dipshit didn't want to have anything to do with me. Hester smiled, "After the abortion, I managed to get his wife's attention…and the cops. But that was a long time ago."

Felicity shook her head. "Hester, you have a belief in yourself that I lack."

She looked directly into Felicity's eyes. The wind had increased so Hester raised her voice to make sure Felicity heard every word.

"This evil man, your *father,* you *must* expose him."

"I am not as strong as you, Hester."

"Felicity, please spare me that, 'I am not strong as you, Hester ' garbage. What if he's diddling….No. Wait. Now I get it. Why you were upset earlier. This is all about Verity, isn't it? Something's happened, right? And you're afraid it's her turn?"

Felicity was staring up into the sky, the wind blowing her black hair across her face.

Hester yelled, "Felicity? Felicity? Answer me, dammit. I'm right, aren't I?"

"I *cannot* do it," Felicity said, her voice adamant, hard.

"You know, you are one, fucking piece of work. For chrissake, at least tell your sister. She probably won't believe you, but maybe you'll plant a seed in her mind about him."

"No."

"What do you mean, no? Why the hell can't you? This is your sweet, innocent sister. Like you were, remember? Do you want the same thing happening to her? O has he already started grooming her? Giving her those sweet hugs of encouragement? Yeah. Things are happening. That's why you're acting like you are."

Hester stood, looking at Felicity's back. The growing wind in the trees the only sound. Rain began to fall lightly. "You know, Sweetheart, you're really…*really* are pissing me off. You ask for my opinion. Okay, no one says you have to take it, but….Son-of-a-bitch, I forgot. There was one more thing you needed to tell me so you could, Christ, I love your phrase, *clear your soul*? C'mon. Let's hear it. Get it off your chest so you can go back to where you keep your secrets."

Felicity turned to Hester. "I know I protect him by not saying anything, but it is not him about whom I have concerns."

Hester took a deep breath. "And? Jesus, Felicity, you have concerns about?"

"Verity, my sister."

"Huh? How are you protecting Verity by hiding from her that her prick of a father might soon be molesting her? Sorry, I don't get it."

Felicity fixed her eyes on Hester's, her face stone-like.

"If I tell Verity about the past, I believe I must tell her everything."

"Yeah. I'd leave out the graphic details, but she needs to be told the truth."

"Truth or denial."

"What?"

"Truth or denial. If I tell her the truth about the past, I cannot deny the other."

"Which is?"

"That she is not my sister."

"Okay, BFD. She's adopted? She's a neighbor's kid your parents raised?"

Felicity looked at the ground and forcefully shook her head back and forth. "No. No. No. Neither of those."

"Okay. Someone left her on the Church's doorstep? I give up. What?"

In an anguished voice, Felicity said, "Verity is *not* my sister…"

"Dammit, Felicity, you've said that."

"Verity is my *daughter*. That is the truth I have been denying. The truth I do not wish her to know, but fear it is too late."

Hester's mouth was open-wide. "Holy shit."

***

"How old were you when it happened?"

"I became pregnant when I was fifteen. Verity is now sixteen. Father took no precautions. 'He, my God, is all the protection I need' is what he said. I had a very regular menstruation cycle. When it stopped, I became very afraid."

"You told your mother?"

"I could not. But when my school sent me home a few times for vomiting, she guessed. Knowing Father would not allow it, she secretly took me to a doctor who confirmed the pregnancy. Since abortion was absolutely forbidden, we discussed what options I had. At times, Mother would sob as she told me how she long suspected what was happening. I knew she had come to my bedroom door more than once, had listened…and walked away."

"Did you ever tell her about that? Her letting you down by her silence?"

"No."

"Of course not. Just keep it all in, huh?"

"When I began to show, Father complained that I was becoming fat and lazy. One night before a Bible reading, Mother turned and looked him in the eye, 'Zane, I have taken my Felicity to a doctor. He examined her and has confirmed that she is pregnant.'"

"What did the bastard say? No, wait. I know He denied you were pregnant. But if you were, you were a slut and made himself the victim."

"He did not move and became very silent. Then, he gripped the sides of the table and slowly rose up. His face very red, he yelled at Mother for betraying him by taking me to some quack who knew nothing. Mother looked down at her open Bible and slowly closed it. Her eyes went back up to his, but she said nothing. He roared at her, 'Answer me woman. You dared this treacherous act without my permission? Now you're spreading this…this willful lie as the serpent lied to Eve in the Garden.'

'Zane, the doctor was right. My Felicity is pregnant. I knew it in my heart even before he told us. I can see it now as her body changes. My Felicity is not fat nor is she lazy. *She is pregnant.*'

"His hands gripped the table even harder as he turned to me."

'If this is true, daughter, you have become a profligate whore in this righteous house of the Lord. A Jezebel bringing shame down upon me. You have copulated wantonly and carelessly with a male, or males for all I know. You have debased yourself and me. In the depths of Hell, Satan is laughing. He knows the reproach I shall suffer. You will leave my sight and this house. You shall be cast into the darkness.'

"Mother stood up. With her right hand, she picked up her Bible and held it out to Father. For the first time in my life, I heard Mother raise her voice to Father.

'Zane…*enough.* I have grown weary, *very* weary of your ranting. Here, take my Bible. Swear on it that you do not know who the father of Felicity's unborn child is. You and I know she is not wanton. You and I both know she is not a whore. Here, take it. Swear you do not know.'

'Do not defile that holy book. Put it down, woman, lest I remind you of the words from Ephesians, *Wives, submit yourselves unto your own husbands, as unto the Lord.* I command you, wife, to sit and place your Bible before you. Felicity, leave my sight at once. After your mother and I finish tonight's verse, she will aid you in packing.'

"Mother continued to stand and glare, her eyes not leaving his. She placed her Book against her heart."

'Zane, I have been a faithful and dutiful wife these many years. I have labored to provide a good home. I have been at your side to help you in your driving ambition to grow your Church and your prestige. I cannot make you admit the truth. That will be between you and God. But hear me. Felicity will stay in this house until she comes to term. I shall not allow her to endure any shame, embarrassment or ridicule from you. I shall enlist the aid of a discrete Christian mid-wife to deliver the child. After she delivers, I shall not bind Felicity here to raise the child that you, I have no doubt, spawned. We shall announce that I have given birth and welcome with love our new child. *I* shall care for the baby. Felicity must have a life away from here, away from you. She will know the child is well cared for. You can tell people and the congregation whatever you wish, God's truth or Satan's lie.'

"Father shoved his chair hard into the table, turned and left the room. He never spoke to me again. He rarely spoke to Mother."

"So, for sixteen years you've been lying to everyone and, I guess, yourself about being Verity's mother?"

"Yes. Mother and I thought that was best for Verity. After her birth, Mother took over."

"And became Verity's mother?"

"Yes."

"And you became her sister? "

"Yes. "

"And you three have just been going along living this lie?"

Felicity hesitated. "Yes."

"And sweet Verity knows nothing about any of this? That her son of a bitch, lying father incested you, is a sexual predator and will very likely sexually abuse her?"

"Yes."

"Well, isn't that ducky."

They walked in silence until Hester shook her head, stopped and turned to face her. "So, Felicity. Now that you've cleared your soul, is there anything left to do? Let's see, you have the pervert ogling your daughter, lusting after her and probably giving her some of his loving hugs, who you can't expose. You have Verity, your sister, no, daughter who you can't tell that she's soon to to have her life ruined. And then, you have...well, you, so weak and so helpless whose lying to yourself is becoming a problem. Hey, are you gettin any signals from heaven what to do? If not, my advice'd be to go home, cut your father's balls off, tell you mother what a failure she was for you and then tell Verity how he raped you and who her father and mother really are. If you're gonna to tell her the truth, you have to tell it all. So, what are you gonna do?"

"Yes,. Verity has begun to work at Father's Church. And he is beginning to do things that make me uneasy." She stared off.

"Yep, there you go staring off again. Felicity, the answer's not out there. What-the-fuck-are-you-going-to-do, *mother*? You know what I think? I think that now that you've admitted the truth to someone instead of denying it, you're gonna pat yourself on the back and do freakin *nothing*. You'll just keep living the lie. Probably tell yourself Jesus will do something. Right?"

"I shall pray. He will show me what path to take."

"Amen, sister. You know, Dr. Steele, for all your holy talking, I think you really don't live your religion, you hide in it. Yep, it's such a darn shame that Verity's gone and grown some titties and brought this 'issue 'back into that safe life of yours."

"I shall pray."

Hester raised her arms up in surrender. "Okay, you want to keep playing the 'I'm powerless' game? Knock yourself out. But I'm done. It's *you* who have serious choices to make, not *God*. Felicity, at least for your daughter's sake, please don't screw it up."

Rain started down harder mixing with the wind that pushed against them . Hanging moss fell from the oak trees and rolled pass them. Felicity looked at Hester. "I thank you for your opinions and concerns. As I attempted to convey to you, I find dealing with emotions troublesome. They interfere with good sense and self-control. Today, feelings evoked in me did just that and disquieted me. In you, I had hoped for a confident, experienced advisor. I believe, now, I have made a mistake in telling you anything."

"Don't knock yourself out about that, *dear*. You've other, much bigger mistakes you need to make right."

Without a word, Felicity made an about-face and rushed away. Hester called after her."Hey, Felicity, you're going in the wrong direction. You'll be lost." Then she giggled.

Felicity kept walking, her eyes straight ahead. She pushed harder, resisting the wind gusts, one cut hand at her side, the other twisting her cross. It'd been so long, she couldn't tell if the wetness was rain or tears on her face.

TWENTY-THREE

Life Has No Remote. Get Up And Change It Yourself
Where Bonny Asks Jack To Take A Trip
<u>Secondary Gain:</u> *Exploiting A Real Problem*
To Your Own Advantage;
I'd Love To Help, But, You Know....

Bonny walked into Jack's home office. "We need to talk,"

Hunched over his computer screen, Jack made the solitaire app disappear, then swiveled his chair to face her. "Bonny, you know those are four words a man never wants to hear. I'm kinda' in the middle of something and I don't think you've an appointment."

She stood looking down at him, hands on her hips.

"Well, if you could fit me in, *please*, we do need to talk."

"Bonny, I'm really not in the mood. You know how exhausted I've been. Let's talk later? Maybe I'll feel better then."

"Jack, you keep saying that. Look, it's Saturday. I've a list of things I need to get done and talking with you is one I'd like to get out of the way. I was hoping that you might've come with me to do errands like we used to. We could've talked then. But since you're still in your jammies, haven't showered and smell a little 'ripe', I guess that's not happening. "

"Bonny, I'm sorry for not coming with you, but this goddamn fatigue has made me a slow-starter this morning. So, unless you *really* need me for something, I think I'll just stay here, maybe take a nap. Oh, while you're out, pick up some tonic?" He started to turn back. "I hope that's okay?"

Bonny crossed her arms in front of her. "No, my poor, suffering baby, it's not okay. On Saturdays, we used to have a leisurely breakfast with time to read the paper, talk about any errands or how else we were going to spend the day. This is the third Saturday when all you've done was make your coffee, go out onto the lanai and sit alone. There was no, 'Hey, Bonny, let me get you some coffee so you can sit out here with me'."

"Bonny, I'm freakin tired. How many times do I have to tell you? It was too much of a chore to do anything this morning."

"Right. You're *tired*. That's been pretty obvious with all your

181

lying around. You know we haven't done anything together for about three weeks. And, outside of your moaning about your terminal fatigue, you don't talk to me. When you do, you're just grumpy. Jack, the Florida sun shines in, but you've taken all the color and light away and replaced it with darkness. I guess I never admitted to myself what a tragic person you could be."

"Look, right now, nothing turns me on. Big deal. And when I start a conversation, you just see it as negative so why should I try? Although right now you're doing pretty well with the bitching."

Bonny sat down opposite Jack, her knees about two feet from his. She leaned towards him with her forearms on her legs, hands clasped between them. Jack didn't see a friendly face.

"Bonny, what's this? An intervention?"

"Close. Jack. I want to tell you that I've been seeing someone."

Jack jumped-up from his slouch. "What? You're seeing a guy? What the fuck?"

"No. That came out wrong. I'm not seeing another guy. I'm seeing a therapist."

"Uh-huh? And why do you think you need to see a goddamn therapist?"

"Human Resources at the my law firm has a social-worker consultant. I've been meeting with her."

"How long have you been doing this? And why? You seem okay to me."

"I started after that patient pulled the gun on you."

"Goddamn it. As soon as I told you about that, you panicked, didn't you? Assumed something would go sour, that I'd go sour. So you went to a 'therapist'. To cry on her shoulder? Say to her, 'Oh, Miss Therapist, how am I going to handle Jack when the shit happens again'? Thanks a lot, Bonny. Doesn't show much confidence in me, does it?"

Bonny looked at him.

"Well,?" Jack said. "You wanted to talk. Talk."

"Please don't get too worked-up, Jack, and use up what energy you have in your weakened condition."

"Cute. Are you going to tell me what this so-called therapy's about?"

"Yes. But I'm thinking how can I be gentle with the obvious."

"What 'obvious'? What 'gentle'? For chrissake, I'm not some fragile piece of glass you have to tiptoe around."

Bonny shook her head. "Oh? You're too weak to tell me what's going on in your head. You stay in here for hours and I haven't a clue what you're doing. This office reeks with garbage thrown anywhere. And you smell most of the time."

"I told you…"

"I know. I know. Don't say it. Now, about the therapy. After Brad did his thing with the gun, you know I had concerns over how you'd handle it emotionally. Since I didn't have a close girl-friend here yet to confide in, and, really, I wanted a more objective person anyway, I started seeing this woman. I don't know. The Brad incident started gnawing at me and brought up past memories. How depressed you got after your patients' suicides up north. Your then telling me of your twin-brother's killing himself to explain your depression. My feelings of betrayal that you hadn't told me about that until after the second one died. How, even though I was angry, I tried to be supportive as you cancelled patients and sat home, *tired*. I got scared that all of that would come back. And I guess I was looking for some validation of my feelings."

"You couldn't talk with me first?"

"Don't you remember? I did. But all I got was, 'Don't worry. I'm handling it Everything's fine."

"So you didn't believe me and went to the therapist?"

"Jack, it wasn't like I hadn't heard, 'I've got this under control' from you before. Like I said, it was for me. My issues."

"So why are you telling me this now, not sooner? I would've been okay with it."

"Uh-huh. Look how you responded when I told you just now?

Therapist aside, my point is you were brittle after the gun thing and worse since Brad killed himself. I know you, Jack. If I mentioned how you were acting, you'd have gotten angry and defensive, like now. You're becoming more and more distant. Even before you took sick time from the Clinic, you'd come home, I'd get a quick 'Hey', but no kiss on the cheek anymore. You'd change your clothes, come in here and only come out to eat. And now we eat mostly in silence.

I'm seeing more vodka bottles in the trash. Jack, it's not a 'tired spell'. You're depressed again and you won't admit it to yourself, just like before. That's the 'obvious' I wanted to talk about"

Jack threw his arms up in the air. "What can I say? Like the good lawyer you are, you've gathered the evidence and you're sure of a conviction. But I'm pleading, 'not guilty'."

"At one point, Fancy called me from the Clinic."

"Oh? Calling you behind my back?"

"She was concerned how you weren't yourself. You weren't answering your cell. You were coming into the Clinic at different times and leaving with patients still sitting in the waiting room. She told me you were rude to people, even to your patients. She said she was trying to cover for you as best she could. She was the one who told you to start taking your sick days to avoid trouble, wasn't she? Now, you're taking vacation days?"

"Yeah. So what? I deserve some time off. Anyway, are you done? Or, are you going to stab me more now that you have your knife out?"

"Jack, are you gambling?"

"What? No, I'm *not* gambling."

"Sorry. I meant are you day-trading? I consider that gambling and you did that before."

"Jesus, what makes you ask that?"

"Joe Faulkner, the banker who oversees our accounts called."

"And? What did he say?"

"He wanted to confirm transfers from our checking to a brokerage account. He just wanted to be sure no hacker had gotten into our account."

"Why in the hell didn't he call me?"

"He said he tried, but you didn't return his calls. He said if it were a hacker, he wanted to get onto it immediately. So he called me. Are you gambling with our money again?"

"That nosy bastard. He probably gets-off peeping into clients' accounts, seeing how they spend their money."

"You are, aren't you?"

"So what if I am? It's my money. I thought I'd make us some more. Maybe we'd take a trip, buy you a new car. Bigger house?"

"It's *our* money. Remember what your psychiatrist up north said about that? When you get down, you day-trade. If the stock goes up, it proves you're a success, back in charge. If it goes down, it feeds your guilt, tells you, 'I'm a loser'."

"Yeah, yeah, I worked through my feelings about suicide a long time ago. That's old news."

"I don't think so, Jack. If you did, why are you repeating the same behaviors after Brad's suicide? Why? What's going on with you?"

Jack sat back and crossed his arms. "Okay, I'll admit that maybe I'm going through some grieving about losing a patient. No big deal. Beyond that, I think I deserve some time off. You know, get out of the daily grind, not shave, stay in my sweats? Do nothing. The day trading? I'm doing it to better our lives. What's wrong with that?"

"Jack, I'm not happy. I don't want to live like this. I want my old husband back. No, I take that back. I want a husband without the drama, the languishing, the brooding and the surliness. I want the guy who's funny, gentle, cares about his patients…and his wife."

Jack nodded his head. "Me too, but it's hard. I'd hoped the time off would've helped my energy return."

She groaned. "Oh, Jack. Poor, wretched, pitiful Jack. Do you ever listen to yourself? We talk and you go right back to your feeble excuses why you're doing things that are affecting our lives. Since you won't face what you're doing, how can I expect you to fix it? To change? And how long is this going to go on? This is what I've talked to the therapist about."

"Great. Someone else butting into my life."

Bonny straightened, her clasped hands tightening. She waited a few heart-beats. "Jack…I want you to leave. Find a motel room, somewhere, to figure out what's going on with you. Your lying around here is going nowhere and I need to do something to impress on you how serious this is. I believe I've been the patient and supportive wife long enough."

"I see. There's a time limit on how long another person has to get better? And I've gone beyond this period that you've dictated?"

"Jack, I've said what I've said."

"That therapist sure put a bug up your ass. You want me to leave? What the hell are you talking about? This is my house too. Why should *I* leave?"

"Because I am asking you to. Because I won't live like this. And, even if you come out of this 'episode' and become 'good-ole Jack' again, I don't want to continue with the threat that it'll happen again. Sooner or later, there's going to be another patient suiciding. That comes with the territory no matter how good a psychiatrist you are. When it happens, I'm not going to be waiting and worrying…again. Jack, I don't believe you ever worked through your issues. I've always felt there was something else still eating at you."

"So you're talking, what, a separation? Is this your idea or did the goddamn therapist put it into your head?"

"Jack, I know you're hearing my voice, but you're not listening to me. I have choices. My first is to be married to you. But, not like this. Strange as it may seem, my asking you to leave is my way of keeping our marriage together. To get you to look inside yourself and deal with whatever keeps eating at you. You want to keep kidding yourself? Your choice. But I'm not going to be around watching you mope and find something new to blame it on."

Their silence was broken only once by the computer beeping a stock trade confirmation.

***

Jack let out a long, guttural sound and stood. He shook his entire body trying to loosen his muscles. He walked over to the doorway, rapped his hand on the frame, turned and came back to sit down to face Bonny. He reached to take her hands in his, but she pulled back, shaking her head.

Jack gazed down into his lap. "Okay. I get it. You're right. There's stuff I haven't told you. Stuff I never told anyone."

"Dammit it, Jack. More secrets?"

"Bonny, I didn't let you on on certain things because, well, because."

"Yeah, Jack, It's that 'because' that worries me."

"Okay, you want me to share it all? Do you?"

Her hands clutched the arms of the chair. She stared at him and waited.

"It goes back to my brother Although we were twins, we were different. He was outgoing. I was shy. He was popular. I had my friends, but I wasn't part of the 'in' crowd like him. He had a way with people. They just liked him. I had to work at fitting in. He was smarter. I was smart too, but he'd always get the 'A' and I'd get 'A-'. There was this one girl, Rachel. I had the hots for her, but I was too shy to talk to her. My brother didn't have to do anything Rachel came up to him. I'd watch them talking and joking."

"Okay, Jack, I get the picture. Two brothers, one better at things than the other. One's jealous of the other. Happens in families all the time. Either you grow out of it or you stay bitter. Do you have a point other than how you suffered as a teen?"

"Bonny, It wasn't just sibling rivalry. As we went through high-school, I grew to hate him. I hated him, really hate him."

"He's better than you at things, you hate him for it. Got it."

"We were juniors when he started changing. He wasn't being his lively self. He became less interested in things, quit some sports, was less social. I didn't see it then, but that was when he started getting depressed. Some of his friends asked me if he were okay. I'd say something funny like, 'it's his hormones'. And I was glad because I could see he wasn't happy. I thought it was what he deserved, for what he did to me."

"Did he talk to you?"

"Yeah. Not knowing about my resentment, he thought he could confide in me. He said he was sad. He didn't know why, but everything just seemed gloomy. His grades were slipping and he felt guilty about letting our parents down. He was worried that if he didn't keep being sociable and funny, no one would like him."

"What did you say? I hope you were supportive."

"Nope. I played right into his self-doubt. I told him that I always thought he was putting on an act."

"Jack, that was mean. Your brother's hurting and you hurt him more? I'd never have thought that about you."

"One day, he told me that everything seemed hopeless, that, sometimes, he wished he were dead. I know now he was going through his own identity crisis and that was his confusion talking."

"Did you tell your parents?"

"I did. They asked him if anything was bothering him. He said that he was fine and gave them some bullshit story about being stressed-out because of mid-terms."

"You didn't tell them he was lying? How he'd seemed depressed to you?"

Jack looked away. "No."

"Were you really such a bastard? Your brother was…."

"Goddamit! Let me finish. We were at school. I remember it was a Tuesday. There had been a freezing-rain the night before. I was in the cafeteria watching the maintenance guy cut up some tree limbs that'd fallen. I saw him sitting by himself, his lunch half-eaten. I went over and sat opposite him. He said, 'I want to just leave it all. I can't do it anymore, Jack'. I didn't know what he was talking about. School? Activities? He said, 'There's some rope in the garage. I've been playing around with it. Making different knots, playing putting it around my neck. Thinking what it would be like. Mom and Dad won't be home until dinnertime. I'm going home right after school. I want to see if the knots work. I'm telling you so you can let Mom and Dad know I love them, but that I just couldn't take it anymore.' I thought that his old-self was coming back and he was kidding me. Bonny, he used to play me, set me up believing something he'd said. Then he'd laugh in front of others at how I fell for it and leave me feeling like a jerk. That day, I told him he wasn't going to trick me this time and make me feel like an idiot. He didn't say anything. He just got up and walked away. I ate my lunch and went back to class. The rest of the afternoon, I kept telling myself he was joking and that if I went home, he'd be there laughing and telling me what a dumbass I was."

"So, you didn't do home?"

"No. I told you. I stayed at school. Afterwards, when I thought about how I was so jealous of him, hated him, the twin that got all the good stuff, I believe a part of me wanted him dead. That I BS'd myself that he was tricking me so I wouldn't go home because I wanted him to die. Bonny, all I had to do was go home. If it was a joke, okay, he got me. But I didn't. Later that day, my parents came home and found him hanging in the garage. I could've stopped him, but I didn't. Bonny, I killed him."

Bonny turned her eyes away from Jack. She saw candy-wrappers and a brown apple core scattered on his desk. Should she get new curtains for this room? She looked outside. A sailboat was motoring by on the canal behind their house. The man at the helm seemed to be the father, the woman coiling lines in the bow the mother. Two kids about six and eight sat in the cockpit with their bright red life-vests on. Dad said something and the two kids grinned. She could see the wind moving the palm fronds. That family's headed for a good day of sailing.

Bonny let out a long, have breath, pushed against her chair and got up. She crossed her arms and stared down at her husband, his head bowed, rocking, eyes fixed on his hands in his lap.

"Jack, I'm trying to get my mind around what you just told me. How to convey to you all that I'm thinking and feeling about it. I'm shocked, bewildered, puzzled and... *doubtful*. That *you* are responsible for your twin's death? That *you* killed him? That you actually can believe that?

But, what I really need to express is how incredibly angry I am at you. It's one more betrayal. One more shoe dropping."

Jack looked up. "Sure, think about yourself first, not me. You just can't let that betray shit go, can you?"

"No dammit, I can't. And I think I shouldn't have to. It's not that you lie It's that you conveniently omit certain significant events from your past. What's going to be next? That you fathered a child in your teens who wants to visit? That you've another wife you've never divorced? What little trust I have in you just keeps eroding away."

"But I finally do tell you, don't I?"

"Jack, the issue is about *trust*. My being able to rely on you and not keep wondering if you're hiding more things from me. Why did you tell me this fantastic tale now? Your profound guilt? Or are you playing me?"

"What the hell does that mean?"

Bonny hesitated. "Jack, my ebbing trust in you is just part of my concerns. It horrifies me to think that I don't really know the man I'm married to. But what sickens me is that I don't believe *he* knows himself. Or that he wants to."

"That's bullshit."

"Jack, I can understand how patients' suiciding can be upsetting for you. I can see how memories of your brother's suicide could distress you."

"Yeah? So?

"So what I don't get is how these admittedly disturbing events get you into such a huge tail-spin. It's like you over-inflate your feelings about what's occurred. Look what happened up north. Your depression got worse after each suicide. Then, out of the blue, you announced you're not cut-out for private practice and we're moving to Florida. I don't think those things were unrelated."

"Where're you going with this, Bonny?"

"Where I'm going? What I said earlier. That I don't believe you entirely worked through your problems in the times you were in therapy. There's something deeper going-on in you that's affecting you. Look, Brad kills himself and you start getting nasty and irresponsible at the Clinic. It gets so bad that Fancy suggests you take some time off. And now, three weeks later, you've been just lying around. I think that's a little long for grieving. And today, this, 'I killed my brother'? What's that all about? Two more weeks to languish?

You know, Jack, there've been times I've had this dumb notion that brooding somehow comforts you. That it gives you like an escape, a place to hide."

Jack stopped swiveling in his chair and glared at his wife. "Bonny, I was extremely ashamed to tell you what I did. I held it back so long because I was afraid of how you'd respond. Would you hate me? Would you understand and give me support? No. Instead, I get your never-ending suspicion and doubt accusing me of *using* it in some way. Then you hit me with how I over-inflate my feelings? I guess there's only a certain amount I'm allowed? That they're not valid? That I use how I feel and what I've gone through to play you? And as an escape? Jesus-Fucking-Christ, Bonny."

"If you want to play victim, you're right about one thing. I have no sympathy. I've run out of it. Jack, I know I keep saying it, but, please, please stop BS'ing yourself. Figure-out what's going on with you and be the husband I know you can be."

" Bonny, you know, maybe it's like you said, you really don't know me."

She smiled. "Jack, you need to find out where that misery's coming from. If you won't do it for yourself, do it for me, for us. Honey, please?"

"So you're giving me an ultimatum? Behave a certain way? Feel a certain way? Or else?"

Bonny rolled her eyes and sighed. "What the heck, one more time. I am telling you that I cannot go on living like this. And that I am not the one who needs to change to make things better. That's what I'm saying. You're free to interpret it anyway you want."

"And if I choose not to? What? Divorce? "

"Actually, Im discussing that in therapy. I don't know right now.""Planning ahead, huh? Son of a bitch. Instead of supporting me...."

"Yeah, like *you* supported your brother. Stop the freakin' drama, Jack. I want us to be together. But *I* can't make that happen."

"And it's my fault if we're not."

"I wouldn't put it that way, but yes."

Now standing, they faced each other.

Jack said icily. "You're still throwing me out?"

Bonny's eyes bore into his, her voice barren of any warmth. "Yes, Jack, I want you to leave, to be out of here, to be absent from this house as soon as you can." Turning away, she left him standing there alone.

TWENTY-FOUR
Let Go Of My Ego
Where Max Looks To TheFuture
<u>Compartmentalization</u>: Separating Conflicting Thoughts Or
Emotions To Avoid Anxiety; Okay, I'll Put I Love My wife In That
File-Drawer, My Affair In That One.

Max turned away from the newly hired young woman at the front desk. "Remember my invitation is always open to you."

"Thank you, Doctor."

"*Mierda*. What a waste of time introducing myself and giving her my dazzle smile. The bitch is married, with two kids. How could I've missed her wedding ring? Eh. There's always that sexy what's-her-name drug-rep for tonight. She's ready. I'll do my usual seduction. Take her to my cousin, Pepe's, nightclub. I'll charm her. We'll eat. Pepe'll make her drinks stronger. We'll dance as foreplay. Then maybe a less noisy place to go. These women are so easy. Scripts for screwing.

Max leaned down from his office chair and opened his, 'spreading the love' drawer. Everything was in order, nothing missing. He pulled three letters from a folder labelled *muy caliente*. After reading them, he sat back and pictured being with each. How they played and enjoyed each other's bodies. Ah, *todo bien*. He rose to make himself a *café Cubano* in the kitchen.

He heard his name and quick steps in the hallway. "*Señorita* Martha, you shouldn't move so quickly. You're breathing so hard."

"I'm glad,' she gasped, "I caught you, Doctor. You didn't ," she panted, "answer the intercom."

"No, I'm going for coffee. Care to join me?"

Martha took a deep breath. "No. I mean, no thank you, no coffee right now. And I believe no coffee for you. Dr. Kingston-Smith wants to see you in his office immediately."

But, surely I have time…?"

"That's why I was running, Dr Hernandez, you need to be in his office *now*."

Martha entered the office first and went around to sit at her desk. She pressed a button on her phone. "Dr. Hernandez is here, Dr.

Kingston-Smith. Yes, I'll tell him."

She turned to Max and nodded toward Smith's door. "Go right in, Doctor."

As he expected, Dr. Smith, wearing a bright pink sport coat, sat behind his desk. But these two men standing next to him?

"Good afternoon,". They deserved only his semi-dazzling smile.

Smith pointed to a single chair in front of his desk. "Dr. Hernandez, please sit,"

Max sat and leaned forward, staring at Smith, intent. He wore his sincere face. "Dr. Smith, as soon as I learned you wished to see me, I came immediately."

Smith sat twisting his mustache. After a few minutes, he steepled his hands in front of him tapping his fingers together. The two men hadn't moved. Max put on his serious face.

Smith glanced at the men standing beside him. "I have summoned you at the request of these two gentlemen. Would you introduce yourselves, please?"

Both had short haircuts and wore white shirts, dark suits and black ties. They stood erect on either side of Smith with their hands behind their backs. One was much taller than the other. They stared at Max, their faces revealing nothing.

"Doctor, I am Special Agent Tom Lankersham. To my left is Agent George Taylor. We're from the DEA, the Drug Enforcement Agency. Perhaps you've heard of us?"

"Of course. I'm a licensed medical doctor here in Florida. I've also my federal DEA number to prescribe controlled substances."

"Would you like to see our I.D.'s?"

"Not necessary," Max's smile increased. "You both appear quite trustworthy."

Smith said. "Dr. Hernandez, these agents thought it best for me, as Clinic Head, to be included in their meeting with you. In fact, I've a few things to talk to you about when these men have finished with you."

Smith turned to the agent on his right. "Agent Lankshim, would you care to begin?"

"Dr. Kingston-Smith, that's Special Agent Lank-er-sham."

Smith looked down at the cards both DEA men had given him.

"Mmm. Quite right. Désolé. Please, Special Agent Lankersham?"

The agent drew his words out. "Dr. Hernandez, we're from our Tampa office to discuss with you some dire concerns we have."

"Yes? And what might these *dire* concerns be, Special Agent Lankersham?"

"About some of your prescribing practices."

Max leaned back and put on his puzzled face. "Oh?"

"C'mon, Doctor, don't be coy. You know exactly what this is about," shorter Agent Taylor cut in.

Lankersham continued. "The Justice Department empowers the DEA with enforcement of the Controlled Substances Act. This Act mainly concerns itself with abused substances. As you know, Doctor, drugs listed under Schedule I, like LSD, peyote, MDMA are experimental. Although MDMA , 'X' or ecstasy is out there. my partner, George, Agent Taylor, and I mostly investigate the Schedule II drugs, primarily narcotics and amphetamines. Consequent to opiate-abuse along with Schedule IV anxiolytics like Xanax becoming so rampant in the U.S., combatting it has become the DEA's number one priority."

Sitting more erect in his chair, Max nodded and put on his helpful face. "I understand, sir. You bear a heavy responsibility. But, how does this relate to me? Unless...of course, it must be that. Knowing you are very experienced agents, I believe that it won't surprise you that sometimes doctors help out friends or co-workers with meds. One of the secretaries comes to me and says, 'Doctor, I'm having another UTI. I know the symptoms. I get them a lot. My regular doctor usually gives me this med. Would you mind?' Kind-hearted that I am, I give her a small prescription or maybe I give a Z-Pack for a bad cold. But, I say, 'This one time only'. I tell them that if things worsen, they must see their regular doctor. That's why you're here, isn't it?"

"Certainly, Doctor, we know that happens although, strictly speaking, you should have documentation for all of this. Do you?" Agent Lankersham said.

"No. No. Like I said, it's among friends, a favor." Max grinned and shrugged, "You know what I mean, eh?"

"No matter. That's something for the Florida Board of Medicine. What's brought us here today, Doctor, isn't about your writing antibiotics for a friend or a secretary."

Max put on his troubled face. "Then I am very confused."

"Still gonna play dumb, huh, Doctor?" Agent Taylor said.

"George, let's help the Doctor with his confusion." Lankersham said. "Doctor, it has come to our attention that you have been prescribing what the DEA considers an *inordinate* amount of schedule II and IV medications."

"Please? What does that mean?"

"It means, Doctor, that in the last three-months you've written at least 700-plus prescriptions for narcotics, amphetamines and tranquilizers."

"Is this true, Doctor Hernandez? In *my* Clinic?" Smith shrilled, mustache flaring.

" Forgive me, but I do have ADD patients who require various Schedule II amphetamines. And, as a psychiatrist, I treat anxiety disorders which may require tranquilizers."

"Please, Doctor, forgive *me* if I was unclear. We're primarily here about the narcotics and the amphetamines you write prescriptions for. The anxiolytics are secondary. Although, I might add that your prescribing 'xanny bars' , that high dose Xanax, far exceeds all other Doctors here in the Clinic as well as all of the psychiatrists in the community combined, Fancy that. But, it's those darn opiates we're wondering about today."

"Yeah. We find it just a little peculiar that a psychiatrist would be treating so much pain, emotional and *physical*. Makes a person wonder. Does it make you wonder, Doc?" Agent Taylor said.

"I'm sure you can see that you're an outlier here, Dr. Hernandez. Would you care to elaborate on what's occurring?" Lankersham said, putting on his confused face.

Max lowered his head and raised his right hand to pinch the bridge of his nose as he stared at the floor.

After a minute, Agent Lankersham said, "Doctor?"

"Yes, yes. Obviously, you have a paper trail of all the Schedule II meds that I've written for. You must understand. Many of my patients have depression. Many of them are depressed secondary to their chronic pain. With Florida's crackdown on opiate prescribing, I've found many doctors now under-treat that pain. Since I couldn't improve their depression while they continued in physical discomfort, I made the bold decision to treat the w*hole* patient. Sirs, when I became a doctor, I took an oath. I *had* to help them. So, yes, I've prescribed various pain medications to relieve their suffering. I am a licensed physician in Florida. I have a DEA number to prescribe. I broke no law, did I?"

"Dr. Hernandez, I very much appreciate your candor. I certainly admire your zeal, dedication and concern for your patients. But, please, if I may ask?" Agent Lankersham said.

Max moved one of his arms and rested it on the back of his chair. He looked up at the man and nodded, "*Anything* I can do to help."

"We've discovered that the majority of the prescriptions you've written are *not* for Clinic patients. Some were for personnel here at the University. And some, actually most, were for people who have no apparent 'professional' connection to you." Agent Lankersham scratched his head. "That perplexes me. Am I correct in saying that you've written, are still writing narcotic prescriptions as well as scripts for speed and Xanax for people who are *not* your patients? Not family members? Not friends? Not even secretaries?"

"I thought HIPPA protected a person's medical information from you?" Max said.

"Well, Doctor, it's like this. There are databases to which we have access. In them, we have the names, the drug prescribed, how many pills given and the doctor prescribing them. Florida has similar information as well. FYI, we did a little homework on you before we dropped by and gathered a list of people for whom you solely wrote prescriptions. We referenced that with a record of University personnel and, to our surprise, some names popped-out as getting narcotics from you. Other names outside of the University we recognized as known 'doctor-shoppers', known drug abusers and even a few dealers. Imagine that? This clinic has many Medicaid/Medicare patients. Accessing those files, we did find *one* person for whom you prescribed opiates who actually was your patient. Not the many you described."

"Weren't we surprised to find even one." Agent Taylor said.

"We called several people on the list with your name as prescriber," Agent Lankersham said.

"You called them? You intruded on their sacred privacy?" Max said.

"Bingo, Doctor. We were looking for a drug-pushing M.D. and hoping some of your customers might help us," Agent Taylor said.

"When we informed them we were DEA, a few hung up. Many, after we explained that we were investigating you and not them, cooperated. They verified that they received Schedule II drugs from you and that they were not regular patients here at the Clinic. Apparently, you told them to stop-by if they needed something and try to catch you between legitimate patients. 'Like the drive-thru at a fast-food place' is how one woman described her 'appointment' with you." One guy volunteered you paid him to fill an amphetamine script and return the pills to you. That you bragged how they give you 'incredible sexual energy'. I must admit, Doctor, that after you had a similar incident with us a few years back that you'd have learned your lesson."

"What?" Smith said wide-eyed.

"Dr. Smith, Dr. Hernandez has a past history of overprescribing. Back then it was amphetamines. Florida dinged him with a year's probation. The DEA disallowed his prescribing Schedule II meds for two years." Agent Lankersham said.

Smith only shook his head.

"Looks like he suckered you, Dr. Smith," said Agent Taylor who'd just finished counting how many plaques, pictures and awards Smith had on his wall and was adjusting his tie in Smith's gilt mirror.

Max sat up and raised his chin. "If I may speak?"

"Of course, Doctor," Agent Lankersham nodded.

"If I am guilty, I am guilty of wanting to ease the suffering of my people."

"But, Doctor, these were not *your* people. They were not *your* patients on whom you are obliged to keep documented records. These were people off the street," Agent Lankersham said.

Taylor shook his head. "Doc, please cut the crap. You're pushing drugs. By the way, how much did you charge for being so devoted and giving to your, 'walk-ins'?"

"Some would offer me money out of gratitude for my caring."

"And, you took it?"

"I did not want to insult them."

"So to be clear, you took the money?" Taylor said.

Max shrugged.

"Hmm.The people we talked with never mentioned their 'giving', only your taking. That you charged cash-up-front per prescription. That money? I assume you didn't leave a paper trail? Did you invest it somehow? Spend it?" Agent Taylor said.

Max's face saddened. "I regret disappointing you, Agent Taylor. I gave it to the local Latino church where I live in Miami."

"You're so unselfish, Doc. Wouldn't have any record of that?"

"I did it anonymously. I am a modest man who seeks no attention."

"Modest, my ass. How much did that gold chain you're wearing set you back?" Agent Taylor said.

The two DEA men looked at each other and nodded. They came around to face Dr. Smith intent of scribbling notes with his Mont Blanc. Each stood aside Max. Smith finally noticed them and looked up, his mustache drooping.

"Dr. Kingston-Smith, we want to thank you for your time. It was a pleasure seeing an administrator showing such interest."

"I demonstrate leadership by example. I appreciate your including me in this confab. You both should know how impressed I am with the skills you've displayed today. I'd be happy to share my opinion with your superiors."

"Coming from you, Dr. Smith, that's really high praise," Taylor said.

" Perhaps we might brainstorm together?"

"Perhaps," said Lankersham. "Our department will convene and decide how we'll proceed with this. We'll also alert the Florida Board of Medicine of our findings plus the University. We've several more people to interview who, we believe, will further corroborate our suspicions."

"Being an integral part of this, I shall receive an update as well, *n'est-ce pas?*"

"*Bien sûr.* We'll copy you on our decision. *Je vous remercie.*" Lankersham bowed before turning to leave.

As he followed his partner out, Taylor bent towards Max and

said, "You'll be hearing from us. That's money you really can take to the bank, not the Church, *Doctor*."

Annoyed, Max ignored the Agent. Why must they pick on me? I'm doing such little harm compared to my friends in Miami. Maybe this nuisance will get lost somewhere in government bureaucracy? Yet, these agents seem a little too tenacious to let this go. I'll need to call my father. He still has his contacts. He'll understand. It's just business.

Max started to leave.

"Stay seated, Doctor, we're not done here How long has this been going on?"

"Dr. Smith, aren't I innocent until proven guilty?" Offended face.

"In court, but not with me. How long, Doctor?"

Max liked at his shoes. I think it's time for a new pair. Tonight, I'll wear my bikini briefs or, maybe go commando? Some women love that. He looked up at Smith, pained face.

"I swear on my mother, I only did it to help people."

"*How long?*"

"Maybe six months? Nine months?"

"How many people were you supplying?"

Max raised his hands and shrugged. "I had some steadies. But, people come and go, you know druggies."

"Were you writing any opiates for people here at the Clinic?"

"The occasional antibiotic or diuretic, but no pain pills or speed. I do have my boundaries."

Smith grunted. "Yes, like you have your oath. *Primum Non Nocere*, First Do No Harm'."

"Yes. That's the one. I'll remember it. Are we done? I've my responsibility to patients."

Smith opened a folder. "No."

Max stifled a yawn.

"About your enhanced social life outside of work?"

"You know I lead an active life after hours. That it's all consensual and I've those letters as proof. Is there some silly issue?"

"There's more than one, Doctor. And they've landed in my lap. Two women have filed complaints with the University against you for sexual harassment. Tell me, Doctor, how could your innocent spreading love ever be seen as harassment?"

"Passion can make a woman crazy. She's not getting enough from me? Could that be harassment? Maybe in her mind."

"One woman works for the Vice-Chancellor. She states that she first thought you a stalker from the way you were ogling her. That after you approached her and she learned you were a Doctor here, she relaxed and found you amusing and personable. She asserts that you met for dinner and drinks and that, as the evening progressed, you suggested finding a motel where you might be intimate. When she refused and requested to leave, you began yelling loudly in Spanish and appeared threatening to a point where she feared for her safety. You called her a *puta*, Doctor?"

"The woman is a liar. I know I become more passionate with lively music and dancing. But I respect women. Anyway, it didn't happen on University property."

"True. But when the Vice-Chancellor gets word of this, and he will, he'll ask *me* if I've a sexual predator working for me? And when the DEA informs the University about your using my Clinic to supply dope to people on campus and the street, I'm certain he'll become quite vexed."

"I'll explain...."

"Stop. The other complaint is from a drug rep. She contends you insisted that you meet with her after hours at a quieter, less distracting place. That this would definitely induce you to prescribe more of her product. Her statement reads that you met at a small, downtown club and had drinks. That as she tried to show you data on her product, you'd interrupt commenting on her looks, her perfume, how she dressed. That you made her uncomfortable touching her cheek as she talked. She notes a fellow she assumed was a waiter kept stopping and asking if you wanted to order any 'special' drink for her."

"It's my cousin's place. I like to go there. So?"

"This woman, a professional who works for a large corporation that funds research grants to this University, swears that she'd been 'roofied'. I've come to learn that a 'roofie' is considered that date-rape drug put in drinks. And the next thing she knew was waking up in some motel room naked. She maintains there was evidence that sex had taken place. She's adamant that someone raped her since, being unconscious, she was unable to give consent. She did have a rape kit done. Comments, Doctor?"

"This is a very sexy woman who wanted more business. She knew where the evening might take us. She's now claiming that she was this naïve and innocent girl who I took advantage of? I clearly am the victim here of an unscrupulous woman pushing her drug. I guess I didn't prescribe enough of it satisfy her."

"And someone giving her what sounds like a 'roofie'? She made that up?"

Max looked at the ceiling. "Don't you see? She's a woman who cannot handle her liquor and is blaming me because she was stupid."

"Did you have sex with her?"

Max sneered. "Of course. Why else have dinner and drinks? We ate, we danced, we drank, we had sex."

"Is that when 'someone' gave her the drug?"

"Like I said, she drank too much, got out of control and now blames me. Women are like that."

"Doctor, she may press charges. You might consider a lawyer."

"A lawyer? Why? I prescribe a lot of her medication. Her company will make her rescind her complaint so they won't lose the business. You'll see."

"Nonetheless, complaints of sexual harassment and rape have been filed. You've tarnished the splendid reputation for my Clinic."

"So, you won't support me?"

Smith leaned forward, "*No.* You've done a decent job here. I've tolerated your acting the innocent because of that. But these complaints, and who knows if more will be forthcoming, have caused embarrassment to me and the University."

"If I play humble and innocent. You play the great leader. We all do our acting, no?"

"Doctor, I'd be careful with my words. As of this moment, you are on probation. Sign this document to acknowledge it. Another psychiatrist will be scrutinizing your charts. Henceforth, you will cease writing any schedule II drugs."

"But my ADD patients? What about them?"

"Fancy will transfer them to other doctors. You will be closing your 'side-business' immediately. I expect the DEA will keep me informed should you write any Schedule II scripts. I am meeting with HR and shall be pro-active in speaking with the Vice-Chancellor and seeking his recommendations. And, to be sure, we'll wait to hear what the DEA's going to do about you."

"So I'm to be like an animal confined in a cage of rules. I'll not be a man. I'll have a minder telling what I can and cannot do? Someone watching me? No. I am a doctor."

"That's what probation is, *n-est-ce pas*? Since I have more weighty issues to deal with, one of your colleagues will oversee you."

Max nodded his head in a barely discernible way. His lips parted slightly.

"Sign the acknowledgment, Doctor."

An odious smile contorted Max's face. "I am guilty of nothing. I will sign nothing. I will not be treated like a child. There will be no probation. And you will not be the hero saving his ass."

"Oh? And what do you envision happening?"

Max stood, laid his hands on Smith's desk and stared at him. "Me? I see you as continuing to manage , no, think you manage this looney bin of weirdos you call staff for a long, long time." Max snickered. "And trying to keep your mustache from drooping and making you look more the idiot."

"And you?"

"Doctor *Kingston*-Smith. I won't be here."

Smith threw the document at Max, "Enough. Sign it."

Max grabbed the paper and tore it over and over into small pieces that he threw up in the air. "Yes, it *is* enough. *Adiós*, Dr. Smith."

Max turned and stomped out leaving a wide-eyed Smith a trail of paper shards

TWENTY-FIVE

The Mind Can Be So Slippery You Can Roll Around
Forever And Never Get Up
Where Bonny Stays Strong
Assertiveness: A Positive Quality Showing Confidence And Self-
Assurance; Unafraid To Use The "Push" Door

Jack crashed through the staff-kitchen door slamming it into the wall.

"Hello, Jack. That was quite an entrance. Haven't seen you around. How are you?" Gus Cobb was sipping his coffee, careful not to spill any on his khaki, poplin suit or his yellow tie.

"I must've left my goddamn mug here because it's not in my office. If it's not here, I know one of the custodial people swiped it. They don't clean because they're too busy stealing. Goddamn them."

"Jack, *Good morning.*" Gus pointed, "If it's the mug with, 'Never Fear, The Doctor Is Here' on it, it seems someone washed it out for you and left it to dry by the sink."

Jack filled his mug. "Son of a bitch. Nobody ever does that. Morning, Gus. Thanks for finding it."

"How've you been, Jack?'

"Fine. You?"

"I'm excellent. Thanks for asking."

"How nice for you."

Gus moved closer to face him. "Jack, I think you owe Fancy an apology."

"What?"

"When you were at Fancy's desk earlier, I came up behind you. You likely didn't hear me because a patient was having a heated discussion with one of his hallucinations."

"Gus, I've a patient to see."

"Jack, when you didn't immediately see your charts, you turned to her and demanded, 'Where are they?' You didn't see the look of surprise and hurt on her face. When she pointed over to the table and said, 'They're where they always are, Doctor.' You said, 'Well, I didn't see them,' grabbed the charts, turned and stomped off. You were very rude to her. When I faced her, she shrugged, but Fancy wasn't smiling."

"Those goddamn charts weren't in the usual place. She 'd moved things."

"Okay. Even if, Fancy's definitely not the person to pounce on. She goes out of her way…"

"I *get* it. Thanks , Gus. Say, since you're not a jerk anymore, I like your new unofficial role as the Clinic's 'manners police'? Stamping out surly behavior wherever you find it."

"Yeah. I was pretty testy for a while, wasn't I?" Gus smiled. "Takes one to know one, huh? Incidentally, how're you doing with that patient suicide?"

"No problems. There'll be a clinical case conference to review what happened. I'm curious to hear what ole Dr. 'Teflon' Smith will say to ensure no responsibility blows his way."

"Good. I was wondering if the suicide were still bothering you because, Jack, you still don't seem yourself."

Jack sipped his coffee then spit into the sink. "Damn, that stuff's bitter. Well, it could be because my wife, Bonny, threw me out of our house. I'd taken a few weeks off to relax and thought I was doing great. Apparently, she didn't. Can you believe that?"

"Well, that'd certainly explain your brusqueness. Where're you staying?"

"Oh, a local, 'economy' motel. It's clean, if not spartan. Since I won't be there too long, I figured why spend the dough. She'll get over her snit, we'll kiss and make-up and everything will go back to the way it was. In fact, we're meeting later today. I'm taking that as a good sign she's come to her senses."

"Good you're keeping in touch. Jack, piece of advice from a dumb, divorced guy? Don't take her for granted. Not listen to her concerns."

"*Me*? Never. If anything, I think it's the other way around. Anyway, I gotta go."

"Glad you found your mug. Hope all goes well with Bonny."

"No worries."

"And Jack? Please apology to Fancy?"

Jack gave a flip of his hand as he walked out the door. "Sure, Gus, just for you,"

***

Jack was happy *The Java House* wasn't crowded so they'd be able to talk without yelling, if she shows-up. Jack checked his watch again. Goddamit. Five minutes late. Is she screwing with me?

This was the place they came when first moving to town. It was a nostalgic spot and he was hoping to use that. They'd come here before starting to unpack the moving boxes. Some mornings, he'd get two coffees with two croissants and they'd eat breakfast using one of the boxes as a table. Despite the work, moving-in was a fun time. Their being together and setting up their new home. And now she was spoiling it. Jack sat facing the door. He took another sip of his latte. Goddammit.

And there she was. When she saw Jack, Bonny also caught only his coffee on the table. Nodding, she went to buy her coffee. Bonny sat down facing him. She put her keys and a pile of napkins in front of her. She took time to check her cell and then put that down next to the keys and napkins. Bonny started to take a sip from her cup, found it was too hot and put it down. She looked up at Jack, "How've you been?"

"Miss me?" he grinned.

She stared at him. "Not cute, Jack. I asked how you were."

"Just checking if you still cared."

Bonny raised her eyes, sighed, then looked at him. "Last time, how are you?"

"Just ducky. And you?"

"I'm doing very well."

"Lonely in that big, ole house?"

"Actually, with the darkness gone, it's been a joy to come home to."

"Still seeing that therapist?"

"Mm-hmm."

"And?"

"And? She's helping me work through some ambivalent feelings."

"And?"

"And, Jack, it's none of your business."

"Excuse me. But since I must be part of what you talk about, I think I've the right to be curious what this counselor is selling you. I've assumed she pushed you into throwing me out. Is she talking women's empowerment now?" Especially regarding lay-about, lying husbands?"

She shook her head. "Gee, Jack, how'd you know that I spend my entire therapy time talking about you? Are you hiding behind a chair? Maybe have the room bugged?" Bonny snickered. "And do you really think I need empowering?"

"Okay. Let's see. How about this humidity? Pretty bad, huh? There's the Clinic. I'm now back at work, full time. There's been some uproar with can't-keep-it-in-his-pants Hernandez quitting. He just walked out one day. There's old man Cobb gone from bitter old-fart to happy old-fart. There's depression, misery, confused souls seeking help. Take your pick."

"Jack, *you* called me. Why?"

"Just wanted to see how you were coping without me."

"In truth, I'm glad you called. After you moved out...."

"After you threw me out."

She let out a breath. "Okay, after I threw you out, I wondered if you understood why I wanted you to leave. I knew I got out my feelings about your behavior and its effect on our future, but I wasn't convinced you really got it. I don't think I was unclear, but when you called, I figured meeting you would give me opportunity to explain as best I could where I'm at in all of this. Jack, understand that I came here today for me. I've learned in therapy that it's not my job to make you understand or persuade you to change. I can only tell you how I feel, how I want to live. The rest is up to you."

"Impressive speech, Bonny, but I did get your point. While we're apart, I'm supposed to ponder the things I should be doing to change myself to make life better, for you. Right?"

"Well, I guess I was unclear. Jack, you've sorta got the words right, but your singing's way off-key. And your heart's not it.

Jack took a swallow of his latte. He tilted his chair back, put his hands in his pockets and smirked.

"So, enlighten me on how I'm *supposed* to be. What *you* want?"

Bonny leaned forward joining her hands on the tabletop. She studied her husband's face.

"It's not what *I* want, Jack, I want it to be what *we* want."

"Okay. Set me straight on what *we* want."

"No. I'm here to tell you where *I'm* at right now.

I've said this before, I'm done with the past."

"I thought we had a good past. Remember when we used to come in here for coffee?"

"Jack, don't be an ass. I am done with your not facing whatever demons inhabit your head. Those that go deeper than your brother, your 'killing' him, your feeling like a failure with those other patients' deaths and, now, of course, Brad. They're getting dull and monotonous.

When you first got depressed up north, I wondered if it were me. Was I being a good wife? And, Could I make things better for you? Get you moving back to normal. I felt pretty powerless not being able to help. Now, I'm seeing I can only do so much. I can't fix you. I can only fix myself in the choices I make. Jack, I've left my doubts behind. I know now I've been and I am, a good wife to you. I've done what I can to help and support you, but my past enabling you by tolerating your behavior is over. You're on your own with that now. That's what I'm working on in therapy."

"What the hell are you saying?"

She took another sip of her coffee savoring that little bit of cinnamon she always put in it. "I'm going to give you my bottom-lines for what I want in my marriage. I'll try to keep it simple."

Bonny began counting on her fingers. "One, love. Two, caring for each other as that special person above anyone or anything else. And three, trust. I think my goals for a marriage are reasonable. But right now, Jack, this isn't us."

Jack couldn't look at her. "But we do love each other?"

"We do. But not in the way I'm talking about. Like I said, you're singing the words, but your heart's not in it."

"Bonny…?"

"Jack, It's pretty basic. I want to be happy… with you. But the way you are now, I don't see that as happening."

"Okay. How do you see a future day in the life of the Rackham household? How would Jack, if he chose to, win your faith back?"

"Besides knowing you're there for me?"

"Well, isn't that part of the trust issue? I'm talking how I'd be day to day. Humor me, okay?"

She sat back and ran her fingers through her hair. "Ha. let's see. Okay, no more of your sarcastic remarks, your bitching about things, being so negative. Funny stories? Witty comments? Fine. But the ridicule and disdain? No."

Jack shrugged his shoulders. "Child's play. Next?"

"No more hitting me."

"What? I never hit you. What the hell?"

"Never hit me again with one of your, 'surprises from the past'."

"There aren't any more, believe me."

"But that's my point. I can't believe you. But, you know, even if there were more, I don't want to hear about them. They are entirely yours to own."

"Since there are none, that'll be a piece of cake. Anything more?"

"I want you to go back in therapy."

"C'mon? I've been there, done that."

"But not really, have you Jack?"

"Who would I see?"

"Not my problem."

"That's going to be a real pain."

"And, oh yes, lose the melodrama. How life is so cruel burdening you with people who aren't the way *you* want them to be and how they make you suffer. Like the slow drivers you're always bitching about."

"Are you done?"

"Lastly, we talk. You talk. I talk. You know, about our day, what we're doing the weekend. But if you start avoiding and BS'ing yourself and me, couples counseling."

"Well, that went from a day-in-the-life to what sounded like a list of demands."

"You asked. I answered."

Jack drank from his cup. "Crap, now it's cold. Bonny, you really don't know me, do you? *My* needs?"

"Jack, are you doing the 'poor wretched me' drama stuff? You just can't help yourself, can you? You know, maybe you're right. Maybe I don't know you. Maybe I'm just an uncaring bitch."

"Bonny, what the hell are you smiling about?"

"Just a tip. Your drama act loses its impact with latte-foam on your upper lip. Oh, and thanks for the coffee you didn't get me, letting me buy my own."

Jack wiped away the foam. "You're welcome. I figured since you're so empowered now...."

"Jack, think a second, stop with the remarks. This is serious, about us, our future."

"Hmm." He joined his fingers together and leaned forward with a cocky look. And speaking about empowerment, I know your therapist has me on her shit-list, but have you told her about your drunken, womanizing, lying father who wasn't around for you when you needed him? That maybe you're taking anger out on me that rightly goes to that son of a bitch. Whaddya' think about that?"

Bonny sat shaking her head, holding back another smile. "Gosh. Dr. Jack, what an insight for me. I'm taking my angry feelings about my father on you? How could I have missed that? And yes, she and I've discussed him."

"Just wondering."

She sat back and laughed. "You pompous ass. I've told you before that, aside from my father's behaviors, it was how my mother endured suffering in her marriage that left a lasting impression on me. How I vowed to myself that if I ever had marital problems, I'd confront them, deal with them. And that I'd never, ever just *endure*. And that's what I'm doing." She laughed again. "I've gotta' say, nice try with the father angle."

"Thanks for the compliment."

"Uh-huh." Bonny looked down at the table. "It's you and me, Jack. I'm doing what I think's best to keep us together."

"Yeah? Because what I keep hearing are your conditions for me so we can stay together. Sit up, roll-over, beg, go fetch. Is that the deal? Or else, what, divorce?"

Bonny's mouth was dry, her coffee-cup empty. "I've told you what I believe needs doing to salvage us and why. I'm not going to be like my mother. Jack, I love you. But I have beliefs about how a marriage should be which I thought you shared. I still have hope that you feel our relationship is worth it. That I'm worth it."

"Bonny, we were happy."

"Yes, we were."

"Can't we go back to that? I come home. We talk. We move on. Look, we're talking here."

"I'm not changing my mind, Jack, if that's where you're going. And you're definitely not coming home."

Jack's face hardened. "Okay, then. Your deciding how things should be? Your being the judge of right and wrong? I don't know if I can deal with that. That I want to deal with it. Just so *you* know."

Bonny crossed her arms. "Jack, choose what *you* want to do. You can be stubborn or you can have a relationship. I've had this feeling that you were seeing your time out of the house like a little kid whose mother told him to stand in the corner for being naughty. Then, the time'd be up and everything would be fine. I'm glad we met today. Your reaction is telling me a lot."

Jack got to his feet, his chair grating on the floor. "Screw it. I'm done talking. Bonny. You've made your bed. Now, you can lie in it, without me."

As he turned, Bonny said, "Jack, if you want, you can call me after you think about what *you* want to do."

"Yeah, yeah" was all she heard him say as he kept walking out the door.

TWENTY-SIX

Existential Dilemmas Are Overrated
Where Jim Tires Of The See-Saw And Tries The Sliding Board
<u>*Mental Inertia*</u>: *The Tendency To Remain Passive And Do Nothing;*
No Risk, No Worry

Jim reviewed the medical chart and turned to his chronic schizophrenic patient. Despite it being ninety-degrees outside, Frank, in his mid-twenties, wore faded jeans and a heavy, wool sweater. His hair was ratty as was his beard which had bits of food in it.

"How are you, Frank?"

Frank shrugged.

"No problem at the shelter? They haven't thrown you out?"

Frank grunted.

"So, you haven't been talking about the Bible all the time?"

Frank shook his head. "Everything's good. I just keep to myself now, Doc, like you said."

"Okay, Frank, who're you today, Jesus or one of His disciples?"

"I am Jesus."

"Not a disciple?"

"No. I am Jesus."

"Frank, have you been taking your meds? 'Cause when you don't, you're Jesus. When you do, you're a disciple."

"Doc, I've told you. I get like jolts of electricity going through my body with that medicine. I don't like that."

"I understand. I might not take something that did that to me either. Unfortunately, out of all the meds we've tried, it's the only one that works for you. And you know without it, you begin your loud preaching at the shelter and get into trouble."

"Doc, you really don't believe I'm Jesus, do you?"

He smiled. Okay, Jim, how about something other than the psychiatrically-approved response.

"Frank, how about this? Since you're Jesus, if you can give me a winning Powerball number for this week, I'll believe you're Jesus. Weak in faith as I am, I need a sign."

Frank didn't hesitate. "Doctor, I do not do that sort of thing. That is not my Father's work."

Jim laughed. "I understand, Frank. How about we try lowering your med a little? Maybe that'll stop that nasty side-effect, but still keep you calm."

After Frank left, Jim leaned back in his chair, clasped his hands behind his head and looked around. He liked his office. He liked how the sun's rays caught the dust particles and toasted the dead flies on the windowsill. He had a good view of the grounds outside. Maybe he'd buy some floor lamps and shut off the buzzing fluorescents? How about an area rug over the gray tile? Add a few more of his photos to the walls? He liked the casual style, his Hawaiian shirts, the warm weather.

C'mon, Jim. You know what you're doing, doncha? You're telling yourself you're staying in Florida. So, what're you gonna do, pal? Think some more? Uncle Joe'd say, 'A man who thinks too much has a constipated brain'.

Jim checked with Fancy who confirmed he had a no-show. "Fancy, do you have any idea what was going on earlier with Dr. Hernandez?"

As her head swung from her computer, her large, hooped earrings clacked against each other. "Why do you ask, Dr. Jim?"

"Passing his office, I heard a lot of noise. I peeked in and saw him throwing things into boxes and shouting to himself in Spanish."

"Doc, I haven't talked with Martha yet so I don't really know what went on. *But,* there were two DEA agents here when I arrived. They wanted to see Dr. H., but I thought it better to redirect them to Dr. Smith. All I know is that the agents, Dr. Smith and Dr. H. met. That's it. Sorry."

"Hmm, since Dr. H. and government agents dress in black a lot, maybe they were looking for some fashion tips from him?"

She grinned. "That must be it. I take it that when you saw him in his office, you didn't ask him what happened?"

"No." Jim smiled. "It didn't seem like a good time to chat. Fancy, I want to tell you those huge, zebra-patterned earrings look great. But aren't they heavy?"

"Dr. Jim, no worries.A a plus-sized woman like myself can handle weight."

Jim saw a framed picture standing out on her crowded desk. "Are these your kids?"

"Yes. Those two are my loves. His name is Azizi. It means 'precious one 'in Swahili. He can be a little feisty. He takes after my mother."

"And I wonder who else? And your daughter?"

"Her name is Bisa. That means 'greatly loved'. And she is. They both are."

"They're beautiful children, Fancy. I know they have a wonderful mother."

She beamed, "Thank you for that, Dr. Jim."

Hearing someone behind him, Jim turned. "Hello, Ahndrea. Did we have an appointment?"

She shook her head as she caught her breath. "I really didn't mean to interrupt, Dr. Bizby. No, no appointment."

Jim took in her deep-green, silk blouse, her long, black hair draped over both shoulders and a hint of her perfume. Don't look like an idiot, Jim.

"So, if we don't have an appointment?"

"Oh, it was on an impulse, my dropping by. I was so hoping to catch you between patients. And, lucky me, here you are. I just had to tell you...."

She smiled as Jim took her arm. "Why don't we stand over there away from Fancy's desk. I'm sure she has things to do."

Fancy nodded. "You're definitely right about that, Dr. Jim." But she kept watching them.

"Ahndrea, is everything all right? Are you having problems with the med?"

"No. Nothing like that. Actually, it's just the opposite. I desperately needed to share with you how well I'm doing. I got my prescription filled right after you gave it to me." She touched his arm. "I feel *so* much better. Thank you."

Feeling her hand, Jim thought about pulling away. "Well, you certainly seem happier."

"I am. I definitely am. It's just like before with my friend's Adderall. My appetite's decreased so I've no anxiety about eating too much." Ahndrea snapped her fingers. "It's like magic. My thinking and worrying about food have disappeared. I feel like I've got some control back in my life. It's wonderful. And I have *you* to thank."

"And the purging?"

"No hurling since I started the medication. No need."

"But, you are eating? You're not starving yourself?"

She raised her right hand. "I swear that I am eating decent portions of food. It's not like before when I'd eat and fight myself not to eat more even though I rarely did. It's not an issue. Thank you, thank you, thank you."

Jim smiled for the first time. "I'm pleased you feel better. You're taking the prescribed dose?"

"Yes. The extended release capsule lasts the day for me."

"Besides the decreased appetite, are you having any other side effects? Overly stimulated? Jumpy? Tremors? Your sleep okay? Constipation?"

"Well, maybe a little of that last one, but it's not a big problem."

"And your depression?"

"It's markedly less." She smirked. "Just like I told you it would be, remember? I feel more in control of my life. I have hope again."

"Okay. Ahndrea, I really need you to be truthful here. You're not getting a pleasant 'buzz' from the Adderall and confusing that with lessened depression? I don't want it giving you a false sense of well-being."

She pouted. "Dr. Bizby, you *still* don't trust me? After I opened up my soul to you? I am *not* getting a buzz. And, just so *you* can feel better, I don't like that overly stimulated feeling anyway. I was depressed because my life was getting out of control and, well, those 'other' things from my past. But, like I said, now that I'm feeling more normal, whatever that means, my depression is less. Okay? Dr. Bizby? You look so serious. Aren't you happy for me?"

"Ahndrea, those profound issues from your past. We will continue to talk about them, won't we?"

"Of course I want to see you again. Can't a girl stop by to tell you how good she feels and express her gratitude for having you as her doctor? I just couldn't wait for the appointment. I hope it was okay to do and you're not mad at me?"

Before Jim realized it, she'd come closer and was hugging him. At first, he stiffened. But he reminded himself to relax and enjoy the moment, a patient just expressing her gratitude.

Too quickly she stood back. "I look forward to our appointment. Sorry I barged in. Thank you again. *Really*."

"You're welcome, really. I only hope this continues."

She smiled at him, spun around and left the clinic. As Jim looked after her, he heard an, 'Ahem'.

Jim turned. "You've a comment, Fancy?"

"Things seem to be going well for Miss *Ahndrea*."

"Yes, maybe a therapeutic success."

"Well, that hug looked like a *lot* of things and I guess 'therapeutic success' could be one of them. I'm glad to see someone besides me smiling around here, especially a patient."

After seeing two more patients, Ahndrea entered his mind. She did seem better, happier. He felt good seeing the improvement in her. Did I wait too long before giving her the med? But, would she have opened up to me about her past?

The intercom buzzed and he heard Fancy's voice. "Dr. Jim, that patient who 'dropped by' earlier? *Ahndrea?* She's on the line asking to talk with you. She wouldn't leave a message and said she was having a problem with her med. That you'd want to know about it. Do you? Because I can tell her, again, that she can leave a message. She sure looked fine to me earlier."

"I agree, Fancy, she did look better. But, who knows? Something might've happened. I'm free now. I'll talk with her."

"Okay. Line five, Doc."

"Dr. Bizby? Thank you for taking my call. I'm *so* sorry to bother you."

"No worries, Ahndrea. What's up? There's a problem with the med?"

"Dr. Bizby, is everything okay with you?"

"Yes, Ahndrea. Thank you for asking. Why are you calling?"

" Please, don't be mad at me. I told a little white lie to your secretary. I'm not having side-effects. I'm fine."

"Then, what is it, please?"

"I just wanted to thank you again."

"You're welcome, again. I'm just hoping all continues to go well. We can talk about all of that in our next appointment."

There was a long, pause. "That was the other reason I called."

"Oh?"

"Mmm, I was kinda' wondering...do I *really* have to wait until my next appointment before we talk again?"

"No. You can reschedule an earlier appointment with the people up

front. I can transfer your call if you want."

Another long silence.

"Ahndrea?"

"No, it's not quite that. I'm sorry. I'm not being too clear, am I? I'm wondering if we could talk sooner, but...outside the Clinic. You know, somewhere else?"

Jim started swiveling back and forth in his chair.

"Ahndrea, what exactly are you talking about?"

"I know this is a little out of usual realm of treatment."

"More than a little I'd say."

"Dr. Bizby, have you ever done anything, I don't know, out of the usual routine? I know the answer's 'yes' because you've already taken a chance in your prescribing the Adderall for me. That was a bit away from the norm, wasn't it? Perhaps even a little risky? You did something more creative in your therapy that you thought might help me?"

It was Jim's turn to be silent.

"Dr. Bizby? "

"I'm here, Ahndrea. I'm listening and I'm curious. Where are you going with this?"

"Your simply meeting with a very grateful patient outside of the clinic?"

"Ahndrea, you've been in therapy before. You know there are boundaries. Rules I need to follow."

"I do. And I want to apologize if I went beyond and made you feel uncomfortable in the waiting room. That's why I asked if you were okay."

"I'm sorry?"

"You know. First, when I touched your arm. Please, believe me, that was totally spontaneous. I sensed you wanted to pull away. Then, when I gave you a hug. I thought about whether I should do it, if it was okay? Was it, you know, 'proper'? But I felt so good after these many months of misery, I thought, 'what the heck, let me show him how thankful I am'. You seemed to respond in a caring way, yet I sensed your still being reserved. I know you try to do things in the 'correct' way. I really didn't mean to embarrass you or overstep."

"No, I…well, I'll admit that you did catch me by surprise. And you're right. A touch, and especially a hug are not the usual things I do."

"I have to say I was a little flustered myself. You know me and my self-control issues go way back. I thought all spontaneity was beaten out of me as a kid. But at that moment, it felt like such a natural way of showing my gratitude. You just brought it out of me. I'm sorry."

"Ahndrea, no need. I hope it feels great for you to know that you don't have to be in control all of the time, that if it feels right, acting a little impulsively isn't the end of the world."

"Doctor, is it possible? Maybe you could be a little impulsive too? And see it isn't the end of the world?"

"We have a doctor-patient relationship. I really shouldn't do anything like you're suggesting."

"But would you make an exception? Just this one time? There are more things from my past I'd like to share and ask you about. As nice as your office is, it's till hard for me talking there."

"Ahndrea, I don't see how it's doable." But even as he said this, Jim was remembering times during his training when he'd walk outside on the hospital grounds with patients. How they became more relaxed, talked more about themselves.

"Please, Doctor. Only this *one* time. I'm feeling so much better I want to share things. I've never had the courage to discuss before. I'm afraid this urge'll pass and you'll have to drag them out of me. We both know that's not fun."

"Ahndrea, I just don't know. It's way out of my comfort zone."

"Think about it as trial 'technique' that will help me. Please? Take a chance?"

Silence.

"Dr. Bizby?"

Jim had stopped swiveling and was staring outside at nothing in particular. He was thinking too much. Uncle Joe'd say, "Jim, you can't sit around forever waiting for a choice to show up."

Jim took in a deep breath, "Okay."

"Okay, you'll think about it? Or okay, we'll meet?"

"Okay, we'll meet. Just this one time though."

"Of course. Is there any place where it'd be okay to talk? Where you'd feel comfortable? Ha, look at me, actually sensitive to someone else's needs. Maybe I really am better."

Jim tried to focus. "Across the river on Tamiami, there's a place called *The Red Gator*. Their outside seating usually isn't too crowded."

" I know it, on the right, going north? Big red alligator sign?"

"That's it."

"After work? About six o'clock?"

"You mean tonight?"

"That's what I thought. Would that be okay?"

Jim started swiveling again. He nodded. "All right. See you there about six o'clock."

"Thank you, Dr. Bizby. I'll see you then."

Hanging up, Jim kept swinging around in his chair, back and forth, back and forth. Outside, there were some students walking by on their way to class, a few couples holding hands, strolling. All was right with the world.

It was done. He'd made his decision. Darn it. He wasn't going to regret something he didn't do.

He jumped as Fancy came into his office.

"Sorry, Dr. Jim. I didn't mean to startle you."

"No worries. I was just shooing-away some 'extra-thoughts'. Sometimes I get too many of them and if I don't put them in a box fast, I get into an existential dilemma."

"I don't think I've ever had one of those type dilemmas, whatever they are."

"For me, it's like running through a maze, trying to make the right turns to finally get to the center even though I don't know what that really is. Anyway, what's up?"

"I saw you'd finished your call with *Ahndrea* so I thought I'd bring you some charts you left on my table. A few patients will be running out of their meds before their appointments. One needs a call-back."

"Thanks. I'll get them right back to you."

"You okay, Dr. Jim?"

"Not quite yet, Fancy. But I will be," he gave her a rueful grin. "as soon as I get rid of those darn existential dilemmas."

"Okay, Doc. I hope you have good luck with that," Fancy said as she left.

"So do I," Jim said to the empty room. Even his Uncle Joe wasn't there.

TWENTY-SEVEN

The Fish Only Sees The Bait, Never The Hook
Where Jim Doesn't Stop The Plow To Catch The Mouse
Epiphany: A Sudden Insight Into The Essential Meaning of
Something;
The 'Aha' Experience.

Jim looked at his watch. He was late. But he already knew that. He'd been sitting in *The Red Gator's* parking-lot for twenty-minutes watching people go into the bar.

"Jim, what are you doing here?"

"I've been asking myself the same thing, Uncle Joe."

"You know, the way your life is right now, this is the last place you should be. But this is supposed to be 'therapy,' huh?"

"Yeah, I thought...."

"Jim, why don't you leave right now? Save you some thinking energy for other things."

"Yeah, Ahndrea and I could discuss the psychodynamics around this in our next appointment. But, darn it, Uncle Joe, I promised to meet her. And you know me and decisions. A promise is a promise, isn't it? Anyway, I don't have her cell-phone number."

"Yep, sure good reasons to stay."

"Actually, Uncle Joe, this meeting might enhance our therapeutic rapport and facilitate discussing her issues."

"Uh-huh."

"But I'd have to be careful about her developing too much positive transference towards me."

"Well, Jim, I'm confident you'll know 'right' when you see it. Just make sure nothing's pulling on your reins to drive you in another direction."

Jim watched two drunks leaning on a pickup. As they argued, their beers kept spilling over their enormous bellies and dripping onto their flip-flops.

He laughed. I guess I'm not getting answers watching these guys, am I, Uncle Joe? He got out of his car.

Ahndrea sat outside at a glass-topped table shaded by an umbrella. She wore large sunglasses with one arm casually lying on the chair next to her. A small ray of sun lit up part of her green silk blouse and made her gold necklace blink. Gold barrettes pulled her hair to the side allowing more of her face to show.

Jim took a deep breath and walked to the table. Looking up, she gave him a wide smile. With slow, deliberate movements, she removed her sunglasses and placed them to the side. As he sat down opposite her, Jim caught the unrushed crossing of her legs and the slender hand adjusting her skirt over them through the glass table-top,

"Hello there. I was wondering if you'd had second thoughts, rejected me."

"Sorry. Some last minute things."

"No problem. Two guys hit on me. I told them I was waiting for someone 'special' and they left."

"I can understand their actions. You look very nice."

"Thank you."

"Have you ordered anything?"

"I've been waiting for you."

After ordering, Ahndrea said, "Dr. B, is your chair okay? You keep moving around in it."

"I just can't seem to find the right spot. But, no worries, I'll find it."

Besides Jim's tapping his fingers on the table-top and his squirming , both were quiet until the wine came.

"Cheers," Jim said, raising his glass to hers. He tried not to gulp it down. "Nice weather we're having," a wry grin on his face.

"Yes, less humid. Do you think it'll rain?" she smirked back.

"Okay. Should I say, 'Come here often?'." Jim kept fidgeting. "I'm not good at small-talk."

"Thank you for meeting me. It's like an affirmation you care."

"How so?"

"Hmm. Because you were willing to go beyond the 'guidebook for psychiatrists' to meet me. Because maybe you see me as more than a name in a medical chart. That you want to help me."

"Ahndrea, I do want to help you. As far as seeing you outside my office, in the past when I treated inpatients, I'd take them outside to walk around the hospital grounds and have a session. But that was a bit different from Florida-bar-therapy."

"Where was this?"

"Up in Cleveland."

"Ah. I know Cleveland, home to The Rock and Roll Hall of Fame."

"Not many people know that. I'm impressed."

"One of my co-workers comes from there and she talked about it. I've always wondered why they built it there? No disrespect, but Cleveland?"

Jim chugged his wine, saw the server, ordered another. Ahndrea passed. The chair felt better. "In the early 80's, some music industry people wanted to build a 'Hall of Fame' to rock and roll. Cleveland heard about it and heavily lobbied to be the site. Their big claim being it was where Alan Freed came from."

"Who?"

"Alan Freed. One of the first disk-jockeys in the early 50's, the guy who originated the phrase, 'Rock and Roll'. But I think it really came down to huge financial incentives from the politicians. It opened in 1995. Did you know IM Pei designed it?"

"And he is?"

"He's a world-renowned architect best-known for his glass and steel pyramid at the Louvre. By itself, I like it, but in that classic setting, no." Jim, you're talking too much. Slow down. Stop showing off. He drank more wine.

"Wow, Dr. B. I'm amazed by your knowledge of Cleveland."

"Aw, shucks. There's really not much to know. It has a nice riverfront, some parks. Oh, how could I forget? More than the Hall of Fame, Cleveland's never-to-be-forgotten draw is, are you ready, a monument to President James Garfield complete with casket, his remains remaining inside of course, on display for all Americans to view." Jim, stop. Relax.

"Gosh, Garfield's remains and casket," Ahndrea pretended to write on the table. "I'm putting 'visit Garfield's casket' on my to-do list right now."

He slouched more into his chair as they laughed. He gazed around. This bar was old Florida. The fake fish-netting, plastic starfish and seashells hanging from the ceiling and broken propellers, miniature crab pots and mermaids on the walls. He drank more wine.

She was watching him. "You made a good choice, Dr. B. I like the casual atmosphere. I think it's helping you open up a little."

"It is. And thank you for suggesting this. I would've never...."

"I know, I know. Your silly ethical code."

"Ahndrea, I'm glad you were finally able to open up to me about your past, about the abuse you suffered. It helped me put into context your depression, the low self-esteem, your concerns about your body image. It also helped me understand your issues with control and trusting."

"Dr. B, I've hinted at things with other therapists, but never gotten too far into them. When we first met, you seemed so distant and stiff, I thought this is definitely not going to work. I never *dreamed* I'd open up to you as I did."

"Alas, that first appointment can be a bit clinical. I need to know why you came in, get some background, do you have a psych history while also trying to get a sense of who you are." He smiled and raised his eyebrows. "And, Ms. Ahndrea, as I recall you weren't too forthcoming about yourself. It was sorta, 'I'm depressed, maybe a little bulimia, I want Adderall so write the script and I can leave.' When you said you wanted the Adderall, that's probably when I got distant, suspicious of your being drug-seeking. What'll also make me more guarded, and, I is when it's a beautiful woman asking for a specific med."

"Okay. But if I were drug-seeking, wouldn't I've come right out and told you about my wretched past? Play the sympathy angle? In fact, Dr. B, when I did reveal it, you wrote me the prescription."

Jim ordered another wine. Ahndrea passed. "I did. But that was after I knew you better. I knew you didn't like to share much, so when you did open up about your past, I felt some trust between us. That did make me sympathetic."

"So it did work. No. Just kidding, Dr. B. Just kidding. Anyway," now she raised her eyebrows, "why would a beautiful woman make you more guarded? You're a proper, trained professional."

Jim hesitated. "Are you teasing me?"

"Absolutely not. Please, Dr. B."

"Well,. *I* have found that 'fetching 'women...."

She grinned. "And by 'fetching' you mean a woman who's

appealing, alluring, fascinating and enticing?"

"Yep. Easily get men's attention. And, because they're so 'captivating', men fall over themselves for them. As your doctor, I didn't want that to happen." He paused, "C'mon, Ahndrea, you've admitted as much to me. We both know you've all those 'attributes'."

She lowered her head, feigned a guilty look. "It's true, Dr. B. I do get my way a lot. But, since *you* didn't fall over yourself to write me the Adderall, I'm guess neither my beguiling nor my suffering impressed you enough?"

"Like I said, I try to careful not to get sucked-in." Jim drained his glass.

Ahndrea leaned forward, rested her hands and arms on the table. "So, Dr. B, which type did you suspect me being? The irresistible seductress using her sexual trickery? Or the woeful beggar, faking her depression?" She deepened her voice. *"To get my drug*? I thought I did a little of both, actually."

Jim drew his chair in, looked into her blue eyes. "Ahndrea, you were a little of both. And played them pretty darn well too. But I never labelled you one or the other." Jim winked. "Remember, you can play all sorts of roles. I was just watchful. Was your depression real? Or were you acting to get the drug? The 'professional' explanation for my being distant is that I was unsure what was going on and stood back to observe."

"So there's another explanation why you were aloof, detached and rude at one point? I'd love to hear that one, Doctor." She was half-smiling, twirling a lock of hair.

"I was rude and I apologize for that. To be honest, the reason I was that way was your" he sighed, " attractiveness. Usually, when a patient comes in who's pretty, I notice that. But then I refocus and get into my evaluation. But with you...."

"But with me, what?"

Jim waited, drank some wine. "I know I shouldn't tell you this, but in our first session, your looks distracted the heck out of me." He shook his head. "I should *not* have let that happen. I couldn't refocus on anything else. That really rattled me. I knew I *had* to get myself back to normal, so I detached. I had to. I need to stay neutral and put you in a singular place *beyond my reach* in terms of my thoughts and feelings not relating to therapy. I'm sorry if I seemed aloof and cold but that was the reason. I'm not that way with patients."

Ahndrea leaned closer to him. She reached out and placed her hand on his. Her voice almost a whisper. "But, Dr. B., at this moment, I'm *not* beyond your reach. I'm right here, thankful to you. Grateful to you for my new life."

her hand was soft, warm. He looked at the long, slender fingers and wanted to place his hand over hers. He smiled. "I guess we didn't get much therapy done, did we? But, it's been very pleasant for me being here, talking with you." He shook his head. "maybe too pleasant because I'm thinking I've talked too much." His hand didn't move.

"Well, Dr. B., you've confirmed another thing for me, that psychiatrists are human too. Thank you for sharing what you did. I didn't sense you an unkind person so it puzzled me why you did what you did. Now I understand." She nodded her head. "Apology accepted."

She squeezed his hand more tightly. "Dr. B, I really need you to know that I am functioning better with the medication. I don't get a buzz. I'm even. I don't think about overeating. Thank you again for trying the medication and thank you for the compliment."

"What compliment?" Jim sat up and slowly pulled his hand from under hers.

"About my being attractive. It's always nice to hear," her long fingers now running up and down the stem of her wine glass.

"Ahndrea, you're bright and you are attractive. You've a good sense of humor and, I bet, many wonderful qualities inside. You've been afraid show that real Ahndrea because your hateful mother's poisoned your mind."

"Oh? So now you're seeing I've some good qualities? And before, in your office? What did you see?"

Jim smirked, "Why, an emotional cripple of course."

They both laughed and enjoyed the quiet that followed.

"If you pardon me, I have to make a trip to the ladies room."

Jim smiled. "I'll be here." He watched as she uncrossed her legs, stood and walked from the table. She is a very appealing woman.

He looked at his empty wine glass. Holy-moly, did I drink three glasses of wine? That's why I couldn't shut up. He peered into the glass, began moving it slowly around in circles, around and around on the table-top. He made the exact, same circle each time. Around and around.

He stopped and stared more deeply into the empty glass. His eyes widening, he let out a long, quiet whistle. He knew Uncle Joe was laughing.

As he watched her return to the table, Jim was experiencing an emotional stew of feelings. Desire, regret, loss. Yet hope, enthusiasm, resolve.

"Dr. B, I see your glass is empty. Should I call the waitress over?"

He was looking at her, his face rueful.

"Dr. B.? Another wine?"

"No. I think three'll be my limit today. But you go ahead if you want one."

"Dr. B., where were you just now? I thought you were looking at me, but you weren't, really."

"Oh, I was just thinking" A small, close-lipped smile crossed his face. "Ahndrea, this has been great. I've genuinely enjoyed being with you." He looked down into his wineglass. "And, as much as I'd like it to continue...."

"I understand. You have to get home."

"No, it's not that."

"Then what?"

He looked away, then back at her. "I'm sorry. I...I can't do this."

Ahndrea moved closer to the table. "I don't understand. What is the 'this' you can't do?"

"Our being here, together like this. It's wrong. No, not wrong like *bad.* It's just that it's not *right.*"

"Pardon me, Dr. B, but what's wrong with two people sitting, having a glass of wine and talking? I thought we were enjoying the pleasure of each other's company. I was. You said you were. Now you're making this sound, I don't know, a bit tawdry."

"Please, Ahndrea, I don't mean it that way. There's no moral judgment or anything like that. Damn, you've had enough of that in your life. I just shouldn't be here with you."

"Because you're married? Is that the trite cliché you're gonna use?"

"No. It's definitely not that. Believe it or not, it's because I want to keep us together, as psychiatrist and patient. I can't be your friend and your psychiatrist. Our sitting here, shooting the breeze and enjoying ourselves impacts on my neutrality. And... if something happened and I became..."

"Became what?"

"Became *more* than a friend."

"Doctor, don't flatter yourself."

"But that's exactly my point. *My* thoughts are intruding there, *my* feelings, *my* issues. If I'm to help you, that can't happen. I *must* stay objective."

Ahndrea's long fingernails began making loud, tapping sounds on the table. She sneered,"So, I'm back to being an object observed from a distance? Was I dumb thinking you were seeing me as a real person, an *individual*. Getting to know *me* so you could discover what makes *me* do the things I do and help *me* change, be happy. But I guess I can't expect that from someone who puts himself in a box? No, from someone who puts *me* in a box to observe and analyze. Who treats me like an object, a thing, like Mother.

Where's that warmth, concern, compassion now? That caring you talked about? And as far as my trusting you? Hah.

Doctor, why did you agree to meet me? You were initially so tentative on the phone. But then you agreed. Why? Did you have some agenda beyond our just talking? Using me for some reason? You mentioned *your* feelings and *your* issues. These went beyond my 'allure' or anything sexual, didn't they?" She took a deep breath. "And you see yourself as a dedicated psychiatrist? I see you more as a deluded psychiatrist."

"Ahndrea, I understand what you're saying, what you're feeling. Why I agreed to meet you? I did have an agenda. But now I see there was more to it. Please, let me explain."

"Just keep it *appropriate*, Doctor."

"When you called and first brought up meeting outside the Clinic, I bet you could hear me stiffen-up even over the phone. And that was the reason I gave myself to get together with you. My issue. To be able to loosen up, be less rigid. Thinking more out of the box like taking a chance with the Adderall off-label. I told myself, look how great that turned out. But, I also knew I wanted to see you. Because of," he smiled, "your allure. I pictured me, the shy psychiatrist and you, the beautiful woman, talking and laughing. Me relaxed, loosened up. You, relaxed, sharing more about yourself. I kept telling myself what a good 'therapeutic' session it'd be, for both of us. And, I swear, if I had an agenda when I walked into this place, that was it. I know now I was crossing the ethical line, but at that moment I was BS'ing myself what a good idea it was."

"But everything seemed fine. We *were* talking, laughing, relaxing. What happened that turned you from smiling to serious? I wasn't in the ladies room that long. But that was when your conscience found you and turned you back into an Eagle Scout, wasn't it?"

"When you left, I sat thinking how enjoyable it'd been. Being away from work, feeling good. How this helped me put out of my mind some unpleasant things in my life right now.

How this has been such a great distraction from that. That's when it happened. Thinking of distraction led into my thinking about avoiding. And then it hit me. My issue."

"Okayyy?"

"Those unpleasant things in my life ? I keep evading them. When I told you I can't do this? Beyond the ethical side, I can't keep avoiding. As delightful as this has been, it's been me dodging what I have to do again. And if, and I know I am flattering myself too much, something physical did develop between us, that would've been a fabulous way to avoid. I need to bring closure to these things before I can enjoy myself."

She sat focused on her hands flat on the table.

Jim smiled. "Ahndrea, I guess I've gotten the therapy today. Thank you?"

She stayed silent.

"Pleased know that I do not see you as an *object*. But I have to stay objective. You are a living, feeling person who's endured vile abuse from parents who should've loved and cared for you. People you should've been able to trust. I'm concerned that you might not now trust me. Helping you has to be about you, not you and me in a bar, me distracting myself. I hope you'll allow me to continue to help you. I rambling, aren't I?"

She looked at him. "Dr. B., there's absolutely no doubt in my mind that I don't like what you're saying. And it's because I know it's right. You really want to help me get into my problems, don't you? Damn. You want to talk about avoiding? Now that my mood and eating are better, I had thoughts that I could've drifted along in therapy. We'd make conversation. I'd flirt with you a little. We'd talk about the Adderall and leave it at that. I'd never have to go down into that ugly abyss of my past that I know still affects how I deal with people. And you don't want that to happen. That said, I'm still angry that you met with me."

She tilted her head. "You know, I feel like I'm breaking-up with a boyfriend? And only after the first date. How silly is that? Maybe, *unconsciously*, I wanted something more? You, my protector, keeper of the meds, the wise, confident one who'd guide me, keep me 'normal', whatever that is." Ahndrea grinned, then shook her head. "Hmm. But that wouldn't really work, would it? My needs met through you, not me. Damn, I still don't like this."

Jim smiled. "Wowie-kazowie. Such insights in this old Florida bar. Maybe this *is* a good place for therapy."

"So, we'll meet here again?"

"Nice try, but no. We can meet in my office though."

Andrea gave him a closed-mouth smile and nodded. She reached across the table and placed her again hand on his.

"Please, don't pull away, Dr. B. This time, I *really* am expressing my gratitude. And, I'm sorry about coming-on to you earlier."

"Oh?"

"My saying I was, 'within reach' with my hand on yours. I was testing you. Were you 'easy'? Or could I trust you? Another person might've taken advantage of the moment."

"Yep. Another person might've."

"When you later said you couldn't do this, I felt rejected. But it's not rejection, is it? You're telling me you're not falling into any of my alluring diversions and really want to help me. That you care." Pulling her hand away, she pouted. "But, I'm still mad at you."

"Well, we can discuss that in our next appointment."

She stopped frowning. "Of course."

Jim checked the time. "I have to go. You? Staying? Going? Another glass of wine?"

She'd been watching her fingers tapping slowly on the table. She nodded."Yes, I'll have another glass. I'd like to stay a bit longer."

"Okay. I'll pay on the way out. See you?"

"Yes."

"And we'll talk? About you?"

"Do you have any doubts, Dr. B.?"

After starting his car, he laughed at himself. You know, Jim, you might still develop post-*dramatic* stress disorder having Ahndrea as a patient. But cowabunga, today you undeniably did some darn good therapy on yourself. Uncle Joe said, "Remember, Jimmy, *you* always have the key. It's which door you unlock that's important."

TWENTY-EIGHT
It's Not Wise To Bang Heads In A Tête-A-Tête
Where Jim Becomes A Dragon-Slayer And Slays What He's Been
Draggin
<u>*Sublimation:*</u> *Transitioning From Annoying, Constipating Worries*
To Positive Behavior And Thoughts; It's Time For me
To Get off My Butt

After the light turned green, Jim waited and watched the herd of old geezers in black-leather, more hair on their faces than on their heads, rev their engines for a testosterone high and roar away. He grinned. Retirees livin the dream. Good for them.

The seashell base of his driveway crackled as he drove to his house. There was Anne waiting for him at the door, kiss ready, eager to tell him about her day and what she'd cooked for dinner. Who am I kidding? I should put over the driveway's entrance Dante's warning, *Abandon all hope, ye who enter here.*

As he drove around some potholes into the garage, he saw the same old stuff. The lifeless grass, the brown dust lying thick on the never-used porch chairs, the grime on Anne's car. When was the last time I started it? Doesn't matter. He took off his sunglasses. They had a few smudges. Reaching down, he wiped them on his Hawaiian shirt, the part with the hula-girl on it. Gee, I hope I didn't hurt her. Maybe I tickled her? That'd be nice. He whistled as he walked to the front door. Really, where should I put that Dante quote? Maybe add some snarling devils' faces?

"Anne, I'm home."

No answer. Okay, one more time, just for fun. "Anne, sweetheart? Your ever-constant yet hope-abandoning husband has arrived. Where are you, you rascal?"

The living room was dark except for the eerie light radiating from the blasting TV. All the shades were drawn. He walked over and looked down. Anne, wearing the same wrinkled blouse and shorts from yesterday, sat fully back in her recliner looking over her chest at the TV, an empty wine glass and her phone beside her. A family album and some dirty plates laid on the coffee-table. She stayed fixed on the TV.

He smiled. This was pure Dickens. And Jim, you'd played the character with great expectations.

Anne grumbled, "The evening news is over, so I know you're later than usual."

"I called."

Jim couldn't see the remote. "Anne, could you turn the TV down or mute it for a few minutes?"

Groaning, she grabbed the remote jammed between her leg and a cushion. With a grand movement of her hand she pressed the mute button. "Okay, your majesty?"

"Thank you. I left you a message about being a little late."

"Oh, yeah, Saw your name. Didn't listen to it. I've already eaten. Had some soup. There's some left in the pot on the stove if you want it. Otherwise, dump it."

"No worries. I think there's some vegetables in the fridge. I'll make myself a salad. Or, I thought I'd go down the road and get take-out from that new Japanese place."

"Jap food's too greasy. I can smell it a mile away. I wouldn't eat that crap. But you do whatever you want. You're good at that."

"Yeah, tempura can be greasy, but I thought I'd get some sashimi. That's not greasy."

"You know, Jim, I was just fine. Then you walk in, late, and start an argument."

"Anne, could you look at me at all while we talk?"

"Why?"

"Mmm. I guess if I have to explain that, never mind. I'm going to get a glass of lemonade. Now don't you stray off and hide on me. Be right back."

"Whatever. Get your freakin lemonade. Just don't come back to start another argument. Oh, get me another glass of wine."

Jim put his lemonade on the coffee table and handed her the wine. She pointed to the table next to her. "Put it there."

He pulled a chair over to sit opposite her, trying not to block her view. "Would you please elevate yourself in that recliner so we can sit face to face?"

"Why? I'm comfortable."

"I need to talk with you."

"Talk? Not argue?"

"Anne, my saying all Japanese food isn't greasy wasn't to start an argument. It's true."

"Jim, admit it. Deep down you're angry at me. That's why you won't move back. To be mean."

"Hmm. Deep-seated anger, huh? Maybe I should get some therapy because I thought I was in a pretty good mood."

"You do that. You'll see."

"Anne, I need to say a few things to you. You don't have to talk at all. Please, could you sit up?"

She made a throaty noise and pressed a button on the side of her chair until their heads became level with each other. Reflecting the rapidly changing colors from the TV, her pretty face seemed grim, bizarre. That's the kind of face I should put on my Dante sign. No one would come down the driveway for sure.

"Anne, could you look at me? Please?"

Inch by inch, she turned her face to him. "Happy now?"

"Thank you."

She turned back to the muted TV. "Start talking whenever you want."

"I'm sorry. I meant, look at me for more than a few seconds. Shut the television off until I'm done?"

"Jim, I muted it for you. *Wheel of Fortune* is starting. I'll miss seeing what Vanna's wearing tonight. They're in Hawaii."

Jim reached over, took the remote and pressed 'off'. He turned on two lamps. Her face was sullen, but, she *was* looking at him. "Anne, I've thought of all different ways to tell you...."

"I know already. You're having an affair. You found some hot babe who's screwing your brains out. That's why you're late. Well, you can go live with her because you're not staying here."

Jim laughed. "No, Anne, I'm not having an affair."

"What then?"

Jim sat with his legs apart, hands folded between them. "I want to be clear...."

She let out a loud groan. "Jim, just say whatever bullshit you have to say, please?"

He let out a long breath. "Anne, we've been miserable for a while.

I know you're unhappy here...."

"Wow, I think I'm gonna cry."

"I thought your homesickness would lessen. That you'd start seeing all the things to do around here, people to meet. That we'd make a home."

"For chrissake, Jim, I came here to humor you for a few months and then we'd return to Cleveland to live happily ever after. I told you that. Why would you *ever* think otherwise?"

Jim nodded. "You're right. I kept hoping, trying to get you interested...."

"Yeah, yeah, yeah. Anne downed some wine and began to reach for the remote. "Now, if you're done?"

He put up his hand. "No. Anne, I'm *not* done."

"Okay, then, Jim, what's your freakin point?"

"I can't go on living like this. I refuse to."

"You gonna move out? Like that'll solve anything."

"Anne, why haven't you moved out? Gone back to Cleveland? After all, you're so miserable here."

She sighed loudly. "Okay, smartass, why? I know you're just itching to tell me."

"Your pride. Not going back with your obedient, doctor husband in-tow. Although I think you're wily enough to work the 'victim' angle and still look good."

"You're really are full of shit, Jim. I'm just waiting. You'll come around."

"Don't bet on that, Anne. My waiting's over. I *do* want to live apart."

"Right. You're so goddamn needy, that won't last."

"But, not just separating...."

"And? Come on, Jim, you can do it. Finish the sentence."

"Anne, I want a divorce."

Anne dropped the remote.

"You can't be serious? You, the psychoanalyst from the famous Cleveland Institute can't make a relationship work? A divorce? Tell me, really, you're not having an affair?"

"No."

"You're drunk. I thought I smelled wine on you."

"No."

"This can't be you. C'mon, who? Who goaded you into this?"

"Anne, this is me talking. We're not happy. And neither of us is going to change. I want a divorce. If you want, I can give you a list of attorneys available to the Clinic."

"Forget that. I don't want some guy who deals with your whackos. You really mean it? You want a divorce?"

"Yes."

"You son-of-a-bitch. You're going to dump me, just like that. Jesus. All this time I wasted waiting for you to come around. Boy, was I a sucker. That's why I need to go back, *family*. I can trust them to care about me." She thought a minute. "Well now, Jim. What I'll do is call my father or one of my brothers, probably all of them. They'll know somebody who knows somebody. Don't you worry, *they'll* look after me. They want me happy."

Jim turned and picked up his lemonade. He saw the glass had left a ring. He smiled and left it. "I'm done now,"

As he started to get up, Anne's voice was tight. "Hold on. I want you to know I think you're a total prick for not taking care of me. You've *never* been the husband I'd hoped for. For all your 'doing the right thing' bull-shit, you really let me down. Just so you know. Now, get the hell outa here."

She turned away and found the remote.

Trying to be heard over 'I'd like to buy a vowel', Jim said, "I'm contacting a lawyer tomorrow. I assume once your family finds someone, you'll do the same. I think the sooner we get this done, the better. We've gotta get you back to all those caring people in Cleveland."

Jim almost skipped into the kitchen. He dumped the cold soup and the wrinkled, brown vegetables into the disposal. He was going to that Japanese place for some take-out sashimi.

Waiting for his order, Jim heard Uncle Joe. "Jim, I always get to where I'm going by leaving behind where Ive been."

He smiled, he grinned, he beamed. He told the fellow behind the counter to change the take-out order. He was going to sit at a table and eat with people around him. He ordered a Sapporo beer. He started a conversation with the couple next to him.

Why rush? There was nothing for him where he'd been. And now he knew where he was going.

TWENTY-NINE

When Talking To A Blind Man, It Doesn't Matter If You Nod Or
Shake Your Head
Where Jack And Jim Share A Beer And Other Things
Avoidance: Behaviors To Escape From Difficult Thoughts And
Feelings; I Think I'll Join The Circus

First it was the smell, then he'd see it. The green dumpster-oven, sitting there, letting the Florida sun do some baking. Jack plodded with pizza box, some Chinese take-out cartons, empty beer cans and wine bottles to make his donation to the cooking garbage. He side-stepped the debris left by his motel-mates who met nightly to rant and drink. And keep him awake... what's not to love?

Back in his room, Jack laid down on the bed careful not to tear the threadbare spread. He turned-on the radio looking for any station that wasn't playing goddamn country-western or some preacher spreading God's word. One song, *Clean Sheets and Dirty Movies,* caught his attention. The country-boy mourned:

When she threw me out,
She left me all alone;
Now I'm sittin' in this motel room with just
Clean sheets and dirty movies to call my own.

Jack smiled. Finally, a country song I like.

Now what? It's Saturday. I've had lunch. Lying around this crap-hole isn't an option. "Jim. Glad you picked up."

"Hey, Jack. How're you doing? It's been a while."

"I'm doin'. Sorry to bother you on a Saturday afternoon."

"No worries. I was just leaving for the car-wash. Don't you and Bonny do errands on Saturdays?"

"Not lately. You don't know, do you?"

"Don't know what?"

"Bonny threw me out of the house. I've been living here in town. I didn't think I'd be out of the house for long so I'm living, if you can call it that, in an 'economy' motels to save money. There's no free-breakfast. My bathroom has shower-head with, maybe, five openings that aren't clogged, a shower-curtain with mold so thick I think I hear

241

it breathing at night and paper-thin towels that could double as sandpaper. But I'm gettin along."

"Jack, I knew you're out and then we kept missing each other when you were back. Gus Cobb mentioned something in passing, but didn't tell me much."

"After Bonny made me leave, I did take some time. Then I decided to get back to work, keep busy. But that didn't last too long. I had Fancy rework some things and I'm taking extended leave right now. I thought I'd give you a call. Maybe get together for a beer? How about after the carwash? Whenever's good. My dance card's pretty open."

"Excellent. Hey, after the beers, how about I help you move to a better motel? Yours sounds pretty bare-bones. Why suffer?"

"Nah. If I can't be home, I'll stay here."

"Whatever you say, Jack. How about right now? *The Lusty Pelican*? I was going down to the harbor anyway to look at some boats. Ten-fifteen minutes?"

"Looking at boats? Nice. See you there. And Jim?"

"Yeah?"

"Thanks."

***

Jim saw his friend sitting at a waterside table. His friend with the uncombed hair, unshaven face and wrinkled shirt.

"Hey, buddy, how'd you luck-out getting us this great table outside? I pictured us inside with the fourteen blaring TV's, yelling to hear each other." Jim pulled in his chair. "Should I get the waitress? Hey, you okay with the sun right in your eyes?"

"I've already ordered us beers. And this table wasn't luck. I wanted it for its great view of the harbor to finally give me a little enjoyment. But I had to wait in line with the tourists and their screaming brats. So, I eventually get the table, you'll notice the sticky floor from the spilled beer, I sit down and, goddamn it, next to me some drunken, sun-burned tourists start yelling and waving at the boats going by. Dumbasses. Like they'd never seen a boat before. Then, once they leave the goddamn sun drops into my eyes and there goes my view."

Jim pointed to another chair. "Why don't you move over here? Sun-free."

"Cause I don't want to move. The sun'll go behind that building soon. I can bear it for now." Jack was squinting, hand over his eyes.

Jim smiled. "Okay, Jack, endure your misery. The sun'll set and your suffering will end... by and by."

"Another one of your Uncle Bob's pithy sayings? What the hell's it's supposed to mean?"

"If you want to suffer when you don't have to, knock yourself out. But maybe you'll wise-up...'by and by.' And it's my Uncle Joe, not Bob. Actually, I just made that up. I can see the book now, *Dr. Jim's Apothegms to Live By*. Cool, huh?"

"Jim, I thought we were going to relax and shoot the breeze?""Yeah?"

"Then why are you busting my balls about some sun in my eyes as soon as you sit down?"

"Uh-huh."

"Uh-huh? What?"

"Okay, driving over, I thought how really great it'd be to catch up. In fact, I've something interesting to share."

"But?"

"But, as soon as I sat down, I felt the tension. Okay, I told myself, he's out of his home, he's stressed. But then I thought, this attitude's nothing new. Only it's worse."

"Me? Attitude? What the fuck?"

"Jack, you always complained about things. The lousy drivers, our dirty kitchen, dead bugs on the windowsills, your squeaky chair. And people, Hester, Smith and especially Felicity."

"So?"

"And you could be witty, amusing."

"Oh? I'm haven't been scintillating?"

"No. I thought we were going to relax, catch-up too. But since I sat down. I've sensed an angrier edge to you. Look, I know your life isn't the way you want it right now, but, Geez, all you've done is tell me about how much you're suffering in one way or another. I say, 'Great table, Jack' and I get how you're *finally* getting a crumb of enjoyment after enduring some waiting, screaming brats and asshole tourists waving at boats. How the sun ruined your pleasure. Did you move? No. You just sat there. On the phone, you got right into bitching about Bonny and your dumpy motel. You won't move from there either. Jack, this isn't relaxing, it's boring."

"Christ, Jim. Those things'd bother you too, wouldn't they? Anyway, do you have a point somewhere in all your bullshit?"

"Everyday, things happen that we don't like, right?"

"Right. I've always wanted to be emperor to prevent that."

"Cute. We can either do something or let it go. Like you and the tourists or the sun in your eyes.

"Okay, Jim. Point? What's pissing you off?"

"You do a third option. You don't do anything, like changing motels, but you don't let it go either. You grumble and suffer. Keep gathering reasons to be angry when you could be doing something. That's what pissing me off.

Jack, what's wrong? You're unhappy. I know it. Your anger's just a front."

"So, since sitting your ass down, you've decided that I've turned into a bitter, miserable guy who resents the world? Christ, I knew the sun would set. Why move and lose the view? And, FYI, I'm used to that motel. Why leave? I'm just waiting on Bonny."

Jim put up his hands. "Jack. You're right. It's not for me to judge. I'm sorry. You said you ordered the beers? There's a server, I'll have her check on them."

"Yeah."

"So Jack, what's cookin? What's with the beard? You heading down to KeyWest to be in the Hemingway look-alike contest?"

"Nah. Just don't feel like shaving."

"How long have you been out of the Clinic?"

"Three weeks. When I went back, I don't know, I started seeing the whole place differently. I got bored listening to all that daily sadness and misery. The challenge wasn't there. Do they ever *really* get happier, Jim? Or is it we're just people they can bitch to who won't argue back? So I said, screw it and took the time. Fancy arranged something."

"The motel? You've been there how long?"

"Two months."

"What do you do with yourself?"

"I get up. Walk across the street, get a Boston-creme and coffee. The bagels suck. The café has wifi, goddamn motel doesn't, so I read the paper online. The gym got boring so I stopped that. I do some wandering, take walks, drive around. Seen some really nice homes. Some real dumps too. I've seen houses so covered with mold I thought they were painted black. Jesus, how can people live like that?"

"Kinda like your motel's shower curtain, huh?"

"That's different. Do you want to hear what else or be an asshole?"

"I'm all ears."

"I'll drive around the campus, check out the babes, see if they've any movies or talks going on. Or I go read. I've found some nice, isolated places on the grounds. If I go back to the room, I'll watch some TV."

"What happened? That you're in the motel?"

"Between Bonny and me?"

"Yeah?"

"Short and sweet, she asked me to leave ," Jack mimicked a woman's voice, 'to think about things'."

"I know Bonny had some issues about the gun-guy?"

"So did you, Jim." Jack shot back. "That was all bullshit."

"Okay, it was bullshit. But what got so bad Bonny asked you to leave?"

"Okay. Brad's suicide affected me. I took sick leave and, I admit it, I wasn't the very best company. I was tired a lot, didn't feel like talking. I'd snap at her if tried to make conversation. I didn't give a shit. About three weeks into it, she confronts me. Tells me my lying around and being pissy have gone on long enough. Like she's some depression referee.

So I tell her.

"Tell her?"

"You remember my brother killed himself?"

"I do. You were twins, early teens."

"I told her how it was me who'd killed him. How that guilt still haunts me and was the reason I was acting like I was."

Jim crossed his arms. "Uh-huh. You killed your bother? Should I call the cops? Or is this more of your dramatic BS?

"Well, I didn't actually *kill* him, but I could've stopped him and I didn't. And that's on me."

Jim forced a yawn. "I'm sorry, pal, but all I'm hearing with this 'confession' is more pain and misery for Jack. If it's not the world making him suffer, he's always got himself."

Jack gave a nasty laugh. "How curious. Bonny said something close to that."

"Right. Bonny? Why are you out of the house?"

"There was no sympathy or compassion. She didn't even rant about my keeping secrets from her because she didn't believe what I told her, bitch."

"Fancy that."

"That's when she said she wanted me to leave."

Jim put his hands together as though praying. "*Why*, Jack, did she want you out?"

"According to Bonny, after weeks of brooding, no matter what the goddamn reason, I should be coming around. And, listen to this, the reason I'm not is because I've something deeper bothering me inside that I won't admit to myself so it keeps on smoldering. Get this. That I *use* these suicides as an excuse to whine, brood, complain and stay depressed instead of facing my problem. Like I *enjoy* feeling this way? Jesus Christ. That I get some weird, fucking comfort avoiding this stupid-ass *deeper* issue? C'mon."

Jim smiled, leaned forward. "My dear Doctor Rackham, I've heard somewhere that a deep-seated fear can subconsciously affect a person's behavior." Jim stroked his chin. "That perhaps, just perhaps mind you, said person might play-up a less threatening yet worthy issue, maintaining it's the cause of his problem. And, by clinging to this problem, for fun, let's use 'guilt', he successfully avoids confronting his more profound issues? Then he really does find a weird *comfort* in his misery. Anyway, Bonny threw you out because?"

"So I could meditate on what my problem is and do something about it. And then we'd live happily ever after."

"And you've been homeless for two months?"

"Yeah, we met once for coffee. Watta waste."

"Oh?"

"She told me she was seeing a goddamn therapist."

"Mm-hmm. Wonder why."

"But you wanna know what really pissed me off?"

"No."

"She gave me a list of *her* demands how I should behave if we're to stay together."

"Jack. Stop. I don't care to hear them. I'd rather hear about your 'meditating'. If you've done any, that is."

"Oh yeah I have. And things *are* getting clearer for me."

"Yeah. I can sense how much more mellow you are."

***

"You know, Jim, I've been surprised how much I've actually enjoyed being away from work."

"Taking a little break from work? Who wouldn't enjoy it?"

"It's not that, Jim. I'm fucking fed-up with the Clinic. It's a dump. From the entry doors with their caked-on spit, the overflowing trash-cans, the urine-stained waiting-room furniture right down to the 56 flies on my windowsill and that goddamn squeaky chair nobody'll fix. And the University? They spend their money on transplants, cancer, research and don't give a shit about us. You know they're all afraid of psychiatry, the loonies. They're scared they might see themselves in some of the people.

Then there's our colleagues. Hester of the spirits, praise-Jesus Steele, macho-man Hernandez and our mirror, mirror on the wall boss, Reginald Kingston-Smith. Damn, how do you stand them?"

"Sure, Jack, the Clinic could do with better cleaning. And our coworkers? I agree. They do have their...eccentricities."

"Eccentricities? Jesus. How about *oddities*?"

"But somehow we get things done, don't we?"

"And that's another thing. The big one. I'm sick of psychiatry. I'm done with it"

"But I thought you loved it? Dealing with patients? The give and take? What the heck happened? It couldn't've been losing Brad."

"He was part of it. One more person I couldn't help."

"Jack, you know we really can't prevent a determined patient from killing themselves."

"Okay, but how many people do we really help to feel better, happier? You know, I think I became a psychiatrist because of my brother's suicide. I had this naive idea that I could help people from feeling so bad. Maybe I thought it'd somehow redeem me."

"Happens all the time. Kid's in the hospital, sees the staff helping people, decides to be a doctor."

"Yeah, but, with all the freakin emotions in me then, I think I pushed myself into it. It wasn't *my* choice, whatever that would've been. And now when I see how little I can really help, it's like, why do it? What's the sense?

Like I've this patient, Ken. I did help his OCD. Then his wife dies and his grieving begins. His feeling of loss is almost palpable. I've tried to help, but I can't take his pain away. He still comes in for his med and we chat. That's all I do."

"Jack, you can't *cure* a loss like that. I'd say your being there for him helps."

"Yeah, sure. And what about the patients who were mentally, physically, sexually abused? Told they were worthless, never wanted? Given no love, kindness, caring, security? They grow up and come to us to be fixed. We try, but know it's a futile fantasy that we can take away such deep hurting, erase the scars. The best we can do is to help them live with it. Dammit, that's not enough for me."

"Jack, I'm stunned. You really are this disillusioned with psychiatry?"

"Yeah. Bonny was right. I wasn't facing my deep discontent, feeling useless, empty, the constant frustration. Well, now it's over. "

"So what are you thinking?"

"Something without direct patient involvement. No more piece work."

"Like?"

"Administration maybe? Look at Smith, a pompous idiot with no organizational skills, but someone who's learned to play the game. I'd have people working for me, doing what I say and getting things done. No more futile fantasies."

"No suicides."

"Yeah, right. Faculty lunches."

"You'd still have responsibility."

"What? Protocols, procedures, heading meetings? Piece of cake. Or I can change specialties, really kiss-off psychiatry. There's anesthesia, pathology, radiology. Not much patient contact there. And they all have that sweet appeal where you do a task, complete it, have a sense of accomplishment."

"Yep. Accomplishment. Just makes you feel all goody-good inside. Anyway, good luck in your quest for fulfillment. Let me know what you decide."

"So you're not gonna support me?"

"Support your being more of a jerk? No. If you want to leave psychiatry, which I believe you love doing, because you're unfulfilled and disenchanted, go for it. But changing specialties? You're not gonna do all that training. And you're not gonna take kindly to people telling you what to do. And what about Bonny? It sounds like she's trying to do all the right things to keep you two together. But you? You sound like a two-year-old yelling, 'you can't make me'. You think she's just gonna say, 'all is forgiven' because you've seen the light? Jack, I don't know what you're trying to prove, but I think you're being a real ass about all of this."

"Well, thanks and fuck you too."

"Oh, and Jack, I thought your calling our treating patients, 'doing piece work' demeaning to me and my patients. Whatever you think, I help people."

"Sure, Jim. I'm so glad you can keep believing that." Jack moved closer to the table, put on a broad grin. "So, how's sweet Anne? Better yet, how are *you* and sweet Anne?"

Jim grinned back. "Thanks for asking. I'm divorcing her."

Jack's eyes widened. "Un-fucking-believable. So you finally did it? Damn. I thought I noticed something. Yeah, not so hesitant. More confident? When did this happen?"

"About ten-days ago."

"How? Why? I mean I knew things weren't good between you. But I always saw ole Jim just plodding along...*enduring and suffering*."

"Takes one to know one, huh, Jack?"

"What happened to get your ass moving?"

"Let's just say something occurred that gave me a good kick in the butt and leave it at that."

"C'mon, Jim, what happened? It must've been really something."

"I finally admitted to myself that we'd hit a brick-wall that was never coming down. That our lives, *my* life was going nowhere. So I decided our divorcing would be the best thing to do. Then we, no, *I* could start living again."

"Curious, isn't it? I've that same 'brick-wall' feeling with Bonny."

Jim sighed. "I don't know about that, Jack. I think there's still a lot of room for compromise with you two. I believe whatever Bonny's doing, even asking you to leave, it's to keep you together. But, in the end, it does come down to do you want to be with Bonny or not? I realized I didn't want to be with Anne. And that that was okay."

"Yeah, well stay tuned about that."

Jim smiled. "I've assumed you haven't mentioned any of your exciting, new ideas to Bonny?"

Jack shrugged. "Why? So she can make fun of me like you did. We'll talk when *I'm* in the mood to talk."

"Right. When's that? When you finally emerge from whatever stupid hole your minds in?"

Half-listening to Jim, Jack turned to glare at the guys at the next table. "Could you guys keep the goddamn noise down? We're having a conversation here."

The guy nearest to Jack said, "This is a bar, jerk-off. It's *supposed* to be noisy. Leave if you don't like it." And went back to his friends.

Didja see that, Jim? Now some dickhead bar-fly's giving me shit. Jesus. Hey, have you moved out yet?"

"Why? If anybody's leaving, it'll be Anne. Right now, we're co-existing in the house, just like before." He shook his head. "except now I'm not trying."

"What's Anne done about the divorce?"

"Like I figured. She called her family and they found a lawyer for her. One brother flew down two days ago. I'm assuming they met with the attorney yesterday. He's coming over today to help her pack. That's why I wanted to get out of the house. She hates it here so much, I'd guess she'll be gone quickly."

"And here you are, soon-to-be bachelor Jim getting his car all spiffed up, strolling the docks looking to buy a boat. Damn. A free man. You know, maybe I should file for divorce? That'd frost Bonny's cookies. Make her come to her senses."

Jim stared at him. "Jack, how do you do it?"

"Do what, my liberated friend?"

"Go from playing the pitiful wretch to thinking you're a master of the universe so seamlessly?"

"Hmm. I dunno." He winked at Jim. "Maybe it's a gift I have, like my being so witty. I'll meditate on that and let you know, okay?"

"Jim shook his head. My Uncle Joe'd say, 'It's better to let people think you're stupid than to open your mouth and prove it'."

"Jim, screw you, screw your Uncle Joe… and screw Queen Bonny."

"Ops, sorry, Jack. I was in the middle of a yawn. Did you say something? Look, it has been good to see you, but I do have some things I want to get done. I'm gonna walk the docks, see what boats are for sale. Check-out the store that carries the Hawaiian shirts I like. There's a camera I want to look at since I'm doing more photography. Then, after I wash my car, I'll find a nice place to eat." He got up to leave. "Like I said, it's been good to see you and catch up." Jim went over and patted him on the back. "Jack, and I really mean this. Work on yourself, please? God knows it took me a while. But I feel so much better coming clean."

Jack watched him leave and scoffed. The bastard makes one big decision and now he's the fucking wise man on the mountain-top?

Jack grabbed his beer, looked at the guys next to him and moved his chair over. "Hey guys. Sorry if I sounded pissy earlier. My friend was being a dick. Hey. What game's on?"

THIRTY
Mirror, Mirror On The Wall
Where Dr.Kingston-Smith Earns His Hyphen
<u>*Identity*</u>: *The Sum Of One's Thoughts, Feelings And Actions; Self-*
Awareness Not Included

Hester Snopes stood at Martha's desk pulling at her astrology ring that had snagged on her macrame vest. Martha looked up. "Hello, dear. Can I help you with whatever it is you're doing?"

Hester ripped the ring free, stuffed the torn yarn back into the vest. "Got it. Thanks though."

Hester continued standing, looking at the secretary. "How do you do it?"

Martha raised her eyebrows, "Do what, dear?"

"Stay pleasant? You never seem flustered about anything."

"What would I be flustered about, dear?"

"This place. The people? The staff? Don't they get on your nerves? Dr. Smith? He seems to need a lot of tending to."

"I just take one thing, or person, at a time, dear, and do whatever I can."

"You don't find the people running in and out of here wanting something a pain in the ass?"

"Why no. People are all so very interesting, don't you think? Oh my, how silly I am telling a trained therapist about people, bless your heart."

"*Mademoiselles, s'il vous plaît?*"

Chin raised, Dr. Kingston-Smith stood in his office doorway. Hester couldn't tell if the little shit had to do it to look up at her or to strike a superior pose, probably both. Those high-heeled cowboy boots peeking-out from his gray slacks really didn't help his being short.

"Martha, hold my calls and take messages while I'm in conference with Ms. Snopes. However, if one certain administrator calls."

"I'll immediately put him through, Doctor. That's the crucial call about when and where for luncheon?"

"*Exactement.* And Martha? Some nefarious villain has parked in *my* designated spot with *my* name on it. Call the campus police and see what they can do about apprehending this malefactor."

Martha smiled, "I'll do it immediately, Doctor."

He looked at Hester. "Please come in, Ms. Snopes." Then turned to settle-in behind expansive desk. Smith pointed with his *Mont Blanc* to the leather chairs in front of his desk. "Ms. Snopes, take one please."

As she sat, Hester felt one of her sandal straps tear, the sandal falling free. She started sandal-squirming trying to get her big-toe back in while not pushing it farther away, but stopped to look attentive. She'd get it back on once they'd finished with whatever was bugging him.

Smith had opened a blue folder and spread several papers across his desk. In time, he looked up. "*Merci* for meeting with me, Ms. Snopes. I presume you know what this is about?"

"Nope. When Martha called, she said it was a 'clinical matter' and left it at that."

"I see. Might you speculate on why we're meeting?"

"Dr. Smith, we got a lot of complainers around here, patients and staff. I'd guess one of them started whining about me and you wanted to give me a heads-up."

Smith looked at his watch and sighed. "*Hélas,* I shall explain. You see this array of papers before me?"

"Yeah?"

"These pages goes beyond idle grumblings and whining." He looked down and began scanning, twisting his mustache as he read. After a few minutes, Smith peered up at Hester.

"Yes, these grievances primarily focus on your therapy style."

"Well, ain't that a hoot. Since my therapy style is, *giving my all,* who'd complain about that?"

Smith reviewed more, then stared at her. "There are references here to the use of Tarot Cards? Spiritualism? Seances? Is this true? Attempts to contact the dead? These absurdities, in *my* Clinic?"

"Yeah, but...."

"Do not talk, Ms. Snopes. I'm not done. I've noted that more than one couple have questioned your spending much of the therapeutic-hour talking about yourself, not them." He found one page. "Yes, here it is. One couple described appointments with you as, 'Snopes Sessions of Self-Admiration'."

Hester sat, mouth closed.

"Ms. Snopes, comments?"

"Oh. I've permission to speak now?"

Smith smiled, nodded. *"Oui, s'il vous plaît."*

"Since my main goal is to have my clients open up to me, I've developed an eclectic, therapeutic approach. Basically, I look for what works to get then talking. Like, I had this emotionally constricted client and I thought, what the hell, maybe the Tarot Cards might help get him talking. I had a client grieving over losing her husband. Why not try contacting his spirit to help resolve things, bring her some peace? Dr. Smith, I am an innovator in my field. I care. How could anyone condemn me for that?"

Smith wagged his finger. "My dear Ms. Snopes, although I laud your good intentions, I must insist that they do *not* preclude good judgment. Your 'innovative' techniques are not recognized forms of therapy. Perhaps they'd have appeal at a carnival side-show, but they have no place in *my* Clinic. For me to think you were naïve in this regard greatly strains my credulity. And what about these accusations of 'self-absorption 'averred by several couples."

"Can I explain? "

"Assurément, Ms. Snopes. *Expliquez."*

Hester took in a deep breath. "Dr. Smith, to help and guide my clients, I draw on my vast life experiences. I describe past challenges in my life, how I faced and solved them. Acting as a role model, I direct my clients in what they should do to live life as successfully as me. I call it my, 'Positive Attitude Therapy'."

"Hmm. So rather than help your clients learn what drives their behavior so they can change it for the better, you simply tell them what to do? Is that a fair statement?"

"Yes, but Dr. Smith, these are dependent, needy people. I'm giving them what they need, direction. That's what I do. I direct them how to live."

"Mm-hmm. Thus, in order to give these desperate, needy people the direction they direly need, talking about yourself is *essential?"*

If only she had that sandal. "Dr. Smith, I find your remarks...."

He raised his hand. "Ms. Snopes, notwithstanding your imaginative explanations, the tenor and intensity of the complaints before me have raised grave concerns about your clinical judgment in our therapeutic setting."

"Sorry to hear that," Hester scoffed, "But...."

"Your being sorry has no importance here. My Clinic and its reputation does. Now, if you could kindly stop twisting in your chair, here is what I propose. You will return to the classic, proven methods of therapy you learned to become certified. You will cease all of your 'innovative' treatment approaches."

"But...."

"They will *cease*. Understand?"

Hester's mouth tightened. But then she smiled. "Yes, Doctor, *completely*." She stretched for the sandal. "Is that all?"

"No." Smith cleared his throat. "Henceforth, I am placing you under the supervision of one of our senior psychiatrists. You will meet with him regularly to review your charts and discuss your proposed treatment strategies."

"And this senior psychiatrist is?"

"Dr. Rackham."

"Dr. Rackham? Are you...?" Hester stopped.

"Ms. Snopes? A comment?"

"No. Except, why Rackham?"

"I believe that's my concern. You will speak with him about your supervision sessions. You may leave now. Thank you."

"No, thank *you*, Dr. Smith." Hester gripped the arms of the chair to push her bulk up and out. Watching her leave, Smith wondered why she was limping. And carrying a sandal? Eh, *ça ne fait rien*. He swiveled to his mirror and nodded. He'd done commandingly well with Ms. Snopes.

***

"The yacht club's my favorite place to lunch. More relaxing than the University's executive dining room. Don't you agree, Reginald?"

Smith was taking in the dining room. "*Certainement*, Vice-Chancellor. Although this is my first time here, I definitely concur."

"I see you're admiring the pennants on the wall. They represent each club belonging to the Florida Council of Yacht Clubs. They lend an aura of elegance and charm. Don't you agree?"

Smith was watching a motor-yacht tie-up at the Club's dock. "I was thinking the exact same thing. Are you a boater, Vice-Chancellor?""Indeed. My wife, Baxley, and I just did the 'small loop' from here across Florida through the Caloosahatchee River locks, across Lake Okeechobee to the East coast. Then, down to Key West returning up our west coast. Seeing Miami from the water at night is truly majestic."

"It sounds sublime. I've longed to get into boating."

"Let me know when, Reginald. I'd be glad to help you find something. We're still on for this Saturday?"

"Yes, Vice-Chancellor. I'm looking forward to playing that course. You've filled out the foursome?"

"Indeed. The Dean of Student Affairs and the Provost will be joining us."

"Excellent," Smith said, buttering his roll.

"Reginald, before lunch arrives, I'd like to review a few University business items with you. Shouldn't take too long."

"*Bien sûr.*"

"In reviewing the minutes of the department heads meeting, I read about your recent, *multiple* personnel issues. Your mental health clinic is a valuable resource to the University and the local population. How're things going?"

" I've kept my Clinic on," Smith looked at the room's pennants, "a very steady course."

The Vice-Chancellor nodded

"It's been a trying time. But the dedicated and loyal group of professionals I lead have rallied to maintain my Clinic's quality of care."

"I'd expect nothing less. What's your personnel status presently?"

"We lost Dr. Maximo Hernandez, someone I'd had my eye on. The DEA was investigating him for writing narcotics and amphetamine prescriptions for people off the street.'""

"Yes, go on."

Smith was buttering another roll. "Additionally, Dr. Hernandez faced allegations ranging from rape to inappropriate sexual behavior with a variety of females. I'd previously confronted him about these issues."

"What did the Doctor say?"

"Things, I'm certain, you've encountered in your vast academic experience. He denied, prevaricated and feigned ignorance of any wrongdoing. However, after the DEA agents, who were extremely professional I might add, presented him with the evidence against him, he admitted to his actions."

"You said you'd been suspicious and had had discussions with him?"

Smith gave a serious nod. "I questioned him rigorously about his using discretion in his sexual activities."

The Vice-chancellor eyebrows narrowed. "What defense did he offer about his inappropriate prescription writing?"

Smith choked. "Sorry. A bit of roll down the wrong tube. I did not have the opportunity to interrogate him in that regard. Information about that did not reach my office until the DEA agents arrived."

"Hmm. And the sexual matters?"

"In his mind, everything was consensual and he, blameless. He was 'helping' women with their loneliness. As he termed it, 'spreading the love'. He labelled the female drug rep who'd filed rape charges a, 'spurned woman taking jealous revenge'."

"And the University women who filed complaints of sexual harassment and stalking? One works in my office."

" Man-hating, butch lesbians or naïve women who simply misinterpreted his innocent wish to socialize."

"This man is a scurrilous sexual predator. Don't you agree?"

" And calculating. He kept numerous letters that he enticed women to write professing their love and anticipation of their next tryst as proof that any sex was consensual. He said that he'd drop any woman who wouldn't write such a letter."

"Reginald, I presume you've reached closure on these sexual issues?"

Smith smiled broadly. "Indeed I have, on both of them. The drug-rep dropped her charges. I suspect her pharma-company pressured her fearing alienating the University and my Clinic. They didn't want to risk any profit loss if we decreased utilization of their product. Incidentally, they transferred the rep."

"I understand. One must make choices in business."

Smith drank some water, patted his lips with his napkin. "And the other University women? Once HR showed them their lascivious *billet-doux* to the Doctor, the matter quickly disappeared."

"Then that matter'll be kept in-house? Nothing adverse about the University will reach the public? The papers?"

Smith shook his head. "Absolutely not. *I* pressed HR to have the women sign non-disclosure agreements."

"For the good of the University. Brilliant, Reginald."

"I try, sir."

"And Dr. Hernandez?"

"After the DEA left, I outlined for him my plan for his probation. He vigorously rejected it as some sort of assault on his manhood and left my office in a fury. By day's end, he'd packed-up his office, save for those love letters, left his resignation with Martha and exited the Clinic."

"And his patients?"

"Having foreseen that possibility, I'd already designed a contingency plan which I implemented immediately. No patient went without. I am currently interviewing worthy applicants to fill his position."

"And the DEA?"

"They've prohibited Dr. Hernandez, from writing Schedule II prescriptions, opiates and amphetamines, for two years. Instead of being incarcerated, he's currently doing community service somewhere in the middle of the State. I suspect that was a result of some 'family connections' ."

"Can I conclude that we are free of the DEA at this point? That they've no further interest, perhaps, in how the Clinic didn't catch on to him?"

Smith cleared his throat. "None in the least, sir."

"Excellent, Reginald. And your other staff members?"

"Dr. Felicity Steele is currently taking a leave of absence. Apparently, some complicated family matters arose to which she had to attend. We expect her back soon."

"And?"

"Hester Snopes, one of our most creative counselors, will be receiving supervision by one of our senior psychiatrists. I believe this area of Florida has not attained the psychological sophistication to appreciate her imaginative style of therapy. The supervision is to ground her a tad."

"Besides Dr. Steele, you had one other psychiatrist out?"

"That'd be Dr. Rackham. He's now back full-time. He'll be supervising Ms. Snopes.

He has a good, critical eye and is well-grounded psychiatrically. Poor chap. One of his patients committed suicide and he took it hard. He needed some time to rekindle his spirits. He knows that I'm there for him anytime. My other two psychiatrists, Drs. Bizby and Cobb appear to be thriving. Despite increased Clinic demands, both seem to have a new energy and optimism about them."

After lunch, the Vice-Chancellor stood and came around the table to shake Smith's hand. "Reginald, I was a little apprehensive reading about the number of personnel-related occurrences at your Clinic. However, after hearing your description of what occurred and your timely control of things, I'm greatly reassured as to your organizational abilities."

Smith gave a little bow. "Thank you, sir. I do my best."

The Vice-Chancellor was about to turn, but Smith held on to his hand. "Might we huddle again to ideate further on some ideas I have?"

Unlocking from Smith, the Vice-Chancellor turned towards the exit. "I'll see you Saturday at the Club?"

"*Bien entendu.*"

"I'm sorry?"

"Of course, Vice-Chancellor. I'm looking forward to it."

***

Hester sat in her office reviewing her Tarot cards making sure she remembered their meanings. She'd closed the blinds and dimmed the lights with only the soft sound of her small mist-generating fountain in the background. Today's mist had a hint of the eucalyptus oil to calm her after meeting with Smith.

Just back from a weekend seminar on *Tarot Cards And Life* in Cassadaga, she was set to try out what she'd learned. Next weekend, she'd be back there for *Understanding Spirits Through Mediumship*.

She drew an angel, the 'Judgement' card. That meant a time of resurrection and awakening when one period of life ends making way for a new beginning. Then, the 'Star' card, a woman with a star shining above her signifying renewal, purpose and hope in life. Hester stopped and thought of Felicity. These cards should be for Felicity. After she'd abruptly left town, Hester had texted, but got no reply. Whatever's going on with her, Hester hoped it was a new beginning and new hope in her life. And less of that,'Praise Jesus' crap.

After shuffling the cards and putting them nearby, she went out to meet the new couple waiting for her. Hester wouldn't start right off with the cards. She'd slowly introduce them into their sessions, that this is how she got to know people. Then she'd smile and say, "Trust me."

THIRTY-ONE

There's Small Change. There's Loose Change. And Sometimes
There's No Change
Where The Sun Goes On Rising Every Morning And Setting At Night
Personality Disorder: An Unhealthy Pattern Of Thinking And
Behaving Which Only Satisfies The Person's Emotional Needs;
People Who Play By Different Rules

"Fancy, *mi amiga*, so good to hear your voice again."

Fancy paused. "Ah, Dr. Hernandez, what a surprise. After you left without an *adios* to anyone, we all thought you'd disappeared forever. I hope you are well."

"*Excellent, gracias.* Please forgive me for leaving so quickly. Things happened that required it. They prevented me from thanking you for all your wonderful help.""Uh-huh. And I'm guessing you're calling today for more help?"

"Only to hear your voice would've been enough. But, I want to be certain the Clinic has my correct address to forward me any important mail."

"Okay. Anything specific?"

"Perhaps some things from the government. I've been corresponding with them about employment."

"Should I look for any particular government agency, Dr. H.?"

"No, just anything that looks official. Thank you. I've taken a modest job at a community clinic deprived of psychiatric services here in the Central Florida farmlands. I felt a desire to give even more of myself to people in need of my care. The work here fulfills me."

"That's nice."

"Although I love the work, I may not be here too much longer."

"Can I get that address from you?"

"My father and I have been talking a lot about the future."

Fancy put him on speaker and started other work.

"He believes I'd do better using my excellent people skills working with him in Miami where he has a well-established financial investment business. After we iron out a few things, I'll be leaving here to have more time with my wife and children."

263

"So, no work for the government? Will you still practice medicine?"

"Ah, if I go into my father's business, I must leave medicine behind. That makes me very sad."

"I understand. But I'm sure working for your father will still allow to practice your skills. Can I get that address, Doctor? Even though you may be leaving."

That done along with reassurances how much the Clinic missed him, Fancy hung up. Remembering her lemonade in the staff-fridge, she put her, 'I'm Not Here' sign on her desk and headed to the kitchen.

"Hey, Fancy, who's minding the store?" Hester said seeing Fancy come in.

"Why, I am. My pleasant, recorded voice says, 'Please press 'one' and leave your message'. Ms. Hester, how're you doing?"

Hester put a teabag in her cup and poured in boiling water as Fancy got her lemonade. When she turned to Fancy, her dream-catcher earrings caught in her hair. But with a practiced shake of her head, she untangled them.

They sat down at the table. "I'm doing pretty well, Fancy. I just finished with one of my, 'let them rant' couples and really need a cup of my echinacea herbal to rouse me from my stupor."

"'Let them rant'? What's that about?"

"I've seen this twosome forever. And they never change. As soon as they sit down, one starts bitching. Then the other one gets going. I let them rant for about ten minutes. Since it's the same stuff each session, I stopped listening a while ago. I think about what I'm making for dinner. Do I need to stop at the grocery store? What I doing the weekend? At ten minutes, I interrupt and say something about how working together might be better for their relationship than blaming. They nod, sit quietly for a few seconds and then restart insulting each other until the session's over. I think arguing's the only thing that holds them together. They're too afraid to be alone if they divorced."

"Have you used the Tarot Cards with them?"

Hester looked to her left and right, whispered, "You can't tell anyone because Smith told me to stop using them. But I am, but not with this couple. It'd be work. You've heard Smith got some stupid complaints about me? Well, because of them, Dr. Rackham's supposed to 'supervise' me. What BS."

"Dr. Jack's already asked me to try and coordinate your schedules so you might meet."

"Crap. I was hoping he'd have forgotten about it. Rackham'll just make sarcastic comments and call it supervision."

"Hester, I've got my lemonade and need to get back to my desk."

"Fancy, do you know when Dr. Steele's coming back? *Is* she coming back?"

"I know you two were sorta' friends, so I will tell you that she left a message asking me to have her leave extended another week. I guess those family issues are taking up more time than she thought. You know, she never calls when we can talk. She always leaves a message after hours."

Hester blew on her tea. "I finally got a text. She was going to stay in her hometown area, but then thought it best to return here. She said she was making some arrangements."

"Arrangements? I thought she was settled-in here?"

"Apparently, she's bringing her...sister to live with her. Something about getting her out of their small town. Letting her see more of the world. The arrangements probably have to do with her."

"Well, that'll be nice, having some family here instead of far away."

" I agree. Fancy? Did I overhear you talking with Dr. Hernandez?"

"Yes I was."

Hester looked up. She'd been digging in her bag for some honey for her tea. "Hah. I thought he'd left this place long behind?"

"He called to give me his new address. He said he was practicing in Central Florida, you know, farms, dust and heat country. Providing service to a needy community, giving back."

"Uh-huh. *I* heard he was doing community service as part of a plea bargain with the DEA."

"Oh, I can't comment on that," Fancy said. "But I think everybody knew about his writing narcotics prescriptions."

"I remember passing a few of his customers in the hallway. They looked a little scary." Hester sipped her tea.

"Dr. H. told me that his father wants him to come to Miami and join his investment firm. Use his, 'excellent people skills'."Hester nodded. " I bet his ole man's one sharp-cookie getting his son to join him, do some fast-talking and make him more money. Hernandez always had a talent for 'selling'. I'd bet Dad also wants him closer to home so he can keep an eye on him."

"Hester, if Dr. H. moves to Miami, won't he be breaking his community service stipulation? Risk losing his license?"

"I think so."

Fancy laughed. "He told me this morning that he'd be leaving medicine because he couldn't do both jobs and how very sad he was."

Hester shook her head. "I think medicine was more a hobby for him. Now, he'll have something where he can smile, rip-off people even more and it's all legal."

"Hester, do you think his living home will bring him closer to his wife and kids?""Nah." Hester grinned. "There'll be too many beautiful women around."

***

Back at her computer, Fancy looked up. "Good morning, Dr. Jack. It's good to see that you're back into your normal routine again."

"Good morning back atcha. Fancy. Great day, isn't it?" Jack sang, "Summertime, and the livin is sweaty. Fish are jumpin and the humidity's high."

"Your different look, Dr. Jack. The shorter hair-cut, your retro-style blue and black shirt"

"Yeah.?"

"Looks good."

Jack bowed. "Thank you, Ms. Fancy. I'm working on a new look, both outside and in. That inside part's taking a little longer, but I'm hopeful." After going over to the medical chart table and scanning his schedule, Jack looked at his watch and picked up his charts. "Fancy, I see I've still a few minutes to get a coffee and prepare myself for stamping out mental illness. Please excuse me."

"Dr. Jack, you back to your old *zip-a-dee-doo-dah* self?"

Jack stood and thought for a minute. "Fancy, I do want to get that *zip-a-dee-doo-dah* feeling, but, you know, I don't want my 'old self', well, maybe a little bit of it, back. Like this morning…I'm sorry, do you have two minutes?"

"I'm okay, Doc."

"Like this morning, the humidity. I knew my shirt'd be sticking to my back by the time I got here. So, instead of getting irritated because, Geez, it happens everyday in the summer, I told myself to turn up the AC and hope for the best. My shirt still clung to me, but that's okay cause it'll dry. Then, instead of tail-gating one of those old slow-driving geezers, I slowed down and took in the beautiful day. You know, by not rushing, I saw two new coffee places and a bakery where I might get a decent bagel. You see? I want to be my old self, but *not* my old self. Never mind. I'm not clear on that yet. Sorry for taking up your time." As Jack turned, he said, "Thanks for having the charts and my schedule ready. See ya' later."

Fancy tilted her head and raised her eyebrows as she watched him walk away.

Jack put his charts down on his desk, took a tube of lubricant from his pocket. Turning his chair upside down, he placed it on the desk top and put some soft, greasy paste on anything he thought might rub when he sat. He put the cap back on the tube, put it back in his pocket, turned the chair over and sat down. He leaned back, right, left, spun around. He smiled. Hot-damn, the squeak's gone. Man conquers squeaky chair.

As he headed for the staff kitchen, he met Gus Cobb.

"Morning, Gus. You seem to be moving kinda fast this morning."

"Good morning to you, Jack. I've got a lot to do before the day is done. And I know it's going to drag for me."

"What's up, Gus?"

For a few seconds, Gus looked down. When his face came back to Jack's, he had a wide grin. "Okay, now don't laugh, but I've a date tonight. Imagine, someone's willing to go out with this old fart?"

"That's fabulous," Jack put his hand on Gus's shoulder. "I'm really happy for you. Hope you have a great time."

"Thanks, Jack. You know, I talk to people all the time, but I'm already getting the jitters about making conversation."

"I have no doubt all will go well."

"And I owe it all to you, Jack, and your sour-puss personality."

Before Jack could respond, Gus turned and rushed away.

Pouring himself some coffee, he saw Hester cornering one of the secretaries telling her how she'd found her psychedelic tie-dyed dress at a yard sale put on by two aging hippies.

Jack looked at the boiling tea-kettle. "Hester, is this your water? Can I bring it over and warm-up your tea?" The secretary escaped.

Hester looked at Jack, took a bite of her carrot, crunched opened-mouthed, swallowed, crunched some more, swallowed. She lifted her cup to Jack. "Yes, that'd be nice."

Jack poured the water and sat down. "Hester, how's your day going so far?"

"The usual."

"That's nice." Jack sipped his coffee. "I'm not disturbing you, am I?"

Hester smirked. "Not yet."

Jack nodded, gave her a small smile. "I deserve that. Hester, I'd like to make things better between us. Especially since we've this 'thing' Smith's ordered us to do. I was hoping he might've forgotten about it, but he asked me how things were going yesterday."

"What'd you tell him?"

"Oh, I told him we're scheduled to meet. We need to do that by the way."

"Well, since you've already told him a lie, why not just continue? Tell him we're meeting and discussing things."

"I wish I could, but apparently these complaints have rankled some higher-ups."

Hester rolled her eyes. "I'm just a plain therapist. I wouldn't know about, *higher-ups,*"

Jack took a breath. "Well, someone above Smith learned about these complaints and is on Smith's butt for progress reports. So Smith, with his paranoia about his reputation, is on my mine. Hence, we *do* have to meet. Smith wasn't altogether clear. Something about your returning to a more ,'traditional' style of therapy?"

"If that's what he said."

"We're supposed to go over some of your clients and your treatment strategies for them? I'm to review some random charts? Is that your understanding too?"

"If that's what he said."

"Hester, I know you'd prefer that this not happen."

"Very perceptive, Doctor."

Jack nodded. "Me, too. But, since we're stuck with each other and have to meet, can we make the best of it?"

"If you say so."

"How's this? I'll talk with Fancy to schedule our meeting once a week. I'll review some of your charts and we can talk?"

"Uh-huh. What about?"

"Well, I'd like to hear more about the Tarot Cards. There's a psychological test...."

"I know, the Borchaulk."

"The Rorschach Test. Yes. But I was thinking of the TAT, the Thematic Apperception Test. The tester shows the person a card with something happening on it. Like, one has a woman staring out of a window into a field. Another has a man and a woman holding each other, but the man is turning away from her. The tester asks the person to tell a story about what they think is happening in the picture."

"Like what I do?"

Jack searched for the right words. "Yes, but..."

"But what? That's exactly what I do, uh, did, with the tarot cards."

"Yes, you did. But I'm wondering, from what little you told me, if you were a little too quick in giving *your* interpretation rather than give the person time to respond. Am I wrong about that?"

"At first I waited, let them talk about what they saw in the card. Since the cards are pretty dramatic, I expected the clients to get right into it and share things. But, no. They'd say stupid things like 'That's scary' or 'She's so beautiful' and miss my whole point. So, when I kept hearing that crap, I went ahead and did my interpretation of the card for them. See if they'd bite onto that."

Jack sipped his coffee and nodded. "I know you really want to get in there with the patient."

"I do. With the *client*. Something wrong with that?"

"Nothing, Hester, nothing. Your enthusiasm is great."

"But? You're going to make some sarcastic remark, aren't you?"

"No, Hester. I want us to work together. But, in getting your clients to talk, you might consider asking why they see the card as scary or why the the woman beautiful. See if you can draw them out that way."

"Why? I told you, they'll just make stupid remarks."

"Okay, just a suggestion."

"Besides, I need to direct them down the right path," Hester scoffed.

Jack thought, that's you, Hester. *Your* goddamn needs. *Your* goddamn direction. He raised his hand in mock surrender. "I agree, Hester. We need to guide our people. But, might it not be better to show them there are many directions and then let *them* chose which one is right for them? I know you've the best interests of your clients at heart."

Hester sat facing Jack in silence. She sipped some tea and wiped her mouth with her hand. "I still don't see why we have to do this. I know all this stuff."

"Hester, like it or not, we have to meet. Maybe we can make a case for your using the Tarot cards, but…."

"But what?" Hester hissed.

"But, dammit, contacting spirits, telling fortunes with the cards? I have to tell you that's just bullshit in a University-run mental health clinic." Jack took a breath to slow himself down.

"Look, Hester, here's the deal. Like I said, I'll have Fancy arrange a time so we can meet weekly. And we'll go from there. And, Hester, I'll expect you to show up."

"Or?"

Jack sighed. "Let's not go there. Please, let's just get this done, okay?"

Hester Snopes pushed her chair out. Grunting, she bent over and put her box of tea and honey into her bag. She grabbed the bag's handles, checked that her flowing dress hadn't caught on anything and pushed herself up. She glared down at Jack, "Dr. Rackham. I can't wait to hear more of your wise and expert suggestions." She turned leaving her stained cup, a crumpled paper towel and a used teabag for someone else to clean up although ants had already started on the spilled honey.

***

He walked down the hallway. Jack, let it go, just let it go. You can't expect Hester to be your best friend after all the BS you've given her in the past. Deal with her one step at a time. This isn't about you. He stopped. A voice was pulling him from his thoughts.

"Well, well, Dr. Rackham, it's good to see you've emerged from your wandering and rejoined our dedicated band, rooting-out mental afflictions wherever we find them."

Jack turned and saw a grinning Jim Bizby and covered his eyes. "Jim, my sight may be ruined. That's one of the gaudiest Hawaiian shirts I've ever seen. Actually, it's so ugly, it's almost, and I say, almost, beautiful." Jack gave Jim a hug. "It's good to see you, man."

"Jack, even though it's only you and me in a hallway, you've just fulfilled one of my life's dreams, being the center of attention. Thank you, thank you. And it's good to see you too."

"Jim, that shirt's certainly going to make you the center of something."

"You're right. I have gotten a lotta, well, comments today. I bought it at that shop near *The Lusty Pelican* after our last get-together. When I walked into the store and saw it, it was love at first sight."

"Does it glow in the dark?" Jim pointed proudly, "Look closely. You'll see it has *everything* on it. Palm trees. Hula girls with leis tastefully hiding their breasts. And, here's the seaplane landing in the lagoon, the smoking volcano in the background. They're outriggers, some fish and a parrot, all on a background of deep blue. I'd never tuck-in a shirt like this. I'd be hiding so much of its rich pattern from the world."

Jim poured some coffee and sat down. They both were still smiling.

"Jack, how *are* you? In our last episode, you looked like crap. I say that only because you look so much better."

"Thanks. Jim, I feel better. Hey, when will you be wearing sandals and shorts to work?"

Jim shook his head. "Alas, my friend, Smith's official dress-code memo, hidden among the myriad memoranda on the bulletin board, strictly forbids sandals and shorts."

"Okay, why don't we form a committee of two to get that changed?"

"Excellent idea. I'll have my people contact yours. You know what else it forbids?"

"String-bikinis?"

"No. We're forbidden to wear a tuxedo to work. We don't want others to feel inferior, do we?"

"Who'd have thought to put that on the list?"

"Undoubtedly, a fellow who never had a date for the prom."

They stirred their coffees, quiet.

"Really, Jack, how are you doing? I felt bad the way we parted company last time. I was going to call you, but then thought it better that you work things out on your own."

"Today, I'm...I'm 'cautiously optimistic' about where I'm at. I think I've made some 'therapeutic discoveries'. Nah, that's too clinical. What's happened is I've faced some things, *real* things, not the BS I was spouting at the bar, that I've avoided for a long time. But right now I'm a work in process. Stay tuned for further updates. Maybe, if you dare, over a beer?" Jack winked, "In the shade of course."

Jim closed his eyes, moved his head back and forth. "I see two rugged guys just back from safari. Elephant rifles beside them, they're sitting at a table, beer foam on their upper lips. They're smiling through the foam. Exotic native-girls dancing girls in the background, wild animals about." Jim opened his eyes. "Yes, I'd fancy a beer with you."

Jim's face turned to concern. "How are things with you and Bonny?"

Jack shook his head and breathed out heavily. "I'm still 'motel Jack'. Bonny and I haven't talked. And that's my fault because she'd left it to me to call when I was ready. Honestly, Jim, I've been afraid to do it. What she might say. I was pretty pissy to her the last time we met.

However, ta-da, in a brief moment of lucidity, I did call her. And, she agreed to meet me. Tonight, in fact. We're going to have a cup of coffee and talk. At least, I'm going to talk. I've a lot I need to tell her, if she'll let me. I'm trying to be optimistic, but I know I've been a real shit to her, to you, to most people around me."

"Jack, just that Bonny's willing to meet with you sounds hopeful. I'm sure all will go well." Jim patted Jack on the back. "Look, I've gotta get going. Fancy squeezed in one of my patients who's having severe panic attacks."

"Jim, before you go, what's happened with you and Anne? I've been concerned how you've been handling all of that. The divorce's still going forward?"

"Oh yes, the divorce is surging ahead moving at tsunami speed. You know, I obsessed about how guilty I was going to feel about it. But right now my divorce decision ranks as one of the best choices I've ever made."

"Along with buying that outrageous shirt?"

"That's second. Thanks for your concern."

"I'm glad you're doing so well."

"You know, it surprised me how quickly Anne was out of the house. As I expected, one of her brothers flew down, got them both motel rooms in town." Jim smiled, " Not where you're staying though. Anne packed an overnight bag and left, left without a word. They waited until I wasn't around, that Saturday when we met, to pack items she'd take on the plane and boxed-up things she'd ship. They must've met with a lawyer because a few nights after she left, I come home and see an empty wine bottle on the kitchen counter. Under it, there's a note. A freakin' typed-note telling me not to touch the boxes she'd packed and that she'd arrange their shipping. She gave me her lawyer's name and number and said I should expect to be served, even though I wanted the divorce. The legal papers would have her demands. It was amazing. For months, Anne sat doing nothing. Then, whoosh, she's gone. And that was that. Jack, she didn't even sign the note."

"Pissy to you right to the end, huh? But, really, you're doing okay?"

Jim laughed. "Sometimes I'll feel guilty about *not* feeling guilty. Funny, huh? But, yes. I'm not only feeling good, I'm feeling extraordinary."

"Well fancy that. Good guys can be assertive and still be good guys."

"Hey, I've joined a camera club and enrolled in an adult-ed photography course here on campus. And, hold on to your pants, I bought some bib-overalls."

"Holy hayseed, what's next for this boy? A John Deere hat?"

"Maybe, cause I have my eye on this John Deere tractor. Perhaps they'll throw the hat in to sweeten the deal. I'm getting rid of the weeds in that plot I dug up for Anne. I'm gonna plant a garden with some vegetables and a lot, a *lot* of flowers. I want to see a mass of colors when I leave in the morning and come home at night.""And that boat?"

"Who knows? I'm thinking about one of these flats boats with a low draft. I could get in close to shore, take pictures of birds and stuff. Take some pictures of people fishing. I want more life, more people in my photos."

Jack gave his friend another hug. "Jim, I'm delighted how things've turned out. Look, I know you need to go. Let's get together soon."

Jim grinned, "Count on it," as Jack saw a blur of color rush down the hallway.

***

Jack scanned the waiting room. The plants were still dusty. The chairs still stained. The fluorescents were still sending out their blue-white, surreal hue onto everything. It is what it is. He laughed to himself. And it does have a certain 'one-of-a-kind' quality to it.

He turned to Fancy looking intently into her computer screen. Its dull glow draining the vibrancy from the orange, yellow and black colors she wore.

"Excuse me, Fancy. My next patient? Cancelled?"

"Dr. Jack, probably a 'no-show'. Remember it's a good fishing day."

"Right. Priorities." Jack scanned her desk. "Fancy, I guess my being on sick-leave affected my memory. I forgot to check out your daily saying earlier and now, I don't see it."

She swiveled around, reached into a pile of clutter and pulled it out. Jack read, 'Savor All That Is Happening In This Very Moment'.

"Fancy? What happened to your smarty-pants sayings?"

"Dr. Jack, there'll still be times when I want to say to someone, 'I may be looking and nodding, but I'm sure not listening '. Never you of course. But I got to thinking. Those kinds of thoughts were more from my past. And I wanted to show how I feel now."

"So, savor the moment?"

"Yes. The past is over and gone. Every morning, I tell myself, Fancy, today's a day you've never lived before. Let's see how it unfolds itself."

Jack returned her calendar which she put beside a picture of her little girls. She peered up at Jack and smiled. "Is there anything else I can help you with right now, Dr. Jack?"

He gave her a closed-lipped smile and shook his head. "Thanks Fancy, but there's nothing you can help me with right now."

Jack slowly looked around the room, sighed, then turned back to her. "I guess I'll go do some paperwork."

THIRTY-TWO

*A Smart Person Knows A Tomato's A Fruit. A Wise Person Knows
Not To Put It In A Fruit Salad
Where Jack Tells Bonny, If I'm Not Me, Who Am I? And If I'm
Somebody Else, Why Do I Look Like Me?
Inadequacy: A Self-Induced Feeling Of Not Being Good Enough;
But, Really, Who Is?*

Twenty minutes early, Jack got out of his car and felt the thick, moist Florida air enveloped him. Ha, maybe I'll get into *The Java House* faster if I try swimming instead of walking. I just don't want to meet her with my shirt sticking to me. No worries. Once inside, it'll be so cold, I'll see my breath. He laughed again. Then, it'll be ice-crystals on my shirt.

Jack bought two coffees and sat near the entrance. The water condensing on the cafe's windows made it hard to see into the parking lot. He got up, tried to brush away some water, but it didn't help. He didn't want to miss Bonny when she came in, if she came in. No, I know my wife. She'll be here. I could always trust Bonny. He smiled wryly, just like she could always trust me.

In between the shrill A*aaaaaaa* of the espresso machine frothing milk and people ordering a peppermint cappuccino with double whip or a medium caramel latte with oat milk, no whip, Jack was pleased the place was quiet enough to talk. He kept moving his chair around to get the best angle on the door. He started to sip his coffee, then put it down untasted. He checked his watch, looked at his phone to confirm his watch was right, then checked the door again. My hands? Should I have them on the table? Folded, serious? Or open, welcoming? Maybe put them in my lap? Should I sit away or close to the table? No keys, phone on the table, no barriers. She said she'd meet me. She'll be here.

When Bonny came in, Jack almost pushed his chair over backwards as he stood up. Seeing him wave, she came over to the table.

He smiled. "Hi, thanks for coming. You know, for a split-second, I had an impulse to come around and hug you. But I thought better of it."

Bonny stood facing him across the table. "You made a good choice there, Jack." Her voice detached, her face without a smile.

Sitting down, Bonny stacked her wallet, keys and iPhone in front of her on the table. Jack pointed to the cup in front of her. "I got you your usual black coffee. I hope it's not too hot. I remembered you liked a dash of cinnamon, so I put a little in. I hope that was okay. If it's too much, I'll change it."

Bonny looked at the coffee, tilted her head and crimped her lips. "Hmm. Thanks. "

Jack wanted to move closer to her. But as he pulled his chair in, it screeched against the floor. He tried again and it screeched again. He stopped. He took a deep breath and wrapped his hands around his coffee cup. He was shivering. Must be that low AC.

Bonny sipped her coffee. "I like the cinnamon. Thanks for remembering to add it. And thanks again for the coffee. Seems to me the last time we were here, you only bought one coffee, for yourself."

Jack nodded. "Sure did, didn't I? I remember thinking, if she wants to be so independent without *me*, let her buy her own freakin' coffee. I was hurt and I was angry. I know now my anger was because of how afraid I was. Of course, I wouldn't have admitted any of that at the time." Jack paused a few seconds. "What a dickhead I was, so petty not getting you a coffee when I bought mine. For a time, I was pissed at everything and everybody. I see it as my *depraved-period* because that's what I was, depraved. "

Bonny had been gazing down into her cup. She moved her eyes up slowly to look at him. "So? Jack. You wanted to meet."

"Yes. And again, thanks for coming."

"You're welcome. This is important to me, Jack, so I'm here."

"Bonny, seeing you, meeting with you is very important to me too. I called because I needed to talk with you. Tell you what's been happening with me over the two-months that I've been out of our home…and apart from you."

Bonny picked-up her cup, sat back and looked at him. "Jack, before you start your 'sharing', tell me, how are you?"

"Like I said, I wasn't too ducky for a while. I was all over the place with my emotions. I'd be angry, then I'd be calm. I'd feel sad, then I'd be happy. I'd feel alone, then independent and free. Looking back, I know at the heart of it, no matter what BS I was telling myself, I was confused and afraid not knowing what was going on inside of me nor what to do. But right now, in this very moment, I believe I'm doing and thinking better. I'm hoping I'm on the mend. And you? How are you doing? Have you been busy?"

Bonny narrowed her stare at Jack. "'On the mend'? Ha. I do believe you've given me that line before, haven't you? And more than once?" Bonny put down her cup chair and crossed her arms. "I hope you've got some new material, Jack. Because right now, I'm feeling pretty skeptical about meeting with you."

"You know, as soon as I said it, I knew it was a mistake. It suggests things are just passively happening, doesn't it? Bonny, that's not what's going on. I'm actively working on things in myself. Things I've been avoiding for a long time, for *too* long a time."

Bonny relaxed her arms a little, yet kept them crossed on her chest. She looked at him in an appraising way. "Well, to your credit I see you've shaved this time and you've gotten a haircut. I like it shorter on you. I don't remember your having that shirt though. Something you bought? It's a nice change from the polos you wore all the time. And the rest of your clothes don't seem wrinkled. I guess that shows some work, at least on your 'outside'."

Her head bobbed back and forth. "Me? How am I doing? My job has kept me pretty busy. The work I'm doing at the legal office and the staff have turned out to be a great fit for me. I'm very happy there. I've two women co-workers who have many of the same interests as I do, so I'm working on developing some new friends."

"I'm glad to hear that."

"I've started running again in the mornings before work. With the days getting hotter and more humid, I've had to get up earlier which is hard.

He nodded. "Yeah. I do remember how much you like your sleep."

"I've finally found a comfortable pair of running shoes that give me the support I wanted. I threw away my old running outfits, mostly because they were getting too big on me."

"I thought you looked a bit thinner when you came in." Jack

smiled. "You look, very nice."

"I've been out to dinner a few times with some colleagues from the office. Otherwise, in the evenings, I either go over legal briefs or catch up on my reading. So, my days and nights have been pretty occupied."

"Great. I hope you're hydrating when you run?"

"Yes, especially now that it's getting hotter and I'm sweating more. I remembered your nagging me about that and I really need to. Otherwise, I get very tired later in the morning. And you? Still going to the gym?"

Jack nodded. "Mm-hmm. I stopped for a bit, but restarted last week. I can't believe how tough it was getting back into my routine."

"And?"

"And? Well, I go early in the morning. I bring my clothes and shower there, dress and get to work. On the way, I pick up a coffee and a plain bagel. Can't do poppyseed and then have that poppyseed smile."

"I know. Looking into a mirror at work and seeing all those seeds in your teeth."

"Exactly. I found this new bakery. You'd love it. Maybe we could...." Jack stopped himself.

"And? I'm waiting to hear you complain about the old farts who yell because they don't hear well. Or that toxic cloud of Ben-Gay that hangs in the air."

"They've become non-issues. I bought some noise-cancelling earbuds and, believe it or not, I've become a little fond of, 'essence of Ben-Gay.'" He grinned. "mainly because I had to start using it when a restarted working out. I focus on getting into the gym, doing my routine and leaving." He smiled. "And I do make sure to shower off all the Ben-Gay."

He nodded to her with his eyebrows raised, hoping for some response. But, outside of resting her chin on one hand and having a curious look on her face, Bonny just looked at him.

Jack hands started twisting in his lap. He looked around the cafe. There were two people on their laptops and a few others having casual conversations. He looked at his coffee. He picked it up, then put it down. He watched the droplets of water flow down the windows.

"Do you want to hear the news from the Clinic?"

"No, Jack, I don't. What I want to hear about is why you wanted to meet. I want to hear about *you*."

Jack licked his lips. How did his mouth get so dry? He wanted to reach across the table and hold her hands while he spoke, do something to impress upon her his sincerity. A few months ago, that would've been such a natural thing to do. How things change. And how things will change, he told himself.

"I know. Small-talk time is over. There's only so many times I can look around the room, huh? I so want to talk to you, but I'm afraid. How you might respond? What you might say back? Will you believe me? Why *should* you believe me?"

"Jack, you don't make the basket if you don't take the shot. I'm listening."

" Okay." He sat straighter in his chair, placed his hands flat in front of him and forced his eyes to meet hers. "First, I want to tell you that you were right."

"Oh? About which part, Jack?"

He gave her a diffident laugh. "About everything." He nodded. "Everything. Getting me out of the house for starters. I did need time by myself to step back and think about things. And my lazing, my brooding in my office at home wasn't going to do it."

"Could you say that again?"

"What? Which part?"

"The part that I was right. It's not to rub your nose in it, Jack. *I'm* hearing it. But I want to make doubly sure *you're* hearing what you're saying."

"You want to know if I'm sincere?"

She nodded. "Uh-huh. I believe that's what I mean."

"Okay. *You-were-right.* My being out of the house jarred me out of my...what? My complacency? My smugness? For a time, I was pretty angry with you, interrupting my 'comfortable' world like you did. But, when I finally admitted to myself how ridiculous and boring my righteous indignation at you was, the anger passed fairly quickly. Leaving that behind, I came to discover how brittle my world, the world in my head, was. I really was a big jerk when we were last here, wasn't I?"

"I think you used the word, 'dickhead'? That works for me because you were. I couldn't believe this was the guy I married. Anyway, don't let me interrupt."

"Okay. There's a lot I want to tell you, to convey to you about where I'm at. But I don't want to ramble on and on about it. I've been practicing so I think I can keep it fairly concise. But please bear with me? I want to get it right."

"Let's see how it goes, Jack. If you start rambling, you can be sure I'll let you know."

"Thanks. I mainly want you to know how right you were on three things. One was getting me out of the house to get me to think about things. Two was how dumb I was behaving and three, the most important, that I did have something inside me that I kept avoiding. That one made me pissed at you the most, because it was true. I want you to know, as well, that I'm working hard on these things, not running away like I used to."

"You've my attention so far, Jack. Look, I don't want to say I'm 'happy 'you've been stressed, but, truthfully, I am if it means you're confronting yourself with some things."

Jack drank some coffee. Damn, his mouth was dry. "Like you said. I'm the expert on the human mind, but don't know much about my own."

"Mm-hmm. And you thought I was deliberately provoking you?"

"Yes, I did. What a dumbass, huh?"

"Actually, I was trying to provoke you hoping it'd get you to look at yourself. But I don't disagree about your being a dumbass. Keep going."

"After I left the house, I tried to go back to work. But I started arguing with people, blowing off patients and being a general pain. Fancy advised, no, 'ordered' me to take more sick time. So, as I stared at the motel walls more, I started telling myself that, maybe, I really liked being alone. I was away from people, staff, patients, everybody. I didn't have to be concerned about being funny or what anyone thought of me or whether I was measuring up. I'll get to the 'measuring up' part later. I wasn't spending every day listening to people's suffering. Being alone let me do whatever I wanted to."

Bonny's face stayed neutral. "Uh-huh. You're saying you really *liked* being alone?"

"At the time, I was ticked-off with everything and everybody, so, yeah, that's what I was telling myself. And, it gets even better. I began thinking seriously about changing jobs. Something where *I'd* be in charge, like administration. Putting a budget together? Running meetings? Nice and clean stuff. Tell people what to do. Then, I progressed to my 'screw psychiatry' period. What was the point of it all? Trying to figure people out? Did I ever really help anyone?"

Bonny raised her eyebrows. "Why stay in an imperfect profession where people kill themselves despite what you do."

"That's where I was going. Change to a specialty with minimal people time. I was looking to be master of my destiny, free of what others wanted from me. No more smiling, encouraging, trying to give hope to the hopeless, laboring at changing the unchangeable. I even fantasized about moving to some low population state, like Montana. I'd have a spread of land out in Big Sky Country, drive all-around in my big pick-up with the gun-rack, not see a soul. I'd do tele-psychiatry. Me, home in my underwear and doing treatment over the computer. No direct people contact. Depraved, huh? I still can't believe where my mind was. Like being alone was being free."

Bonny sat unmoving yet attentive. Pushing her coffee aside, she brought her hands together and tightly clasped them on the table. "So? People were the problem. Getting away from them, maybe becoming the lone cowboy, independent and free, was the answer? That was your becoming a master of your destiny? Whatever the heck that means."

"I know you don't like my stories…"

"I like your stories, Jack, when they're funny. It's when they become harangues where you bitch about something. Those I hate."

"None of that. Promise."

"Uh-huh. Go ahead. Let's see."

"Basically, some things happened, nothing earth-shattering, just simple things that, for some reason, struck a chord in me. In telling you about them, I'm hoping you'll see how they helped realize things about myself."

Bonny clasped her hands more tightly, sighed. "Okay, Jack. I'm all ears."

"Okay. Okay. I'm living in this cheap motel room. I didn't think I'd be there long so I figured why spend the money on something more expensive."

"You thought you'd be home pretty quickly, didn't you? That I'd change my mind?"

"Yeah, I did. More bullshitting myself."

"Mm-hmm."

"Even when it was clear that my being there wasn't going to be short, I stayed on. The place was a dump from its thread-bare quilt to the squeaky bed and the moldy shower curtain. And drug deals at night in the parking lot."

"Jack. Okay. It was a seedy place. If I'm supposed to start feeling sorry for you, it's not going to happen."

"No, Bonny, it's not. This is not about drama, it's to set a scene. I had the money and certainly could've moved to a better motel any time. I met with Jim one time for a beer and told him about the rat hole. He said right-out I was a jerk for not moving. Of course, I got defensive and gave him some lame excuse about staying. All he did was shrug and say if I wanted to suffer, it was my choice. Driving back there, I thought about what Jim said about it being my choice to live in that hole. Then it hit me that, dammit, he was right. Staying in that dump fed right into, kept alive my 'poor suffering Jack' persona. And I loved it. You'd even confronted me on that."

"I did, didn't I? The non-mental health expert strikes again."

"Then I realized that my staying there symbolized what was the deeper issue. I wasn't 'worthy' of a better room. That I never felt deserving. That, compared to others, I was inadequate, a fuck-up. I started to wonder if that's why I chose to work in that gloomy Clinic with its grimy windows, dead bugs, gray walls and squeaky chairs. I could've found another place to work down here, but I stayed... and bitched."

"Okay, I can see that. But Jack, you keep alluding to 'inadequacy' and 'not measuring up' and just now, 'unworthy'. You're a successful doctor and have done pretty well. I'm trying to get past the drama of how this all sounds. Help me out here to understand."

"Better than anyone else, you know that I can be very fault-finding of people."

"You? Judgmental? Disdainful? Hmm, never crossed my mind."

"I see now that it's not them who don't measure up, it's me. Being judgmental, finding flaws in others is my defense. Being critical let's me puff out my chest and tell myself how better I am."

"And?"

"And why do I have to do that? Keep telling myself I'm better? Why do I feel inadequate? It's so dumb because it's the same old thing I deal with everyday in patients, the, 'I make mistakes. I'm not as good as someone else. I'm no good because I'm not perfect' cliché."

"Come on, Jack? You?" Bonny kept on staring at him. "Wait, is this where you bring in your brother, patients suiciding and guilt? Look for sympathy by reciting your tale of woe?"

"No, no. Not at all. All my brother stuff was," Jack nodded to her, "just like you said, 'something to blame so I could avoid'. My comparing myself and seeing others as better was in me way before what happened with him. I remember feeling, 'lessor' back to kindergarten. Some kid had a cleaner eraser. That meant he made fewer mistakes than I did."

"You remember that? You were depressed then? That young?"

"Bonny, depression runs in my family. I think I've had a smoldering depression for a lot of years. And, by the way, my brother? He *was* better than I was in many ways. A lot of people are better than I am. I *get* it now, at least trying to get it now. Why compare myself to anyone? What good does that do? I can only be me. You know, I find I've these two voices in my head. One telling me how good I am at this or that. Like, man, I'm in so much better shape than he is or that music, I could've written that. The other constantly criticizing so I can feel superior. A guy drives by in a big Mercedes and I think, 'What an asshole. Thinks he so hot. I bet he can't afford it. He can't even drive right.' But what I'm really fighting in my head is, 'That guy in the big Mercedes? He's more successful than I am. I don't measure up to him."

"Jack, that's ridiculous. The car doesn't...."

"Bonny, I know. I *know*. It's dumb, *really* dumb. But this is what's in my head. It's so obvious to me now. But it's been happening automatically for so long, it was my 'normal'. I freakin' never noticed it. And I discuss this with patients all the time. Talk about feeling like an idiot."

"Wait. I'm still confused. You're good with people. You joke. You laugh with them. They like you at the Clinic. It sounds like your patients like you."

"That's where I wonder if it's me or an act for approval, attention. And if it's not me, who am I? "

"Jack, we all get down on ourselves. At least I do. If something unnerving happens, like I've a confrontation at work, I play it later back in my mind how I might've handled it better, said something so incisive it would've shut the other person up. I look in the mirror to see how I look. I get envious when someone's articulate in a meeting. How is what you're talking about any different?"

"As long as one isn't *driven* to look good. Bonny, you're able to keep things like you mentioned in perspective, probably see it as an experience you can learn from. I go right to my being flawed, lacking. Look how I handled Brad's suicide. Okay, I should've felt bad. I should've wondered if there was something more I could've done. But in my head, I went right to how I failed him. Into that melodrama you saw. And I denied."

"Okay, but…"

"Bonny, I don't want to make this about drama and brooding. I'm *done* with that crap. What I want is for you to know is that I *am* looking at, facing, finally, those negative things that drive me. Facing and doing something positive about them. It's funny how sitting alone in an empty motel room can make you hear the squeaky wheels turning in your head and how they need some oiling."

"Jack, what you're saying, that you're seeing your issues and doing something about them? I have to say that there's a little, nagging voice right now in *my* head. It's wondering if this 'not measuring up', this 'not being worthy', even though you said you're done with it, is it going to be the new theme for Jack's brooding? You know, woe is me, am I *really* doing better?"

Jack smiled ruefully and nodded his head. "Ahh, the drama of my brooding. I was good at it, wasn't I?"

"I won't say no."

"Perfect segue, first story about insight. Next, about brooding."

"A *short* next story about brooding."

286

"Short, cross my heart. I told you about that middle-aged fellow, Ken, with OCD whose wife died after they moved down here?"

"Okay."

"I first saw him for his OCD, but then his wife's death became the main issue. They were two, very shy people who somehow found each other. They'd no children and relied entirely on each other for support. And they were happy, very happy. When she died, he not only lost a wife and best-friend, he lost a large part of himself. They were as one. When death wrenched her away from him, his grief was enormous."

Bonny tapped her fingers on the table top. "Okay, grieving husband. Where is this going? I hope not, 'Jack, the grieving husband'?"

He smiled. "Bonny, I understand your cynicism, but listen, please? He'd visit her grave everyday. He told me that when he talked to her, he'd touch a tree near her grave, hoping the tree's roots would carry his words to her there in the ground."

"That's touching, really. A story about how much a man loves his wife." Bonny started looking at her phone for messages.

"For weeks, he continued to grieve, but no socializing, no support groups, no talking with neighbors. He kept on working. I was frustrated what to do for him, but he wanted to keep coming in to talk. Then, the other day...."

Bonny looked up. "You're back in the Clinic?"

"Yep. Started full-schedule two days ago. The other day, he came in and said, 'You know, Doc, I think I'm better, not grieving so much.' When I asked him what'd changed, he said, 'I know the pain of losing her, that emptiness, will always be inside me. That it'll, like you say, lessen with time. But, now, when the sad thoughts come into my mind, I'm trying to just let them go. I used to fight them by making myself remember what we had. But, you know, I wasn't thinking about us so much as fighting my sadness. One part of my mind wrestling with the other. I think that's why I was always so tired, using up my, ' mind energy'. Now I try my hardest not to pay any attention to them. Get the thoughts to pass through me and out of my mind. Even the good thoughts because if I go there, I'll get sad. I'm still doing my part-time driving people around to appointments and such. I go to the cemetery,

I do my things around the house. Thoughts come up. Feelings come up. I try to recognize them and let them go. To accept what's happened is now in the past, gone'. Then he said, 'Really, Doc, when I can do that, I'm at peace. I'm able to live in the present. I see the things around me, the sky, the people, what I'm doing. I just *am'*. "

"Jack?"

"Almost done. But I really want to tell you about this part. Ken's been delaying having a headstone made. Before he did, he asked me to read what he was putting on it, something he saw somewhere. Can I read it to you?"

"Only if it's shorter than *The Iliad*."

Jack took a piece of paper out of his pocket, unfolded it. "It moved me so much, I had him write it down. It's called, *Beloved*.

Before I never knew, you were ...and in love's marvelous time, we found us.

Ever since, in myriad days time devours, in our sharing of one-soul dreams, I've

Loved you; I still long for your closeness, desire your always nearness.

Over rapid years in our lives' hoping, planning and living, I still wonder at the

Very magic that we shared.

Even yet and always, you are with me; you are love, laughter, smile, gentleness,   goodness; you in me, now less without you.

Dreams past are fulfilled because of you, because of us."

Bonny had looked up from her phone. "That's beautiful."

"Isn't it? He told me how he felt that death, in a way, was a good thing."

"Oh?"

"That her death had made him more aware of life. That he had a certain amount of time left and what was he going to do with it. Then he said, 'Doc, I hope you're not going to put me in the looney bin for what I'm saying?'" Jack shook his head. "And I'm thinking, this guy has discovered the meaning of life."

Bonny put down her phone.

"Okay. Interesting stories, one about an epiphany in a dingy motel room and the other about a patient who broods no more because he's found the meaning of life. But why are we here?"

"Can I get you another coffee?"

"No. You can get me an answer to my question."

"The guy with the poem. He made me think about how selfish I've been. Secretive, afraid to share things. It would seem like I was doubting your love for me but, really, it was my doubting myself, my deserving of your love. That poem helped me see all the more how much I love you and what we have. How my insecurities, my holding things back because I was afraid of losing you were the things that might cause me to lose you."

"But I thought you wanted to be the lone Montana cowboy, riding the range, away from anyone who'd make you feel not good enough?"

"Yeah. A master of my destiny, yet all alone, a prisoner of my fragile ego,."

"Sounds like a good time."

Jack snickered. "Some real crap there, huh?"

"Uh-huh."

"Bonny, what I saw in my patient was his accepting each day as it unfolded. But most of all, his acceptance of himself just as he is."

Bonny, silent, still serious, searched Jack's face. Had he been making any sense to her? And even if he were, did it matter?

"Quick story."

Bonny sighed. "Really?"

"Jim and Anne Bizby are divorcing. You know she was never happy with the move here?"

Bonny's eyes widened. "This is true? Wow. Though, in a way, I'm not surprised."

"Why?"

"I met her only that one time when we brought over that house-warming gift. She seemed pleasant enough. But, you know, what struck me, and I thought it silly at the time, was that she really wasn't in a hurry to unpack. I remember when we moved, I couldn't wait to open the boxes, get things organized and get on with life. How's Jim? It must have hit him hard when she told him."

"Actually, Jim is, in his words, extraordinary. And he's the one that asked for the divorce."

"Jim? Amazing. I'd have thought he'd never stop trying to make it work."

"He said that Anne wouldn't even try to adapt. And he wasn't going to live like he was."

"I assume you saw some similarities, Jim's situation and ours?"

"Yes. I realized that I wouldn't have wanted to live with Anne either."

Bonny stared at him. "Jack."

"Bonny, I know now I wouldn't have wanted to live with me either. Thank you for hanging-in there."

Bonny placed her hands out in front of her, palms flat on the table. "Okay, Jack. It's clear you've been thinking about a lot of things. I'm genuinely pleased to see that although a few times I did have that, 'is this too good to be true feeling'. So, now that you've told me your stories, is there something else? Let me put it this way. Is there something you want me to be thinking about as I drive home tonight?

Jack leaned forward and laid his hands on the table up to Bonny's phone, wallet and keys wall. "Bonny, I want you to know that I've come out of wandering in the desert. That I've emptied the sand out of my head and am hopefully wiser for the experience. I'm trying hard not to be the jerk that I was." Jack paused. "I've been thinking a lot about a lot. Stuff clunking in my mind like sneakers in a dryer. Why I do the things I do. Why am I in psychiatry? Ha. Was I looking for free analysis? My keeping people at a distance. Of course, my guilt rears up. But I'm paying much less attention to all of that. Like you've said, it's boring and, really, it doesn't go anywhere."

Jack swallowed hard. "You were so right all along about so many things. My hiding behind my bitching and moaning, the whining and complaining and the drama, especially that outrageous crap about my killing my brother. My holding back things from my past *was* a betrayal based on my moronic fears you'd love me less. I'm seeing that I'm a just a looney wretch like the people I treat. Ha, probably like most people. Concerned about what the other guy thinks. Geez, what an astounding, mundane revelation I've had, huh? Jack, you're not perfect. Live with it. Bonny, what I've told you have been insights for me. Nothing profound. Just life. I'm embarrassed about my dumbness. Guess I'm just a slow learner.

Bonny, driving home, I wish you'd think about since I have changed. But I know you'll still be wondering can you believe that. I *want* to, *need* to change even more. Be different. A better different. Accepting myself. The disdain, the denial, the BS'ing myself? They're still lurking inside. But now, when I hear one screaming to come out, I don't fight it. I just don't pay it any attention. I'm trying to let it pass through me and disappear. Like my patient said, those negative thoughts use up too much brain energy. One looney helping another looney." Jack grinned. "He'll never know he was helping me more than I helped him that day." He stopped, slumped back in his chair and looked at his wife.

"Bonny? Is that a hint of a smile I'm seeing?"

"Ha, don't push it, Jack. Are you done?"

"I am. It was about Jim divorcing Anne. That was the lightning-strike that scared the hell out of me. Why I called to meet. Before that, I was too afraid."

"You thought I might divorce you?"

"Bonny, you're a bright, patient, caring woman who's put up with a lotta crap from me. But, at some point , even I would've divorced me."

Bonny lifted her chin a little. "Jack, I won't lie to you. If you continued to behave as you were, divorce *was* an option. I wasn't going to live with a drama-king who'd kept me out of his life."

Jack's face hardened as he sat up, hands pushed hard down into the table. He'd said the word in his mind, but hearing Bonny say, 'divorce' aloud stunned him. A life without her?"Since you're looking so awfully solemn, Jack, let me say that I see a hint, a flicker, maybe even a twinkling of hope here."

"Oh?" Jack's eyes widened.

"Although a couple of times, I saw a little strain on your face, I was impressed that you made no smart-ass comments this whole time. And, you didn't interrupt. Well, you did, a little. But, of course, you were doing most of the talking."

Bonny pressed her lips together. "Now what, Jack? You seem more insightful and honest with yourself."

"But?'

"But, Jack, you've talked about being 'better' before. And…."

"And you trusted and believed me. All I can say is that this time, *this* time, you did get my attention and that I'm seriously working on myself. In the past, I mouthed the words, but just kept doing my dance of denial."

"Okay? And?"

"Well, I've joined Gamblers Anonymous," he smiled, "not that I needed to."

"What?"

"Sorry, not the time to joke. I *needed* to."

"Interesting. That must've taken a lot of, I was going to say humility, but I think honesty is a better word. Good."

"I called Dr. Lankersham, my old psychiatrist up north, asked him if he knew anybody around here I could see for therapy. Turns out he has a few friends who migrated nearby. One's in Sarasota."

"Well, aren't you full of surprises? But wouldn't that be a drive for you?"

"It's only an hour each way. I've already called the Doc and have an appointment with him next week. I asked Fancy to work something out in my scheduling so I can get to those appointments during the day."

"My, my. I thought you'd use the distance as an excuse."

"I'll work it out."

Bonny stared at her car keys.

"Oh, and I bought you a water pistol."

"Because?"

"Because, not that it'll happen, if I start whining or bitching, you can shoot it at me."

She nodded, almost smiled. "I like that idea. I hope you won't have to carry around a towel."

"Me, too."

When Bonny didn't say anything more, Jack pushed on. Anything to keep her sitting across from him, listening to him. "And, I'd like it if we can talk more. I need to talk. About how the day unfolded. About what I'm learning in therapy. But, honestly, to let you see how I'm doing." Jack felt a palpable silence intruding between them. He saw looks of seriousness, confusion and sadness contorting her face. *Did I overdo selling myself? I probably did sound too good to be true. Too good to believe?*

"Jack, you're talking like we're going to be seeing each other?"

He looked away. Then slowly turned to her.

Looking severe, she said, "I don't know, Jack. Since you're not perfect and just a mere mortal, I'm thinking that maybe you really don't deserve *me*." Bonny held her solemn look for a few seconds to see his reaction. Then, she smiled.

Jack let out a very long breath. "I'm so sorry, Bonny, for being such an idiot."

Bonny raised her hand. "I disagree. You certainly were an idiot. But, what you really were was a *bastard*. I appreciate the apology, but I'll delay accepting it right now if I may."

"Okay, because?"

"Because, Jack, the best apology is changed behavior. I can't tell you where I heard this, but there's a quote from Mae West that goes, 'An ounce of performance is worth pounds of promises.' When I see your promises truly turn into performance, that's when I'll accept your apology."

"I understand."

"Jack, I may have joked a little there, but I'm very serious about this."

"Bonny, I *am* trying."

"That's nice, but read my lips. Trying is good. *Doing* is better. Jack, you hurt me by not telling me things and then keeping me out of what you were feeling. It's going to take a while for me to trust you. And it's going to take a while for that hurt to go away."

"I get it. I do. As long as *we* have time for me to show you I'm doing what I need to do. To prove myself. Our having time, that's what I'm hoping for."

"Jack, maybe I shouldn't have joked about our seeing each other. I don't know."

"Don't we have to see each other to…."

"I know. And then there's the issue of your coming back into the house, unless you're growing fond of that motel?"

"Oh, no, no, *no*. The sooner I leave that cockroach breeding ground, the better. But, if you think it might be a while yet, please let me know because I *will* move out of there."

"Let me think about things for a little bit, okay? I came here with one mindset. And you, ah, definitely surprised me out of it. I'll call you."

"Okay. And I'm sure you'll want to talk about it with your therapist?"

"Ah, *finally*, the smartass comment. Couldn't help yourself, could you?"

Jack instantly put his hands up in surrender. "No. No. I didn't mean it that way at all. I want to make things work between us. I think it'd be good that you discuss it with her. I want you to be sure."

"Gadzooks, Dr. Jack. You sure are full of surprises today."

"Gadzooks, Attorney Bonny. I've never heard you use gadzooks before."

Both pushed back their chairs, got up.

"Bonny, I know a hug is out of the question."

"Jack."

"Can we just shake hands, please?"

She thought a moment, nodded. "That'd be okay."

Jack sprung for her hand, held it until she pulled it away. As they headed to their cars, he laughed.

"Something funny?"

"When I had all that time on my hands, I watched a lotta garbage on TV. As a kid, do you remember ever watching *Popeye The Sailor* cartoons?"

"Mm-hmm, I think so. Olive Oyl was his girlfriend? Wimpy ate hamburgers?"

"Yep. I was just thinking. Perhaps, underneath Popeye's salty exterior lived a wise, mariner-philosopher. And I've just decided that I'm adopting his credo. Remember it?"

"Ah, 'I'm strong to the finich cause I eats me spinach?'"

"Nope. He'd say, 'I yam what I yam and that's all what I yam'.

Pretty metaphysical, huh? Like a Buddhist mantra? It's going to be mine, too."

Bonny smiled, ducked down and got into her car.

Jack waited, waved then watched her drive away.

Maybe, just maybe, I'm getting to 'Zip-a-dee'. But now, I've gotta get that, 'do-dah' part right.

About the Author:

 Stan Kapuchinski is a psychiatrist living in southwest Florida. His other published work includes the non-fiction, self-help book, *Stop Your Misery. Recognize People Who Make You Miserable And Eliminate Them From Your Life For Good!* Which describes people with personality problems and how they manipulate and control others.